W.A.Harbinson was the Chief Associate Editor of Paul Raymond's *Men Only* and *Club International* from 1972 to 1976, when the magazines were at the height of their popularity. He left to become a full-time professional writer, producing many books, including the best-selling novels, *Genesis* and *Revelation*, and a Number 1 US best-selling biography of Elvis Presley. Though born and bred in Belfast, Northern Ireland, Harbinson now resides in West Cork.

Web Site: www.waharbinson.eu.com

For Poul Madsen

Foreword

Back in the late 1970s, a few years after leaving my job as Chief Associate Editor of *Men Only* and *Club International*, I decided to write a comic novel based loosely on my four years with those magazines. I had wanted to do so for a long time but had always been discouraged by Tony Power, the off-the-wall Managing Director and Editor of Paul Raymond Publications.

Tony was a tall, attractive, curly-haired bad boy who was essentially good-natured, but he'd had too much success too early. By the time I went to work for him, he was already drinking to a degree that would have made most hardened drinkers seem teetotal. He was also into any kind of upper or downer and well on the road to cocaine. His affairs and other misadventures were legendary amongst those who knew him, though he had a great talent for getting out of trouble as easily as he appeared to get into it. Tony had never written a book in his life, but he had developed an obsession about writing a novel based on the men's magazine business and he was convinced that I, a published author as well as his Chief Associate Editor, was going to steal his idea. In the end, I did so, but only after it became perfectly clear that Tony had gone far beyond the pale and was incapable of writing anything, let alone a novel.

I knew this definitely when Tony, still in his mid-thirties, underwent a major surgical operation. After the operation, he wasn't supposed to smoke or drink alcohol, but when I arranged to visit him, mere days after he'd been chopped up, he asked me to bring along a bottle of brandy – which, rightly or wrongly, I did. Once at the hospital, with the bottle hidden under my coat, I guiltily entered his private room to find it stinking with cigarette smoke. Surrounded by flowers, including a wreath sent by friends as a joke, Tony was sitting upright on the bed, grinning and obviously under the influence. There was a half-finished liquor bottle resting on his bedside cabinet and other bottles were hidden here, there and everywhere.

Scattered around him on the bed were a lot of those small red notebooks with lined pages that were used in schools years ago. When I asked him what they were for, he insisted that he was writing his novel and extracted from me another promise that I wouldn't write a novel on the same subject. I meant to keep my word, but a few years later, when both Tony and I were long gone from the magazines and Tony was a mess – unemployed, in debt, constantly drunk or stoned – I knew that the game was up and so decided to proceed with my own novel.

The resultant work, *Deadlines*, was an outrageous, over-the-top black comedy that satirised pornography, male chauvinism, female liberationists, and even the SAS before that regiment gained its high public profile. Unfortunately, the published book was packaged like a Harold Robbins novel, with the cover showing an unsmiling model wearing sunglasses. I failed to see how such a cover could possibly illustrate the zany black comedy inside; and it is my belief to this day that if *Deadlines* had been packaged properly, particularly as a hardback, it would have received more attention that it did. In the event, coming as it did shortly after my best-selling novel, *Genesis* and a few months before its successor, *Revelation*, it was turned down by Corgi, the publisher of those books, where it was felt that it would only confuse my readers. Subsequently purchased by another publisher, NEL, it was treated as a run-of-the-mill paperback that was not, to the best of my knowledge, even sent out for review. Needless to say, my disappointment was acute.

My daughter, Tanya, has read all of my books but insists that *Deadlines* is her favourite. I am therefore republishing it mainly for her, but also because I feel that it deserves a second chance. In the words of the SAS: 'Who dares wins.'

W.A.Harbinson
West Cork, Ireland

2009

Deadlines

Internal Memo

From: The Man Ed
To: All members of staff

(1) It has been noted by the Managing Editor that by 09.50 this morning not one member of the magazine production staff had arrived on these premises. By 10.00 – the official starting time as laid down in your contracts (which will, incidentally, be drawn up in the near future) – not one member of staff had yet materialised.

(2) This memo is being composed at precisely 10.30 and it is noted that the premises are still devoid of all staff, including the Managing Editor's secretary (terms of employment still negotiable), which has caused the Managing Editor to type his own memo.

(3) The switchboard operator, who is, according to her letter of employment (not yet completed due to certain queries re: Para 16), obliged to start at 09.30, has still not been seen, and numerous incoming calls have therefore been missed.

(4) The Managing Editor has still not had his morning coffee. The tea girl, who is, according to our agreed terms of employment (not yet typed up – an unfortunate omission), supposed to be in the kitchen by 09.45, has

still not arrived – nor has she had the decency to phone in with any sort of acceptable explanation, though if she *had* phoned in she would not, due to the absence of the aforenamed switchboard operator, have been able to get through to anyone.

(5) The Managing Editor was almost locked out of his own office upon his arrival, *in good time*, at these premises. This was due to the fact that his office door had not been unlocked by the cleaning lady. Luckily the Managing Editor keeps a spare key behind the loose tile in the Monsieur's, but this hardly detracts from the fact that the cleaning lady, who is supposed to be working a five-day week and whose hours of employment are from 07.00 to 09.00 (by verbal agreement but subject to instant change) is in point of fact only working about two days a week and, according to unverified reports, normally leaves within thirty minutes of her arrival.

(6) It has been brought to the attention of the Managing Editor that the general office message boy (hired for a four-week probationary period, terms of employment to be discussed at a later date) was given a packet of black-and-white photographs (tit shots, bum shots and crotch shots, reference Volume 94, Number 2, pages 22-28, 41-45 and 66-73 respectively) to be delivered to Reinholt and Gross last Thursday, and has not been seen since, nor has any explanatory communication been forthcoming.

(7) It has been conveyed to the Managing Editor, who was not present on Friday afternoon, that no members of the editorial staff were present on Friday afternoon. This information was conveyed by our esteemed Publisher,

who was, of course, in his office all Friday, not to mention all evening, and who also presented the Managing Editor with firm evidence that the Boardroom had, that very same afternoon, been used for purposes other than the purely creative. Found in the Boardroom after the exodus of the editorial staff were seven empty wine bottles (four red, three white), a crate of crushed beer cans, one bottle of Pernod, one bottle of brandy (an extremely expensive Remy Martin), innumerable cigar and cigarette butts, and at least one obviously used contraceptive. Further, someone had carved into the Boardroom table the words 'I love Sugar Daddy' (the characters were clearly feminine and the instrument of vandalism was a Silver Morton surgical knife of the kind commonly used by the Art Department) and the viewing box of the copy scanner was redolent with what appears to have been marijuana fumes. It is also noted that the slide projector has been left on all weekend, that the bulb is now extinct, and that some colour transparencies of a rather dubious nature were found on the floor of the Picture Editor's office.

(8) This shit has to stop.

1

The Managing Editor was in early this sunny Monday morning, which meant either that his wife had thrown him out of the house again or that he simply hadn't been home since Friday. Dennis knew that the Managing Editor, generally known as the 'Man Ed' or 'the Ed', was in early because he had just found a memo on his desk. The Ed didn't like memos. He rarely read them and hated writing them. In fact, the Ed only composed memos when he was extremely agitated, and he was always extremely agitated when he came in early.

Dennis lit a cigarette. It was the ninth one that morning. He coughed and slumped down behind his desk and gazed straight ahead. It was a functional office: white walls and bookshelves. There were no pinups on the walls, the shelves were stacked with back issues of the magazines in his charge, and the desk was littered with letters and manuscripts. Dennis wanted it that way. His office was businesslike. It had the appearance of a dentist's waiting room and it intimidated the writers and gave Dennis a little edge in negotiations. Dennis picked up the telephone.

'Yes?' a girl said.

'Hello,' Dennis said.

'Who is this, please?'

'This is the Chief Associate Editor.'

'I thought you weren't in yet.'

'I thought *you* weren't in yet.'

'Well, I am.'

'Yes. So am I.'

'It says here you aren't.'

'Where?'

'In this memo.'

'A memo?'

'Yes. From the Ed. It says no one is here.'

'A *nasty* memo?'

'Yeah. I think so.'

'And the Ed. Have you seen him?'

'No.'

'He's probably in his office.'

'Really?'

'Really.'

'Oh, God.'

Dennis smiled and put his feet on the desk and asked the girl to give him an outside line. When this was done, he languidly dialled a London number and listened to the low ringing tone. He closed his eyes, but promptly opened them again. His eyes were blue and they turned all soft and misty when he heard Laura speaking.

'Yes?' Laura said.

'It's Dennis,' Dennis said.

'Oh,' Laura said.

'And how are you, dear?'

'Fine,' Laura said.

'I just thought I would call, dear.'

'Yes... That's nice.'

Dennis smiled and inhaled on his cigarette, keeping his voice soft and soothing, sounding quite tender.

'And you feel all right?' he said.

'Yes,' Laura said. 'Wonderful.'

'Good.'

'It's real nice of you to call.'

'My pleasure,' Dennis said.

'I mean, so soon after... I mean, you only *left* me an hour ago.'

16

'I wanted to talk to you,' Dennis said.

'That's nice.'

'I'm all aglow,' Dennis said.

'Are you?'

'Yes.'

'That's nice to know.'

'And you?' Dennis said.

'Well, yes, glowing… and hurting a little.'

'Vaseline,' Dennis said. 'The next time we must try a little Vaseline. It eases the – '

'*Don't say* it!' Laura hissed. 'Just don't mention it! I still don't believe I actually let you… *Lord*!'

Dennis grinned, hearing her embarrassment, then inhaled on his cigarette.

'Love me?'

'Oh, yes,' Laura said.

'That's nice,' Dennis said. 'Well, I'll ring you.'

Dennis put the phone down and it instantly rang again and he picked it up and heard the switchboard girl.

'I heard that,' she said.

'Really?' Dennis said. 'Have you been listening in again?'

'It was an accident.'

'I see.'

'I couldn't help it.'

'I see.'

'Sounded like a good night.'

'Tut, tut.'

'Vaseline… What on earth do you use *Vaseline* for?'

'Don't you read the magazines we publish, dear?'

'No.'

'Well, you should. For a start, you work here. Secondly, they are really most instructive.'

'Gee, your voice is so sexy.'

'Mmmm.'

'When are you going to take me for a drink?'

'You're speaking to the Chief Associate Editor. And you *are* being impertinent.'

'Really?'

'Really.'

'All right, then.'

'*Don't* you read our magazines?'

'No.'

'Why not?'

'They're filthy. I don't read filth like that. And my mother, if she found out, would kill me.'

'You still live with your mother?'

'No.'

'Oh... Where do you live?'

'In a bedsit. In Notting Hill Gate.'

'A wicked area.'

'That's why I live there.'

'Really?'

'Really.'

'I see.'

'Yes.'

'Can you make coffee?'

'Sure.'

'Could you make me one?'

'You mean here or in my bedsit?'

'Here.'

'No. I'm not allowed to leave the switchboard.'

'Who says so?'

'It says so in this memo.'

'Ah, yes, the memo. I must read it.'

Dennis put the phone down, leaned back in his chair and stretched himself, inhaled on his cigarette and studied the phones on his desk. There were two phones, one red and one yellow. The yellow was connected to the switchboard and the red was an outside line. Dennis quietly cursed himself. He should have used the outside line. The switchboard girl was obviously a gossip and he didn't like that. Dennis picked up the yellow phone again.

'Yes?' the switchboard girl responded.

'It's me again,' Dennis said.

'Who?'

'The Chief Associate Editor.'

'Gee, your voice is so sexy.'

'Mmmm.'

'You want a line?'

'No. I want you.'

'Pardon?'

'A drink. I want to take you for that drink.'

'What? *Now*?'

'No. Tomorrow. I thought you might like a treat. There's a party tomorrow evening – for a rock group – and I thought you might like it.'

'What group?'

'The Orgasms.'

'Gee, well, I…'

'I thought you might like it. I thought it might be a pleasant change for you. Meet the rich and the famous, the weird and the wonderful, the beautiful. Have a bite, have a sip, have a smoke, on a boat, on the river.'

'Well, I…'

'The boat's named the *Renown*. It's docked at Charing Cross Pier. I want you to be there at six o'clock sharp and I suggest that we meet on the boat, inside, by the smorgasbord. I have a few prior appointments. I may not be around the office. But I'll meet you on the boat and introduce you to everyone and you'll enter the world of your dreams.'

'Gee, I…'

'But keep it a secret. You must promise me this. Not a soul in the office must know. Do you understand that?'

'A… *secret*?'

'Yes, a secret. It must remain our secret. I'm the Chief Associate Editor and I receive these invitations and everyone wants to come with me. I shouldn't really be taking *you*, but I will, but no one in the office must know.'

'Gee, why *me*?'

'Because your voice is so sexy.'

'Well…'

'You've been here three months and I still don't even know your name…'

'It's Rosie. Rosie Teasedale.'

'… and I like you and I think we should get to know each other.'

'Gee.'

'Right, Rosie. Now tell me, dear, what will you look like?'

'Well, nice hair, not too long, not too short; green eyes, pretty sweet but nothing special; five feet two, but look taller 'cause I'm slim; two ears, one nose and sexy lips.'

'That sounds delightful, dear. But tell me. What will you be *wearing*?'

'What I'm wearing now.'

'Which is?'

'Oh. A Marks and Spencer sweater, low-cut and pretty tight, black, some white stitching, blue jeans and pink socks and stiletto-heeled shoes, with a badge that says how much I love the Rolling Stones. You want my underwear?'

'No, thank you, dear, I think that will be quite adequate – and you've certainly struck up a pretty picture. I'll see you tomorrow.'

Dennis put down the yellow phone, stubbed out his cigarette, lit another and picked up the red phone and dialled a number. He heard Anna's sweet voice.

'Hello?'

'It's Dennis.'

'Dennis!'

'Yes, dear.'

'Welcome back!'

'Pardon?'

'From your trip, silly.'

'Oh… Yes… Paris. Last night.'

'Yes. Was it awful, love?'

'Bearable.'

'You poor magazine editors. Working even on Sundays. You must be so tired, my pet.'

'Yes, well…'

'I missed you.'

'Really?'

'Really. I missed you inside me.'

'That's nice.'

'Deep, deep inside me. I keep thinking it's still Saturday night. I still feel you inside me.'

'Yes, me too.'

'My tongue?'

'Yes.'

'Down your throat?'

'Yes.'

'And my lips, too?'

'Your lips, too.'

'Down there? All around you?'

'Oh, yes.'

'I can't wait until tomorrow night. I can't bear to wait that long. I want you inside me. I want you all around me. I want you on top of me and under me and beside me. I want you to eat me.'

'Ah, yes, well that's why I'm – '

'What about my story? Have you read it yet?'

'Your story?'

'My short story. For one of your magazines. You said you were going to read it on the plane to Paris.'

'Ah, yes, of course. Well, I did.'

'And?'

'A definite improvement. But it still needs some work. I think we should go over it again.'

'But I'm getting close?'

'You're getting close.'

'Oh, darling, you're so sweet. I don't know what I'd do without you. You've been so patient, so kind, and all for an amateur. I'd never have come this far without you. Do you *really* think you can publish it eventually?'

'Absolutely certain. It just needs some more work. Another couple of drafts and we'll be there, dear.'

'*More* drafts? Oh, God! It all seems like so much work. We've been working on it together for three months now. Is it *always* this difficult?'

'Always. Always. But we're close, dear.'

'Oh, yes, we are that.'

'About tomorrow, dear.'

'The boat trip?'

'The boat trip.'

'I can't wait.'

'It's all off, dear.'

'Pardon?'

'I can't make it. There's this damned emergency at the printers and I've got to go out there. There's a fault on some proofs and I've got to go out there and check them. And I'm informed that I can't do that until tomorrow evening.'

'Oh, no!'

'Yes. It's so annoying.'

'I can't bear it. I haven't *seen* you since Saturday.'

'This is only Monday.'

'Precisely. It's been *years*!'

'I know, dear. I know. But it's only the boat trip. I'll try to get to your place tonight. I don't know what time. Tennish... Eleven. I have to work late on some page-proofs, so I can't be too sure. But I'll get there. I'll make sure of that. I can't wait to see you.'

'Oh, you poor dear. You must be so tired.'

'It doesn't matter.'

'I love you, Dennis.'

'Really?'

'I do.'

'Well, that's nice. I'll call you.'

Dennis put the phone down. The intercom started buzzing. Dennis lit another cigarette and coughed and looked around for the intercom. It was on the floor, buried beneath a pile of manuscripts. Dennis threw the manuscripts aside and picked up the intercom and pressed a button. The intercom stopped buzzing.

'Yes?' Dennis said.

'Well, hello there!' a male voice said heartily. 'Can it be true that the Chief Ass is in? I just don't believe it!'

'You're late,' Dennis said.

'That means you were in early.'

'And how is the Assistant Editor of *Suave* this morning?'

'The ass of *Suave* is feeling rough this morning.'

'A bad weekend?'

'I don't know. I can't remember.'

'There's a memo on your desk, Harvey. It might help you remember. There was a party on Friday afternoon.'

'Really?'

'Really.'

'I don't believe it.'

'You weren't there?'

'I don't know. I wasn't home. I know *that* much. I woke up in the back of someone's car. That was three hours ago.'

'What sort of car?'

'A Renault.'

'I don't know her.'

'I feel sick. Can I have the day off?'

'No. Read the memo.'

'What memo?'

'There's one on your desk.'

'Really?'

'Really.'

'I can't see it.'

'Did you touch your desk this morning?'

'Yeah. I was trying to find my electric shaver. I stuck my hand beneath the pile and the papers all moved and I probably lost the memo in the shuffle.'

'You'll never find it again.'

'I'm overworked. That's what it is. That's why there are so many papers. Manuscripts, letters, PR handouts and invoices – it's all too much for one man. I need some assistance.'

'Read the manuscripts, reply to the letters, burn the invoices and that just leaves the handouts – which can be of use.'

'Are you accusing me of not working?'

'I wouldn't dream of it.'

'Was the memo from you?'

'No. From the Ed.'

'You mean he's still here?'

'Yes.'

'I thought he was in New York.'

'No. He came back five weeks ago.'

'Gee. I must go down and say hello. And how is the mad bastard?'

'Pretty mad.'

'Why?'

'Because we're all late.'

'Late? What's he talking about? I'm here already and it isn't even lunchtime.'

'How's the next issue of *Suave* coming along?'

'Smoothly. Smoothly.'

'I mean schedule-wise.'

'I wouldn't know. I'm only the Assistant Editor. You better ask that bitch of a Production Editor.'

'Okay. I will.'

The telephone rang. Dennis switched off the intercom. He picked up the phone and Rosie informed him that three people had rung him. The first was a literary agent who wanted the

urgent decision on a manuscript that Dennis had promised him
six weeks ago. The second was a writer who wanted to be paid
for an article that had been published in *Gents* four months ago.
The third was the printers who were now running late because
layouts for Section 2 of *Suave* had still not been delivered.
Dennis told Rosie to tell the literary agent that he was out for the
day, to tell the writer that he was holidaying in Marrakech, and
to tell the printers to contact the Production Editor. Dennis
waited for ten minutes and then he buzzed the Production Editor.

'Yes?'

'It's Dennis. And how are you, my dear?'

'Awful. Just awful. Can I come and see you?'

'No. I have someone with me at the moment. What's
happening to the schedule?'

'Awful. Just awful. We're running late on delivery of
Section 2 and the printers are driving me nuts. They've just
called me again.'

'That's silly,' Dennis said. 'That's really most annoying.
I've told them repeatedly to call *me* when this sort of thing
happens.'

'I know, luv. That's really sweet of you. You're the only
one who'd do that sort of thing. I really appreciate it.'

'So. What's the delay?'

'It's that fucking Harvey. He's a bastard. He really is a
bastard. I mean, it's a simple matter of cutting some over-matter
on the continuation page of "Going Down to Get It Up", and he
won't let me do it myself, and he promised to do it and give it
back to me a week ago, and he's never in his bloody office, and
when he *is* in he's too busy to do it.'

'He's in now.'

'I know. I've just been to see him. He said he gave it back to
me a week ago and *I* must have lost it. But that's not true. You
know it's not true. It's probably still on his desk, but his desk is
such a mess, it'd take a month to sort the stuff out. He's only
interested in his perks, that's the problem. I mean, his whole

desk is overflowing with PR material about watches and clothes and hi-fi sets and tape-recorders and cameras and other shit, and he's always on the phone trying to get himself some freebies on the pretext that he'll cover them in the magazine. I think you should talk to him.'

'I'll do that.'

'This morning?'

'This morning.'

'Thanks, luv. You really are a dear. I mean, I don't know how I'd stick it out without you. I've been on pills all weekend. My nerves just can't take it. My boyfriend says I'm underpaid, my doctor says I'm overworked, and the doors in the house open and close on their own and we still get those noises in the attic.'

'The doors still open and close?'

'Yes.'

'And you still get the noises?'

'Yes.'

'Any manifestations?'

'Not yet. But then I haven't actually gone up to *look*.'

'And this doesn't worry you?'

'No. But the magazine does.'

Dennis cut her off and then he tried buzzing Harvey, the highly devious Assistant Editor of *Suave*. There was no immediate reply, so Dennis started thinking that perhaps Harvey had already gone for lunch, which would mean he wouldn't be seen for another week. However, Dennis buzzed around the whole building and finally netted one of the accountants who said that Harvey was there with him, claiming some petty-cash and demonstrating a pocket-sized tape-recorder that he was offering the accountant at half-price. Dennis told the accountant to put Harvey on.

'Hello?' Harvey said.

'Is that the Ass of *Suave*?'

'It is.'

'Your friendly Chief Ass here. There have been some

complaints that you're spending too much time and petty-cash entertaining PR people for the purpose of obtaining free products, and that you're not so much interested in such products as material for the magazines as you are in selling them cheaply afterwards. Any truth in this, Harvey?'

'That bitch of a Production Editor.'

'No, it wasn't her. I swear it wasn't her.'

'The Ed?'

'No.'

'Okay,' Harvey said. 'Let me tell you about that. It's true that I work myself to death entertaining certain boring farts from various retail companies with a view to obtaining publicity copy and pictorial matter on numerous products of interest to a male readership, but I *would* point out that I'm filling three pages of *Suave*, not to mention three pages of *Gents*, with free copy and pictorial matter, and that a study of the differences between my petty-cash expenditure and time against the overall cost of six pages of *purchased* copy and pictorial matter would reveal that I'm saving this publishing company a fucking packet. That I happen to pick up the odd freebie here and there is coincidental.'

'What's this tape-recorder you've got?'

'It's a Hamatachi SLR stroke 08800 RFO stroke HY742 with one-touch operation for action under the worst conditions, special anti-rolling mechanism to eliminate sound distortion caused by vibration of the tape, a built-in condenser microphone, pause control, automatic recording level control, 5-cm damp-proof speaker, electronically controlled DC motor, high reliability IC circuitry, Thumbmatic recording, frequency response 100 to 8000 HZ and output power of 350 MW... You want one?'

'Free?'

'Free.'

'Yes.'

'Say no more.'

'Right,' Dennis said. 'I also have a complaint from the

printers who rang me personally to say that they are being delayed on Section 2 of *Suave*.'

'Don't know anything about it. Ring the Production Editor. After all, it's that bitch's *job*.'

'I rang her. She says the delay's due to the incomplete continuation page of "Going Down to Get It Up", which page was given to you over a week ago for cutting of some excess text. Apparently she's still waiting to get it back.'

'What that bitch needs is a decent cock up her.'

'I'm afraid I can't oblige.'

'It's all the Art Editor's fault,' Harvey said. 'What happened is that our dumb Production Editor, the lovely Lavinia, brought me the offending page, which needed forty lines of excess text cut, and which she had arrogantly taken it upon herself to cut. She wanted me to praise her work and I said I wouldn't even look at it because she shouldn't have made the cuts in the first place, this not being her job. She went off in a huff and I cut a different forty lines and immediately, repeat *immediately*, took it back to her. An hour later she brought it back and said that the Art Editor, revered by, and known to us all as, the Artful Ed, had decided to put a cartoon on that page because he didn't like to see a full page of type, and that this meant another cut of 150 lines. I rang the Artful Ed to say I couldn't cut another 150 lines and the Artful Ed – through his assistant, the great man himself not being in his studio – informed me that it was *you*, the Chief Ass, who had insisted on having a cartoon in. The Artful Ed couldn't get a cartoon until Wednesday, this being two days later, so I gave the page back to the lovely Lavinia and told her to give it back to me for cutting when she had received the cartoon from the Artful Ed. I haven't seen the thing since, so I think someone should prod the Production Editor and give her less cause for frustration.'

'*I* didn't ask for a cartoon to go in,' Dennis said.

'Well, *someone* did,' Harvey said.

'And how's the wife?' Dennis said.

'I'm not too sure. I haven't seen her since Friday morning. She rang me this morning to say she was leaving home, and I said, fine, I'll see you around. She'll cook dinner tonight.'

'A Renault?'

'A Renault.'

'I can't place a Renault.'

'She was blonde and her teeth were too big and my cock looks like chewing gum. Apart from that, I can't remember a thing.'

'Where was the Renault parked?'

'Outside the Inn on the Park.'

'Do you think she was at the party?'

'I don't know. Were you?'

'I don't think I'll answer that.'

The yellow phone rang so Dennis cut Harvey off and picked up the receiver and listened. Rosie informed him that there was a new girl in Reception and that she had come to start work in some unspecified editorial position. The girl had been sitting there all morning, but Rosie had forgotten to tell Dennis, which wasn't her fault since the new girl had been very quiet and she, Rosie, had been busy at her switchboard. Apparently the girl had been told to ask for Dennis, and Rosie now wanted to know if Dennis knew anything about the new girl. Dennis said that he didn't know anything about the hiring of a new editorial member of staff but that he would come down presently to see her. In the meantime, could he please have an outside line. Rosie gave Dennis an outside line and Dennis dialled a North London number. The phone was picked up and he heard muffled murmurings and pounding rock music in the background.

'Yes?' a male voice said suspiciously.

'Would that be the Art Editor of *Suave*?'

'Who is this?' the male asked suspiciously.

'This is your friendly DJ, Dennis the Menace, ringing from the House of Sin in decadent Soho and wanting to know why you're still not at work.'

'Dennis?'

'Dennis.'

'What the fuck are you doing ringing me at home?'

'You're not *supposed* to be at home. You're supposed to be at *work*.'

'Why? What's the time?'

'Eleven-thirty. In the morning, I mean.'

'So? What's the rush?'

'The rush is that you're supposed to start at ten.'

'I worked late on Friday.'

'You were at *the party* on Friday.'

'It's all work to me, mate. I was entertaining clients. I heard there was a party in the Boardroom, so I took them downstairs and introduced them to the staff.'

'Some introduction.'

'They loved it.'

'Was I at the party?'

'Oh, yes.'

'And what did I do?'

'I won't tell you.'

'What are you doing at the moment, Artful Ed?'

'Pardon?'

'What are you doing?'

'I'm just getting out of bed. I'm having a cup of coffee. Am I *allowed* to have a cup of fucking coffee?'

'You're working, aren't you?'

'That's right, I'm working.'

'On some of your outside jobs. You're doing some of those record-album covers on our time and with our equipment, and that's why you haven't come to work yet.'

'What a thing to think,' the Artful Ed said. 'Listen, Dennis, let me tell you something. The reason I'm still at home is that I had to bring a lot of fucking work home from that studio because I spent all week doing nothing except try to get some corrected page proofs off that bitch of a Production Editor.'

'Lavinia.'

'Right. And I didn't get them until Friday when she told me she needed them straight away because the printers were screaming for them. So I brought them home and I've been working all weekend, *on my own time*, trying to complete the fuckers, working half of last night, which is why I'm having a late breakfast. As a matter of fact, I wanted to talk to you about that. I think I've been getting too much work lately, particularly since I'm now doing half of that fucking American edition and haven't received an extra penny for it. I think it's about time we discussed a raise.'

'You mean *money*?'

'Well, I don't mean my dick.'

'I don't know, Artful Ed. That *could* present me with difficulties. There *is* a rumour going around that you're spending half your time building up a little empire of your own. From what I hear, you've got album covers, book jackets and posters on the side, and most of it's being done on our time, not to mention our premises.'

'That bitch of a Production Editor.'

'No, it wasn't her. I swear it wasn't her.'

'The Ed?'

'No.'

'Okay,' the Artful Ed said. 'I think that's a neat line in bullshit you're pulling. I'm asking for a raise and you're trying to wriggle out of it by pretending that all this extra work I'm doing is my own. Now you *know* that's not true. A man's entitled to a little spare work on the side, as long as it doesn't interfere with the magazines and doesn't require the use of the Company's facilities. I work my ass off for this Company, and you know it, but you just won't admit it.'

'You frighten everyone,' Dennis said. 'Everyone says you're difficult to work with. They all think you're a weirdo.'

'I don't frighten the Ass Ed of *Suave*. I only frighten neurotic bitches like that fucking Production Editor, Lavinia, and that twat who pretends to be the Assistant Editor of *Gents*, and that spineless wonder who ponces up and down and pretends to be the Art Editor of *Gents*. I mean, I have my standards, I'll fight for what I believe in, but I'll listen if I respect the person talking. As I said, I don't frighten the Ass Ed of *Suave*. Old Harvey, he knows his job. He's a good boy.'

'Well, I think that's most generous of you to say that.'

'Praise where it's due, Dennis.'

'What's that music in the background?'

'The Rolling Stones' latest. Pretty good, eh?'

'Pretty good. You just buy it?'

'No. Harvey gave it to me. A review copy.'

'I see.'

'Yeah.'

'Sounds like a fantastic hi-fi set.'

'One of the best,' the Artful Ed said. 'Four-channel Matrix Circuitry and Two-Speaker Systems, with FM/MW/LW tuner, a 25-cm turntable with automatic return tone arm and oil-damped cueing control, fantastic treble and bass controls and a tape-monitor switch for externally connected tape-deck – though it *does* have its own cassette tape-deck section with automatic recording-level control circuitry and auto-stop at end of tape, with MPO total of 17W and RMS of 7.5W, normal market price being about 750 quid, though I got it for forty percent less.'

'From Harvey?'

'Yeah.'

'I see.'

'So,' the Artful Ed said. 'What are you ringing me about?'

'I have a little problem with *Suave*.'

'*Suave*'s running smoothly. Don't worry.'

'*Suave*'s running late.'

'Really?'

'Really.'

'I didn't know that.'

'I spoke to both Lavinia and Harvey and it all has something to do with the continuation page of "Going Down to Get It Up", which is the only uncompleted page on Section 2 and consequently is holding up the whole issue. It originally needed forty lines cut, so Lavinia stupidly cut them herself and then gave them to Harvey, who was most annoyed, this being a purely editorial function – '

'Dig.'

' – and so Harvey cut a different forty lines just to spite her and then passed it back. Lavinia then returned it, saying that *you* wanted to put a cartoon in, which necessitated another 150-line cut which Harvey thought was impracticable. He then rang you and you told him, through your assistant, you not being present at the time, that *I* had ordered the cartoon, which I had *not*, and that it would take you another two days to get a cartoon. Apparently no one's seen or heard of the matter since. That makes five days' delay.'

'It's all my fucking assistant's fault,' the Artful Ed said. 'I mean, I don't mind having an assistant if I can pick her myself, but when you get these dumb cunts turning up in your studio, usually unannounced, saying they're your new Assistant Art Editor, and you ask them who hired them and they say it was the Ed, and that they haven't had any previous experience, but that they met the Ed at some party or other and he, what with the brandy and the moonlight, offered them the job, doubtless after a quick gobble and grope, then what the fuck can you expect?'

'What indeed?' Dennis said.

'Anyway,' the Artful Ed continued. 'What happened was that this stupid bitch assistant was told to ring some cheap-skate cartoonist and get him to knock off a slick bit of shit about a shark going down on the hard-on of a dolphin – you know, *Jaws* and "Going Down to Get It Up" or something like that – and she did this, and the cartoonist delivered it Wednesday as expected, since I did, I can assure you, *lean* on him, and then the stupid bitch assistant, instead of marking her instructions on the *back* of the cartoon, put the instructions all over the *front* of it, thereby necessitating another fucking cartoon. That second cartoon arrived on Friday morning, and I'm going to mark it up myself as soon as I get in there – '

'I thought you said you took your work home.'

'Different work.'

'Oh.'

' – and as soon as I've done it, I'll deliver it to that bitch Lavinia and she can give it straight to Harvey – *if* she catches him before lunchtime – and he can cut the 150 lines and send the page off. And as for the delay, there wouldn't have been a delay in the first place if *you* hadn't asked for the last-minute addition of a cartoon, since that page, *as designed originally by me*, was complete.'

'*I* didn't order a cartoon,' Dennis said. 'I didn't even see the layout.'

'Well, *someone* ordered a cartoon,' the Artful Ed said. 'And if it wasn't you, I'll bet my balls it was the Prod Ed herself – who is, of course, frustrated and needs a decent cock up her, and who probably just *said* that someone had ordered the cartoon so she could get her own back on Harvey by making things difficult for him. I think you should talk to her.'

'I'll do that.'

'This morning?'

'This morning.'

'Good,' the Artful Ed said. 'I don't mind telling you, Dennis, you're the only bastard there who seems to be able to get things done. I was just saying to the Ed the other day, if it wasn't for our Dennis what the fuck would happen to the mags? That's what I said, Dennis.'

'You saw the Ed?'

'No. I spoke to him on the phone.'

'And you were at the party?'

'Yeah, I was at the party.'

'You actually *came in* for the party?'

'No,' the Artful Ed said. 'I went in because I had to pick up

34

my wages and some petty-cash and entertain some very important clients, and then, when I heard there was a party going on in the Boardroom, I thought it would be a good chance to introduce these clients to the staff. I saw the Ed there.'

'So you spoke to him.'

'No,' the Artful Ed said. 'He was at the other side of the room and I didn't dare interrupt.'

'Why?'

'He was down on his knees, that's why.'

'With whom?'

'The popsy who carved "I love Sugar Daddy" on the Boardroom table.'

'And which one was that?'

'I don't know. I never saw her before.'

'That's because you're never here.'

'I'm a very busy man.'

'I don't think the Ed knows he was at the party.'

'The state he was in, I don't doubt it.'

'And you're coming in this afternoon to finish that page?'

'On second thoughts, I can't,' the Artful Ed said. 'Thing is, I've got this photo session this afternoon. It's a fashion spread. We've got a lot of kinky gear there. It'll take all afternoon and probably half the night, so I probably won't get into the office. What I'll do is, I'll ring this stupid fucking assistant of mine and tell her *exactly* what to do and then she can take it straight to Lavinia.'

'I didn't know there was a photo session this afternoon.'

'I'm doing too much work, I can tell you.'

'No one told me about a photo session,' Dennis said.

'It's a special deal between me and the Ed. He wants it kept secret because it's actually for *Gents* and he doesn't trust their Art Ed to do it. You know what that prick's like. I mean, he's the fucking Art Editor, but he's frightened of naked cunt and so he just lets the photographers get on with it. The Ed wants me to handle it.'

'You're not going to stick your great horny cock into one of those juicy little models, are you?'

'I wouldn't do that. I'm professional.'

'Where are you shooting?'

'I can't tell you that. It's a special studio and it's pretty fucking expensive, and the guy who owns it wants it kept secret because he doesn't want to be hassled by a lot of tit mags. He only lets it be used for special jobs, and me knowing him and all – '

'We'll know his address when he invoices us.'

'No, you won't. Because he's not going to invoice you direct from his own address. He's going to put the invoice care of my address and then I'll pass the payment on to him.'

'You mean you're using a pseudonym and your own apartment and charging us twice the normal rental.'

'You're a suspicious fucking bastard, you really are.'

'We'll expect you tomorrow, then.'

'Well, I don't know about that,' the Artful Ed said. 'I'll have to check my diary. Between *Suave* and the American mag and the work I shouldn't have to be doing for *Gents*, I'm being run off my fucking feet and I've got a full book. I'll check it out and ring you back. And I *do* think, Dennis, that I should get double wages. I really should. Just bear it in mind, mate.'

'I'll do that.'

The intercom buzzed so Dennis cut the Artful Ed off and pressed the receiving button. Rosie informed him that two more people had called him, one being the Circulation Manager who was hysterical in Torremolinos and the other being a writer who wanted an interview with a view to doing some sordid work for the magazines. Also, the accountant wanted to see him regarding some queries on his recent monumental petty-cash claims, the Administrative Manager wanted to speak to him regarding the over-use and/or theft of typing paper, carbon paper, typewriter ribbons, pens and a couple of missing typewriters, and the girl who had arrived for unspecified editorial work was still waiting in Reception to see him. Dennis told Rosie to ring the writer back and tell him to make contact through the mailing system, to tell the girl to go and make herself a coffee and sip it until he could get to her, to inform the accountant and the Administrative Manager that he would buzz them as soon as he was free, and to give him the phone number of the reportedly hysterical Circulation Manager in Torremolinos. Dennis jotted down the Circulation Manager's Spanish number, agreed with Rosie that his own voice was indeed sexy, then reached out and buzzed the Artful Ed's assistant. The girl who replied sounded vague.

'Yeah?' she drawled.

'Good morning, my dear,' Dennis said. 'This is the Chief Associate Editor.'

'Oh, hi,' the girl drawled.

'I know we haven't met yet,' Dennis said, 'but I just thought I'd check that you're settling in okay.'

'Well, yeah, I suppose so. I mean, I've been here three months. I suppose it's okay, you know?'

'Good, good,' Dennis said. 'And how are you getting on with the Art Editor? Is he showing you the ropes, my dear?'

'Well, he certainly keeps me busy. I mean, he's always on the phone, but I never actually *see* him, you know?'

'Yes, I know. It must be terribly frustrating. But then he *is* a *very* busy man.'

'Yeah, I suppose so, but it *is* a bit *weird*. I mean, I'm up here on my own, day in and day out, and I keep getting this voice on the phone, telling me to do this and do that, and I haven't actually *met* him so I don't like to say too much, but I don't really know what he's talking about half the time and I *thought* he'd be here to teach me something. It's weird, man. It's *freaky*.'

'You sound American,' Dennis said.

'I'm from Putney,' the girl said. 'But I spent a bit of time over there. A few weeks in Los Angeles.'

'Ah,' Dennis said.

'That's where I met the Ed,' the girl said. 'He was over

37

there on one of his business trips and I was wagging my tail in this topless bar on the Strip and he came in pretty loaded, I mean really far out, and we sort of got friendly, I mean what the hell, we *fucked*, and then he gave me this address and told me to drop in if I came back and he'd give me a job as a model. Well, that's what I wanted, to be a real live model, so a couple of weeks later I knocked on his door, in the office, I mean, and he sort of glanced left and right, not remembering me, you know? And then gave me this job to familiarise me with the mags and said he'd have me photographed in a few days time. That was three months ago.'

'And you like this work?'

'You mean the Art Department?'

'Yes.'

'Well, it's not exactly being a *model*.'

'Well,' Dennis said, 'the Ed's not a man to break a promise, and I'm sure he hasn't forgotten you but is merely waiting for the right, for the *best*, the most *trustworthy* photographer to turn up and do the job properly. After all, you *are* new to the business, and too many pin-up photographers simply can't be trusted, and the Ed doubtless feels a certain responsibility toward you, and I *do* find that admirable, don't you?'

'Yeah, well, I suppose…'

'Thing is, my dear, that I *do* have this serious problem with the schedule of *Suave* and I think you're the only one who could sort it out for me.'

'Really?'

'Really.'

'Well, gee, it's really nice of you to say that and I'd really like to help, but I don't know that I can because the Artful Ed's just been on the phone to me again, saying he forgot to stick a cartoon on the continuation page of "Going Down to Get It Up" and asking me to pull one out of that great pile of spares that he keeps in his desk drawer and get it sized up and then sent straight down to the Production Editor of *Suave* – who is, incidentally, a domineering bitch who drives me nuts and is probably frustrated and needs a decent bit of cock up her.'

'Mmmm,' Denis said.

'Anyway, I'm going to do that right now, but I don't particularly want to take it down to that bitch myself and was going to give it to the message boy instead, except the message boy apparently disappeared about a week ago, so I wondered if maybe you could tell that bitch to come up here in five minutes and she can pick the cartoon off my desk and we won't have to talk.'

'Well, I think I can manage that, dear. I'm sure I can. I'm surprised, actually, that the Artful Ed even *wanted* a cartoon on that page, this not being his particular style, as it were.'

'He *didn't* want a cartoon on that page, because when I rang him and told him you wanted a cartoon, he told me to do nothing about it for a few days and then maybe you'd forget the whole thing. He said he was surprised that you even *wanted* a cartoon there, this not being your normal style, he said.'

'I must confess,' Dennis said, 'that I *don't* normally like cartoons on a page of type facing the first page of a girlie set, and I'm quite surprised myself that I might have ordered it.'

'Yeah, well, anyway, when that bitch Lavinia came up and said you had insisted on having a cartoon in and that we'd better find one fast, 'cause we were running late and all, I just said okay and then rang the Artful Ed – who was working at home at the time – and he told me what I just told you he told me.'

'I certainly don't like to suggest it, dear, but it *does* seem to me that a somewhat over-zealous Production Editor has taken it upon *herself* to put a cartoon in and used my name to push it through.'

'Right.'

'Right.'

'Anyway, I'm just going to pull a spare cartoon out of that pile that the Artful Ed keeps hidden in his desk drawer – all drawn by himself, incidentally, under various pseudonyms, and pretty damned good, if expensive – and I'll have the Art Editor of *Gents* size it up in two minutes flat and then that bitch can come up the stairs and collect it.'

'Well, I must say that's really terribly decent of you, dear, and I'll send Lavinia up in five minutes.'

'Say,' the girl said, 'can I come down to your office and discuss this further? I mean, we haven't met yet and you sound really sweet and this might be a good time to get acquainted.'

'That *would* be nice, dear, but I have someone with me at the moment and the subject under discussion is most urgent. Why not let me buzz you later on?'

'Okay, then. That's cool.'

Dennis cut the girl off and leaned back in his chair and put his fingers to his lips and smiled slightly. He then picked up the red phone and dialled the printers and asked their switchboard girl to put him through to the Production Manager. The man who came on the line sounded harassed.

'Yes, yes, hello,' he said.

'Mr Pearson?'

'*What?* Yes, yes, that's me. Pearson.'

'Ah, Mr Pearson. This is Dennis Elliot, the Chief Associate Editor of Saturnalia Publications.'

'Really?'

'Really.'

'Ah, yes, well, I...'

'Mr Pearson, I'm ringing because I believe you were trying to get in touch with me earlier on and were told to ring the Production Editor of *Suave* instead.'

'Oh, yes, right, I remember...'

'First and foremost, Mr Pearson, I would like to apologise for the embarrassing ignorance of our relatively new switchboard operator who put you on to that junior member of staff without even telling me you had called. Naturally, had I known you were on the line, I would have taken your call, knowing, since *you* were calling *personally*, that it must be a matter of some importance. Naturally the switchboard girl has been reprimanded.'

'Oh, well, that's all right. I mean, I didn't – '

'And this urgent matter, Mr Pearson. Not trouble, I hope. Not on a Monday.'

'Ha, ha, not on a Monday, a good one. Well, thing is, Mr… ah…'

'Elliot.'

'Elliot, that we're running rather late on the current issue of *Suave* because of a delay your end regarding the final section, Section 2. I've rung your staff repeatedly during the past week, trying to get it off them, but no one seems to know what's going on and I'm at my wit's end. We're ready to roll, you see.'

'I'm very sorry to hear that, Mr Pearson, and I must say I knew nothing about it, although, as you know, that sort of information is normally conveyed to me via the Production Editor who has, in this instance, been appallingly lax, not having mentioned a thing to me. But you spoke to her this morning, I believe. What did she say?'

'Frankly, Mr… ah…'

'Elliot.'

'Elliot, she didn't say anything that made sense. All I could get out of her was that she appreciated my problem and was trying to sort it out, but that she was getting no co-operation from her fellow workers. Apparently she's been waiting for an over-matter cut and a cartoon, but now your editorial and art departments are denying all knowledge of the original layout, which could mean that the girl herself – who strikes me as being a bit hysterical, that Assistant Editor, Harvey, by contrast, being a real nice chap to talk to and pretty sharp at rustling up the odd tape-recorder – has lost it and is trying to cover up.'

'That sounds very likely, Mr Pearson, and I must say I'm deeply perturbed to discover that all of this has been going on without my knowledge. As I'm sure you appreciate, Mr Pearson, finding production staff with any kind of competence is not at all easy, but what I'm going to do is sort this whole matter out myself and ring you straight back. Give me five minutes and no more.'

'That *would* be appreciated.'

Dennis dropped the phone and buzzed straight through to Lavinia who answered with her customary efficiency.

'Yes?'

'Hello, dear. It's Dennis.'

'Oh, hi! Can I come in now?'

'No,' Dennis said. 'I have someone with me at the moment and the subject under discussion is most urgent. I'm simply buzzing you because I know how terribly worried you are about the delay on Section 2 and to tell you I've sorted it out. What I did was personally ring an old friend of mine who runs his own cartoon agency, very exclusive, very expensive – I'm going out on a limb here – and normally very difficult to get, but because I'm a friend he sent around one of his better cartoons by taxi. Also, I had that cartoon delivered direct to the Art Director of *Gents*, who has already sized it up and left it on the desk of the Artful Ed's assistant – '

'That bitch.'

'Quite – for your immediate collection. Now I want you to go up there and collect it and take it immediately to Harvey to have that over-matter cut. I don't want you to talk to Harvey. He would just try confusing you. And nor do I want you getting in touch with the printers. I think that another phone call to the printers would just be humiliating for you, and since I want to avoid that, and since I'm extremely annoyed with Harvey for his negligence in this matter, I have already instructed him to make the cuts immediately and to then personally phone the Production Manager of the printers to apologise and tell him that the layout is on its way. I think that this should save you embarrassment, my dear, whilst also teaching Harvey a lesson.'

'Gee, thanks,' Lavinia said. 'That's really great. I don't know what I'd do without you, Dennis. You're the only guy in this hellish place who knows his stuff.'

'Not at all, dear.'

'I must say, Dennis, I think your suggestion about putting a cartoon in the middle of that page was really brilliant. It's just a pity that those other farts weren't more co-operative and thus caused all this unnecessary delay.'

'Well, you know how it is, dear,' Dennis said. 'Everyone's defending his own position. You try to suggest these things and you're met with resistance until you're forced to go over their heads. I'd just like to add that I appreciated your assistance in this matter and will certainly bear it in mind when an editorial vacancy next comes up.'

'Do you *really* think the Ed will eventually let a woman on the editorial team?'

'I'm working on him, dear, and if I succeed you'll be first on my list.'

Dennis cut her off and then he started buzzing around for the Ass Ed. He had trouble finding him because Harvey had moved on from the accountant, filtered through the typing pool, meandered up to the Art Department, and eventually disappeared down the stairs again. Dennis eventually located him in the kitchen.

'I didn't know there was an intercom in the kitchen,' Harvey said.

'The Ed had one installed last week,' Dennis said, 'because he felt it was the only place he was likely to find us.'

'He told you that?'

'No. His secretary told me.'

'I think that shows a great lack of faith in his staff.'

'And what are you doing down there?' Dennis said.

'I'm making a coffee,' Harvey said.

'Is that all?'

'Yes.'

'You're lying.'

'Well, actually, I'm thinking of running an up-front article on this new 5-inch portable TV set, integrated circuitry, three-way reception, 8.5-cm round dynamic speaker, collapsible rotating telescopic aerial and three hours continuous viewing with an ordinary National Hi-Top dry battery. I got one off this rep I took out to an extremely boring lunch – just to try it out, you understand – so I've closed the kitchen door and pulled the curtains across and I'm in here with the Ed's secretary having a look-see.'

'Why the Ed's sack?' Dennis said.

'She's in here making a coffee for the Ed and she says to tell you that the Ed wants to see you when you're free because he's annoyed about everyone either coming in late or not coming in at all or hiding in the bog or the kitchen and not doing any work and about the fact that he's installed an intercom in the kitchen and wants to know if it's helping.'

'I want to talk to you privately.'

'Okay,' Harvey said. 'Just a mo… Listen, angel, could you just step outside for a…? Yes, lovely… Okay, Dennis, she's gone.'

'Right,' Dennis said. 'About the delay on Section 2.'

'Oh,' Harvey said. 'That.'

'Yes,' Dennis said. 'That. And I want to warn you, straight off, that Lavinia is after your guts.'

'Wrong. She's after my cock.'

'She's after your job.'

'Okay. So?'

'Well, I've managed to sort out this mess about the delayed layout and so on. What's now happening is that I've arranged for a cartoon to be delivered to her, and she's just going to put that, plus the layout, on your desk for immediate correction.'

'Good. I'll make the bitch wait.'

'No,' Dennis said. 'I don't want you to do that. If you do that, you'll be playing straight into her hands. Thing is, I never asked for that cartoon in the first place, but I think *she* did – just to give you more work and to screw you completely because you wouldn't let her cut that over-matter herself. Now, what I've done is ring and inform their Production Manager of this fact, putting the blame squarely on Lavinia's shoulders. I also told their Production Manager that the Editorial Department was not responsible for any of this since Lavinia hadn't informed us of the delay, but that I've since informed *you* of the delay and you've already sorted the whole mess out. At the moment the printers are extremely annoyed with Lavinia – and will doubtless pass their annoyance with her back to the Ed – and are very impressed with you. However, not wanting them to think I was taking sides in the matter, I told them that I had only informed you of the delay – but not the reason for it – and that I didn't want you informed for fear of causing interdepartmental antagonisms. They appreciated this discretion, so they're going to studiously avoid discussing the matter further with you, and I'd appreciate it if you would give Mr... ah...'

'Pearson.'

'Pearson a ring, apologise for the delay, and say that the material is now on its way. This way, they'll think I'm the soul of discretion, you're the height of efficiency, and the lovely Lavinia is someone to avoid. That *should* sort her out.'

'Brilliant,' Harvey said. 'That's really fucking brilliant. I've got to hand it to you, Dennis, and I always did say it, you're the only bastard in this lunatic asylum who knows his job. And that *should* teach the bitch.'

'Yes, well, you'd better get up here straight away and finish the layout.'

'I'll be up in two minutes.'

Dennis pressed the OFF button and picked up the red phone and rang the printers and asked for Mr Pearson.

'Mr Pearson? It's Dennis Elliot of Saturnalia Publications, and I'm just ringing back, as promised, to tell you that the whole sorry mess has been sorted out and the layout is now on its way.'

'Wonderful. That's magnificent, Mr... ah...'

'Elliot.'

'Elliot, that terrific.'

'Now what I did, Mr Pearson, was bring everyone concerned with this lamentable matter into my office and personally, and severely, reprimand them. I then located the missing items, to wit, the cartoon and the layout, the latter being with the incompetent Assistant Editor and the former with the supposed Production Editor, and I made them redesign the whole page there and then. It is now being sent to you by motorcycle messenger, and I think you'll be receiving a personal apology from the Assistant Editor.'

'Well, that's first rate, Mr... ah...'

'Elliot.'

'Elliot, and I really do appreciate it. As a matter of fact, I have to ring the Managing Editor of your group in a couple of minutes to discuss the recent, and if I may say so, *regrettable* increase in our charges, and I will certainly pass on to him my appreciation of your co-operation and efficiency in this matter.'

'I don't think that's really necessary, Mr Pearson – although, if you insist, the gesture would certainly be appreciated. However, since I am particularly annoyed that my Assistant Editor should have let an incompetent Production Editor's fiasco pass unnoticed, and since a gentle reprimand your end could only add weight to my own, I would appreciate it if you could, when he calls to apologise, listen to his apology but hang up immediately if he starts elaborating on the fuller details of the matter. That should encourage him in the belief that you are seriously annoyed with him and perhaps discourage him from a similar carelessness in the future. I'm sure you appreciate the importance of this.'

'Indeed, I do, Mr... ah... *Elliot*, and I must commend you for your astute grasp of the politics of administration. I shall, as you instruct, listen silently to the young man's apology, wait until he starts offering his explanation – or, more likely, his denial of his personal involvement in the fiasco – and shall then immediately hang up. And, again, *do* accept my thanks for sorting this matter out so promptly and efficiently, and rest assured that my appreciation will be conveyed forthwith to your esteemed Managing Editor.'

'Thank you, Mr Pearson.'

Dennis dropped the phone and waited. Five minutes later he was buzzed by Harvey who informed him that the over-matter had been cut, that the layout and cartoon had been sent off to the printers, and that he, Harvey, was now chortling over the thought of that bitch Lavinia stewing. Dennis thanked Harvey and two minutes later he was buzzed by the lovely Lavinia who informed him that she had just seen Harvey giving the layout and cartoon to the motorcycle messenger, that the motorcycle messenger had now left, and that she, Lavinia, was now chortling at the thought of that bastard Harvey sweating. Dennis thanked the lovely Lavinia and then, noticing that it was noon and feeling that he had done a good day's work, decided to go downstairs and invite the Man Ed out for a drink.

2

The Man Ed's office had no windows, the fluorescent lighting stung his eyes, and the two electric fans that were his sole source of ventilation were blowing the papers off his desk. The Man Ed, more economically referred to as the Ed, didn't like papers. He hated letters and manuscripts. He let them blow all over the floor, and he cursed and lit a cigarette and looked at the wall straight ahead and saw the vagina. It was a very large painting, covering the whole wall. The vagina was blood-red and it resembled the Grand Canyon, and the Ed wanted to run in there and get lost until he saw the door opening.

'Holy shit,' the Ed said, 'a human being.'

Dennis walked in and he was slim and well dressed and he didn't have a beard and his eyes were blue and innocent and the Ed didn't trust him an inch. The Ed knew that little bastard. That little bastard was just like him. That little bastard was sharp and he wrote filthy novels and he gave them good reviews in the mags and the Ed didn't like that.

'Jesus, mate,' the Ed said, 'it's good to see you. How are you, mate?'

'Fine,' Dennis said. 'Not bad at all, Ed. And you? You got through the weekend okay?'

'Jesus, don't mention it. I just don't want to know. I mean, I've been home all weekend, working on these fucking mags, the French edition, the American edition, *Gents* and fucking *Suave*, and I didn't even have time for my kids and now I feel whacked.'

'I read the memo,' Dennis said. 'A real classy bit of work.

Brief, precise and to the point. It should travel far.'

'Well, *Jesus*, I mean *really*, what do you expect? You're working your ass off all weekend on these mags, no assistance, no sleep, no time for your own kids, and then you come in early to implement your ideas and there's not a fucking soul in the building. I don't mind telling you, Dennis, that the Big P is disturbed, the Big P is annoyed, the Big P is in his office and he's sending *me* memos so fast you'd need a computer to get through them. I feel like a punch-bag.'

'I sympathise, Ed. I understand your problems. You're caught between the Publisher and the staff and nobody's helping.'

'Too fucking true. I must say, Dennis, and I always *did* say it, you're the only bastard in this place I can trust. I mean, you get things done. You know what's going on. As a matter of fact, I just this minute received a call from that guy at the printers, Mr... ah...'

'Pearson.'

'Pearson, and he was telling me what a great job you just did in sorting out that godawful mess on Section 2 of the current edition of *Suave*, and what a right pair of fuck-ups Harvey and Lavinia have been, and I said to him straight, I said that Chief Ass of mine is the only guy in this whole building who knows what the fuck is going on. That's what I said, Dennis.'

'Well, it's quite surprising that Mr Pearson should tell you that, Ed, and I really do appreciate it. Thing is, it was the usual sort of confusion – or, should we say, *lack of communication* – between Harvey and Lavinia, and that *does* happen too often for my liking. I don't really like to say this, not wanting to be *negative*, but I'm really having problems with those two. The Prod Ed's obviously a bit hysterical, what with the doors opening and closing in her house and the noises in the attic and so forth, while the Ass Ed *does* strike me as being a bit too involved in his own interests, namely tape-recorders, wrist watches, TV sets and dildoes, to take any real interest in the actual work. I *do* have my doubts there, Ed.'

'Sit down, Dennis. Take a pew. Rest your ass.'

'Thanks, Ed.'

Dennis sat down and offered the Ed a cigarette. The Ed took it and Dennis lit a match. It was Dennis' last match and it started to flicker out so Dennis tore the front page off someone's manuscript and lit it and used that instead. He then threw the burning paper on the carpet and vigorously stamped it out, and he and the Ed sat back and smoked greedily.

'Well, Dennis,' the Ed said, grateful for any bastard to talk to, 'I must say I agree with you, and I'd just like to add that I appreciate you keeping me informed like this, since, as you know, I very rarely get upstairs, let alone out of this office. I'm too busy dealing with paper manufacturers, hassling with the printers over their costs – which, incidentally, they are trying to increase again – fighting various obscenity and libel suits, keeping the finger on our incompetent distributors – which, I might point out, is really the job of the Circulation Manager who went to Paris last Monday and was supposed to be back on Friday but hasn't been seen or heard from since – and, of course, trying to keep the Big P from sacking half the fucking staff because they never seem to be here or do any work when they *are* here, which is why he still hasn't given them the contracts they keep moaning about. As a matter of fact, the only person the Big P *doesn't* want to sack is *you*, because, if I've told him once I've told him a thousand times, that Dennis, I said, he's the only bastard in this place who knows what the fuck is going on.'

'Most kind of you to say so, Ed.'

'Not at all, Dennis.'

'And can I assume from that, Ed, that the Big P will soon be signing my contract?'

'I'm pushing him, Dennis. I'm pushing hard. Thing is, the Big P doesn't mind giving you *your* contract, but there *are* a few clauses he first needs to check out with his solicitors, it being, as you well know, that our esteemed Publisher is a very fair individual with a strong sense of responsibility who wouldn't want you signing anything that might, even inadvertently, work against you in the future. But we're pursuing the matter, Dennis. We're on top of it.'

'Well, that's really great, Ed. I *do* appreciate that. As a matter of fact, that's one of the things I keep trying to drill into the staff: the fact that you are, as it were, the only contact we have with the Big P and that you are obviously trying to do your best for us and that it certainly can't be easy and that we should all appreciate your efforts a little more. I tell them these things, Ed, but they just don't respond. They're trying to grab all they can. They take everything out and they put nothing in and they're only in the work for the money, they have no other motive.'

'Too fucking true, Dennis,' the Ed said. 'Now, you and me, we're proper magazine people, we have no other interests, we're obsessed with nothing other than our work and that's as it should be. But the staff, Dennis, the staff, they're just not in the same league. They're hassling me for raises and they're moaning about their contracts and they're always asking for longer holidays and threatening me with the NUJ, but they don't appear to want to work for it, they're just never around. I hear rumours, Dennis. I hear disturbing stories. I hear that certain staff members, no names, no pack drill, are using their positions not to improve our magazines but to further their own selfish ends.'

'Really?'

'Really. For instance, I *have* noticed an uncommon amount of *female* writers in the magazines recently and, since our mags are for men, and since whores generally haven't a fucking clue how to write for men, the Big P is beginning to suspect that certain of the editorial staff are simply putting these articles in in return for certain intimate, not to say *sexual*, favours from these particular female writers. Of course, I *personally* don't believe this for a minute, Dennis, but the Big P, well, he's a bit disconnected from everything happening upstairs, it being, as you know, that he rarely comes out of his office and is always too busy to see anyone when he's in there, and so he's bound to suspect certain things from the evidence before him. I just think, Dennis, that there's a very great danger that certain staff members, particularly those not quite as mature as ourselves, might be *tempted* into abusing their privileged positions in such a manner, namely putting their own interests before those of the magazines, and so I think you should keep your eyes open with regard to this matter.'

'I take your point, Ed,' Dennis said. 'That was really most perceptive of the Big P. I *do* have a tendency to place too much trust in my staff and I don't always check out what they buy. But I would be most disturbed if I discovered that the features you mentioned were bought for anything other than their literary merit. Still, as you say, the possibility *is* present, particularly when you're dealing with individuals like Harvey, the Ass Ed of *Suave*, who is, not to put it too harshly, a bit of a hustler and who certainly has exposure to the various temptations you mention.'

'Really?' the Ed said.

'Really,' Dennis said. 'Now, as you well know, Ed, I don't like to be negative, but there *is* the disturbing fact that various products are being featured in the up-front section of *Suave* – cameras, wristwatches, hi-fi sets, and so forth – about the same time as the Ass Ed has acquired, not to say *been given*, those products for his personal use, and I have at times found myself wondering if there couldn't be some connection between the two – although, of course, it isn't the sort of thing I would normally bring to your attention until having first ascertained the full facts. Incidentally, Ed, I've always been hugely impressed by this amazing hi-fit set you have here in your office, mainly because I'm thinking of expanding my own unit at home, and I was wondering if perhaps you could give me some information as to where it was obtained and, if it isn't too personal a question, how much such a unit would cost me.'

'Dennis,' the Ed said, back-pedalling with some dexterity, 'I *do* appreciate your concern over the possible, not to say *suspected*, culpability of our venerable Ass Ed, but I would recommend that you tread with a certain delicacy here, since the Ass Ed *does* strike me as being – apart from his suspected, but *as yet unproven* misdemeanours – one of the few occasionally constructive editorial members of staff we have, and he certainly seems to be doing a good job of filling up those front sections with a lot of colourful, not to say *free*, material of the kind that would normally be extremely difficult to obtain.'

'A good point there, Ed.'

'And after all,' the Ed continued enthusiastically, 'it does seem to me that any abuses of his privileged position would surely come to light in good time, and in the meantime, we *do* have more serious problems with those members of staff who, like that all-too-feminine Production Editor, Lavinia, spend most of their time being hysterical about schedules and making *everyone else* hysterical about schedules, with the result that no one knows what anyone else is doing and everyone's too hysterical to ask. Now that disturbs me, Dennis. I don't like that at all. As a matter of fact, that stupid bitch, the Production Editor, who is, if you don't mind me saying so, hideously frustrated and needs a good cock up her, is spending most of her time on the intercom, about every five fucking minutes to be exact, asking if she can come in and see me to discuss something important, and apart from the fact that, as you know, I don't like to see the staff during working hours, I don't want to see that whore of a Prod Ed because I know she only wants to ask me if she can have an editor's position, which she can't, since I do not believe in having hysterical women on the creative side of male-interest magazines, and I'd tell her that except I can't, because she'd just become hysterical and I wouldn't like that, so I want you to express my views to her and stop her tormenting me.'

'I agree with you, Ed, that we certainly can't have females on the editorial side of the magazines. I mean, just the other day, being very pressed for time because I had to take the afternoon off to endure a long lunch with an extremely boring literary agent – '

'Male?'

'Female.'

'I see.'

'So I let Lavinia write up a couple of picture captions, and when I returned to the office, the next day, I found that she'd written something about "the divine Charles Bronson displays his adorable torso in this absolutely dreamy film" and I thought, Lord, what on earth are the readers going to think? Is it a group of homosexuals running *Suave* and *Gents*? And I realised, then, Ed, the wisdom of what you've just said to me.'

'Right.'

'Right,' Dennis said.

At this point in the proceedings the Ed's intercom started buzzing and the Ed cursed and pressed the receiver button and he and Dennis listened patiently to Rosie, the switchboard girl.

'Mr Prince?' she said.

'*Of course* it's Mr Prince! This is *my* office, isn't it? Who the fuck do you *think* it is? Mary Whitehouse?'

'I'm very sorry, Mr Prince, but it's pretty difficult to work out just who's supposed to be in that office, particularly since the Assistant Editor of *Suave*, that cute Harvey, often uses the office in your absence, usually for the purpose of entertaining various businessmen, and when I was in there one day last week, during your all-afternoon lunch break, the Ass Ed was having a conference with some such men, and I noticed that he had photographs of his wife and children on your desk, and that his nameplate was on your door, and that he was pouring the men drinks from your bar and passing around your cigars, and I just thought that maybe, you know, he had been *promoted* or something, so I'm never too sure who's in there.'

'Miss… ah…?'

'Teasedale.'

'Teasedale, please note that Robert Prince always was, still is, and hopefully always *will be* the Managing Director and Editor of Saturnalia Publications, and the fact that he occasionally lets certain executive staff members use his office in his absence is no indication that he is about to abdicate. Now what do you want?'

'Well, Mr Prince, I have quite a few messages for you, most of which have come in since Friday lunchtime when you told me you didn't want to take any calls because you were busy in the Boardroom with the staff, ha, ha, and I just thought, since some of them seemed pretty urgent, that you might want me to read them out to you.'

'I don't recall giving you any such instruction, Miss Teasedale, since I am, of course, always willing to take incoming calls, it being that most calls to the Managing Director and Editor *are* of some importance, so please give me the messages received.'

'Right,' the redoubtable Rosie said. 'Our solicitor called to say that he is particularly offended by the photograph on page sixty-six of the current issue of *Suave* and wants it either removed from the print-film or touched up in a manner that renders it less suggestive than it is. Apparently the photograph shows two naked girls in an amorous embrace on a silk sheet, and although the solicitor is willing to pass lesbian poses that are redeemed by a certain subtlety in the photography, and although he doesn't mind photos of young girls engaged in lesbian – i.e., *oral* sex – he finds it gravely offensive that the girls should be smiling – i.e., *displaying pleasure* – while so engaged. He would therefore like the lips touched up to appear turned down as well as having the somewhat glaring sexual organs painted out to the point where they can't really be seen. And he says that either you do that or he must insist on having the aforementioned photographs removed, even understanding, as he does, the inconvenience and expense this will cause at this stage of production, it being that the offending photographs are already on film and ready to roll.'

'Bastard.'

'Right. There's also a message from a Mrs Allbright of Liverpool who claims that the incident related in "The Cleft", a short story we published two months ago in *Gents*, actually happened, but not to the heroine in Guatemala as related in the story, but to her, Mrs Allbright, in Manchester in 1943, and not with a Brazilian who used a cane but with an American GI who used a whip, and she wants you to ring her back with a view to discussing compensation for the use and subsequent abuse of her hideous experience.'

'Bitch.'

'Right. I also have a few other calls which are probably not that important. From your wife, who was trying to locate you all Friday afternoon and now wants to know where you are; from your Bank Manager, who is threatening to cancel all your credit cards unless you ring him back by five o'clock Friday, which day has passed; from a photographer who turned up with two models at a location recommended by the Artful Ed only to find that the Artful Ed wasn't there and that the location didn't really exist but was in fact a North London branch of the Labour Exchange; and from our esteemed Publisher, the Big P, who was trying to get you all Friday afternoon to tell you there was a noisy party going on in the Boardroom - a message I couldn't pass on to you because you had told me that you would be in the Boardroom with your staff, ha, ha, and weren't to be interrupted. Finally, a message that *could* be of some importance, having been phoned through this morning from a hotel in Piccadilly, saying that two Norwegian paper manufacturers, neither of whom speak remotely decent English, are being held at the hotel pending payment of a bill for three nights in residence – ordered for them, apparently, by the Artful Ed, after he had escorted them to the hotel from the party in the Boardroom, signing them in in your name and telling them that you would doubtless contact them in the morning. The Norwegians, both of whom are married and are usually teetotal, are reportedly in a state of shock due to the fact that they have been drunk all weekend, they suspect they were also drugged, and the two ladies recommended by the Artful Ed stole their wallets and travellers' cheques. The hotel wants you to ring them.'

'That cunt,' the Ed said.

'Right,' Rosie said.

'Okay,' the Ed said. 'I would like to commend you for your efficiency in taking down all those messages, but at the moment I'm engaged in a very important conversation with the Chief Associate Editor and I don't want to take any more calls. Is that understood?'

'Yes, Mr Prince.'

'Good.'

The Ed pressed the OFF button and inhaled on his cigarette and coughed and ran his fingers through his hair, his youthful face a deathly white.

'Jesus,' he said, looking for an ashtray and failing to find one and stubbing the cigarette out on someone's manuscript. 'I just don't believe it. I mean, you work your ass off all weekend on these mags, from morning to night, not sleeping, not seeing your kids, and you come in here hoping for a clear run and you're buried in shit before you can breathe. I tell you, Dennis, I don't know that it's worth it. I'm twenty-six years old and I'm in hock to the bank, I can't pay my mortgage, I smoke sixty fags a day, I drink enough to sink a battleship, I fight constantly with literary agents and printers and the Law, I haven't time for a meal, I never get enough sex, my parents have disowned me, my wife's threatening to leave me, and now I'm stabbed in the back by my staff. It's a glamorous life.'

'Your wife's threatening to leave you?'

'That's right.'

'Well, I'm very sorry to hear that, Ed. I mean, that's one very fine woman you have there, well-bred, intelligent, wonderful with the kids, and she keeps a beautiful home, lovely furniture, great cooking, and it would be a shame if you lost that.'

'It's all the fucking Artful Ed's fault.'

'Really?'

'Really.'

'I didn't know that.'

'Yes, well, you know what I'm like, Dennis, you know that I like to keep my finger on the pulse, to stick *close to the action*, as it were, and although the Artful Ed is pretty slick at staying out of the office but still getting his work done – at least *someone* must do it because the magazines *do* come out – although he does this and is, if I may say so, spectacularly good at it, he *is* a fucker who has to be watched closely, which is why, when I'm not here in the office, during which times it is, apparently, being used for underhand purposes by that prick of an Assistant Editor, I am running around the city trying to catch up with the Artful Ed, particularly when he's involved in photo sessions at which, were I not present to prevent him, he would most likely abuse his privileged position by trying to stick his great horny cock into one of those juicy little models. So I have to go along to keep a tight rein on things and also, it being that it is extremely rare to actually *get near* the Artful Ed, to discuss the general art side of the magazines and, of course, the Artful Ed being what he is, before any discussion of value can get off the ground he's poured the wine and rolled some fucking joints and then two, three days later, the whole experience a blur, I waken up in this office minus money and good health and wonder what the hell I've been doing and when I was last home. That's why the wife's leaving me.'

'I must say, Ed, that sounds really terrible.'

'Quite.'

'Quite. And as a matter of fact, Ed, not wanting to spread any ill-found rumours, particularly about the Artful Ed who is, as you know, a gentleman to respect, but it *has* been brought to my notice that the Artful Ed – though undoubtedly busy with the mags, which is why he spends so much time out of the office, giving his *personal attention*, as it were, to every last detail of every last photo-shoot – is also very busy with his own affairs and is, in fact, building up a private empire with, according to unverified rumour, a lot of design work for record companies and book publishers and advertisers, not to mention illustrations for *rival* magazine companies, this all being the fruits of a general design studio that he runs in partnership with a young lady who is, according to unverified rumour, another member of our staff and who also helps him out in his reportedly lucrative sideline in the selling of Letraset, 35-millimetre film, layout sheets, tracing paper, felt-tip pens, sketch pads and crayons, all of which comes from our Company supplies and has almost doubled the Art Department's expenditure. I *do* have my doubts there, Ed.'

'Dennis,' the Ed said, tugging at his beard and running agitated fingers through his hair, 'I appreciate you telling me this because I did indeed have my own doubts, and not only about the Artful Ed but about most of the other members of staff as well, particularly since it becomes increasingly clear to me that more and more of our executives, tricky fuckers the lot of them, are abusing their privileged positions and my trust by concentrating more on their own interests than on the overall interest of the magazines in a manner typified, and possibly even *encouraged*, by the otherwise highly talented Artful Ed.'

'True, Ed,' Dennis said.

'Now you, Dennis, you don't do that at all. You write your novels and you do them in your own time and you never let them interfere with the job, and I admire that, I *respect* it. I also respect the fact, Dennis, and I don't mind admitting it, that you keep your private life to yourself, you go your own way, and you keep a decent and, if I may say so, a *dignified* distance between yourself and the other members of staff, particularly those of the female persuasion. I want you to know this, Dennis, because the thing I find most *shitty* is the realisation that certain editorial staff members – no names, no pack drill, but take Harvey as an example – are utilising the glamorous image that adheres to their privileged positions in order to impress, not to say *fuck*, certain of the more impressionable female staff members, no names, no pack drill, and I'm pleased to note that this is not a vice practised by yourself.'

'Thanks, Ed.'

'I trust you, Dennis. You're the only one I can trust. I know that I can turn my back on you without having to worry that you're going to abuse my trust and your privileged position by purchasing stories from no-talent female writers in return for sexual favours, or stealing items of equipment from the office for your own use at home, or slipping reviews of your own books – all written under pseudonyms, I gather, and very good reading at that – into the mags, or last but certainly not least, taking over my office and pretending it's your own as reportedly that fuck-rat Harvey has been doing. I don't think that's fair, Dennis.'

'Ed, I must say I'm gratified by your faith in me and by your willingness to put it on record, and I would just like to state, regarding the last item in particular, that I fully agree with you and that I think it's about time we dampened down the *ardour*, as it were, of an increasingly exploitative Assistant Editor, and I shall certainly take this matter in hand myself, without further delay.'

'Dennis, I appreciate your courage in being willing to do this,' the Ed said with some fervour, 'but it does seem to me that the various abuses we've mentioned have only come about through my own, admittedly innocent, omissions in that I *did* tend to place too much trust in the staff, with the result that they now think me not benevolent, but *soft*, and that I should therefore take the matter in hand myself by *personally* disciplining the recalcitrant members of staff, starting with that smart fucker, Harvey, who will shortly feel my whip on his back. And, since you are the only one I can trust, and since obviously you are the only one I can leave in charge in my absence, I would like you to remain here and observe how the shit hits the fan.'

'Okay, Ed.'

'Okay, then.'

Clearly feeling more positive and dynamic, the Ed tried buzzing the shifty Ass Ed, but received no immediate response. Figuring that Harvey was not at his desk, since he very rarely was, the Ed buzzed the message boy, remembered that he was missing and tried buzzing someone else instead. After going through the Ass Ed of *Gents*, the Production Editors of *Gents* and *Suave,* and the advertising and circulation secretaries of all the magazines, none of whom were at their desks, he finally reached his own secretary who was having a coffee in the kitchen. She informed him that the Ass Ed had just left the kitchen carrying a great little 5-inch portable TV set and half a pint of coffee in a new dildo-shaped thermos flask that lit up in the dark and could, if the central section was withdrawn through the bottom and three normal HPS batteries were inserted, be used as a sophisticated high-speed, low-speed vibrator, and that he had stated his intention of returning to his desk, sampling the coffee, and getting on with some overdue work.

The Ed promptly buzzed the Ass Ed's desk again and got a strange girl who told him, between hysterical giggles, that the Ass Ed had offered her some brandy-laced coffee from an illuminated, vibrating dildo and had then disappeared up the stairs, taking with him a life-size inflatable rubber doll with removable breasts, vagina and blonde wig and additional male wig and testicles, designed specifically for frustrated married couples, transvestites and bisexuals, and that he intended trying selling this to the mysterious teetotal bisexual editor who sat at an empty desk in the Art Department's studio and worked ceaselessly at unspecified tasks for various unnamed magazines.

The Ed cursed and buzzed the mysterious teetotal bisexual editor who replied promptly by saying that the Ass Ed had just given him a life-size inflatable bisexual doll, truly delicious, in return for the crate of brandy that had been sent to the mysterious teetotal bisexual editor from a gay liberation magazine that had appreciated the coverage he was giving them in the various unnamed magazines that he worked on for Saturnalia Publications. The mysterious teetotal bisexual editor also said that the Ass Ed had just been seen disappearing into the Picture Editor's office, carrying the crate of brandy and an expensive Minolta SRT 303B 50-mm f1.7 camera that he wanted to give to the Pic Ed in return for a free trip to the Bahamas with one porno photographer and two sexy models, which would, the Ass Ed had said, result in a superb picture spread for *Suave*, this being devotion to duty and truly most admirable. The Ed cursed again, threw a fierce look at Dennis, then buzzed the Picture Editor's office. Harvey replied.

'Yes?'

'Is that the Assistant Editor of *Suave*?'

'Who is this, please?'

'This is the Editor.'

'The *Ed*?'

'The *Editor*.'

'Well, hello there! Good to hear from you, Ed! As a matter of fact, the Chief Ass told me you just got back and – '

'I got back five weeks ago.'

'Right. And I said, I really must go down and say hello to our old buddy. So how are you, Ed?'

'I'm fine. And you?'

'Not bad. Not bad at all. A bit overworked since you've been away, what with Dennis not being here most of the time and *someone* having to do most of the work, though I don't want to burden you with that now, Ed, you just having come back and all, and me not being the type to rush you.'

'Most kind of you, Harvey.'

'Not at all, Ed. So how was New York?'

'Busy.'

'Two girls to every guy, all ready, willing and able. Did you pick up some true love and syphilis and did you enjoy it? Now tell me the truth, Ed.'

'I would really like to discuss something quite serious.'

'Ed, I've got this great idea. Let me tell you this great idea. As you know, Viking is due to land on the Moon tomorrow – '

'Mars.'

'Right. And this being such a large leap for the machine, such a small step for mankind – '

'An historic occasion.'

'Right. So I thought it might be a nice idea, *timely* as it were, if we could rush in a short satirical piece relevant to the subject. I mean, *funny*, certainly, but *serious* as well, a sociological and scientific study of what might happen if – and we're just supposing here – we *did* discover Little Green Men up there, and if, say, they were homosexually or even, God forbid, *bi*sexually inclined, and then, of course, us being humans and all, and what with the difference in our gravitational pulls – I mean, how high would a hard-on *rise* up there? And what happens if you're trying to poke it in and the fucking thing keeps floating about in that rarefied atmosphere? And so on and so forth. And so, you know, we could pull this nifty little number on how the Moon – '

'Mars.'

' – with its admittedly *hypothetical* Little Green Men could alter the whole emotional and physical sexual drive of Mother Earth and lead to a whole new fucking species. And I thought that maybe we could call it something like… well, bearing in mind that we don't want *New Scientist* getting one up on us… I thought, "Slipping it up a Martian Canal" or something like that. You dig, Ed?'

'Wonderful.'

'Well, Ed, I'll get straight on to it. I'll have it commissioned and on my desk by Friday, and I just want to say, Ed, that I've really appreciated your valuable comments on this idea and I'm sure I'll be seeing you real soon.'

'*Don't cut me off!*' the Ed shrieked.

'Pardon, Ed?'

'I haven't finished yet,' the Ed said, settling back, wiping his sweaty brow, a tall, thin, schoolboy-handsome wreck. 'I want to talk to you.'

'Really?'

'Really.'

'Well, Jesus, that's great, Ed. I mean, you only back five weeks and already wanting to tell me all about it. But I *am* pretty busy at the moment, Ed, so why don't I call you later and perhaps we can both slip out for a quiet drink or something?'

'That sounds like an excellent idea, Harvey, but at the moment I'd just like to discuss the fact that apparently you've been using my office in my absence.'

'That's right, Ed, and I'm sorry you heard about it since I wasn't going to tell you myself, not wanting you to feel *indebted* to me or anything, because there *was* an awful lot of unattended business piling up on your desk during your absence, and what with Dennis not being around most of the time, and understanding the *importance* of your correspondence and so forth, I felt that *someone* had to go in there and sort it all out. As a matter of fact, Ed, at one stage I was doing so much work in there I was hardly getting near my own desk, and, you know me, Ed, a devoted family man and all, I even found myself taking that picture of my wife and kids down with me, just to comfort me, as it were, and I must say it was a pretty dismal time, particularly when I had to entertain certain of your business associates, most notably the paper manufacturers I was with the day the switchboard girl came in and looked puzzled, and that really was one pretty exhausting day, Ed, though I don't want you thanking me.'

'What paper manufacturers?'

'Thing is, Ed, I never took their names down because although at first they seemed genuine, it *did* begin to dawn on me that maybe they weren't quite on the level, that most likely they were just three guys from the Vice Squad come in to have a look around – something more or less confirmed when the Artful Ed rang me and told me that *he* was going to be entertaining some paper manufacturers on your behalf a few days later – so I just poured these guys some drinks and told them a few tales and sent them on their way without offending them too much – '

'Very wise.'

' – but I didn't want to tell you, Ed, because I didn't want you to feel *indebted* or anything, though I *would* like to have that drink so we could discuss the extra work and responsibility that your absence placed on my shoulders, particularly since Dennis was rarely around, probably at home writing his novels, ha, ha, and I feel that perhaps some form of remuneration in the form of, say, a raise and even, hopefully, the signing of that overdue contract, would not be remiss, so how about three this afternoon?'

'I really can't confirm at the moment whether or not I'll be available at three this afternoon and, of course, I couldn't discuss your contract anyway since, as you know, the contracts are still being perused by our esteemed Publisher, the Big P, who is gravely concerned about certain aspects of the contracts that might be detrimental to the employees and who would therefore appreciate a bit more time to sort these points out, not being able to tackle the job immediately because, as his secretary has stated, he is constantly engaged in numerous complex negotiations which will ensure the long-term viability of this Company and thus the security of its employees, something he holds close to his heart.'

'And how *is* the Big P, Ed?'

'Our esteemed Publisher is, according to his secretary, in the best of health and in optimistic frame of mind, but since, as you know, the Big P rarely comes out of his office and is always too busy to see anyone when he is in there, I can only add that my personal contacts with him, via memos and messages conveyed through his secretary, have been more than a little cordial – though he *has* recently expressed certain grievances about the laxness of particular staff members regarding time-keeping, petty-cash expenditure, interdepartmental relationships, general creative input to the magazines, and the overall production costs.'

'Well, I don't blame him there, Ed' Harvey said. 'I mean, I can hardly spend any time at my own desk because I'm always running around from one department to the other, doing everyone's job but my own because no one's ever in the fucking place. I rarely have time for breakfast, I'm lucky if I get sleep, I run around the city collecting pictures, seeing literary agents, hassling cartoonists and illustrators because no one else is willing to do it. Now that isn't my job, Ed. It's the Art Department's job. But you get these people, they're slipshod to say the least, and you find yourself doing it yourself because you want the job done. I'm glad you brought the subject up, Ed. I think it should be discussed. I mean, you get these people, they're not professional like you and me; they think of nothing but having free meals and free drinks, but they don't want to work for the privilege. That's what's happening, Ed. That's why our costs are rocketing. Too many of the staff are fucking hustlers and we've just got to stop them.'

'Your concern in this matter is most laudable, Harvey, and, since you've brought up the subject, perhaps it would be appropriate if we started our investigations along these lines by clearing the air over certain matters that have arisen during my absence, most notably the situation regarding the use of advertisers' products in the up-front section of the magazines, it being that our esteemed Publisher is concerned about the possible connection between products featured in those sections of the magazines and the sudden acquisition of such products by certain members of the staff.'

'That's a very good point, Ed,' Harvey said agreeably, 'and it's one I was going to bring up with you myself when we had that drink at three o'clock, it being that although, as you know, I have been particularly successful at filling three pages of each magazine with *free* copy and photographs – a saving of approximately five-hundred quid per page, six pages per month, total save of three thou per month and all for a few quid from petty cash – although I have, as I say, been particularly successful at this, I *am* finding it increasingly difficult due to the fact that more and more manufacturers are complaining about being exploited by the staff of our magazines, many of whom are reportedly ringing up and requesting certain products, most notably record albums and books, on the pretext that they are working for me and want them for review purposes, the items, naturally, never being reviewed, with the result that the manufacturers are closing their ranks, I'm left out on a limb, and the possibility of having to actually *buy* up-front material – which would mean an additional cost of three thou per month to the Big P – looms larger every week – and I tell you this, Ed, because, as you know, I take the up-front sections very seriously, I believe they enhance the magazines, and I don't want them to be fucked up because of the selfishness and greed of certain, as yet unnamed, members of staff... Incidentally, Ed, how's your hi-fi set?'

'Pardon?' the Ed said, looking shifty.

'The hi-fi set in your office,' Harvey said. 'I always did say it, Ed, and I say it again, that you shouldn't keep that particular item in your office, that it's much too valuable to be left around, that you should keep it at home where you could appreciate it properly, it being that it was such a good bargain – 800 quids worth of the best of Japanese, but yours for 200 plus VAT, no hassles, no strings – and I would also point out that that's just one of the many benefits that will disappear if we don't clamp down on the staff and stop them exploiting their privileged positions and my hard-earned friendships with the numerous manufacturers who are really extremely concerned by it all.'

'Harvey,' the Ed said, again back-pedalling with great dexterity, 'the possibility that what you say is true is really most disturbing, and I must say I'm gratified to learn that you have the situation in hand and are going to do something definitive about it. I *do* feel, given what you've just told me, that we should discuss this matter further when time permits, and in the meantime a tentative memo to all members of staff might be appropriate, reminding them that you and you alone are in charge of all reviews and product profiles and that under no circumstances is anyone else to contact manufacturers or record, movie or book companies, and that, should they *definitely* need to contact such companies for, say, general information on release dates and castings, they are only to do it through you.'

'Right.'

'Right. And now, Harvey, I'd just like to say how sorry I am that I haven't been able to get up there – '

'Down.'

' – to see you since my return, but then I am, as you know, extremely busy at the moment, what with the increasing difficulty in trying to obtain printing papers and the various obscenity and libel cases I'm trying to defend and the growing complexity of our distribution outlets and, of course, the numerous problems that come to my desk in the shape of various staff members, most of whom are extremely selfish and avaricious and ungrateful for their privileged positions, but I *do* hope to see you soon, Harvey, and when I do, perhaps we can discuss these important matters further. Incidentally, how's the wife?'

'Who?'

'The wife.'

'She's threatening to leave me.'

'Well, I'm very sorry to hear that, Harvey, since that's one very fine woman you have there, well-bred, intelligent, wonderful with the kids, damned good with the housework not to mention the cooking, and I always did respect her, as you know.'

'It's the job, Ed,' Harvey said. 'She doesn't understand the problems. As you know, Ed, I take my work very seriously with the result that I'm more or less at it all the time and, of course,

Dennis not being in the office often, being very *busy* as it were elsewhere, ha, ha, and what with guys like the Artful Ed never being in the vicinity for consultation with their staff, well, Ed, I find that more and more of the staff are coming to *me* for assistance, and so, no doubt about it, I'm being run off my feet, I never get a minute's rest, and I'm rarely at home and the wife wants to leave me and I think you should give me a raise. I would like to discuss this, Ed.'

'Harvey, I appreciate the difficulties you must be having at present and I certainly would like to discuss the possibility of a raise, but I really don't think I can approach the Big P at the moment since the Big P is, as his secretary has confirmed, extremely busy with the broader aspects of the Company and should, I feel, be allowed a little more time to resolve such problems before being burdened with individual requests from isolated members of the staff, although, as I'm sure you appreciate, I will certainly bring your problem up at the first available opportunity.'

'That's fine, Ed,' Harvey said. 'I really do appreciate that. And how is the wife?'

'Who?'

'The wife.'

'A few difficulties there, Harvey. A few traumas…'

'Well, I'm very sorry to hear that, Ed. I mean, that's one very fine woman you have there, well-bred, intelligent, wonderful with – '

'Harvey, I wonder if, since I've got you on the buzzer, you could tell me precisely what you're doing up in the Picture Editor's studio, it being that I have a few urgent jobs of a more important nature, and the kind of jobs that I could only trust *you* to handle, but, of course, I wouldn't drag you away from what you're doing at the moment if it were even *more* urgent and important. So please fill me in, Harvey.'

'Thing is, Ed, I've got this expensive Minolta SRT 303B 50-millimetre f1.7 camera that I was thinking of reviewing in the up-front section of *Suave* and, also, since the Pic Ed was saying that he could do with just such a camera for instant test shots on possible models, and since the manufacturers of this product have kindly agreed to let me have it free of charge in return for a brief techno-profile in the up-front section, I thought it would save the Company a bit of money – in that we'd fill at least two columns of the mag with free copy and a pic and, also, negate the cost of an extremely expensive piece of equipment that is desperately needed by the Pic Ed – by accepting their generous offer, and so I'm up here checking the camera with the Pic Ed himself by doing some test shots on this sweet young lady who was invited in by the Pic Ed for some test shots.'

'You have *a model* up there?'

'That's right, Ed.'

'*Undressed?*'

'Well, Ed, she *does* want to model for *our* magazines.'

'Harvey, this is really most disturbing, not to say *shitty*. If I've told you all once, I've told you a thousand times, *no* models are to be either interviewed or photographed in the absence of the Editor, and when such models *are* to be interviewed or photographed, this is to be done by one of the photographers we have on a retainer and *not* by the Picture Editor or, for that matter, by anyone else, least of all members of the editorial staff.'

'Jesus, I'm really sorry, Ed, I didn't know that. I just… hold on a second… What? Right… Well, Ed, the Pic Ed says to tell you he's very sorry, that he wouldn't normally have gone ahead on his own with such a shoot, but that in this case he felt it best to go ahead since we urgently need a centre spread and, aware of the fact that you've just been back a few days – '

'Weeks.'

' – he didn't want to disturb you and thought he would just knock off a few quick shots and then send them down to you for your perusal at your convenience, although, now aware of your presence and interest, he certainly would welcome you up here to view the young lady under discussion.'

'Hold on. I'll be right up.'

The Ed pressed the OFF button and looked intently at Dennis who was idly doodling on the first page of someone's manuscript. 'You just wouldn't believe it,' the Ed said self-righteously. 'I mean, you can't trust those fuckers at all. I've said it before, Dennis, and I don't mind repeating it, you're the only bastard in this building I can trust. They have a girl up there, Dennis. The girl's naked and defenceless. If I didn't know about it, they'd have her on the floor and then we'd all have a scandal on our hands. They have no discretion, Dennis. They just want some nooky. They'd have her on the floor and they'd both be on top of her and she'd leave that office screaming about rape and then we'd all be up Shit Creek.'

'I must say, I'm shocked, Ed. I'm shocked that they'd do that without your permission.'

'They don't give a fuck, Dennis. They don't respect my position. You turn your back and they go their own way and then the shit hits the fan.'

'Well, Ed, as you know, I always check personally with you before tackling anything outside my normal area of jurisdiction. But these people, Ed, what can I say? They're just irresponsible.'

'That's the word, Dennis. It keeps me awake at night. You trust them and they slip the blade in, and the word's *irresponsible*.'

'That's what it is, Ed.'

'And you heard that *whole* conversation, Dennis?'

'Yes, Ed, I did.'

'So you must have heard that little bastard Harvey slipping the blade into your spine?'

'Yes, Ed, I heard that.'

'That's what they're like, Dennis. You can't trust them for a minute. They pretend to be your friend, but the first chance they get, they try to have you hung, drawn and quartered. I don't like that, Dennis. I think it's cheap and nasty. I think it's trying to buy credit at someone else's expense, and I think it shows a lack of self-respect. I want you to nail that bastard.'

'Well, Ed,' Dennis said sweetly, 'I must say, I feel no animosity, since it's only human nature after all. These people, they're not professional like you and me; they lack confidence and so they try to impress you. You know how it is, Ed. Everyone's defending his own position. It's not nice, but it *is* understandable, and I don't mind at all.'

'I respect that, Dennis. You retain your objectivity. You don't let ambitions or resentments detract from the main issues. That's why I trust you, Dennis. You never try to shaft anyone. You get on with your work and keep yourself to yourself, and don't look for praise or revenge. I really respect that.'

'Well, I certainly appreciate that, Ed.'

'I think we'd better get up there, Dennis. I think we'd better get up there and see what they're doing and check that that girl's still a virgin. I don't trust those bastards.'

'That's very wise, Ed.'

The Ed buzzed the switchboard girl and informed her that he and the Chief Associate Editor were going up to the Picture Editor's office and were not to be disturbed for any reason. The switchboard girl, the redoubtable Rosie, told the Ed that she had quite a few new messages for him, which messages had been mounting up all morning because the Ed had told her not to interrupt him, and the Ed, after listening with furrowed brow to this weighty news, informed Rosie that he still didn't have time to attend to the messages. Rosie then wanted to know if it was true that the Chief Associate Editor was actually there with the Ed, and when the Ed said yes, it was true, Rosie said to tell him, the Chief Associate Editor, that the girl who had arrived to take up a new editorial position was still waiting in Reception and that the Circulation Manager had telephoned again from Torremolinos.

'I *wondered* where that bastard was,' the Ed said.

'He's in Torremolinos,' Rosie said.

'We know,' Dennis said. 'You've just told us that.'

'What's he doing in Torremolinos?' the Ed asked.

'I don't know,' Dennis replied. 'He rang me this morning but I didn't have time to take his call.'

'Are you talking to me?' Rosie said over the intercom.

''No,' Dennis said.

'He's *supposed* to be in Milan,' the Ed said.

'Paris,' Dennis said.

'Paris?' the Ed said.

'Yes,' Dennis said. 'He went to Paris on Monday and he left there on Tuesday and he was supposed to be back at work this morning and instead he's in Spain.'

'What the fuck is he doing there?'

'I don't know, Ed. I haven't spoken to him yet.'

'I don't trust that bastard, Dennis.'

'Neither do I, Ed.'

'All right. Let's find out.'

The Ed told the switchboard girl, Rosie, to get in touch with the Circulation Manager in Torremolinos and to put the call through to the Picture Editor's office when it came in. Rosie said she would do that, and then she asked the Ed what she should do about the girl who was still in Reception, waiting to take up her new editorial position.

'I don't know anything about her,' the Ed said.

'The Chief Associate Editor knows something about her,' Rosie said. 'As a matter of fact, he said he was going to come down and see her.'

'I don't know anything about her,' Dennis said. 'The only thing I know about her is what the switchboard girl told me, which is that she's here to start in some unspecified editorial position and she was told to ask for me.'

'Well,' the Ed said, 'if she's here to start in an editorial position – over my dead body, I might add – and she was told to ask for you, you must know something about her, Dennis.'

'No, I don't, Ed. The only thing I know about her is what

the switchboard girl told me, but *I* certainly haven't hired anyone recently and I assumed that *you* must have hired her and told her to report to me and then forgot to tell me she was arriving and what she'd been hired for.'

'*I* didn't hire her,' the Ed said.

'Well, *someone* hired her,' Dennis said.

'Do you think she was at the party on Friday afternoon?'

'I don't know, Ed. I wasn't at the party on Friday afternoon.'

'Weren't you?'

'No, Ed.'

'Who *was* at the party on Friday afternoon?'

'*You* were at the party on Friday afternoon, Ed. At least the Artful Ed *said* you were at the party, though I can't confirm this since I wasn't at the party myself.'

'That bastard,' the Ed said.

'Quite,' Dennis said.

'Are you talking to me?' Rosie asked over the intercom.

'No,' Dennis said.

'I *couldn't* have been at the party on Friday afternoon,' the Ed said. 'On Friday I had lunch with an actress and her agent, and, as I remember, it was a long lunch. I still have the hangover.'

'Is that the blonde who makes intellectual porno movies and talks about sexual liberation on the chat shows?'

'That's the bitch.'

'I know her,' Dennis said. 'She walked out of the Boardroom about four-thirty Friday afternoon, starkers and bushy-tailed, and waltzed drunkenly through the typing pool, right past the Big P's door, and came up the stairs and sat down in my office. I must say, I was shocked, Ed.'

'Really?'

'Really.'

'And what did you do, Dennis?'

'I took off my jacket and draped it around her, but

W.A. Harbinson

unfortunately it didn't cover her lower parts. I therefore left her in the office and borrowed a full-length coat from the Prod Ed of *Suave* and put that coat around her and led her back down the stairs to the Boardroom. I did not enter the Boardroom myself, since I did not wish to participate in an unauthorised orgy, so I simply pushed her back in and closed the door and returned to my office. I didn't see her again, Ed.'

'Well, I must say that was extremely decent of you, Dennis, but I'm sure that the girl you saw was not the actress of whom I speak, since her agent is a most possessive man who would not have let her get into such a state, much less out of his sight.'

'Is that the homosexual gentleman with the bald head and gold chains who lisps and drinks gallons of Pernod?'

'That's the one, Dennis.'

'I think I saw him,' Dennis said. 'After returning to my office, I found myself requiring the advice of a member of the Art Department, so I went upstairs to the studio – which was, of course, totally empty due to the party in the Boardroom – and turning to leave again, I heard a commotion from the room containing the back issues. Hoping to find at least *one* responsible member of the Art Department, I glanced in and instead found that mysterious teetotal bisexual editor, who has his own desk in the studio and works at unspecified tasks for various unnamed magazines, lying on top of the bald homosexual agent on the message boy's table, both of them undressed from the waist down, the bald homosexual agent clutching the table with both hands and making odd whimpering sounds while the mysterious teetotal bisexual editor was thrusting in and out at a very specific task, his posterior bobbing up and down in the gloom and the whole table rocking. I must say, I was shocked, Ed.'

'Jesus,' the Ed said.

'Right,' Dennis said.

'I don't think I can listen to any more of this,' Rosie said over the intercom.

76

'Jesus,' the Ed said again.

'It seems to me, Ed,' Dennis said, 'that you must have brought your luncheon guests back to the building for further constructive talks, and then, discovering the party at its height and not wishing your guests to know that it had been organised without your permission, decided to take them to the party and introduce them to the staff – an intelligent political move which unfortunately resulted in you becoming embroiled in the sordid affair in a manner you had not intended and certainly would not have sanctioned had you not been placed in such an embarrassing situation in the first place.'

'That's it,' the Ed said gratefully. 'You've hit the nail on the head, Dennis. The members of staff do these things and they don't think of the consequences and innocent people get caught up in their shenanigans and all hell is let loose. I think I remember it now. It was all the Artful Ed's fault. That bastard was in there with two fat-bellied foreign farts who couldn't speak decent English, and they were starting to look pretty shocked – being teetotal or diseased or something – and I was saying what a pity it was that they couldn't get into the proper spirit of things – just being polite, as it were – and then I moved away, and then I remember seeing that bearded maniac, namely the Artful Ed, dropping a couple of tablets into their glasses of Coke, and I thought, you know, LSD or some shit, and then I had another brandy and it really seemed to hit me, I mean it nearly lifted my fucking head off my shoulders, and I thought, Christ, the bastard's spiked *my* drink as well, and the bastard must have, because the next thing I remember is seeing this really sweet little whore, a total stranger, probably not even staff, probably some cunt's *wife* or something, and she was lifting her skirt up over her hips and swaying and giggling, doing a *mambo* or some such fucking number, that Brigitte Bardot bit from *And God Created Woman*, some piss-take like that, and the next thing I knew, giggling myself as I remember, I was down on my knees with my nose between her legs, and I was... well... sort of...you know… I mean… Jesus it doesn't bear thinking about. You don't think I was…?'

'What colour was her hair?' Rosie asked over the intercom.

'What?' the Ed said, looking confused.

'What colour was her hair?'

'Oh,' the Ed said. 'Brunette, I think.'

'Brunette,' Rosie said. 'She's a brunette.'

'*What?*' the Ed said.

'The girl in Reception,' Rosie said. 'The one who's waiting to start her new job. She's a brunette.'

'Jesus,' the Ed said.

'Oh, well,' Dennis said.

'The Artful Ed,' the Ed said. 'The rotten bastard.'

'That's it,' Dennis said.

The Ed told Rosie to tell the girl waiting in Reception that both he and the Chief Associate Editor were in conference and would not be finished until after lunch and that she should therefore take herself off for a bite and report back to Reception in an hour or two. Rosie confirmed that she would relay this message and that she would also put the call to the Circulation Manager through to the Picture Editor's office when she managed to get Torremolinos. The Ed thanked her and pressed the OFF button and then stared hard at Dennis.

'All right,' the Ed said, 'let's get the fuck upstairs before we have to call for the riot squad.'

'That sounds like the thing, Ed.'

The Ed didn't want to be seen by any members of the administrative staff, so he made Dennis go down and press the lift button and give him a shout when it came up. Dennis did as he was told and when the lift doors opened he called out to the Ed and the Ed ran into the lift and the doors closed again. The magazine offices were located just above an expensive strip club that was owned by the Big P, and standing with Dennis and the Ed in the lift, which linked the strip club to the dressing rooms to the magazine offices above, was a naked stripper who had been carried past the dressing-room floor when Dennis pressed the third-floor button. The stripper had false eyelashes and a long blonde wig on her head and siliconed breasts and sparkle-dust on her pubic hair and she was sweating and chewing gum and at her ease. She was standing close to the Ed, but since she wasn't a member of his staff and therefore did not come under his jurisdiction, he hardly noticed her glorious presence.

The lift stopped and the doors opened and the Ed furrowed his brow and walked out and stood with Dennis in the corridor. To their left was the small dark room that contained the back issues and which also had contained the bald homosexual agent and the mysterious teetotal bisexual editor when they were going at it like two pigs in a trough. The Ed glanced at this room and visibly shuddered with revulsion and then glanced furtively through the two glass-panelled doors that led into the combined Art Departments. The studio was large and spacious with a lot of wooden desks and very few working people, this few being predominantly female. As a matter of fact, the only reasonable facsimile of a male that the Ed could see was the mysterious teetotal bisexual editor who was presently leaning across his cluttered desk and speaking into a telephone and looking bright-eyed, energetic and degenerate. The Ed stared long and hard at this facsimile of a male, and then, glancing around unsuccessfully for some sign of the real article, turned to Dennis and informed him that the male members of staff were all absent and were therefore doubtless in with the Picture Editor. Dennis agreed that this was probably the case, so the Ed straightened his shoulders, glanced around him in disgust, then opened the door just in front of him and quickly walked in.

79

3

Dennis followed the Ed into the Picture Editor's office and saw that it was filled with merry males. Dennis closed the door behind him and waved cigarette smoke from his face and saw the Ed glancing around him and blinking repeatedly. The Picture Editor's office was white and had thick carpet on the floor, the walls covered with pinup posters and ads and some newspaper cuttings. There were also a lot of shelves around the walls, stacked high with yellow plastic boxes that contained thousands of colour transparencies of bum and tit and pudenda: a pornographer's paradise.

The Picture Editor was twenty-four years old and he had cropped blond hair and rimless glasses and a bottle of brandy in his right hand. Dennis saw him wave the bottle at the Ed, and then, studying the smoky scene, he noticed that the chairs surrounding the Picture Editor's desk were all taken, one by Harvey, another by Clive Grant, the Advertising Manager, a third by Les Hamilton, the Art Editor of *Gents*, and the fourth by Rick Walker, the Assistant Editor of *Gents*. All of them, with the exception of the intense, long-haired Rick Walker and Harvey, were knocking back healthy mouthfuls of the brandy that had come from the crate now resting on the floor near the desk. Harvey wasn't knocking back the brandy only because he was slowly, carefully withdrawing a damp photo of the girl – who stood naked at the far end of the office – from the back of an XPB stroke 487 oblique 00 stroke RTV De-Luxe Polaroid camera, while the girl herself, dark-haired and long-limbed and bushy-tailed, stood patiently on a wooden pallet in the hot glare of the spot lights and sipped delicately at her own glass of brandy.

'I've never had *this* before,' she said.

'Don't worry about it, sweetheart,' the Picture Editor said. 'Just knock it back in one gulp and have another and then the work will seem easier. How are you, Ed? Good to see you.'

'Good to see *you*, Stan,' the Ed said.

'Great, Ed. Fantastic.'

'I must say it's encouraging to see so much activity going on up here,' the Ed said, 'though I'm sure that the brandy could have been dispensed with until later and the young lady could have done without the audience.'

'It's lunchtime,' Stan said, pouring the Ed a glass of brandy. 'I told the young lady that I was having a conference during lunch but that she could stay for a drink if she wanted, and she certainly wanted.'

The young lady giggled and the Ed glanced cagily at her before picking up his glass and having a sip and licking his moist lips.

'Well,' the Ed said, 'it's decent.'

'Decent?' Stan said. 'It's fucking great. You want a drink, Dennis?'

'That's really most kind,' Dennis said.

'Not at all. It's on Harvey.'

The enthusiastic Picture Editor, fondly known as the Pic Ed, poured Dennis a dangerously large brandy, and Dennis picked the glass up and had a sip and then stared at the naked girl. The girl was slim and sexy with almost perfect breasts and a naughty little arse and long dark hair and pink pouting lips. She stood on the wooden pallet, looking on with interest as Harvey passed her photograph around the lads, all of whom studied it in an extremely casual manner, dreamily gulping down their brandy and scratching their balls and sometimes running their fingers through their hair and being academically critical.

'Nice tits,' Clive Grant said.

'A cute bush,' Rick Walker said.

'A little under-exposed,' Les Hamilton said. 'We'll have to touch her up, ha, ha.'

'You know,' the Ed said, sitting on the edge of the desk and crossing his legs and gazing directly at the girl, 'this brandy isn't at all bad. Quite a nice drop, in fact.'

'Not *bad*?' Stan said loudly, the light flashing off his spectacles. 'That's the fucking understatement of the year. This brandy's just *beautiful*.'

Stan topped up the Ed's glass and the Ed gulped another mouthful, this being his favourite poison, and offered the naked girl his most winning smile.

'I'm Robert Prince,' he informed her. 'The Managing Director and Editor of Saturnalia Publications, including *Suave* and *Gents*.'

'Really?' the girl said.

'Really,' the Ed said.

'Oh, I'm *so* glad to meet you, Mr Prince. I've read so much about you.'

'A little scandal, a lot of dirt,' the Pic Ed said. 'Ho, ho, ho, let's all drink to that.'

The smile left the Ed's decadent schoolboy face as he turned his head to look down at the ebullient Stan. Stan leaned forward and topped up the Ed's already topped up glass, and the Ed smiled and turned back to face the girl.

'And what's your name, dear?'

'Muriel,' the girl said, brushing her hair back from her eyes and thrusting out her darling little breasts. 'Muriel Beckett.'

'Muriel,' the Ed said. 'Mmmm. Let's call her Lydia.'

'Right,' the Pic Ed said.

'Right,' Harvey added.

The girl smiled brightly and walked over to Stan's desk and stood very close to the Ed. She leaned across the desk and held out her empty glass, and her body, smooth and suntanned and with round, milky arse-cheeks, formed a bridge across the Ed's denimed legs. The Ed had a sip of brandy and cast his gaze along the girl's spine and raised his eyebrows as the girl straightened up. They both smiled and touched glasses.

'Cheers,' the girl said.

'Cheers,' the Ed said.

'The NUJ,' said the sombre Rick Walker. 'That's what we need here.'

'The NUJ?' the Ed said innocently.

'That's right,' Rick Walker said. 'The National Union of Journalists. That's what we need here.'

'Fucking fascists,' Harvey said.

'Fucking right,' the Ed said. 'I mean, those bastards, they're all out to get us. They hate private enterprise.'

'We need a union,' Rick Walker said.

'Like a hole in the head,' Harvey said.

'Rick hates me,' the Ed said. 'I can feel it. It's a blade in my spine.'

He stared briefly at Rick Walker, his innocent blue eyes like lasers, then turned away and smiled fondly at the girl, a slight bulge in his pants. Rick Walker glanced around him, silently pleading for support, but the other lads, the unprincipled bastards, all chose to ignore him.

'Have a look at this photo,' Harvey said. 'I think it's a winner, Ed.'

'You mean Lydia or the camera?' the Ed said.

'Both,' Harvey said. 'Two items well worth the running, Ed. I think I'm earning my wages.'

'I didn't know you had a Polaroid as well,' the Ed said.

'I just got it this morning,' Harvey said. 'I brought it up with the Minolta SRT 303B 50-millimetre f1.7 to show them both to the Pic Ed, good old Stan here, who is, as you know, badly in need of a camera for instant test shots, and he seems to think that the Polaroid would be more practical, so I'm going to let him have it and I think I'll keep the Minolta back at my own place where it will, as it were, be safe and sound until we can find a place for it in the magazines.'

'That all sounds very organised, Harvey.'

'That's me,' Harvey said.

Harvey slipped out of his chair and walked across the room and handed the colour picture to the Ed. The Ed put his glass down on the desk and held the picture in his left hand and casually dropped his right hand on Muriel's *aka* Lydia's thigh. Lydia was now sitting on the desk beside the Ed, and she had her legs crossed, and Harvey glanced at her dark silken bush and gave her a wink. Lydia smiled at Harvey and seemed oblivious to the Ed's hand as the Ed made humming sounds and studied her photograph and gave her thigh an encouraging squeeze. Lydia sipped at her brandy.

'Not bad,' the Ed murmured. 'Not bad at all.'

'You like it?' Lydia said.

'I like it.'

'I *am* glad,' Lydia said.

The Ed smiled at the naked young lady and put the photograph on the desk. Harvey picked up the photograph and wiped some brandy off the left nipple and went back to his chair and picked up the Minolta. Harvey then proceeded to snap off more pictures around the office, first of Rick Walker, the Ass Ed of *Gents*, who was lying back in his chair with his long legs outstretched and his right hand mopping sweat from his anxious brow; then of Dennis, the dignified young Chief Ass, who was leaning quietly against the door of the office, saying nothing, merely sipping his brandy and looking thoughtfully at the naked thigh being massaged by the Ed's tender hand; and finally at Clive Grant, the Ad Man of all the magazines, who had his own bottle of brandy and was loving it. When Harvey had finished taking their photos, and had received the full weight of their lassitude and indifference, he took some pix of the Ed and the naked girl.

'My God,' he gasped, 'that's good!'

'Yes,' Clive Grant said, 'not bad at all.'

'You mean the camera?' Harvey said.

'No,' Clive said. 'The brandy.'

'Oh,' Harvey said, disappointed. 'I see.'

'Why?' Clive said softly, glancing slyly at Harvey. 'Are you thinking of *selling* the camera?'

'Of *course* I'm not thinking of selling it,' Harvey said. 'This camera has been given to me as a sample by the Hotflash and Lensman Light Company, and I only got in on the grounds that it be used by the Picture Editor for one-column colour pix and that we mention where possible the fact that the pix were taken with the brand-new XPB stroke RVT oblique De-Luxe Polaroid, and that it was not to be used outside the office or without due credit to the manufacturers, and that it was not to be sold or otherwise used for trade. I am therefore passing this valuable piece of equipment on to the Pic Ed, good old Stan here, which is why I was given it in the first place.'

'Well, that's very honest of you, Harvey,' the Ed said, smiling at the naked Lydia before offering Harvey his coolest appraisal, 'although there *is* a rumour going around, certainly *unverified*, that your intention was to give that camera to the Pic Ed here in return for a free trip to the Bahamas, ostensibly for a pic set. Any truth in that, Harvey?'

'No, Ed,' Harvey said, 'there's no truth in that, and I'm sorry to learn that these offices are still vibrant with vicious gossip. As you well know, Ed, I approach my liaisons with the various manufacturers with extreme seriousness, and I stringently avoid offending them by abusing their faith and trust, which I would certainly do if I started using their valuable products as items of barter. No, Ed, I think it would be counter to my own interests – *and* the interests of the magazines in general – if I were to do what you suggest I might be doing, and I'm truly sorry that you think I might be doing it.'

'Hear, hear,' murmured Stan, the Pic Ed.

'It *is* true,' Harvey continued, 'that I *have* discussed the possibility of a trip to the Bahamas with the Pic Ed, but this had nothing whatsoever to do with the camera, but was in fact a suggestion put to me by the Grapefruit and Vine Company, the directors of which, because of my extensive knowledge of their business and particular interest in setting up, with the helpful co-operation of Clive here, a special champagne offer and competition open exclusively to our readers, wanted me to personally fly out, *at their expense*, to the Bahamas, for the purpose of photographing and writing up an accompanying illustrated feature as a prelude, as it were, to the competition offer. This would, of course, have involved us in supplying a photographer and two models at our own expense, but such expenses would certainly have been covered by the revenue anticipated from the returns on the exclusive, if costly, champagne offer. Naturally, this trip, coming as it will at my busiest time on *Suave* – this being when we would normally process the double-size Christmas edition – would be both inconvenient and quite arduous to me, but I *did* initially discuss it with Stan here because I felt that its value was such that I had to place my own welfare aside and think of how it would benefit the magazines.'

'Here, here,' good old Stan said.

'That sounds lovely,' Lydia said.

'Mmmm,' the Ed said. 'All worked out.'

'I must say,' Stan added quickly, 'that I thought it was a great idea and a brilliant *coup* on the part of old Harvey here, since, as you know, we *will* have to start planning the bumper Christmas edition soon and are pretty damned short on unusual photo sets. Now with a place like the Bahamas – you know, the golden beaches, the palm trees, great hotels and sexy birds – added to the novelty of an exclusive competition – the prize, incidentally, according to old Harvey here, being three weeks out there in a five-star hotel with one thousand quid spending money – well, I just thought that it would give us that little extra something for the bumper Christmas edition and make a fucking spectacular cover line.'

'Gee,' Lydia said, 'who are the models? Do you think *I* could go?'

The Ed smiled at the naked angel and gave her thigh a promising squeeze and then turned his coolest appraisal on Harvey, whose gaze didn't flinch.

'And just *who* were you planning to send?' the Ed said.

'Thing is – ' Harvey began.

'A bit of a problem there, Ed,' Stan promptly interjected, pouring the Ed another brandy and then filling Lydia's empty glass and sitting back and taking a swig from the bottle. 'Thing is, this idea we worked out, we decided that the readers would *identify* more with the idea if we used a *male* model as well as a whore. We therefore felt around the situation for a few days, discarding the one-shot geniuses and concentrating on the photographers we have on a retainer, but we only *have* two photographers on a retainer and neither seems suitable. Blomberg's a great photographer, but he's also a raving faggot – incidentally, I think him and that weirdo outside have been having it off on the side – so he'd be good with the male model, but it's almost certain he'd shit all over the girl. We then thought of Mark Hamlyn, who's a fantastic outdoors man, but he's got a cock like a piston and it never stops pumping and the girl wouldn't be able to take her clothes off and he'd leave the guy stranded. A further problem came up in that the company we're dealing with, the – '

'Grapefruit and Vine Company.'

'Thank you, Harvey. The company we're dealing with is insisting that we include a representative from our own advertising department – which is, as you know, a one-man band run by good old Clive here – and since they were insisting on this but didn't want to pay the plane fare, we felt that the only way out of the problem – to cut our own costs, as it were, by which I mean the *Big P's* costs – was to have good old Clive here double up and go along, not only as our Advertising

Manager, but as a perfectly presentable male model, it being that he *does* look the part and is used to the high life and will therefore look natural in the Bahamas and the glories of Kodachrome.'

'And the photographer?' the Ed said.

'Well, Ed, as I've just stated, that looked like a tricky one, and much as it's going to be a right fucking drag, the only photographer I can think of who *wouldn't* try to fuck one of the models, thereby fucking up the other, is *myself*, and so, you know, I thought I'd better go along and do the job, even though this will, I assure you, cause some aggravation with the missus and lead to a pretty unpleasant Christmas.'

'And, of course,' the Ed said, 'Harvey has to go because...'

'That's right, Ed,' Harvey said. 'It's a right fucking nuisance, but they've insisted on me because of my extensive knowledge of their business and because they want a really *tasteful* feature. I tell you, Ed, if the wife wasn't already leaving me she'd leave me because of this trip. But a man has his work, Ed.'

'That's big of you, Harvey,' the Ed said.

'Not at all, Ed,' Harvey said. 'I don't really resent it. I mean, you *are* fighting for our contracts, and you *are* trying to get us raises, and I feel that it's as little as we can do to repay you for that.'

'It really is a nuisance,' Clive Grant said, 'and I just don't know how I'm going to manage it. I mean, I was going to take the wife and kids to Calpe that month, but I had to cancel that because, as you know, Ed, that *is* my busiest month, what with the bumper Christmas edition and all, and now here I am, completely booked out again, lumbered with a trip to the fucking Bahamas, which will just *kill* my family.'

The Ed was deeply moved by these various displays of supreme self-sacrifice and he proved it by gulping down his brandy. The Pic Ed, good old Stan, promptly poured him another and the Ed stared at it and then stared at Stan and the naked

Lydia, blinked and glanced around him and finally let his gaze rest on Dennis, his dependable Chief Ass. Dennis, sensing emanations in the atmosphere, as it were, stepped forward and stood in the centre of the smoky room, sipping his brandy and giving the lads his most tender smile.

'Well, chaps,' Dennis said, 'you all appear to have come up with a particularly good concept, and I'm sure the Ed appreciates your hard work on it. Indeed, I think the fact that you are already, in the middle of July, working on possible features for the Christmas edition is commendable, more so when, given the inconvenience and sheer grind that this project will entail, you are still willing to go ahead with it.'

'Thanks, Dennis,' Harvey said.

'Appreciate it,' Stan said.

'*However*,' Dennis said, 'since the envisaged feature is obviously going to be of such enormous value to the bumper Christmas edition, I *do* feel that, rather than discussing it further at this point, you should all get together, put the details down in draft form, and submit the draft for the Ed's personal scrutiny.'

'Right,' the Ed said.

'After all,' Dennis continued, smiling sweetly at their shifty faces, 'neither the Ed nor myself, though obviously wanting the *very best* for the magazines, would want to cause undue inconvenience or hardship when such inconvenience and hardship might be avoided. Now, I'm *not* saying that your suggestions aren't *sound*; what I *am* saying is that a project of such complexity might have more than one angle and that it should therefore be studied *in depth* by the Ed himself. The Ed, with, hopefully, my own input, might be able to come up with some additions to your basic idea, springing, as they would, from his far broader knowledge of our readership and the likely interdepartmental situation at the time of the proposed trip, thereby circumventing any possible inconvenience to yourselves and avoiding any loss of *maximum impact* in the presentation of the feature. My suggestion, therefore, is that you have the full details of the proposed trip typed out and on the Ed's desk by tomorrow, and then the whole thing can be finalised at Wednesday's editorial meeting.'

'Right,' the Ed said.

At this point in the proceedings, the Pic Ed, good old Stan, darted around his desk and proceeded to top up everyone's glass. The Pic Ed, who was visually orientated, noticed that the Ed's right hand was inching up the naked Lydia's thigh, that Lydia's pert breasts were heaving, that her nipples were stiffening, and that both she and the Ed were rather flushed. Stan thought this was most entertaining, but he dragged himself away and poured the others full glasses, and before very long they were all extremely drunk and obsessed with their work. The telephone kept ringing, but Stan wouldn't answer it because the Ed didn't want to be disturbed since, obsessed as he was with his work, he was examining the naked Lydia, beautifully shadowed in smoky gloom, to ascertain her short-term future prospects.

'So tell me, dear,' the Ed said to the flushed, naked Lydia, 'are those lovely breasts real or supported with silicone?'

'Silicone?' the model replied. 'What's silicone?'

'Ah, ha,' the Ed said, 'then they're real.'

'Real?' Lydia said. '*Of course* they're real!'

The Ed, who was both visually and verbally orientated, leaned closer to the lovely Lydia and carefully studied her taut nipples, his gaze solemn, objective.

'Do you mind?' the Ed said. 'I mean, I just want to feel them. I can't believe you when you say they're for real. They're too perfect for that.'

The girl giggled and nodded, so the Ed raised his right hand and placed it on one breast and squeezed and pressed his thumb down on the nipple and made the girl gasp.

'Oh,' she said breathlessly, 'that tingles.'

The Ed gave the girl a quick smile and looked furtively around him and then moved his hand over to her other breast and felt out the situation, the girl alternately giggling and gasping, while Dennis, who was observing this and who *did* feel uneasy – not wanting the Ed to expose himself, as it were, and knowing of the Ed's tendency to do just that when on the brandy – turned to walk away but was accosted by the very young old bald beardless Art Director of *Gents*, Les Hamilton, who was not drinking anything at all, being somewhat perverse, and who now, stung and shamed by the sight of the venerable Managing Director and Editor massaging that innocent young model's tits, talked obsessively to Dennis about his work.

'And so what I'm saying, Dennis,' Les whispered halfway through his interminable monologue, 'is that if all these bastards fly off on this *obviously valuable* trip to the Bahamas, and do so just when we have to start work on the double-size bumper Christmas issues of *Gents* and *Suave*, then, given the fact that the Artful Ed – who is, as we all know, a real great guy and one of the most creative art directors in this lousy business – probably won't be around, since he very rarely is, then I'll be left all of my own, lumbered with the two mags, both twice their normal size, with no extra assistance and probably no extra bread, and, of course, though I wouldn't *normally* mind doing this – since, as you may have gathered, I already have to do half of the work on *Suave*, not casting aspersions on the Artful Ed who is, beyond doubt, one of my very best friends, but who *does* tend to stay out of the office a lot and, in fact, only comes in for his wages – so, you know, I don't think it's fair to expect me to do the same when both mags are going to be bumper issues. And I tell you this, Dennis, because you're the only one I can trust, you're square and you get on with the job, which is more than I can say for the rest of the staff who don't seem to want to do anything except drink and fool around, even the Ed who makes all these promises and never keeps them and who can't seem to conduct an intelligent meeting, like the one we were hoping to have today, without getting pissed, as he is right now, or turning the whole thing into a disgusting orgy, which clearly he's about to do right now. I mean, just *look* at him, Dennis. I mean, where do you hide your face? I mean, groping about with that *whore*. I mean, it just-makes-me-*sick*!'

Dennis nodded and sipped his brandy and glanced over Les' shoulder to observe that the Ed was, indeed, groping about with that delightfully naked young model, the pair of them still sitting on Stan's desk, the Ed fully clothed, Lydia still deliciously starkers, the Ed flushed and intense, Lydia giggling and gasping, the Ed's hand down between her thighs, his index finger invisible, muttering, 'Mmmm, oh yes, well that's nice, dear,' and Dennis, not wanting to be part of this sordid scene, but intrigued nevertheless, being a novelist and so on, a surveyor of human nature, nodded again and listened to the ebullient Stan who had come up to his side and put his arm around his shoulders and, obsessed with his work, was saying, 'I want you to understand, Dennis, that this was going to be an *orderly* and *highly constructive* meeting until you and the Ed came in and fucked it up by encouraging us to pour the brandy and forget ourselves.' Dennis didn't reply, merely nodded and smiled, and at that moment Harvey came up, holding his glass of brandy in one hand, a glowing dildo in the other, and, obsessed with his work, said, 'Well, Dennis, what with sorting out all these problems that have been troubling us for so long, and sorting out the invaluable Bahamas trip, and finding that great little whore for the centre spread – a real sweet kid, incidentally, though I *do* have my doubts about the Ed there – and I was just wondering if, you know, it would be *politic* to go up to the Ed and ask him, since he obviously has a certain *rapport* with the young lady, if he could try out this incredible new high-speed, low-speed convertible vibrating thermos flask by removing his greasy finger and slipping the flask up instead and then, when he's finished, we can all have a drink and check if the temperature's changed.' Harvey chortled at the thought of this while Dennis looked straight ahead, his expression revealing nothing of his innermost thoughts and his eyes focused clearly on the Ed, who was, at that very moment, placing the young lady's hand on the

W.A. Harbinson

bulge under his denims while the index finger of his other hand disappeared and reappeared and the intercom on the desk started buzzing.

'Yes?' Dennis said into the intercom.

'Who is that, please?'

'This is the Chief Associate Editor speaking.'

'Mmmm. Your voice is so sexy.'

'Mmmm. Quite. And the message?'

'Is the Ed still there?'

'Why?' the Ed said, sounding drunk.

'I have the Circulation Manager on the line. He's calling from Spain.'

'Spain?' the Ed said.

'Torremolinos,' Dennis clarified.

'Ah, yes,' the Ed said, 'that fucking hole.' He whipped his finger out of the girl, sniffed it, licked it, then chortled and picked up the telephone and switched on the loudspeaker. 'Hello?' he said drunkenly.

'*Hello hello*!' said the voice at the other end of the line, emerging and receding out of static. 'Hello! *Can you hear me*?'

'Yes,' the Ed said, 'I can hear you.'

'I can't hear you! Yes, I can! No, I can't! Yes, I can! Is that you, Dennis?'

'Yes,' the Ed said, drinking brandy and grinning crazily, 'this is Dennis.'

'Thank God for that, Dennis. I thought it might be the Ed. If that bastard finds out where I am he'll chop off my balls.'

'Don't worry,' the Ed said. 'The cunt's down in his office. Now, what are you *doing* in Torremolinos? Give me the deal, Frank.'

'Jesus, Dennis, it's dreadful. It's a fucking nightmare. If the Ed ever finds out, he'll kill me, he'll tear out my toenails. It wasn't my fault. I swear to God, it wasn't me. In fact, I didn't even know where I was until the receptionist told me.'

The Ed grinned in a lewd manner at the flushed, naked girl,

94

drank more brandy and glanced at all his lads, clearly enjoying himself.

'Dennis?' the Circulation Manager shouted desperately from Torremolinos. 'I can't hear you! Are you still on the line, Dennis?'

'Yes,' the Ed said. 'I'm still here, Frank.'

'Dennis, you've got to help me. You've got to help me get out of here. I'm trapped in this hotel and they won't let me leave because that bitch ran away with my plane ticket and, incidentally, my wallet.'

'An *hotel*, Frank?' the Ed said.

'I don't know how I got here, Dennis. I just don't understand it. I mean, I saw our French connection. We discussed our mutual interests. We thrashed out their percentage and they agreed to our terms and I felt that I'd done a good job. Then it all went to pieces, Dennis. I don't know what happened. I only know that it was the Artful Ed's fault and I still can't believe it. The Artful Ed was there. I swear to God, he was in Paris. I was going to leave on Tuesday and I went for a walk first and there, lo and behold, was the Artful Ed. It was in the rue de la Paix. The Artful Ed was in a café. He was sitting with two men who were dressed all in leather, and he was selling them a lot of our transparencies. Naturally, I joined them. The Artful Ed was really sociable. He explained that the Ed had sent him over for the day to scout around for photo agents and models. Naturally, we had drinks. Some cognac, a few Pernods. The Artful Ed – well, you know him – he gave me some tablets and told me they would keep me awake if I mixed them with cognac. Things went funny after that. I mean, I felt really high. Things were happening and then they weren't happening and then they were happening again.' Frank stopped to catch his breath, obviously suffering in sunny Spain, then coughed and offered a whimpering sound and started talking once more. 'I remember a room, Dennis. It was near the Place du Tertre. The two men in leather were with me, both with whips in their hands. I didn't like that, Dennis. I mean, they had me tied up. They shoved a golf ball in my mouth and put clothes pegs on my cock and started whipping it and everything went crazy, but boy, did I *come.*' Frank stopped talking again, obviously stunned by this recollection, then he coughed and took another deep breath and continued his tale. 'I remember the Artful Ed. He came back when they'd had their fun. I think they gave him some money – I was too dazed to be sure – and then he drove me to the airport and fed me more tablets and I awakened with this whore in Torremolinos and fell asleep and she disappeared. Dennis, I'm in trouble. My balls look like balloons. My cock looks like it's been through a wringer and I'm trapped in this room. I've just got to get out of here.'

'Good Lord,' the Ed said, rolling the words on his tongue. 'Are you sure you're not putting me on, Frank? I can hardly believe this.'

'Dennis, it's true! I swear to God!'

'The Artful Ed?'

'On my life!'

'Well,' the Ed said, knocking back more brandy and grinning crazily at everyone, 'I must say that it sounds rather odd, but of course if it *is* true – '

'It is! It is!'

' – then it's quite reprehensible and I shall *certainly* pursue the matter further.'

'Don't tell the Ed! Jesus Christ!'

'No, no,' the Ed said. 'Don't worry, Frank. I don't think we have to do that. No. What I think we have to do is arrange to get you out of there – and meanwhile, you can speak to the Ed and give him a story.'

'Right! Right! That's it, Dennis!'

'All right, Frank,' the Ed said. 'Now, what I'm going to do is, I'm going to have this call transferred to the Ed and then you can give him a story. In the meantime, I'll arrange to have some cash transferred to your hotel and when you get it you can book a flight out. Now how does that sound?'

'That's it! That's perfect! That should do the trick, Dennis. I'll give the Ed a fucking story and then tell the dumb bastard that I've just spoken to you and that you're fixing things up for my return. That sounds great, Dennis. I'll do that.'

'Okay,' the Ed said. 'Now how much do you owe the hotel?'

'A difficult one, Dennis. I mean, it's written down here, but it's all in fucking Spanish and I can't work that money out for shit. I mean, it's *difficult*, you know?'

'Come, come, Frank. How much?'

'Fifteen hundred smackers, not counting the plane fare.'

'*What?*'

'It's not my fault, Dennis! It's the Artful Ed's fault! I mean, I was booked in with this whore by the Artful Ed, *at his expense*, and he told the whore to dock up what she wanted, no fucking ceiling mentioned, and she brought in a whole gang of friends. It wasn't an orgy, Dennis – I wouldn't say it was *that* – but it was certainly one hell of a party and went on for two days. The Artful Ed didn't pay. The Artful Ed did not appear. The Artful Ed made the booking and he gave the whore *carte blanche* and he didn't leave a penny for the bill and now I'm stuck here in Shitsville. *Oh, my God, if the Ed found out!*'

'Calm down, Frank,' the Ed said, grinning wildly, his eyes red. 'Just give me the contact details of the hotel and I'll fix it all up.'

The Circulation Manager, Frank Harrison, gave the hotel's details and the Ed wrote them down and grinned wickedly.

'Okay,' the Ed said, 'I've got all that, Frank. Now I'm going to put you through to the Ed, so you can give him your story.'

'Dennis, you're a pal. You're really fantastic. I want to say to you now, and I always *did* say it, you're the best of that lousy bunch, you're the only one a guy can trust, and I'm not going to forget what you're doing as long as I live.'

'Well, it's kind of you to say so, Frank. Now I'm putting

you through to the Ed.'

The Ed pressed a button on the telephone and held it for a few seconds, still glancing at all his lads and grinning wickedly. Eventually he released the button, waited a few more seconds, and then, in exactly the same tone of voice, spoke again to the desperate Circulation Manager.

'Hello,' the Ed said. 'Robert Prince here.'

'Is that you, Ed?' Frank said.

'Yes, this is the Editor of *Gents* and *Suave*, and the Managing Director of Saturnalia Publications.'

'Ed, it's Frank,' Frank said in an admirably authoritative tone of voice. 'Frank Harrison.'

'Ah, Frank! How are you? I wondered how you were getting on. I thought you were supposed to be back here last week. What's happening in Paris?'

'Well, Ed, a few complications here, some unforeseen eventualities, but nothing that won't soon be sorted out. I have, of course, been in lengthy consultations with our current French distributors, and have certainly found these talks to be most fruitful, although, due to the intransigence of certain members of their Board, and to a definite unwillingness to put their cards on the table, there *were* some disagreements as to the terms of the contract, particularly with regard to their percentage, something which you *did* insist should not be increased, and I therefore felt it expedient to stay over for a few more days in order to check out some alternative distributors, which alternatives were to be used not only in the case of an emergency, such as a breakdown in the negotiations, but also as an additional pressure *during* the negotiations, and, of course, in order to do this, and also because, as you had stated, an initial examination of the possibilities of further expansion throughout Europe would be welcomed, I thought it wise to make a quick trip to Torremolinos for exploratory conversations with Herr Mayer, who is, as you may recall, a formidable figure in the Scandinavian and German publishing fields and who is presently residing at this hotel in order to ascertain the possibilities of an opening market for the more advanced erotic publications in the fluctuating but seemingly hopeful new political climate of post-Franco Spain. I *did* think this was worth it, Ed.'

'I must say I agree with you, Frank,' the Ed said, 'and I'm certainly impressed by your initiative, not to mention your *enthusiasm*, in making such a trip when you could have been back home with your family. So, when can we hope to see you, Frank?'

'A difficult one, Ed, and I'm sure you understand me when I say that. Thing is, this Herr Mayer, who is, if I may say so without prejudice, a gentleman and scholar, not at all like your average wooden-headed Kraut, is very seriously considering some sort of merger, most notably with *Gents* and *Suave*, and he wants me to hang around here for at least one more day, since he's attempting to obtain an audience with Juan Carlos himself in order to ascertain the climate – sexual, religious and political – of the current market, from *the horse's mouth*, as it were, and, of course, if this climate seems favourable, then such a merger would be invaluable to us. For this reason I *do* think it imperative that I stay here for at least one more day, as I'm sure you'll agree.'

'Indeed I do, Frank, but I *am* concerned for your welfare. I mean, what's your financial situation, Frank?'

'Ed, it's really decent of you to raise that subject without having been asked, and I certainly do need some cash badly. Thing is, Ed – and I'm a bit embarrassed by it all – this Herr Mayer is, as you know, an extremely powerful man, an extremely *influential* man, and he *does* have a pretty rich life style. To be blunt, Ed, he lives pretty fucking high on the hog, and he *is* in residence with quite a large retinue, and, you know, I have a few drinks with them, a meal here, a hooker there, and before you know it the bill is pretty steep and now I need two thousand quid. I'm embarrassed to ask, Ed.'

'Not at all,' the Ed said. 'I appreciate your directness. And naturally, Frank, when the rewards could be so great, the expenses are cheap at the price. I'll ask Dennis to organise it.'

'As a matter of fact, Ed, I've just spoken to Dennis and he said he would clear it with you and then get it organised. I mean, I spoke to him because I couldn't get through to you and I felt that this matter was an urgent one. I hope you agree, Ed.'

'Indeed I do, Frank, and I'm very pleased to hear that Dennis has displayed his customary initiative and common sense.'

'A great guy, Ed. And loyal to you.'

'Precisely. Well, Frank, keep up the good work and I'll look forward to seeing you when you return.'

'Thanks, Ed. It's heavy, but I'll shoulder it.'

'Well, that's fine, Frank.'

'I'll see you, Ed.'

The Ed dropped the telephone and had a drink of brandy and grinned at the naked model and glanced around him.

'Did you all hear that?' he said.

'Yes, Ed, we heard it,' Les Hamilton said. 'And I must say, it's pretty damned disgusting. You just can't trust anyone.'

'Thank you for that comment, Les, and I do appreciate it, because it *does* seem to me that something fishy is going on over there and that our Circulation Manager – who is of course entitled to travel around this country and Europe for matters relating to distribution and possible tie-ups – is abusing his privileged position by using his freedom for his own ends and then lying to his Editor, who trusted him. Now I don't think that's fair, chaps.'

The Ed smiled at the naked model and the girl smiled back brightly and the Ed put his hand on her thigh and gave it a hopeful squeeze. He polished off his brandy and the Pic Ed refilled his glass and he drank it and licked his lips and kissed the girl's neck. The girl giggled and Les Hamilton looked disgusted and Rick Walker, the Ass Ed of *Gents*, started scratching his balls. Dennis stepped forward and asked the Pic

Ed to top up his glass and he sipped some and then glanced around him and fixed his gaze on the Ed, who was, at that very moment, resting a hand on the naked model's pubic zone and slowly inching his index finger in, a wicked grin on his face.

'This *does* strike me as being a rather unfortunate occurrence,' Dennis said, blandly ignoring the Ed's wandering finger, 'but I think, Ed, that we should suspend any criticism of the Circulation Manager until we've ascertained the full facts. It *is* true, certainly, that the Circulation Manager lied to you, but then you *did* encourage him to do so, using *my* name in the process, and there *is* the added mystery of the Artful Ed's appearance in Paris early last week. Now, as well you know, Ed, I would not normally offer negative comments about the splendid Artful Ed, but he *does* have a tendency to move around quite a bit, doing only God knows what, and I therefore think that this claim of the Circulation Manager should be thoroughly investigated. In the meantime, we should get the Circulation Manager out of there.'

The Ed listened carefully to Dennis, then removed his index finger from the young lady's treasured interior and patted her rump and put him arm around Dennis and walked him away and started whispering melodramatically.

'Dennis,' the Ed whispered, 'I appreciate your comments on this matter and I must say they were more constructive than the comments of that dumb-fuck, Les Hamilton. Thing is, Dennis, I can't trust any of these bastards, they're all out to shaft me, you're the only professional here, the only one with some intelligence, and so you're certainly the only one I can depend on. I'm telling you this, Dennis, because I want it sorted out, I want Frank pulled out of there, and I want to know what the fuck's going on. Thing is, Dennis, I *do* have serious doubts about the Artful Ed, who is, as we all know, an extremely talented guy, a truly *creative* guy, but one who *does* have a tendency to resemble the Invisible Man and can certainly get up to some fishy tricks.'

At this point, the Pic Ed, good old Stan, came up to them and said, 'You want another drink?' and the Ed said, 'Yes, fill it up,' and the Pic Ed, generous Stan, did so and then, laughing crazily, departed. The Ed had a quick snort and said, 'Great stuff,' and then started swaying, but Dennis took hold of his shoulder and straightened him up, and the Ed, looking cross-eyed, started whispering again.

'What I mean,' the Ed whispered, 'is that it seems to me that the Artful Ed, who was certainly in Paris *without* my permission, was over there trying to sell off some of this Company's valuable transparencies to fill his own coffers, and I would even go so far as to say – not for one moment suggesting that he ever sold a woman to *me* or sold me to *someone else*, but, let's face it, given the Artful Ed's nature and all – well, it *is* possible that Frank's garbled story *did* have some basis in fact and that the Artful Ed, a born pimp if ever I met one, actually got him stoned and then *sold* him for an hour or so to those leather-clad kinks who are, if my memory serves me well, a right pair of degenerate sharks and very good at the sadism – *not* that I speak from *personal* experience, just word on the grapevine and so forth – and so, Dennis, I *do* have my doubts there.'

Dennis gently propped the Ed up against the wall and then had a sip of brandy and looked over his shoulder with clear blue beautiful eyes at the Picture Editor's desk where Harvey, the Ass Ed, and Clive Grant, the Ad Man, and good old Stan, the Pic Ed, were gathered around the giggling and wide-eyed young Lydia who, naked and suntanned and glistening with sweat, was staring down between her legs at the glowing device which, held in the artistic hands of the highly creative Harvey, was being slipped into her, humming and vibrating and making her tingle all over, now gasping, now purring, now closing her lovely eyes, while the Ass Ed chortled and the Pic Ed laughed crazily and the Ad Man, who was slick and extremely urbane, smoked a cigarette and tweaked one of her nipples.

Dennis, observing this, delicately shifted his gaze, his

innermost thoughts hidden, and looked instead at Les Hamilton who was clearly disgusted, all flushed and muttering about filthy whores, and who slumped down in a chair beside Rick Walker, the Ass Ed of *Gents*, who, dishevelled and sallow and smashed out of his skull, was muttering about fascists and Mary Whitehouse and Liberation and the desperate need for a Trade Union. Dennis, who had little or no time for the Ass Ed of *Gents*, and who certainly didn't want him present at Wednesday's editorial meeting, smiled at the drunken Ed and spoke softly.

'I understand your concern, Ed,' Dennis said, 'and I believe we can sort this matter out. Now, what I think we should do is – '

'Just look at those cunts,' the Ed said, leaning against the wall and staring with bloodshot eyes at his merry lads. 'I mean, just take a good look at those bastards.'

'Yes, Ed, I see them. Now what I think is – '

'That's disgusting, Dennis. It's a fucking disgrace. I mean, here we are, trying to sort this mess out, trying to conduct a proper meeting and discuss Company business, trying to behave like professionals and face up to our problems and organise what needs to be done, and just look at those cunts.'

'Yes, Ed, I see them. Now – '

'They've no discretion, Dennis. No sense of responsibility. They take that young model, a sweet kid, a *professional*, and they think they can treat her like a whore and they don't care who's watching. I don't think that's fair, Dennis.'

'Well, Ed, I must say I agree with you, and – '

'I must say, Dennis, and I always *did* say it, you're the only bastard here with any morals. You keep to yourself, Dennis. You don't try to fuck the staff. You're not married, but I don't mind that at all, I think you live clean. Now I respect that, Dennis. You keep your cock in your pants. You get on with your work and if you *want* a little nooky you pick it up somewhere outside, though I do have my doubts there. Still, I don't mind. I repeat: I respect it. You're straight and that *is* reassuring and I want you to know that.'

'Thank you, Ed.'

'Not at all.'

The Ed sipped more brandy and smiled fondly at Dennis while the telephone rang and went unanswered. Dennis offered the Ed a cigarette and the Ed accepted gratefully, and they both lit up and looked across the room at the desk. The girl was now lying on her back on the desk and the Ad Man, urbane Clive, was pouring brandy over her navel and the Pic Ed, good old Stan, was French-tonguing her, and the Ass Ed of *Suave*, good old Harvey, was sampling coffee from the vibrating thermos flask and checking that the temperature was right and then the office door opened.

'Oh, boy... Excuse *me*.'

Annie Bedward, the Production Editor of *Gents*, was slim and very pretty and always willing to share herself around. She stood briefly in the bright light from the hallway just behind her, then closed the door and stared at the Pic Ed's desk. Harvey quickly walked up to her and explained that the lads around the naked girl on top of the desk were trying to work out the best angle for a picture set and that he, Harvey, would really appreciate it if she, sexy Annie, would sit down and take some notes and that she might as well have a brandy while she was doing it. Annie Bedward, who had blonde hair, green eyes and teasing tits, studied the girl who was writhing on the desk and then grinned and sat down and crossed her legs. Harvey gave her a glass of brandy and sat down beside her and asked her to take off her knickers and then bit her neck. Annie giggled and the party continued as Dennis talked to the Ed.

'Now what I think, Ed, is that we can't be too sure of just what *is* going on over there in Torremolinos and that, given our mutual doubts about both Frank and the Artful Ed, it might be singularly unwise to transfer all that money across. No, Ed, what I believe we should do, to protect ourselves and to discourage further frivolity, is send *someone else* over with just enough money to cover the hotel bill and get them both back on the next plane out. I do believe, Ed, that in doing this we will be protecting ourselves against further exploitation and *ensuring* the immediate return of the Circulation Manager. I *do* believe this might work, Ed.'

'Just look at this office, Dennis. Have a good look. I mean, we come up here, we try to sort the fuckers out, and they get pissed and now they're having a fucking orgy. I must say, Dennis, that I find this most disturbing, I find it quite disgusting, and I think you should do something about it. I mean, just look at that poor model. She's half out of her head. And now Annie Bedward's here and old Harvey is all over her, and you can bet he's going to stick his great dong in her twat even before the moon rises and his teeth grow long. I don't like this, Dennis.'

'Well, Ed, I'm not too impressed with it myself, and I shall certainly do something about it when we've finished our business.'

'Okay, Dennis,' the Ed said, 'continue.'

'Well, Ed, what I suggest is, we send the Assistant Editor of *Gents* to Torremolinos.'

'That cunt? I don't believe it.'

'Now, Ed,' Dennis said smoothly, 'I know you *don't like* Rick, that you feel he's a pretentious fool who's always talking about the NUJ and complaining about his health, and I must say, Ed, while not wishing to voice negative comments about a fellow staff member, that in certain respects I agree with you. But I *do* feel, Ed, that you're being a little unfair here, that Rick *does* have a few problems, both regarding his lust to form a Trade Union chapel and his indecent concern for the state of his health, and that this calls for a little understanding and should not be ignored.'

'He's a stupid cunt,' the Ed said.

'Well, Ed, he *may* be a stupid cunt, as you so delicately put it, or he may *not* be a stupid cunt, as I would rather not put it, but the point is that Rick, being somewhat preoccupied with politics and the state of his health, is probably a good choice as courier

105

in that he is of an unusually sober disposition and would therefore treat the mission seriously. Further, being the sort who is terrified of foreign food and drink, most of which he seems to think is highly dubious indeed, he would almost certainly stay away from the winos and hookers, the latter, in particular, being a breed of womanhood that often gives him nightmares of syphilis, and we could, therefore, expect him to return here in a reasonable condition.'

'A good point there, Dennis.'

'Thank you, Ed. I would also like to point out, Ed, that, much as *I personally* feel no animosity towards Rick, I know that *you* don't feel quite the same way, that you do in fact find him most annoying, particularly at editorial meetings when he insists on ignoring the realities of our magazines and instead wastes a considerable amount of time on his own, no doubt passionate and sincere, political convictions which drive him to discuss, not possible features of a sexually orientated nature, but the hope that we will turn our extremely popular and profitable magazines into a forum for the liberation of the sexually oppressed and the socially handicapped, none of which we see as our business, and so I would suggest, Ed, that if we were to put Rick on an aircraft as soon as possible it would ensure a much smoother passage through the traumas of the editorial meeting, as I'm sure you'll agree.'

'I do, Dennis. I do. As a matter of fact, I think it's fucking brilliant and I'm going to implement it right this minute.'

The Ed lurched away from the wall and headed toward Rick, stopping only long enough to survey Lydia and Stan, both of whom were stretched out on the latter's desk, the former still naked, the latter with his trousers around his ankles, the former lying back upon a carpet of colour transparencies and letters, the latter pumping away for all he was worth, and the Ed, observing this scene, studied it with some interest, with *professional* detachment, ascertaining the visual aspects, imagining centre-fold staples in Stan's arse, and then he turned away and moved on, almost choking in the smoky atmosphere, and saw Annie Bedward waving her knickers above her head as horrible Harvey slid his hand beneath her skirt, making the Ed take a deep breath before he gratefully stopped at Rick's chair.

'Rick!' the Ed exclaimed, loud and clear. 'How the fuck are you, Rick?'

'It's duodenal,' Rick said. 'The brutes told me that this morning. They shoved a telescope up my ass and jammed a camera down my throat and they said it was a duodenal ulcer and now I feel awful.'

Rick had been engaged in a serious discussion about freedom of the press with the urbane Clive Grant who was fast asleep in the chair beside him, and the Ed, disturbed by the fact that his Advertising Manager should fall asleep during an important meeting, kicked him and received no response. Satisfied that his Ad Man was out for the count, the Ed took hold of Rick Walker, pulled him to his feet, put his arm around his shoulders and walked him to a corner of the room and then started whispering.

'I've been wanting to talk to you, Rick,' the Ed whispered, 'and I don't want these cunts to overhear me.'

'Really? Why not?'

'Thing is, Rick, I *do* have a little problem with that fucking Circulation Manager and I think you're the only one who can help me.'

'Really?'

'Really.'

'Gee, Ed, I certainly appreciate that, but I *do* have a duodenal ulcer and I'd like to go home now.'

'Rick, I'm truly sorry to hear about your ulcer and I must say, and I always *did* say it, that I admire your fortitude and courage in coming to work when you should be in your bed, because, believe me, Rick, I could not in all honesty say the same about the others, most of whom take advantage of my easy-going nature and are always having days off when they're not nearly as sick as you are. Even worse, Rick, is that all these fuckers have been sitting here planning a trumped-up trip to the Bahamas, which would mean you having to do all their work in their absence, and I just want to tell you, Rick, that I do not intend *letting* them make that trip and fuck you up when you so obviously deserve a trip more than they do. So what I'm going to do, Rick – and I'm going out on a limb here – is send you for a nice little trip to Torremolinos with the excuse that you're going to collect the Circulation Manager.'

'*Abroad*?' Rick said nervously.

'Now I know you don't like foreign food, Rick, and God knows I don't blame you, but I just want you to know that you'll fly with the best airline, that they serve good old British tucker on board, and that you'll be staying in a five-star hotel where the grub is pure gold-dust. I just want you to get away, Rick. I just want you to have a rest. I don't want to stand by and see those fuckers getting the perks while you stay behind and sweat your guts out. You'll be leaving this evening.'

'Gee, Ed, that's great. I mean, I don't know what to say.'

'Don't thank me, Rick. I know you deserve it. I know you wouldn't try to go on a trip like this off your own bat, that while these other fuckers waste their time planning such trips you just go right ahead and do your work. That's why I'm sending you, Rick. I feel that you've earned it. These fuckers, they'd go if they could, but I'm not going to let them. As a matter of fact, Rick, it was the Chief Ass himself who suggested that I send you on this trip, but much as I respect Dennis, and much as I am loathe to voice negative comments about him, I must confess that as soon as he offered that suggestion I realised that he had only done so thinking I'd be impressed by his magnanimity and send *him* to Torremolinos instead – a pleasure, of course, that I wouldn't give the sly little bastard. So I'm sending you, Rick. I want you to go. I want you to accept it as a token of my appreciation, and I don't want to hear a word of thanks.'

'Gee, thanks, Ed, that's really decent of you, but Spain's a fascist country and I'm not at all sure that my conscience would let me enjoy the place.'

'Rick, I'm very pleased to hear you say that. I mean, I'm pleased that at least one member of my staff is aware of political realities and has certain moral reservations about the state of them. But don't worry about Spain, Rick. I've anticipated your concerns. I want you to go out there, but I don't want you to be forced into mixing with the fucking Spaniards or eating their polluted food or drinking from the grape that the poor have to trample or putting money into a fascist economy. No, Rick, certainly not. I respect your integrity, Rick, and I just want to point out that this particular hotel is owned by an old friend of mine, a former British Army colonel who fought for freedom in '43, and that the staff are all British and that they get British wages and that the food is all imported and that he fiddles his taxes and that the Spanish don't get a thing out of it. I'm sure you'll enjoy it, Rick.'

'Gee, Ed, if you put it like that, well, I – '

'Fine, Rick, I knew you would go. Now, since the Chief Ass wanted to go on this trip himself, and since I did not appreciate this selfish desire on his part, I'm making him suffer by having him organise the plane tickets and hotel accommodation for you. So, Rick, Dennis will sort out the whole trip and the necessary money and ensure that you get to the airport with some pills for the plane. Okay?'

'Okay, Ed.'

The Ed slapped Rick on the shoulder and then returned to Dennis and told him, omitting the insults conveyed to Rick, what he was planning. Delighted at the thought of getting rid of the troublesome Rick, Dennis instantly phoned through to the account's department and told them what was required. He then crossed the room to Rick and told him to go down to the account's department and picked up the necessary and then immediately make his way to Heathrow airport, adding that he should only phone his wife once he was in the departure lounge and she couldn't complain or try to stop him from going and that he could also purchase some air-sickness tablets with the petty cash provided. Looking simultaneously dazed and scared shitless, Rick hurried from the room. Efficient as always and quietly satisfied, Dennis returned to the Ed's side.

The Ed was surveying his bunch of merry men. Stan and the naked model were both lying on their backs on the desk, Lydia breathing heavily and gazing up at the ceiling, Stan gasping and fingering his wilting weapon. The Ed was quite shocked that his Picture Editor should have disrupted such an important meeting in such an uncouth manner and, feeling that he had to talk to someone other than Dennis, he decided to check out the possibility of some free cassette tapes from the inventive Ass Ed of *Suave*. Harvey was at that very moment being particularly inventive with Annie Bedward, the inventive Prod Ed of *Gents*, the happy couple chuckling and groping one another while Clive Grant snored loudly beside them. The Ed, who was sensitive to young love in bloom, decided to wait for his cassette tapes and instead wandered over to the desk. Stan was lying on the desk with his tongue hanging out, and the Ed tilted his glass and poured brandy down Stan's throat and then looked rather pointedly at his wristwatch. According to the Ed's wristwatch, which was a gold-plated, self-winding, many-jewelled wonder courtesy of Harvey, it was now five o'clock in the afternoon. The Ed therefore decided that it was too late to return to his office and do something constructive, and, since he did not feel like clambering over the body of the exhausted Stan to get at the equally exhausted naked model, he thought it wise to beat a hasty retreat to some nearby watering hole. The Ed was just about to open his mouth and announce his decision to the human flotsam around him when the office door swung open, Lavinia stood there in a rectangle of light, and then, her eyes like lasers, her lips tight and prim, she made the announcement they all dreaded to hear.

'We have a deadline,' she said.

4

With the word *deadline* resounding in his head like a bell of doom, Dennis slipped surreptitiously from Stan's office, leaving the merry lads to deal with the grim Lavinia, and made his way back down the stairs to his office and dark dreams of suicide. Slumping low in the chair behind his desk, his clear, blue, beautiful eyes scanning the white walls all around him, Dennis thought of the gas oven, of wrists dripping blood into a bath, of himself crucified by the unjust world and its cruel mores. Realising that this was the grossest form of self-pity, but worth thinking about nonetheless, Dennis tried to forget that the dreaded word *deadline* had been uttered by a flesh and blood human being and instead reached out for the red telephone, which, being an instrument of plastic and static, protected him from the threat of physical contact and made life more bearable. Dennis dialled a number and waited patiently, wondering if she would answer.

'Yes?' a soft female voice said.

'It's me,' Dennis said.

'You shithead,' the voice replied. 'You rotten bastard. I'm packing right now.'

'I can explain,' Dennis said.

'No, you can't,' the woman said. 'You can't explain anything at all, so go back to your whores.'

'Hardly fair,' Dennis said.

'You little shit,' his wife responded. 'You can stay away as much as you want now – I won't be here to miss you.'

'I don't like it when you swear.'

'I can get my fucks elsewhere.'

'It's not natural when you swear. It doesn't sound right. You're not the type for that kind of language.'

'And of course *you* don't swear.'

'It's not necessary,' Dennis said.

'No, you don't *say* fuck. You just fuck around all over this city with anything moving.'

'It's not my fault,' Dennis said.

'Pardon?'

'It's not my fault. I simply have a very strong sex drive . It's just a physical thing.'

'Oh, Christ!' his wife exclaimed.

'Don't blaspheme,' Dennis said.

'Don't lecture me, Dennis. I can't stand it when you lecture me. God, you're so... so... *Victorian*... You hypocritical bastard.'

Dennis winced and lit a cigarette and inhaled and coughed loudly, wondering why he felt so old at twenty-three years of age.

'I didn't want you to find out,' he said.

'No,' his wife said. 'Obviously not.'

'I didn't know she was your sister, after all. I mean, these things, they just happen.'

'You bastard. You fucked her.'

'These things happen at parties. It was an extraordinary coincidence, I know now, but I didn't know then.'

'Oh, I see. That makes a difference.'

'What?'

'That she was my sister. What you're assuming is that I wouldn't have been concerned if she'd just been some whore.'

'I'm sorry it was your sister.'

'And you want me to forget the others?'

'It's just physical,' Dennis repeated. 'They're not important. It's just sex. I *love* you.'

112

'Oh, Christ,' his wife repeated.

'Don't blaspheme,' Dennis repeated.

'Unspeakable,' his wife said. 'You're unspeakable. I don't know what to say.'

'Say nothing,' Dennis said. 'Just stop packing. Don't be foolish. You know I couldn't bear to live without you... and I just can't afford it.'

'What?'

'Separation.'

His wife slammed the phone down and Dennis winced and glanced around him and inhaled on his cigarette and coughed and then rang her again.

'Yes?' she said wearily.

'I'm sorry,' Dennis said. 'I didn't mean to say that. I really didn't. It just sort of slipped out.'

'You're sick,' his wife said.

'It was a joke,' Dennis said.

'You're a sadist – or mad. I don't know which is worse.'

'I'm neither,' Dennis said. 'I'm just unhappy. I have the middle-aged blues.'

'You're twenty-three,' his wife reminded him.

'I feel older,' Dennis said.

'It's those magazines,' his wife said. 'You shouldn't work there. That whole business is crazy.'

'I have to support us,' Dennis said.

'You could write a few more books. You used to write pretty good books, but now you're just writing filth.'

'A booming market,' Dennis said.

'Educational,' his wife said.

'That's it,' Dennis said. 'Your sense of humour. I always loved that.'

'Don't try to charm me, Dennis.'

'Wouldn't dream of it, darling.'

'They're all mad in those offices,' his wife said. 'Either leave or I pack.'

113

'Hold on,' Dennis said.

The intercom was buzzing, so Dennis covered the mouthpiece of the phone with one hand and pressed the black button on the intercom with the other.

'Yes?' he said to Rosie Teasedale.

'Mmmm,' she said. 'Your voice is so sexy.'

'Quite,' Dennis said.

'You've been busy on the phone,' Rosie said.

'Yes, very busy.'

'Tomorrow night,' Rosie said.

'Yes,' Dennis said.

'I can't wait to see you tomorrow night. I hope you're good looking.'

'Is this the message?' Dennis said.

'No,' Rosie said. 'I have a lady waiting patiently on the other line. I think you know her, ha, ha.'

'I'll ring her back,' Dennis said.

'I said that, but it didn't work. The poor little creature sounds so lonesome. She's *desperate* to talk to you.'

'Okay, put her on.'

Dennis removed his hand from the mouthpiece of the red telephone and, as he drowned in the great wave of self-pity that had been blown in on the knowledge that he was too decent to say 'No' to anyone, said to his wife, 'Sorry. It was the intercom. Where were we?' The yellow telephone rang as Dennis' wife said, 'I was saying that either you leave there or I pack,' and Dennis, picking up the yellow telephone with his hand covering the mouthpiece, said, 'I understand completely. That's fair. But we have to discuss this.' There was no immediate reply, but then his wife said, 'All right. I'll wait until you come home. I'll continue packing my bags, but I'll stay here until we have a talk. When can you come?' While his wife was saying this, Dennis covered the mouthpiece of the red telephone and removed his other hand from the mouthpiece of the yellow telephone and heard the delicious Anna saying, 'Hello? Hello? Are you there,

Dennis? I can't hear anything. Hello?' Dennis said, 'Sorry, pet, a business call on the other line,' and Anna said, 'Oh, God, Dennis, I miss you. I can't wait until tonight. I've been going over my short story, reading that sex scene you put in, and I think I'm learning an awful lot from it and it's got me excited.' Dennis was now thinking in terms of his 'red' and his 'yellow' hands, and subsequently he raised his red hand and said to his wife, 'Sorry, dear, *what* was that?' and while his wife was saying, 'I'll wait, but I won't wait too long, so you'd better come quickly,' Dennis dropped his red hand and raised his yellow hand and said, 'Pardon, pet?' and Anna said, sounding breathless, 'Oh, God, Dennis, I miss you. Can't you come over now? I want you over me and under me and beside me, because that new sex scene is so *hot*.' Dennis tried to explain to Anna that coming over right now might be difficult, but he was having difficulty in speaking since his wife was saying, 'I won't wait here all evening. I won't be made a fool of again. So just answer the question. *When will you be coming*?' Dennis dropped his yellow hand and raised his red hand and said to his wife, 'Well, dear, I think the problem might be that you're still a bit overwrought at the moment, and I was just thinking, you know, that it possibly might be wiser for you to sleep on it, think about it, and then we can discuss it more rationally tomorrow morning.' Dennis' wife, who was the most attractive and interesting woman that Dennis knew, but who didn't see eye to eye with his perfectly harmless sexual proclivities, said, 'That's very understanding of you, Dennis, but I am *perfectly calm* and I just want you to prove that you care by coming over *right now*.' Dennis excused himself with the comment that he had someone on the other line, and then he said to Anna, 'Thing is, pet, that I'm under a bit of pressure at the moment – a late schedule, legal problems, a writer coming about six – and so I don't really think I can get away,' and Anna cried, 'Oh, God, Dennis, I can't wait, I read the new sex scene, it's so *vivid*, such *talent*, God, I don't know what to say, I'm all wet, *come and eat me*!'

'Dennis?' his wife said.

'Yes, dear,' Dennis said.

'Are you still on the other line?'

'Yes, dear.'

'*When*?' Anna said.

'You're stalling,' his wife said. 'I don't think you're on another line at all. You're dreaming up an excuse.'

'We have a – '

'No!' his wife said.

'I'm too busy,' Dennis said.

'Then make me come *now*,' Anna said. 'Bring me off with your *voice*.'

'Pardon?' Dennis said.

'Don't mention a deadline,' his wife said. 'I've heard that line too many times before. It's just a fucking excuse.'

'Remember?' Anna said. 'You did it just like in that movie. The one that had Michael Caine in it. You did it over the phone.'

'No,' Dennis said.

'No *what*?' his wife said.

'I'll close my eyes and touch myself,' Anna said. 'I'll pretend that you're touching me.'

'It's not an excuse,' Dennis said.

'Yes, it is,' his wife said.

'All right,' Dennis said. 'Touch yourself. Pretend that it's me.'

'Oh, God, yes,' Anna said.

'We have a deadline,' Dennis said. 'Really. I'm not lying. It's the truth. We'll probably be here all night.'

'Really?'

'Yes, really.'

'Oh, God,' Anna groaned.

'Yes, pet,' Dennis responded.

'I have my fingers in myself and it's you, Dennis. With my eyes closed, it's you.'

'I love you,' Dennis said.

'What did you say?' his wife said.

'Keep your eyes closed,' Dennis said. 'Just lie back and relax. Can you imagine me? Can you feel me inside you? I'm so *hard*. I must *have* you, pet.'

'Christ,' Anna groaned.

'Do you believe me?' Dennis said.

'Oh, God, yes,' Anna groaned.

'No,' his wife said.

'Yes! Yes!' Anna groaned.

'No,' his wife repeated. 'I can't believe you. I try, but I can't.'

'Trust me,' Dennis said.

'Oh, God, yes!' Anna gasped.

'Your darling clit,' Dennis said. 'I am stroking it. I can feel it. So tender, so moist, so very warm... Please try to understand, Kathy.'

'No,' his wife, Kathy, said.

'I'm licking your nipples,' Dennis said. 'You have to learn to trust me, Kathy. I can change. I *will* change.'

'Yes! Yes!' Anna cried.

'Oh, Christ!' Kathy said.

'Oh, Christ!' Anna cried. 'I can't bear it! Oh, Christ! *Give me everything*!'

'We never talk,' Kathy said.

'Oh, Christ, *talk* to me!' Anna cried. 'Say something sexy or obscene, you sweet bastard, that's wonderful!'

'So,' Kathy said.

'Oh!' Anna yelped. 'Ah!'

'Yes,' Dennis said. 'I suppose you're right. I never know what to say.'

'You're so hard,' Kathy said.

'I'm so hard?' Dennis said. 'It's so hard and it's throbbing, my pet, and now I'm putting it into you.'

'Oh, shit, yes!' Anna cried.

'When are you coming?' Kathy said.

'I'm coming! I'm coming!' Anna screamed.

'I have a deadline,' Dennis said.

Kathy slammed the phone down and Dennis almost shed a tear as he felt his member hardening in his pants and heard Anna's hosannas. 'Oh, Christ!' Anna sobbed as Dennis dropped the red phone and put his head back and stared at the ceiling and let the self-pity smother him. Anna's well-bred, upper-class, nymphomaniacal groanings subsided to a satisfied sighing as Dennis lay back in his chair, his member rigid in his pants, and thought self-pityingly of how he could not, with his finely attuned sensitivity (being a writer and so forth), bring himself to say 'No' to any of the darling girls, and of how they, understanding this, and being wilful, possessive creatures, abused him by exploiting his generous nature and demanding his body and soul. Thinking thus, Dennis, with his clear, blue, beautiful eyes wide open and his innermost thoughts well hidden, but quite poetic nonetheless, coloured with dark visions of slit wrists and gas ovens, murmured, 'Yes, Anna, my pet, I *will* try to make it tonight,' and then dropped the yellow phone, licked his lips and glanced up, and saw a tall brunette walking through the door to tower over his desk.

'Dennis whatsisname?' she sneered.

'Mmmm,' Dennis responded.

'The Chief Associate Editor of these rags?'

'Yes,' Dennis said. 'Hopefully.'

'I've been waiting downstairs all bloody day.'

'Really?'

'Yes, really,' the woman sneered. 'And isn't that kind of treatment typical of you cock-glorifying, cunt-fixated, woman-hating, suppressive, male chauvinist rapist pig bastards who run these disgusting, immoral, regressive, sadomasochistic, male-fantasy so-called magazines, you degenerate shits!'

'Was that a question?' Dennis said.

'No, it was a statement.'

'Ah,' Dennis said.

'Correct,' the woman sneered. 'I've been sitting there all day, and now I've got a good idea of how you bastards treat the women who work here, you contemptuous cock-suckers.'

'You're upset,' Dennis said.

'Too right, I'm upset. I come here for a job and I sit down politely and you bastards leave me sitting there all day until my arse has turned numb. I call that inflammatory.'

Dennis was staring thoughtfully at the imposing brunette, who was possibly twice his size and wore thigh boots and a leather jacket, a white sweater tight against her magnificent breasts, when the yellow telephone rang. Dennis picked it up and, surreptitiously stroking his still throbbing erection to ensure that his zip was done up, listened to the merry voice of Rosie Teasedale.

'Is that the Chief Ass?'

'It is,' Dennis said.

'I just overheard your conversation with Anna. It was an accident, I swear to it.'

'I'm sure,' Dennis said.

'Some conversation,' Rosie said. 'I almost came myself, just listening to it. Boy, oh boy, you're *creative*.'

'I appreciate your comments,' Dennis said, 'but I'm busy right now.'

'You have a visitor?'

'Yes.'

'A brunette?'

'Yes.'

'It wasn't my fault,' Rosie said.

'Pardon?' Dennis said.

'It wasn't my fault,' Rosie repeated. 'Thing is, she's been sitting down here all day, waiting to see someone about that editorial job that someone promised her, and, you know, all of you guys kept putting her off and saying you knew nothing about her, and so, well, I mean after *a whole day* here, she got mad and suddenly stomped up the stairs, determined to see you.'

119

'Ah,' Dennis said.

'Right,' Rosie said.

'Thank you, Rosie,' Dennis said. 'That information was really most helpful.'

'Best of luck,' Rosie said.

Dennis dropped the phone and rested his elbows on the desk and clasped his hands beneath his smooth, beardless chin, his blue eyes clear and candid.

'So,' he said softly.

'Right,' the woman sneered. 'I've been sitting down there all fucking day, and now you'll just have to talk to me.'

'Quite,' Dennis said.

'Right,' the woman said.

'Please accept my apologies,' Dennis said, 'for this regrettable mishap.'

'It was deliberate,' the woman said.

'Not at all,' Dennis said.

'A typical male chauvinist pig trick: she's a woman, piss on her.'

Dennis winced at the profanity, lit a cigarette, inhaled and then blew the smoke out, his blue eyes taking on a hurt look as he stared at the Amazon.

'Don't try it,' she sneered.

'Try what?' Dennis said.

'That big-baby-blue-eyed hurt look. I'm not *that* soft, you prick.'

Dennis, inwardly shocked by the fact that his big-baby-blue-eyed hurt look had failed to work instant wonders with this tall, tight-lipped, attractive brunette Amazonian warrior, sensed that the conversation was getting out of hand and decided to rectify the situation.

'May I ask you something very personal?' he said.

'No.'

'I'm afraid I have to.'

'Okay.'

'Who *are* you?'

'You know damn well who I am. I've been waiting downstairs all fucking day.'

'For a job?'

'Right.'

'What job?'

'The editorial job you promised me.'

'*I* promised you?'

'Right.'

'Are you sure it was me?'

'I was told to ask for you.'

'I gave you my name?'

'Yes.'

'Me, or someone else?'

'All you chauvinist pigs look the same to me... And you were down on her knees.'

'Ah,' Dennis said, 'the party...'

'That's correct,' the woman sneered. 'You were down on your fucking knees where you belong and I was having a good time.'

'I see,' Dennis said. 'And are you the young lady who – ?'

'Not lady – *woman*.'

'Pardon?'

'The word's *woman*. The use of the word *lady* is a typical male chauvinist pig form of condescension suggesting that women, to be attractive, must be as artificial as fucking models. I'm not a lady and I'm nobody's girl: I'm a flesh and blood *woman*.'

'Ah,' Dennis said, 'I see.'

'Good,' the woman said.

'And were you the lady – ?'

'Woman.'

' – who carved "I love Sugar Daddy" on the Boardroom table at the party on Friday afternoon?'

'Right.'

'And who was Sugar Daddy?'

'Sugar Daddy was the stupid prick who went down on his knees and followed my orders to the letter.'

'That wasn't me,' Dennis said.

'Oh, really?'

'I'm afraid not.'

'All you chauvinist pigs look the same to me.'

'Thank you,' Dennis said.

'Not at all,' the woman said.

'You know, you're really very attractive,' Dennis said.

'Oh, yeah?' the woman said. 'Well, don't cream your pants waiting for my thanks.'

Dennis inhaled smoke, thought of rotting lungs and cancer, but was aware that the disease could take a long time in coming and wondered if he could possibly wait that long.

'I think it was our Editor,' Dennis said. '*He* was down on his knees at the party on Friday afternoon.'

'So,' the woman said, 'it was your Editor. Two lips and a willing tongue.'

'That's all you remember?'

'I wasn't interested in his mind. I just wanted a quick gobble where I stood, so I grabbed what was nearest.'

'That must have pleased our Editor.'

'He was scared shitless,' the woman said. 'He was sweating and shaking through it all and I heard his teeth rattling.'

'Excitement,' Dennis said.

'That as well,' the woman said. 'I didn't particularly want to give *him* any pleasure, but it couldn't be helped.'

Dennis was quietly dwelling on the possibility that insanity lurked just around the bend when the yellow telephone rang and his right hand picked it up and the mischievous Rosie Teasedale told him that there was an urgent call on the line, and then, without waiting for his permission, she giggled and opened the line and left Dennis with the sound of heavy breathing.

'Yes?' Dennis said.

'Tits,' a man said. 'I bet you've got huge, luscious tits, you sweet, sexy darling.'

'Pardon?' Dennis said.

'Lovely tits,' the man said. 'I could suck them and lick them and bite them and drive you bananas.'

'I think you've made a mistake,' Dennis said.

'All soft and creamy,' the man said. 'And no bra. You don't need support. Just shove them into my face, you slut.'

'I'm a man,' Dennis said.

'God, that voice,' the man said. 'I bet you're the real big butch type with a cunt like a sewer. I could do with a taste of it.'

'Mmmm,' Dennis murmured.

'You sexy bitch,' the man said. 'If you saw how big it is at this moment, you'd come running and beg me. Then I'd give it to you good. Every bit of my twelve inches. It's a monster and you'd come a dozen times and keep groaning for more.'

'Mmmm' Dennis repeated.

'Fifteen inches,' the man said. 'Hard as rock and keeps going for hours and they can't get enough of it.'

'Lucky ladies,' Dennis said.

'Filthy whores,' the man said. 'They keep their noses in the air when they pass me, but I know what they want: twenty inches and more, the evil harlots.'

'That's a lot,' Dennis said.

'It's a monster,' the man said. 'Just imagine it throbbing inside you, you insatiable wench.'

'What a brute,' Dennis said.

'God, your voice,' the man said. 'You filthy slut, you great big butch whore, you just can't get enough of it.'

'Don't stop,' Dennis said.

'You shameless bitch,' the man said. 'Just a moment, my three minutes are up. I'm putting in some more money.'

'Yes, Dennis,' said, 'do that.'

'Oh, Christ, I'm out of change!'

'You're a real disappointment,' Dennis said.

'You rotten whore! You *castrator*!'

Dennis dropped the yellow telephone and was about to convey a few curt words through the intercom to the mischievous Rosie Teasedale when he saw the imposing brunette in the thigh boots and leather jacket shaking her head disgustedly and slumping down in the chair facing the desk. Suddenly fearful that he, too, might be forced onto his knees to partake of the Amazon's treasures, Dennis removed his hand from the intercom, offered a tender smile, and carefully kept his eyes off the white sweater and magnificent breasts.

'I'm sorry,' he said. 'I should have offered you a seat.'

'Either you have manners,' she sneered, 'or you don't. And clearly you don't.'

'I simply forgot,' Dennis said.

'Because I'm a *woman*,' the woman said.

'You took me by surprise,' Dennis said. 'That's all there was to it.'

'Surprise?' the woman said. 'You call this a *surprise*? I've been sitting down there all frigging day with my arse freezing solid.'

'I'm truly sorry,' Dennis said.

'I'll bet,' the woman said.

'So,' Dennis said, 'what's your name? That *would* be most helpful.'

'Caroline Cooch.'

'Couch?'

'Cooch, you shit.'

'And you've come for this job you were promised?'

'Right.'

'Do you usually apply so aggressively for jobs?'

'I know my fucking rights. And every pig in this office has been inflammatory and made me uptight.'

'An editorial job?'

'Yes.'

'We don't normally have women in editorial positions.'

'Right,' Caroline said. 'Discrimination. I could have you for that.'

'Can you type?' Dennis said.

'No.'

'Have you ever edited before?'

'No.'

'Shorthand?'

'No.'

'Proof-reading?'

'Shit, no.' Caroline Cooch looked annoyed, slammed her shoulder-bag down on the desk, withdrew a packet of cigarettes from her pocket and lit one and sat back, puffing smoke. 'Oh, fuck it,' she said, 'let's stop all this pissing around. It's pretty obvious you don't want to hire a woman, and I can't stand the hassle.'

'Well,' Dennis said, trying not to sound relieved, 'it's really nothing to do with the fact that you're a woman... more to the point is that you don't have any skills or qualifications.'

'I'm a *woman*,' she said.

'You can't type or proof-read.'

'Discrimination,' she repeated. 'You chauvinist pigs are all the same. I could have you for that.'

'I'm sorry,' Dennis said.

'Okay. Let's lay our cards on the table.'

'Yes,' Dennis said, 'let's do that. That *would* be helpful.'

Caroline Cooch was just about to lay her cards on the table when the intercom buzzed. Dennis pressed a black button and listened to the voice of Rosie Teasedale.

'He loved you,' Rosie said.

'Pardon?' Dennis said.

'The deep breather who was on the phone... he obviously loved you.'

'Miss Teasedale, I really do think that in the future you should – '

'Your voice is so sexy,' Rosie said. 'Now I know why...

you're *butch*!'

'Ha, ha,' Dennis said.

'He'll ring back,' Rosie said. 'He's always jerking it off in a phone booth, so I know he'll ring back.'

'Don't put him through again.'

'Why not? You're so *cool*.'

'I really don't think – '

'God, I *love* the way you talk. So sexy, so masculine, so… *butch*. I can't wait till tomorrow.'

Rosie giggled and killed the line and Dennis stared at the imposing Caroline Cooch, offering her a tentative smile, a delicate blush on his cheeks.

'Miss Teasedale,' he explained. 'Our switchboard girl. She's a little bit mischievous.'

'Mzzz,' Miss Cooch said.

'Pardon?' Dennis said.

'It's not *Miss* or *Missus* anymore… The new term is *Mzzz*.'

'Mzzz?'

'M.S. Capital "M", a small "s". You won't categorise women anymore and put them into your pigeon-holes.'

'Ah,' Dennis said. 'I see…'

'And I suppose you're going to violate that young woman eventually?'

'I *beg* your pardon?'

'You heard me: I said *violate*. I suppose you're going to rape her eventually with your huge, mindless cock.'

'Hardly huge,' Dennis said.

'A modest man,' Mzzz Cooch said.

'Well,' Dennis said, 'I would hardly term it rape. I would, at least, wait for her consent: a reciprocal arrangement.'

'All seduction is rape,' Mzzz Cooch said. 'All you pricks are the same.'

Now that his prick had subsided and he could think more clearly, Dennis again found himself pondering the possibility of painless suicide, moved, as he was, by the thought that his delicate sensibilities were being shredded on the sharp blade of experience, and that visitors like Mzzz Cooch, though doubtless with their virtues, were no more than the phantoms in the dream that would soon do him in. There were no windows in his office. He often thought about that. He often wondered if a saner world existed beyond those blank walls.

'I really think we should stick to the subject at hand,' Dennis said.

'What subject?'

'Your job application.'

'Fuck the job,' Mzzz Cooch said. 'The job was only an excuse to get me in here.'

'I don't think I understand,' Dennis said.

'The truth of the matter is that I'm an Associate Editor on the female liberation magazine – '

'But you can't type or proof-read,' Dennis said.

'Don't try those cheap tactics on me,' Mzzz Cooch said.

'Tactics?' Dennis said.

'A deliberate confusing of the issues.'

'You can't type or proof-read,' Dennis said, 'so you can't be an Editor.'

'Okay,' Mzzz Cooch said. 'I'm a freelance female liberationist journalist who contributes to the invaluable contents of *Second Class Citizen*, which is, as you know, a magazine dedicated to the liberation of women everywhere, irrespective of class, creed or colour, and which is currently running a successful campaign against the sort of slimy innuendo, regressive filth and downright shitty, second-rate, mind-polluting garbage to be found in male chauvinist pig rapist magazines such as *Gents* and *Suave*.'

'Good Lord,' Dennis said. 'Caroline Cooch... *Now* I remember.'

'Right,' Mzzz Cooch said. 'Caroline Cooch: leading journalist of the women's liberation movement and founder member of COCK – the Cooch Organisation for Cunt Karma.'

A sliver of dread shivered down Dennis' artistic spine as he stubbed out his cigarette, immediately lit another, sucked greedily and thought of the fearsome COCK. COCK was one of the more extreme of the women's liberationist movements, most noted for its violent demonstrations both outside and inside strip clubs, brothels, football stadiums, boys' schools, gentlemen's clubs, Number 10 Downing Street, the Stock Exchange, Lord's Cricket Ground, model agencies, the Church of the Divine Male Inspiration, and the offices of male-interest magazines. Dennis shivered again when he also remembered that the attractive members of COCK were individually encouraged to send nasty letters to their respective Members of Parliament about the corrupting influence of magazines like *Gents* and *Suave*, blow up the homes of all males suspected of harbouring unclean thoughts, puncture the tyres of all cars displaying the *Playboy* sticker, and rape, with dildoes, decent men in the streets without as much as a by-your-leave. Dennis thought of this with horror. He wanted nothing to do with COCK. The members of COCK were female chauvinist bitches, and Dennis didn't like them one bit.

'Well, now…' Dennis murmured.

'So,' Mzzz Cooch said. 'The real reason I came here wasn't for a job, but to write an exposé of your filthy rags. I only asked that limp prick for a job because it seemed the best way to get in here and see what's cooking, and, since his nose was between my thighs and his teeth were rattling like castanets, I knew he was in no position to refuse.'

'That certainly shows initiative,' Dennis said.

'COCK's pretty fair,' Mzzz Cooch said, 'so credit where it's due.'

'Pardon?'

'The Artful Ed,' Mzzz Cooch said. 'That's one hell of a guy you've got there – and he doesn't hate women.'

'You mean the Artful Ed gave you that idea?'

'That's right,' Mzzz Cooch said. 'The Artful Ed had this

sadomasochistic, limp-dick virginal friend who was letting him, the Artful Ed, use his name and home address for the receipt of cheques for work done by the Artful Ed under pseudonyms for your magazines and who was sadistically threatening to withdraw this benefit from the Artful Ed because he was masochistically yearning to be raped and didn't know who to ask, so the Artful Ed, knowing that my members hated men and loved to rape them, asked me to get the guy fixed up when he was travelling home on the tube from Earls Court to Parsons Green, which I did, and then, the Artful Ed being no woman-hater and always appreciative of the odd little favour, took me to that orgy on Friday by way of a return favour and suggested that I make the Editor gobble me and then pin him down for a job, which is why I'm here now.'

'I see,' Dennis said.

'Right,' Mzzz Cooch said.

'Well,' Dennis said, thinking fondly of the Artful Ed, 'I *do* appreciate the concerns of COCK and *Second Class Citizen* and would certainly like to assist you with your article, since, contrary to what you might feel after a superficial reading of *Gents* and *Suave*, we do, between the lines, as it were, have a great deal of sympathy for our sisters on the other side of the fence and try to present an always reasonable and balanced viewpoint. Also, I would point out to you, Mzzz Cooch, that while our magazines are obviously focused on the *possibly* regressive aggrandisement of certain male fantasies, we ourselves, again contrary to your understandable misconceptions, treat our own female staff members with the utmost respect and courtesy – both in word and deed – as I'm sure you would appreciate if indeed you worked here.'

The expression on Mzzz Cooch's face was beginning to soften just a little when the intercom buzzed and Dennis pressed the black button and listened to the drunken voice of the Ed.

'Hello, Dennis! Hello! Are you there?'

'Yes,' Dennis said.

'Jesus, Dennis, this is crazy. Where the fuck did you go? I mean, that whore Lavinia came in, made her typically female hysterical pronouncement about a deadline, and then, you know, what with Stan and that dumb cunt of a model still being glued to one another and good old Harvey being particularly inventive with that quick-to-come mindless little whore Annie Bedward, and then, you know, that shithead Clive Grant suddenly waking up and offering Lavinia a nice slice of his throbbing meat, well, you know Lavinia, a latent lesbian if ever I saw one – though also frustrated and needing a decent cock up her – well, what can I say, Dennis, she just hit the fucking roof and started yelling about the fucking deadline in that dumb, hysterical, typically senseless female manner, and I looked around and my Chief Ass was gone. What the fuck are you *doing* down there?'

'Well, Ed,' Dennis said, glancing nervously at Mzzz Cooch, 'the thing is – '

'Thing is, Dennis, I'm getting pretty fucking fed-up with all these dumb-cunt, hysterical, typically female neurotic Production Editors, or *Prod* Eds, ha, ha, coming in late because they've had a fight with their fucking boyfriends, or moaning because they have to take their dumb kids to school, or taking days off because they're having their filthy periods, and then, to cap it all, stomping around our fine offices and kicking up a storm over nothing. We can't trust the women, Dennis. All the women are dumb bitches. All the women, we should put them in cages and feed them some bird seed.'

'Well, Ed,' Dennis said, trying to smile at Mzzz Cooch, 'I *do* feel that perhaps the heat of the moment, as it were, has gone to your tongue and is making you say things you don't mean.'

'Let's face it, Dennis, I'm a straight guy, a fair guy, but we have to use these women, brainless whores the whole lot of them, and instead they should have been kept in chains, they're only good for a quick screw.'

'Ed, I really think you should know that – '

'We've talked a lot about this, Dennis, and I know you

130

agree with me, so let's not let the bitches waste our precious time. Thing is, we have to work with them because of the Industrial Tribunal and the National Union of Journalists and all those other fascist organisations, but I *do* feel, Dennis, that something has to be done to terminate their increasing delusions of equality and women's rights, and so, you know, you being *practised* at this and so forth, I do feel that you should take the matter in hand.'

'Ed, I really think you should know – '

'Anyway, Dennis, apart from the fact that that whore Lavinia is a typical example of female neuroses, hysterics and pure, undefiled, cunt-dominated mindlessness, I *do* get the vibration of imminent disaster in the air and can only assume that in this case she's right. We really *do* have a deadline, Dennis, it's a very *serious* deadline, so I'm going to have a talk with this whore and call you right back.'

The Ed cut the line before Dennis could warn him about the presence of Mzzz Cooch, and then, before Dennis could formulate a quick and crafty excuse for the Ed's exotic description of the fairer sex, the intercom buzzed again and good old Harvey was talking.

'Hello, Dennis, my worthy Chief Ass, are you there?'

'Yes, Harvey.'

'Why the fuck did you disappear, Dennis? Things are getting hot up there.'

'*Up* there?' Dennis said. 'Where are you now?'

'Thing is, Dennis, I zipped out of the Pic Ed's office as soon as that whore Lavinia walked in – not wanting to be involved in any embarrassing demonstrations of typically female histrionics – and then, having made good my escape, came back down here to clear up all this work on my desk, which, in the event, I can't do because I've just had a frantic call from the Ed, telling me that that whore Lavinia – who is, of course, frustrated and needs a good pulsating, squirming, squirting, natural-veined, super double-sized vibrating dildo up her – well, anyway, the Ed said she might be right and that we might *indeed* have a genuine deadline on our hands and therefore might have to work all night and tomorrow to get some new, unspecified material ready to go to press by tomorrow evening, and so, you know, I can't really do any of the required work on my desk because I have to make a few phone calls to my wife and some of those unpaid whores that I occasionally satisfy, and so, Chief Ass, I'm back down here at my desk.'

'Harvey, I really feel you should know that I do not appreciate such crude commentary on the female members of our staff and would – '

'Anyway, Dennis, I just thought I'd let you know that while I'm willing to endure the presence of that frustrated cunt Lavinia, and while I'm also willing to risk my mental and physical health by working here all fucking night, I am *not* willing to do so if this so-called deadline is another of those crises deliberately engineered by that bitch Lavinia to make us all feel that she's the only one on top of the situation – since, as we all know, and apart from anything else, it is *we* who should be right on top of *her*, ha, ha – and so, Dennis, well, you know me, I'm real straight, I'll do the work if I have to do it, but I'm a happily married man, a devoted husband and daddy, and I'm not going to risk wrecking my marriage by staying away from home just because that whore is making a power-play.'

'Harvey,' Dennis said, smiling sweatily at Mzzz Cooch, 'I really think we should discuss this matter some other time, and in the meantime – '

'Dennis, I really appreciate your valuable comments on this matter, but I'm going to have to get off the intercom because the Ed is buzzing me on the telephone here – in fact, speaking to me as I'm speaking to you – telling me to get off the fucking intercom since he wants to talk to *you* on the intercom and I'm holding him up. I'll have to cut you off, Dennis.'

The intercom went dead and Dennis just had enough time to notice that the imposing Mzzz Cooch had lost her softer expression and was once more tight-lipped and flushed with anger. Dennis, himself flushed with brandy, emotional exhaustion and increasing tension, smiled at Mzzz Cooch with the false bravery of a condemned man and then twitched visibly when the intercom buzzed again.

'Dennis?' the Ed said.

'Yes, Ed,' Dennis said.

'The shit has really hit the fan, Dennis, and we've got to do something.'

'Ed, I think we'd better discuss this on the telephone.'

'What the fuck's the matter with the intercom, Dennis? Can't you hear me or something?'

'Yes, Ed, I can hear you, but – '

At this point in the proceedings Mzzz Cooch slipped out of her chair and leaned across the desk and pressed the button that turned the intercom off. Still leaning across the desk, still grim and imposing, Mzzz Cooch took a deep breath, her magnificent breasts out-thrust, and gave the speech that sent Dennis to the pits.

'Before you speak to your Editor again,' she said, 'I'd just like you to know that I intend remaining in these offices until I find out just how you bastards operate, that I do not want either the Editor or anyone else to know who I'm writing for, and that in case you're thinking of telling them, I should point out that I know all about you, I know that you're married, and I even know who Anna and Laura are. Now do I have to say more?'

Dennis needed precisely one second to understand that she didn't have to say more, and so, a lot paler than his normal shade of pale, he shook his head and heard the intercom buzzing and pressed the black button.

'Yes?'

'Is that you, Dennis?'

'Yes,' Dennis said.

'I keep asking,' the Ed said, 'because these intercoms are funny and you sound like one of Doctor Who's Daleks.'

'Right,' Dennis said.

'This is no time for jokes, Dennis," the Ed said hysterically. 'That hysterical bitch was really on the ball and now we have to defend ourselves.'

'Pardon, Ed?'

'That whore, Lavinia,' the Ed said.

'I know,' Dennis said. 'But what about her? What did she say?'

'Terrible things, Dennis.'

'Really?'

'Yes, really. The shit's really hit the fan, Dennis, and we have to do something.'

'Please explain,' Dennis said.

'I will,' the Ed said. 'That hysterical bitch was absolutely right and now I'm fucking hysterical.'

'Stay cool,' Dennis said.

'I will, Dennis! *I will*! It's just that the very thought of what's happening is driving me crazy.'

'We'll work it out,' Dennis said.

'That's sound advice,' the Ed said. 'I always knew I could depend on you, Dennis. You always know what the score is.'

'So,' Dennis said, 'what's the score?'

'Terrible, Dennis. Terrible! *Really* terrible! Thing is, the printer's solicitors have rung me to say that they can't possibly take the risk of printing "Going Down to Get It Up", not only because of what they described as "the extremely indecent, obscene, degenerate and dangerously stimulating nature of the article" but also because the accompanying illustration, which apparently is a cartoon depicting a shark going down on the hard-on of a seal – '

'Dolphin.'

' - or some such shit, would offend animal lovers and bring down upon our heads the full wrath of the RSPCA.'

'Good Lord,' Dennis said.

'That's it!' the Ed said. 'You've hit the fucking nail on the head. Now what the fuck do we do, Dennis?'

'Well, Ed – '

'Thing is, Dennis, the next issue's just about been laid to rest and was ready to roll and now we're going to have to pull that feature – *plus* the fucking illustration – and fill that empty hole by tomorrow night.'

'I appreciate your concern, Ed, but I'm sure, given the cordial relations we've always maintained with our printers, that they'll willingly hold off their other jobs until we replace the aborted material.'

'Those fucking printers,' the Ed said. 'The rotten bastards. They won't do a damned thing.'

'Really?'

'Really.'

'And why not, Ed?'

'Because,' the Ed said, sounding wounded beyond words, 'that bastard you spoke to this morning at the printers. Mr… ah…'

'Pearson.'

'Pearson, rang me back and thanked me for our efficiency and thoughtfulness in working our asses off to get him "Going Down to Get It Up" and the accompanying illustration so promptly, and then, having grovelled and thanked me, the filthy cock-sucking, syphilitic, back-stabbing son of a bitch told me that he was going to have to put up his prices, and reminded me, the ungrateful, materialistic, tight-fisted snake-in-the-grass, that we hadn't paid him and his lousy fucking Company a penny for the last three issues, refusing to believe, the miserable lump of steaming, foul-smelling, diseased turd, that this was merely due to the notorious inefficiency of those union-controlled, fascist, anarchist bastards in the post office, who kept losing our cheques, and so, you know me, I told the revolting, stomach-churning, vomit-inducing tub of lard what I thought, and then he, the blackmailing, immoral lump of contaminating slime, said that if we didn't get the cheque to him double-quick he wasn't going to hold up the presses and, further, that contrary to my assertion that the RSPCA, whatever *they* are, could get stuffed, he, the delightful Mr Pearson, would not, cheque or no cheque, make a move on our magazine until "Going Down to Get It Up" had been replaced.'

'Well, Ed,' Dennis said, ignoring Mzzz Cooch's muffled snort of malicious mirth, but cognisant, nonetheless, of the dramatic swelling of her magnificent breasts, 'I'm afraid we'll just have to disturb the Big P by asking him to sign a cheque and then send that cheque by motorcycle messenger direct to Mr Pearson, after which we can get together, work out a replacement feature and, hopefully with the assistance of the Artful Ed, get a new illustration and then, by working right through the night, get it off to the printers by tomorrow.'

'I knew I could depend on you, Dennis, and you've really come through again, which is, I might add, more than I can say for any of those other bastards, namely Harvey, Clive and good old Stan, all of whom, at the mere mention of this grave crisis, disappeared to suck brandy and tit. As a matter of fact, Dennis, apart from all the whores in this establishment being incompetent typists, switchboard operators, production editors and clerks, I also believe that they're a negative influence on the lads by distracting them with bouncing boobs and fannies. I really think you should look into this, Dennis, but in the meantime there are more important matters to discuss, such as the fact that that dumb whore Lavinia threw another spanner in the works by telling me that she had learned from someone she obviously fucked at the printers that the printers were not in fact concerned about "Going Down to Get It Up" – which is, after all, an innocuous little piece about bestiality, necrophilia, paederasty and sadomasochism – but were actually only using it as an excuse for getting rid of our mags altogether to make way for a glossier, even filthier, better-paying lad's mag that's being rushed out by some unknown publisher.'

'A *rival* magazine?' Dennis said.

136

'Right,' the Ed said. 'And I don't have to tell you, Dennis, that if we don't get this issue of *Suave* out on time, those rotten bastards at the printers are going to make sure we don't get it out for another *month*, during which time they would be running off that new, rival magazine, which would, being glossier and more scandalous than *Suave* or *Gents*, steal our whole fucking readership and put us up Shit Creek without a paddle. So, Dennis, as I see it, we're now on War Alert and I've already taken steps to win the battle.'

'Oh?' Dennis said. 'And what are those?'

'Well, Dennis,' the Ed said, sounding drunkenly authoritative, 'my first priority was to ensure that none of these bastards and whores who're supposed to work here leave this building until further notice, in furtherance of which I have informed, by memo, all the whores that they are to remain at their posts throughout the night and that food and drink, when deemed necessary, shall be ordered for them, simultaneously informing Harvey, Clive and that cunt-obsessed Picture Editor Stan that we will all shortly be retiring to Muriel's in Frith Street for an in-depth discussion on the matter.'

'Do you really think that's wise, Ed?'

'What?'

'Muriel's.'

'Well, Dennis, I agree with you that Muriel's, under different circumstances, might be something of a temptation for our merry lads, what with the low lights and brandy, but, Dennis, let's face it, we can't expect our male members of staff to stay awake through what promises to be a very arduous night and morning without *some* modest form of reward and encouragement, and so, Dennis, I felt that a few hours out of the office, with a few drinks and decent food, might do them some good, and, of course, there's no need to worry about the office, since, in our absence, all the whores will be here and we will, not wanting to forget them or appear to be ungrateful, send up some Coca Cola and crisps.'

The Ed's gesture of benevolence toward the female members of his staff, not to mention his choice terminology regarding the dear girls, nearly made Mzzz Cooch come out of her chair again – nearly, but not finally, since she somehow managed to contain herself and instead merely shivered with revulsion (magnificent breasts bouncing beautifully) and lit up a cigarette and then blew smoke directly at Dennis, her unpainted lips grim.

'Very nice,' she sneered. 'Wonderful.'

'Also,' the Ed continued, unaware of the great terrors and passions that would soon fall about him and, in the shape of Mzzz Cooch, leave his every nerve singing, 'I am cognisant of the fact that we must get the Circulation Manager out of Torremolinos and winging his way around this country to encourage, by way of bribery, blackmail or deceit, as many retail outlets as possible to ignore all approaches by the representatives of that new fucking magazine – not least on the grounds that its Publisher is an unknown quantity and therefore clearly not to be trusted – and to take double their normal quota of our very own *Suave* when the fucking thing *is* finally printed.'

'Such integrity,' Mzzz Cooch murmured. 'I am touched.'

'So, Dennis,' the Ed continued, unaware of Mzzz Cooch's presence, 'I'm pleased to inform you that according to the account's department that shithead Rick Walker, who masquerades as the Assistant Editor of *Gents*, has been booked on a Malaga flight for nine o'clock this evening, with instructions to locate that thieving and degenerate son of a bitch of a Circulation Manager in that brothel he pretends is a hotel and bring him back to London on the next morning flight out. The shithead – Rick, *not* the Circulation Manager, who is, of course, also a shithead – is on his way to Heathrow right this minute, moaning about his raw throat and his sore arse and his frigging ulcer, convinced the plane will crash, terrified of Spanish food, but otherwise all set to do the job for fear of losing his balls.'

138

'Charming,' Mzzz Cooch said.

'Finally, Dennis,' the Ed continued excitedly, still unaware of Mzzz Cooch and of the anguish and exaltation that would soon be his, 'I think it imperative that we get the Invisible Man, alias the Artful Ed, into this office, since, apart from the fact that he's the only bastard with enough talent, grease and cunning to get us another layout and illustration done by tomorrow, he is also the one animal, vegetable or mineral likely to know who this new rip-off bastard Publisher is and who might, through his infinite and ruthless knowledge of the Outside World, find a way of blackmailing that cunt or the bastards who're printing him.'

'Delightful,' Mzzz Cooch said. 'Enchanting.'

'So, Dennis, I'm depending on you. I want you to get on the phone right this minute and find out where the Artful Ed is hiding, and then, when you *do* get the bastard, tell him what's happening and insist that he haul his arse around here immediately. Come to think of it, Dennis, the Artful Ed – who is, as we all know, an extremely talented guy, a truly *creative* guy, but also, if I may say so without appearing to be detrimental, an exceptionally *slippery* bit of work and apt to pull some shifty stunts – well, knowing what the fucker is like, I feel it might be wise if I were to come down to your office right now and then, when you contact the mad bastard, talk to him myself. I'm on my way, Dennis.'

'*Just a moment*!' Dennis hissed.

'What's that?' the Ed said.

'Well, Ed,' Dennis began, and then, staring into the cold, clear, relentless threat of Mzzz Cooch's green eyes and, perhaps more to the point, seeing her mouthing the words 'Laura and Anna... I will tell all,' Dennis, licking his dry lips, feeling the fluttering of his heart, his soul plunging into the pits, said, 'Thing is, Ed, I've got a journalist down here, a most attractive and understanding young lady who wishes to do a profile on the magazine for *The Observer* supplement, and, you know, while on the one hand this might be a particularly inconvenient time for something like that, it could, on the other hand, given the pressure and all, be an excellent way of letting her view the creative side of our magazines and could also, of course, lead to invaluable publicity just when we most need it.'

'Dennis, you're a genius,' the Ed said. 'I'm coming right down.'

5

It was love at first sight. Dennis was leaning back in his chair behind his desk, smoking a cigarette and staring at the windowless white walls of his office and wondering if there was a saner world beyond them. Removing his stinging eyes from the walls, he stared at the red phone, the yellow phone and the intercom in turn, thinking, as he did so, that ninety percent of his life was lived in a world of voices, all remote, disembodied, divorced from reality, and that these lines of communication, sometimes living, sometimes dead, were the very blood and bone of his existence. Having thus contemplated philosophically on the tenuous nature of his being, he turned his weary gaze in the direction of the imposing Mzzz Cooch, she of the tremendous boobs and the terrifying COCK, and, in so doing, was reminded of what she knew and thus plunged once again into the pits. Rescued by the entrance of the Ed, he saw Love at First Sight.

It was obvious from the instant the Ed stepped into the office that he had, since Dennis left him, been swallowing something other than simple brandy. Tall, thin and elegant in his trendy denims and tan coat, no tie, shirt unbuttoned, his beard matching his curly dark hair, the Ed walked in and stopped and then stared at Mzzz Cooch with brown eyes that now resembled pinwheels. Staring down at the seated Mzzz Cooch, who stared back up with a smile of Antarctic warmth, the Ed visibly took a deep breath, glanced at Dennis, licked his lips, then stepped forward and stretched out his hand and watched it dangle in the air. Untouched.

'Well, hello there,' he said.
'Mzzz Caroline Cooch,' Dennis said.
'Mzzz?' the Ed said.
'M.s.,' Dennis said.
'M.s.?' the Ed said.
'A term of address,' Mzzz Cooch explained.
'Ah,' the Ed said.
'Right,' Dennis said.
'Hello, Caroline,' the Ed said. 'Charmed, I'm sure. Nice to meet *The Observer*, ha, ha.'

Mzzz Cooch stood up and looked *down* at the tall Ed and then, in that magical moment when their hands met in the air and the Ed, well laced with brandy and spaced out on God knows what, his mind swirling with dark dreams of treachery and ruination, glanced down to see her fingers encircling his own, first gentle, then vice-like, then possibly crushing bone, and stifled a wince that expressed ecstatic pain, and looked up and saw the clear green splendour of her eyes, so searching, so relentless, so afire with cruel mockery, and knew, without doubt (and it was shamefully visible) that True Love had raced into his heart and would make him a stronger man.

'Hi,' Mzzz Cooch said.

The Ed stood there with his jaw hanging open and his bloodshot, pinwheel eyes staring fixedly at the imposing Amazonian lady who was, oh sweet miracle, even taller than himself and who would, oh sweet hope, make him go down on his knees and tear his hair out by the roots and stand naked but for thigh boots and stomp up and down his spine and put needles in his cock and whip him senseless and then show him transcendence. Yes, the Ed obviously knew this when he looked at her and, not remembering her, but torn, like Dennis, by life's cruelties and injustices, and therefore needing love and the redemption of savage lust, felt certain that already he knew her – a miraculous sign.

'Haven't we met before?' the Ed enquired.

'No,' Mzzz Cooch lied.

The Ed rubbed his pinwheel eyes, ran his fingers through his curly hair, and then offered his most charming, schoolboy smile. By way of return, Mzzz Cooch looked him up and down, and then, to his delight, returned his smile with all the warmth of a cadaver just dug out of the snow.

'Well,' the Ed said, searching desperately for words and wanting, in the innocence of his new, transcendental love, to show her what a bright boy he was, 'Well, I must say I'm very pleased that such an esteemed newspaper as *The Observer* is willing to send along such an obviously intelligent and open-minded lady to have a look at how we work and finally, and forever, put into their grave all those terrible stories about how illiterate and uncouth we gentlemen are.'

'I'm interested in the woman's angle,' Mzzz Cooch said.

'The *woman's* angle?' the Ed said, sounding confused.

'Yes,' Mzzz Cooch said, her detestation ill concealed, thus sending tremors of delight down the Ed's spine. 'We're interested not only in your magazines' general editorial attitude towards women, but in your attitude to the women who actually work here.'

'Indeed, yes,' the Ed said, shaking his head and looking sombre, his schoolboy face enlivened with vice and the urge to be pure. 'A good angle. Most laudable.'

'It's not an *angle*,' Mzzz Cooch sneered.

'My God, no!' the Ed promptly backtracked, her contempt making his pecker jump for joy. 'A commitment. Most certainly.'

At that moment, Dennis coughed into his fist and the Ed, blinking repeatedly and coming back down to earth – though not too low for fear of being trampled, the fear exciting his loins – coughed, likewise, into his fist and turned away slightly from Mzzz Cooch and, giving Dennis his most serious, even academic, look - the look of a *real* Editor, as it were - made it clear that he was set for serious business.

'Well, now, Dennis,' he said, his voice dropping a few octaves, 'I think it would be a good idea if we were to let Mzzz Cooch accompany us to Muriel's where we can, in the quiet and dignified atmosphere which that esteemed establishment engenders, perhaps elaborate for Mzzz Cooch's benefit on the vicissitudes of magazine production and the current, though hardly typical, problems of our deadline, and then, of course, once we have returned here, we can let her sit in on the editorial meeting which, as usual, will continue throughout the night and at which, I am sure, Mzzz Cooch will be able to see for herself that we treat all the members of our staff equally, irrespective of position or sex, and thus have what can only be called a happy team.'

'Right,' Dennis said.

'In the meantime, Dennis,' the Ed continued sonorously, desperately trying to keep his pecker from jumping at Mzzz Cooch, 'I think you should get on the telephone and contact our prize-winning Art Directior – known to us all, Mzzz Cooch, as the Artful Ed, ha, ha, and presently out on an urgent photographic assignment – to inform him of our plans and ensure his presence at the editorial meeting. After that, we can all retire to Muriel's.'

'Right,' Dennis said.

'Okay,' Mzzz Cooch said. 'That's fine with me. I'll go to the john while you make your call.'

'Excellent,' the Ed said. 'A very good idea, Mzzz Cooch. I go four or five times a day myself. Please let me escort you.'

'Just tell me where it is,' Mzzz Cooch said. 'I can pull my own drawers down.'

The sneer with which Mzzz Cooch delivered her retort made the Ed blush, not with shame but with ecstasy, and as he babbled the pertinent facts regarding the whereabouts of the toilet, his bloodshot, pinwheel eyes were afire with a light that displayed his more human side and only dimmed when, with a contemptuous up-thrust of the nose and out-thrust of her magnificent breasts, Mzzz Cooch departed to drop her drawers, at which point, more sane, his less benign self returning, the Ed coughed into his fist and stared at Dennis and said, 'God, did you see that?'

'Yes,' Dennis said.

'Christ,' the Ed said, 'what a woman! Real flesh and blood, Dennis.'

'I'd better ring the Artful Ed,' Dennis said.

'Right,' the Ed said.

Dennis picked up the yellow phone and asked Rosie Teasedale to give him an outside line and heard Rosie giggle, a mischievous, dirty sound, and then heard a click and some static and a familiar male voice growling in one long, drawn-out sentence, 'All you sluts are the same, I mean working for those filthy rags, I'm a regular reader and I know, they should be banned, I've got twenty inches all hot and throbbing and rigid right now, so come and get it, you slut.' Then, after Dennis had barked into the phone for Rosie, he heard the man say, 'God, you're butch!' followed by a click, then another giggle, then the sound of an open outside line. Again thinking fondly of suicide, Dennis dialled the Artful Ed's number.

'This is a recording,' said a suspiciously lively, sexy female voice. 'The Artful Ed is not here at present, but will, when and if he returns, answer all messages. When you hear the click, please leave your message or name and phone number. Praise be to Allah.'

Waiting for and eventually hearing the click, Dennis felt his soul sliding down into the pits, and then, when the click had come and gone, to be replaced by a hollow, echoing sound, he said, 'This is Dennis Elliot, the Chief Associate Editor of *Gents* and *Suave*, so please get off the line, tell the Artful Ed I'm waiting, and ensure that he picks up the phone and offers his own voice.'

The hollow, echoing sound continued for some time, until, without a click or the whirring of tape, the same sexy female voice returned.

'This is a recording,' said the suspiciously lively female. 'The Artful Ed is not here at present and therefore, while being unable to personally take incoming calls, has left instructions that, should a certain Mr Dennis Elliot call, he is to wait until he hears the click and then take down the number he will be given. Please have your pen or pencil ready and, when you hear the click, take down the number. Buddha reigns over all.'

Cursing quietly and waiting for the click, Dennis felt his soul sliding deeper into the pits, and then, when the click had come and gone, scribbled down the phone number that was given to him by the same suspiciously real-life female voice and, once having done this, dropped the yellow phone, glanced up at the twitching Ed (whose decadent schoolboy face was a parchment of fear and new-found love) and then, picking up the yellow phone again, dialled the new number. He heard a humming sound, oddly muffled and echoing, then another female voice started speaking without the hindrance of tape hiss.

'This is a recording,' said the suspiciously vibrant voice. 'The Artful Ed is not here at present and, while personally being unable to take incoming calls, at least, in his estimation, until tomorrow, he has left instructions that should a certain Mr Dennis Elliot call, he is to be informed that the Artful Ed will, if required, return Mr Elliot's call within the hour and in person, subject to Mr Elliot leaving on this answer-machine, after due pause and the sound of the click, his estimated whereabouts at the time of the anticipated return call. Please wait for the forthcoming pause and click, and, once having heard the latter, offer clearly the relevant information. The wrath of Kali is merciful.'

Closing his eyes and wallowing deeply in the pits, his hopes centred on sex and suicide and oblivion, Dennis heard the click and said, 'Muriel's' and then opened his eyes and dropped the phone and looked up at the Ed and said, 'The Artful Ed's vanished.'

'*What?*' the Ed said, looking horrified.

'The Artful Ed appears to have vanished. He'll ring back in an hour or so.'

'That bastard,' the Ed said.

'Quite,' Dennis said.

'I would strangle that cunt,' the Ed said, 'if he wasn't so talented.'

'Anyway,' Dennis said, sounding calmer than he felt, 'I'm sure that the Artful Ed will, as his message stated, ring back in an hour or so and will then, as usual, make up for his absence. In the meantime, Ed, I feel I should warn you – '

'I want her to stomp on me,' the Ed said.

'Pardon?' Dennis said.

'Oh, God, I'm diseased, I'm perverted: I want her to whip me.'

'Ed, I really think – '

'Thing is, Dennis, I respect you, I admire you, I *trust* you, and I know I can talk to you, and so, Dennis, I don't mind telling you, I sometimes get the feeling that this constant exposure to all these sex articles and photos of bum and tit and pudenda, not to mention the all too frequent and more intimate exposure to the various models and actresses and female members of our staff – who are, if I may say so, a bit too loose for decency – is possibly breeding the contempt of familiarity in the sense that I'm finding it increasingly difficult to feel excited over normal leg, ass or cunt, and indeed, Dennis, to my horror, find that beauty alone will no longer suffice and that I now fantasise about *other* forms of gratification, most of which, I fear, would shock even the hardest hooker, and so, Dennis, as I'm sure you agree, this life isn't too healthy.'

Dennis was about to reply, with deep and genuine emotion, that he, too, suffered from certain negative impulses and desires (such as suicide or some other form of helpful oblivion) when the imposing Mzzz Cooch swept back into the office, her magnificent breasts bouncing in her tight white sweater, her aggressive sexuality emphasised by the leather jacket, thigh boots and crotch-gripping denims, all of which almost made the Ed slaver as his pinwheel eyes ravished her.

'Okay,' Mzzz Cooch said, sneering, 'let's get the fuck out of here.'

Thrilled to his toenails by the revelation that Mzzz Cooch, though a real *Observer* writer and therefore a superior being, could so casually drop the odd obscene word to show that she could be one of the lads, the Ed nodded his head in a gesture of loving obedience and then pressed one of the buttons on the intercom on Dennis' desk and said, 'Hello? Is that the Big P's secretary?'

'No,' a female voice replied. 'This is Lavinia.'

'Lavinia?'

'Yes.'

'And where is the Big P's sack, Lavinia?'

'Miss Fright has – '

'Not *Miss*,' the Ed said firmly. '*Mzzz.*'

'Mzzz?'

'M.s.'

'M.s?'

'Correct,' the Ed said. 'I will not tolerate the demeaning categorisation of the female members of our staff by allowing the use of such debasing forms of address. Now where is Mzzz Fright?'

'Mzzz Fright has gone home on the grounds that it is now well after five-thirty and she has neither been given in writing an agreement that she will be paid extra for working overtime nor been paid for all her *previous* overtime, and so, understanding the gravity of our present deadline, and wanting to ensure that our esteemed Publisher, the Big P, is on hand should we require him, I have moved temporarily into Mzzz Fright's office to take over her telephone and intercoms.'

'You've *what*?' the Ed hissed.

'You heard me,' Lavinia said. 'We can't have this office

unmanned, so I had to take over.'

Brutally whipped by the cold winds of bloody revolution, the Ed shot Dennis a horrified glance and then glared at the intercom.

'Well, Lavinia,' he said, keeping his voice unnaturally reasonable, remembering the presence of Mzzz Cooch and not wanting her to think of him as a disgusting male chauvinist pig rapist, 'I really do appreciate your initiative in this matter – not to mention your touching gesture of solidarity – but given the fact that our esteemed Publisher, the Big P, does not like to hear bad news when he's in his office, I *do* hope you have not taken it upon yourself to inform him of our present little crisis.'

'Whether or not I tell the Big P about our present little crisis depends entirely on how big our little crisis grows between now and tomorrow's five-in-the-afternoon deadline, which itself depends on whether or not you, the male editorial members of your staff and the Artful Ed can come up with a replacement article and illustration for the aborted "Going Down to Get It Up", this in itself being an issue of considerable doubt.'

'Come, come,' the Ed said, sounding calm, looking outraged, 'surely you know us better than that.'

'You're a bunch of incompetent bastards,' Lavinia said, 'and you're all drunk already.'

'*You're fired*!' the Ed screamed.

'I'm not leaving,' Lavinia said.

'*You syphilitic slut*!' the Ed screamed. '*You filthy whore*! *You dumb cunt*!'

Dennis reached across the desk and turned the intercom off and rolled his eyes in the direction of Mzzz Cooch, trying to save the Ed's love-life. The Ed blinked and stared at Dennis, buried his face in his hands, then removed his hands and looked at Mzzz Cooch, his smile radiant with pain.

'Wonderful,' Mzzz Cooch said.

'I'm *so* sorry,' the Ed said.

'Gross abuse of an employee,' Mzzz Cooch said. 'And all

because she's a woman.'

'A slip of the tongue,' the Ed said.

'Vile language,' Mzzz Cooch said.

'Heat of the moment,' the Ed said.

'You rotten shit,' Mzzz Cooch said.

The Ed naturally flinched from the contemptuous wrath of Mzzz Cooch, and then, this token gesture of basic decency dispensed with, shivered with rapture and thought of the possibilities in her forthcoming vengeance. Dennis saw the Ed's young face, the fear and yearning in his eyes, and understood (being a writer and so forth) that human nature was complex.

'Dear Mzzz Cooch – ' the Ed began.

'You snivelling turd,' Mzzz Cooch responded. 'You raped that poor girl with your tongue. Do you know what that feels like?'

'Pardon?' the Ed said.

'Humiliation,' Mzzz Cooch said. 'All rape is a form of humiliation and I want satisfaction.'

'Let's go to Muriel's,' Dennis said.

'Shut your mouth,' Mzzz Cooch said. 'I'm going to teach this bastard a lesson he'll never forget.'

'I really think – ' Dennis began.

'Down on your knees,' Mzzz Cooch said. 'You're going to get as good as you give, you indecent pig rapist.'

The Ed was stupidly obstinate, being a virgin in such matters, stepping back and offering a pathetic, girlish plea that merely excited his rapist. Mzzz Cooch grabbed him and forced him down, her grip brutal and merciless, then she undid the buckle of her belt and jerked the zip open.

'Stop whimpering,' she sneered.

Dennis closed his eyes and shivered, thinking of the fearful wrath of COCK, and realising, as most bystanders do, that he was too scared to intervene. Worse: while the Ed's acoustic demonstrations of hope and despair and shame and primal lust (first clear, then more muffled, his tongue most brutally abused) were an illuminating summary of the destructive, redeeming and mysterious contradictions of human sexuality, which did, in a certain sense, further Dennis' education, they did not, nonetheless, give him any real assistance when it came to facing up to his immediate cowardice. Indeed, it might be true to say that Dennis, forced to listen to the beastly rapist's yelps of satisfaction and her unfortunate victim's pathetic whimperings, might never have recovered from the shock of the experience had not he been rescued, as so often was the case, by the nerve-shattering ringing of the yellow telephone.

Opening his eyes again, and momentarily imagining that he was watching a Sam Peckinpah movie scripted by Russ Meyer – the Ed down on his knees, his lips and tongue being utilised, Mzzz Cooch with her denims and knickers pulled down, her crotch pressed to the Ed's flushed face – Dennis reached out for the phone, tried to ignore the yelps and whimperings, and, with an admirable display of self-control, spoke his own name.

'Hi,' Rosie Teasedale said. 'It's me.'

'Ah,' Dennis said.

'God, your voice is so sexy,' Rosie said. 'I can't wait till tomorrow night.'

'That's a delightful sentiment, my dear, but I'm busy right now.'

'Why? What's happening?'

'We're having an editorial meeting.'

'Sounds noisy.'

'Yes, they often are.'

'I have a call for you,' Rosie said.

'Not the heavy breather, I hope.'

'Another heavy breather,' Rosie said. 'That bitch Lavinia.'

Being an artistic soul with delicate sensitivities, a writer and so forth, Dennis realised that he could no longer tolerate the brutal rape of the Ed, particularly when the rapist was making it abundantly clear that she was not about to show mercy and was, indeed, intent upon having her whole pound of flesh, pulling it out of the Ed's trousers as if out of a sausage-machine, while the Ed, now on his back, looking up, his eyes like saucers, cried piteously and succumbed to her filthy deeds. Dennis, observing it all, filled with shame and compassion, nevertheless knew that he could not remain an innocent bystander and therefore, wanting cleansed of the sin of omission, took a deep breath and made his decision.

'I'll take her call on Harvey's phone,' he said. 'Tell her to hold on.'

With as much dignity as he could muster under the circumstances, Dennis put the phone down and stood up and walked around his desk, and then, aware that the imposing Mzzz Cooch was making her presence felt with the Ed by opening her legs and lowering herself upon him, equally cognisant of the Ed's pathetic virginal whimperings, and also understanding the terrible truth that fear and desire are one and the same, that a 'no' can often mean 'yes' and that 'right' and 'wrong' are relevant terms, skirted carefully around the groaning couple on the floor and left them to find their own salvation.

The spacious, open-plan office outside Dennis' small, more intimate office was, like Dennis' particular tomb, without windows or clocks. It was therefore no surprise to Dennis that when he entered that larger space he did so with no sense of having changed his environment – though it *was* a surprise to see that Harvey was still at his desk, this unusual event being explained by the fact that Harvey was not actually working, but was, instead, talking to the delightful Annie Bedward, who, sitting on Harvey's desk with her tight skirt pulled up over her beautiful, crossed thighs, was giggling while staring down at the life-sized, inflatable rubber doll, the capabilities of which Harvey was demonstrating by making the pink, ghoulish lips and teeth move up and down an ambitiously large, flesh-coloured, latex-covered phallic vibrator while the doll's long rubber legs quivered over the desk, painted crotch and artificial pubic hair indecently exposed.

'Please cover that lady up,' Dennis said. 'I have to make a few phone calls.'

'This,' Harvey said with a mirthful snort, 'is Angelique, a living body-mould of one of Europe's most famous models and, according to the poetic brochure text, ready to please any distinguished man who can appreciate her unique erotic offerings.'

'Good,' Dennis said. 'Take her to bed. I have to sit in your chair.'

'What's the matter with your own office?' Harvey said, withdrawing the vibrating dildo from Angelique's rubber lips and running it teasingly along Annie Bedward's thigh.

'My office is being used by some others,' Dennis said. 'The Ed and a certain Mzzz Cooch are engaged in serious intercourse over the ever-changing parameters of contemporary male-female interaction.'

'An intellectual activity,' Harvey said. 'I trust the Ed will enjoy it.'

Annie Bedward giggled when Harvey's vibrating dildo slid up under her skirt and then, obviously preferring the real thing (being only eighteen) slid off the desk and lightly slapped Harvey's wrist and said, 'Christ, you're a cheeky sod, Harvey. Let's go to Muriel's.'

'Muriel's is out,' Dennis said.

'What?' Harvey said, looking suspicious.

'Muriel's is out,' Dennis repeated. 'We've no time for that now.'

'You don't mean…?'

'Yes,' Dennis said. 'All night.'

'Without even a *drink* first?'

'I'm afraid so.'

Harvey stood up, his face pale with the thought of work, and then, as Dennis slid into his vacated chair, opened one of the drawers in the desk and withdrew a small plastic bag that was filled with tablets of various colours. Undecided between the red, blue, green and yellow, Harvey simply gave up and promptly swallowed the four pills at once, after which he blinked repeatedly and smiled brightly.

'You want some?' he said. 'I think you'll need them.'

'What are they?' Dennis said.

'God knows,' Harvey said, 'but they're reliable. Of that you can rest assured.'

'How do you know they're reliable?'

'Because,' Harvey said, clearly affronted, 'as you know I only deal in quality goods.'

'You mean they're *legal*?' Annie Bedward said.

'Well, no,' Harvey said. 'I mean, I wouldn't *exactly* say that... Not legal, but certainly trustworthy... a really reliable source.'

'What source?' Dennis said.

'Well...' Harvey hesitated.

'Come on,' Dennis said. 'If they're reliable, you can tell us your source.'

'The Artful Ed,' Harvey said.

Dennis closed his eyes and plunged into the pits, thinking of the Artful Ed, of his genius and madness, of his dark Rasputin beard and his brilliant, stoned eyes, and his shadow trickling over the gutters beneath a full moon. Then, having thus hallucinated, Dennis opened his eyes again.

'I'll take one,' he said.

Democratic Harvey gave Dennis four tablets of different colours, and Dennis, now losing his reasoning and no longer able to count, took the tablets and swallowed them all at once and then picked up the telephone.

'And did you,' he said, dialling Lavinia's new number, 'give any of those little treasures to the Ed?'

'Yes,' Harvey said.

'When?'

'Just before he entered your office.'

'Ah,' Dennis said. 'That explains a lot.'

While Dennis was dialling the last digit of Lavinia's new number, he saw Harvey pick up a camera and then, with one finger to his lips to indicate that Annie Bedward must be quiet, tiptoe across to Dennis' office, an evil grin on his face. Dennis knew exactly what Harvey was up to, and, while under normal circumstances might have felt impelled to protect Mzzz Cooch and the Ed, now, what with the brandy and the tablets and Lavinia's voice, was unable to stir himself into action.

'Yes?' Lavinia said suspiciously.

'Hello, dear. It's Dennis.'

'Oh, Dennis, I'm *so* glad you called!'

'Really?'

'Yes, really. I mean, I sincerely hope, Dennis, that you didn't think that any of those terrible things I said to the Ed about his editorial staff related to *you*, since, as you know, though I think most of those other guys are morons, you're the one person in this building that I still respect.'

'Most kind of you to say so, my dear.'

'Not at all. You deserve it.'

'And *have* you been in contact with the Big P, as stated?'

'Well, Dennis, as you know, I've always wanted to actually *meet* the Big P, but so far I haven't been able to see him because about an hour ago a huge man wearing a leather executioner's mask and steel-studded leather gloves and carrying a pretty bulky suitcase went into the Big P's office, and from that moment the Big P refused to answer either the telephone or the intercom and instead communicated with me by exchanging handwritten notes that he quietly slipped under the adjoining door. Initially, through the medium of these handwritten messages, I was able to convey to the Big P that I was standing in for his normal secretary, the revolting Mzzz Fright, and that I felt we should have a serious discussion about recent and deplorable events regarding the production of the magazines – but there were a lot of strange, muffled noises coming out of the Big P's office, moans and groans, what seemed like whimpering, and then, just after the Big P had slipped me a rather shakily written note asking "What events?", he inexplicably stuffed up the space between the bottom of the door and the floor with what appears to be a damp towel, thus unfortunately preventing any further communications.'

'I see,' Dennis said. 'So he still doesn't know about our crisis?'

'No,' Lavinia said.

'Well, dear, since you've now at least been *accepted* by the Big P as the redoubtable Mzzz Fright's stand-in and are therefore now in a position of some authority, I believe it would be helpful if you were to use your new-found authority to impress upon our reluctant accountant the need for that long-overdue cheque to be sent to the printers.'

'Dennis, that's brilliant. I mean, you really give me confidence. I mean, you're the only bastard in this building who gives a damn about what's happening, and tomorrow, when I've had my talk with the Big P, I'll ensure that you, at least, will remain on the staff.'

'Well, now, that's really very kind of you, Lavinia, and we really must get together soon and discuss this at length... But tell me, how are you otherwise?'

'I'm on pills all the time. My nerves just can't take it. My boyfriend says I'm underpaid, my doctor says I'm overworked, and the doors in the house open and close on their own and we still get those noises in the attic.'

'The doors still open and close?'

'Yes.'

'And you still get the noises?'

'Yes.'

'Any manifestations?'

'Not yet. But then we haven't actually gone up to *look*.'

'And this doesn't worry you?'

'Well, it didn't before, but it's starting to worry us now because the noises in the attic are much louder.'

'What sort of noises?'

'We've been halfway up the stairs, but no farther... I mean, the stairs up there *shake*.'

'So,' Dennis said patiently, wanting to humour the loony lady, 'you must have heard the noise pretty clearly.'

'A sort of roaring... a clanging... pretty muffled... and the stairs just keep shaking.'

'I really think you should send your boyfriend up,' Dennis said.

'Well,' Lavinia said, 'he *did* phone me this afternoon to say that the noises were now going on throughout the day and – '

'They'd only occurred at night before.'

'Right. And so, you know, he tried to screw up his courage and actually managed to get about three-quarters of the way up the stairs.'

'And?'

'He lost his nerve. I mean, I don't really blame him. I mean, he's been to see *The Exorcist* and he's frightened that if he goes up there some spirit-being might *vomit* over him or something... So, you know, he came down again.'

'I think you should encourage him up farther.'

'I don't know... He's so delicate.'

'Well, dear,' Dennis said, 'I *do* hope you can resolve this disturbing matter soon, as I'm sure you will resolve the matter of the overdue printer's cheque.'

'Oh, yes, Dennis, I will.'

'I'll ring you again, pet.'

Dennis dropped the telephone and cast his eyes to the left and observed, with an exaggerated, slightly unreal clarity, that Harvey was now down on his knees at the door of Dennis' office, his eye at the viewfinder of the Polaroid camera, the camera itself pointed into the office where Mzzz Cooch and the Ed were still happily at play. Shivering at the thought of the kind of pictures that such a sight might produce, and then, having shivered, feeling the hint of an erection, Dennis noticed (his

157

erection hardening) that the delightful Annie Bedward was kneeling on the floor beside Harvey, trying to stifle her mirth... Then the telephone rang.

'Yes?' Dennis said.

'Harvey?'

'No. Dennis.'

'This is Rick, Harvey.'

'Pardon?'

'Rick Walker.'

'Who?'

'Rick Walker – the Assistant Editor of *Gents*.'

'Ah, yes,' Dennis said.

'What the hell's the matter with you, Harvey? You sound pretty strange.'

'Oh, I'm fine,' Dennis said.

'Okay, Harvey. I just tried to get that slimy, so-called writer Dennis on the phone, to tell him that I'm now at Heathrow and my plane is taking off for Malaga in ten minutes – but, of course, as usual, there's no one in his office and so, Harvey, since I'd rather speak with you anyway, and since you're the only one in that whole building that I can trust, I'd just like you to know that I'm going to get on that plane and then, if it doesn't crash, make my own way from Malaga Airport to Torremolinos, and then, if whatever maniacal Spanish taxi-driver I pick up manages to get me there in one piece, or if I don't get mugged or poisoned, I'll find that frigging Circulation Manager, and then, if my murderous ulcer doesn't kill me, I'll bring him back, as instructed, on the first available flight tomorrow – and so, Harvey, you know, tell them I'm doing the best I can, which is all a man can do, and then, if you would, ring my wife – who's presently not speaking to me because of this damned trip – and tell her that if I don't make it back she'll find the insurance policies in a plastic bag stuck behind the toilet cistern and that every last instalment has been paid.'

'Right, Rick, I'll do that.'

'Thanks, Harvey. You haven't heard anything odd on the radio?'

'About what?'

'Heathrow Airport.'

'No.'

'That swine Dennis wouldn't tell me if *he* had.'

'I haven't heard anything, Rick.'

'I'm only asking, Harvey, because there seems to be an awful lot of people milling about here and I'm wondering, you know, if there's been an *accident* or something.'

'No, Rick, I've heard nothing.'

'A lot of *policemen* here, Harvey.'

'There always are,' Dennis said.

'You think *hijackers*, Harvey?'

'No, Rick. Stolen suitcases. A lot of luggage gets stolen at Heathrow. That's why there are policemen.'

'Okay, Harvey, say no more. That's good enough for me. I'll take my chances just like all the others. And I'll ring you from Torremolinos.'

'Fine,' Dennis said.

The line went dead and Dennis sighed and studied the door of his office and saw Harvey climbing back to his feet and holding on to Annie Bedward, the pair of them chortling, wiping tears from their cheeks, their eyes glued to the Polaroid pictures that Harvey held up in his left hand. As they returned to the desk, supporting each other and shaking with heartless mirth, Dennis studied Annie Bedward with a clarity that had hitherto fore eluded him, and noticed that she was, with her short-cropped blonde hair and rather large violet eyes and small breasts and narrow hips and long legs, quite extraordinarily attractive. Indeed, so attractive was she that Dennis, filled with brandy and the Artful Ed's mysterious tablets, felt like strangling good old Harvey who had obviously, in the crassness of his Philistine nature, explored that enchanting terrain. Nevertheless, though feeling this way, Dennis suppressed his baser instincts and, as

Harvey and Annie rocked together against the desk, retained his customary business-like demeanour.

'Christ!' Harvey exclaimed. 'What a sight! Just take a look at these photos!'

Dennis studied the photographs, his innermost thoughts hidden, and saw a crystal-clear mosaic of writhing limbs and naked genitalia, the Ed's eyes almost popping out of his head, Mzzz Cooch's dark hair disarrayed, and he shivered, feeling shame for all humanity, his tender soul scorched.

'Quite athletic,' he said.

Harvey and Annie both roared with laughter, clinging helplessly to one another, and Dennis, who was shocked by their heartless amusement at human frailty, lowered his pained gaze to the desk and hoped that time would dissolve him.

'We have a deadline,' he said.

'So I've heard,' Harvey chortled.

'It's a very *serious* deadline,' Dennis said. 'I think you should know that.'

'Oh, I know that,' Harvey said. 'You don't have to tell *me* that. I took one look at the Ed and that whore on the floor, and I knew, from the tension in their faces, that matters were urgent.'

Annie Bedward laughed raucously, shocking Dennis all the more, as Harvey opened one of his desk drawers and dropped the photographs into it.

'And where is the Picture Editor?' Dennis said.

'Who?' Harvey said.

'Stan.'

'Good old Stan,' Harvey said, 'at least when last seen, was stretched out on his desk, belly down, on top of Lydia, heavily engaged in constructive interaction with that hopeful young model.'

Sweet Annie Bedward laughed raucously at this while Dennis, his innermost thoughts hidden, kept his eyes modestly lowered.

'And Clive Grant?' he said.

160

'You mean the Advertising Manager?'

'I believe that's his function,' Dennis said.

'Good old Clive,' Harvey said, 'at least when last seen, was stretched out on the floor of the Picture Editor's office, a bottle of brandy between his legs, snoring loudly and oblivious to the interaction of the Pic Ed and Lydia.'

Sweet Annie Bedward laughed raucously again while Dennis, floating outside himself, thought of madness as being perfectly normal.

'We have to have an editorial conference,' he said.

'For *Suave*?' Harvey said.

'Yes, for *Suave*.'

'Right,' Harvey said.

'And do we have any remote possibility of awakening our industrious Advertising Manager and, perhaps, while we're at it, interrupting the obviously valuable interaction between the Pic Ed and that young model and getting them all to come down to the Boardroom?'

'I'll put a squib up their asses,' Harvey said. 'They might jump at the sound of it.'

'Excellent,' Dennis said. 'And perhaps we could have them down there in half an hour?'

'Say no more,' Harvey said.

Dennis raised his widening eyeballs from the vast terrain of the desk, and then, as Harvey and Annie chortled hysterically and disappeared, he heard the telephone ringing and picked it up and wondered how he could painlessly kill himself.

'Hello,' Dennis said.

'Harvey?'

'No. Dennis.'

'Oh, Dennis!' Laura said. 'I'm *so* glad it's you. I thought it was that rotten bastard, Harvey.'

'No. This is Dennis.'

'Oh, good. I'm *so* glad.'

'And how are you, dear?'

'Fine,' Laura said. 'Just… you know.'

'Hurting a little?'

'That's right,' Laura said. 'Hurting a little… but wanting some more. When can I see you?'

'I only left you this morning.'

'It seems an *awfully* long time. And I miss you… on top of me, inside me… you know just what I need.'

'And he doesn't?' Dennis said.

'No, he doesn't, the rotten bastard. He's so crude, so self-centred compared to you… and stays away from home all the time.'

'That's terrible,' Dennis said.

'He doesn't care,' Laura said. 'He'll go with any tart who doesn't charge, but you're not like that, Dennis.'

'No,' Dennis agreed.

'You're so sweet,' Laura said.

'I'm busy right now,' Dennis said. 'Can I ring you back later?'

'Oh, God, yes,' Laura said. 'Even better: come around here and spend the night. The bastard's not coming home again.'

'Are you sure?' Dennis said.

'He just rang me and told me. He said he couldn't get away from work, but you know what that means.'

'I couldn't say,' Dennis said.

'That's why I love you,' Laura said. 'There isn't an ounce of malice in your bones. You just can't condemn anyone.'

'It's not my place, dear.'

'You're so sweet, my angel.'

'I'm really busy,' Dennis said. 'I'll probably ring you later on. Even better: I'll try to get around there.'

'Bring some Vaseline,' Laura said.

Dennis dropped the phone and heard the intercom buzzing and pressed the button and heard Rosie Teasedale and had an instant erection.

'*Vaseline*?' Rosie said.

'You naughty girl,' Dennis said.

'I wasn't deliberately listening in,' Rosie said. 'It was an accident – I swear to it.'

'And you wanted me?'

'Yes... and your Vaseline and your charm... besides which, there's another call waiting, this one from your wife.'

'Put her on,' Dennis said.

He closed his eyes and breathed deeply, floating languidly in space, his erection shrinking back in humble worship of the glorious cosmos. Then he heard Kathy's voice, a gentle music in the silence. Then he opened his eyes and looked across the room and saw Mzzz Cooch with her clothes on.

'Dennis?'

'Yes, Kathy.'

'I'm not angry.'

'I'm glad.'

'I was angry when you said what you said, but I'm not anymore.'

'That's good,' Dennis said.

'It's not good, but it's a help. I've finished packing and I just thought we should talk before I make my decision.'

Dennis blinked and looked again and saw Mzzz Cooch at his office door, zipping up her denims and marching out, the Ed trailing behind her. The Ed was clearly in raptures, his clothes dishevelled, limbs trembling, looking upward as if expecting to see stars, but viewing only the ceiling. Then Mzzz Cooch, the imposing creature, suddenly turned back to face him, barked something and kneed his nuts, and the Ed doubled up, clutching his nuts and yelping ecstatically, and, after watching her stomp out of the office, straightened up and hobbled over to Dennis, his eyes still like pinwheels.

'I want you to believe me,' Dennis said.

'Believe what?' Kathy said.

'I want you to believe me when I say I can't talk now, but that I *will* ring back soon.'

163

'Oh, horseshit,' Kathy said.

'It's the truth,' Dennis said.

'Okay.' Kathy sighed. 'One last time. I'll wait here for an hour.'

'Thanks,' Dennis said. 'Later.'

The Ed hobbled up to Dennis, one hand cupping his battered balls, the other waving to grip thin-air as he stumbled and fell. Dennis jumped up just in time, slipping sharply around his desk, and looked down as the Ed performed a pirouette and let his arse find the chair.

'God!' he gasped. 'What a woman!'

'Where's she gone?' Dennis said.

'She's gone to change her diaphragm,' the Ed said, 'but she's coming right back.'

'That shows initiative,' Dennis said.

'God, I love her!' the Ed said. 'She raped me, Dennis – yes, I'll admit that – and now I'm her willing slave. I can't help myself, Dennis. It's shameless, but it's *real*. She raped me and kicked the shit out of me and made me a new man. Now I know what love is, Dennis. It's always having to say you're sorry. It's taking all the kicks and all the blows and apologising for loving it. God, I love her... She's *masterful*!'

Dennis wondered if he, too, could find his redemption in a truly spiritual love, but then, gazing into the Ed's pinwheel eyes and seeing, in their luminosity, the awesome splendour of such redemption, dropped his weak, mortal gaze to the life-sized inflatable doll on the desk, drinking in her ruby lips and gleaming teeth and pumped-up breasts, her painted crotch and artificial pubic hair, and realised, with horror (and even as the Ed also saw her) that he was having yet another disgusting erection.

'There's a woman on the desk,' the Ed said, 'and she has no clothes on.'

'It's Angelique,' Dennis said.

'It's Harvey's desk,' the Ed said. 'And I warned that little bastard before to keep his hands off the models.'

164

'She's just a doll,' Dennis said.

'This is scandalous,' the Ed said. 'I just have to turn my back for two minutes and this is what happens.'

'She's not real,' Dennis said.

'She's fucking exhausted,' the Ed said. 'The poor bitch can hardly move a muscle, and it's that bastard's fault.'

'She's made of rubber,' Dennis said.

'He used a rubber?' the Ed said. 'Well, I can't say that makes up for much. I mean, look at the *state* of her!'

Angelique smiled at the Ed, a foam-lipped, ghoulish grimace, and the Ed, blinking his stunned, pinwheel eyes, came back down to Earth.

'A real doll?' he said.

'Yes, a real doll.'

'You mean one of those dolls you *play* with?'

'That's right,' Dennis said.

The Ed sighed with relief and sat back in his chair, his left hand fondly stroking his unfortunate, raped balls, his other hand rubbing his bruised lips.

'Well, thank God for that,' he said.

Yet even as the Ed was coming back down, if not to Earth then at least to a reasonable level of sanity, Dennis was finding it impossible to take his eyes off the delectable Angelique and thus, perhaps impelled by his throbbing erection, was remembering the Ed's former outburst about the negative effects of their vocation and wondering, with deepening dread, if the bum, tit and pudenda, the stapled arses and tinted pubes, were indeed driving him away from all normal desires and gradually turning him into a strait-jacket case. Luckily, such evil thoughts, *and* his throbbing erection, were subdued by the shrill ringing of the telephone.

'Don't answer that, Dennis,' the Ed said.

'Pardon?' Dennis said.

'Don't answer that telephone, Dennis. We don't want interruptions.'

'It might be important,' Dennis said.

'It's not important,' the Ed said. 'The important thing is to find the Artful Ed and get the bastard back in here.'

'That might be him,' Dennis said.

'Never mind,' the Ed said. 'We don't want that bastard playing his tricks while we're trying to get organised.'

'I see,' Dennis said.

'I'm glad you agree,' the Ed said. 'We've got a crisis on our hands, there's not a minute to spare, and those bastards, both upstairs and down, are just frigging around.'

'Right,' Dennis said.

'Where's Mzzz Cooch?' the Ed said. 'You don't think she's decided to go home just to punish me further?'

'I don't think so,' Dennis said.

'I'd still be proud of her,' the Ed said. 'I'm shameless and I'd ring her and say I'm sorry and beg her to whip me.'

'I think she's downstairs,' Dennis said.

'Don't answer that telephone, Dennis. The only important thing is to find the Artful Ed and nail his feet to the floor.'

'Right,' Dennis said.

'Downstairs *where*?' the Ed said.

'I think she's probably waiting in the Boardroom. I think she's waiting for both of us.'

'*Both* of us, Dennis?'

'Yes, Ed,' Dennis said. 'We're having an editorial conference to sort out all our problems.'

'Dennis, you're a genius.'

'Thanks, Ed,' Dennis said. 'Now why not go down and talk to her, and I'll follow on later?'

'Dennis, I'm *touched*.'

'Pardon?'

'I'm near to *tears*. I'm shameless and you show me compassion and deep understanding. You're a human being, Dennis. I'm a whore, but you forgive me. Instead of casting stones, you see the love behind my sins, and you offer me,

166

without making it obvious, a few more minutes alone with her. I am touched. I am *moved*.'

The Ed wiped tears from his eyes and stood up and sighed deeply, reached out and placed his hands on Dennis' shoulders and shook him gently, with love. Then, without a word, indeed too choked up for clichés, he turned around and hobbled to the door and limped down to Nirvana.

Dennis stood there, bemused, the tablets working their wonders upon him, then he heard the ringing telephone, picked it up, blessed the silence, then put the magical instrument to his ear and heard pounding rock music.

'Dennis?' the Artful Ed said.

'Yes,' Dennis said.

'You were supposed to be at Muriel's, you little cunt. I just wasted a phone call.'

'Sorry,' Dennis said.

'I want a refund,' the Artful Ed said. 'I can't afford to pay for all these calls when you bastards go missing.'

'How are you?' Dennis said.

'Not bad,' the Artful Ed said. 'The sun's shining through the window right this minute and I'm having a massage.'

'Pardon?' Dennis said.

'What's the matter? Are you fucking deaf?'

'I'm just looking at my wristwatch,' Dennis said. 'It's nine in the evening.'

'Four,' the Artful Ed said.

'In the morning?'

'Afternoon.'

'If the sun's shining on Notting Hill Gate, then you're obviously stoned.'

'*What?*' the Artful Ed said.

'Pardon?' Dennis said.

'The sun's shining and the sirens are wailing and I'm having a massage.'

'The sun's shining on Notting Hill Gate?'

167

'No… On New York.'

Dennis closed his eyes again, took a deep breath, tried to think, felt exhausted and stoned and insane and wished that love would rescue him. Then he opened his eyes again, saw the open-plan office, no windows, no clocks, just the silence: a perfectly normal asylum.

'New York?' Dennis said.

'Are you fucking deaf?' the Artful Ed repeated.

'I spoke to you at eleven this morning – and you were there in your flat.'

'That's right,' the Artful Ed said. 'So what's the confusion? I caught a flight to New York an hour later and arrived here at one.'

'In New York?' Dennis said.

'Local time,' the Artful Ed said. 'The sun's shining and the sirens are wailing and I'm having a massage.'

'A *massage*?' Dennis said.

'That's right: a massage. Am I *allowed* to have a fucking massage after a seven-hour flight?'

'You didn't mention New York,' Dennis said.

'You didn't ask,' the Artful Ed said.

'When I asked you to come in this afternoon, you said you were shooting a photo-session.'

'That's right,' the Artful Ed said. 'In New York… I picked up this really kinky gear and it suits Broadway great.'

'Is that where you are now?'

'I'm on West 44th Street. I'm staying in some dump called the Algonquin, so it won't cost too much.'

'Christ,' Dennis said.

'That's what *I* said when I arrived. I took one look at this fucking museum and knew they wouldn't like rock 'n' roll.'

'The music's loud,' Dennis said.

'They keep complaining,' the Artful Ed said. 'At least they did until I pissed down the stairs and now they're too scared to bother me. So, why the call?'

'A few questions, that's all.'

'I'm not guilty,' the Artful Ed said. 'They're always hassling me, those fucking bastards, just because I'm so talented.'

'The Circulation Manager,' Dennis said.

'Who?'

'Frank Harrison.'

'A nice guy. I met him in Paris. I sort of showed him around.'

'So he told us,' Dennis said. 'He's still suffering from the shock. Your nice friends tied him up, shoved a golf ball in his mouth, put clothes pegs on his cock and whipped him off. His teeth are still rattling.'

'Sounds like fun,' the Artful Ed said.

'You sold him,' Dennis said. 'You slipped drugs into his drink and then sold him as part of some package.'

'That's a terrible accusation.'

'It's the truth,' Dennis said.

'It's not the truth, Dennis, and you know it and you're just trying to hassle me. The *truth*, Dennis, is that I was in Paris attempting to rustle up some really kinky gear for an exceptional picture spread, and so, you know, I met these fucking perverts who'd been recommended to me by the Ed after he'd met them at a party at my place, and they, being in the business both financially and socially, offered me some incredible, knock-out kinky leather gear in return, not for filthy lucre but for some of our left-over transparencies, and so, Dennis, being efficient and thinking only of the good of the mags, I was finalising this remarkable deal at a café in the rue de la Paix when, lo and behold, the Circulation Manager turned up, obviously plastered out of his skull and making a jack-ass of himself, and so I just completed the deal and walked away in utter fucking disgust.'

'He ended up in Torremolinos,' Dennis said.

'That's right,' the Artful Ed said. 'He ended up in Torremolinos. And he wouldn't even have made it that far if it

169

hadn't been for me. Now that isn't my job, Dennis.'

'Tell me about Torremolinos,' Dennis said.

'Thing is, Dennis, I did, much to my embarrassment, receive a phone call from those two perverts, telling me that Frank had, when I left, refused to leave them alone and insisted that they take him back to their apartment and whip him – a very nice place, incidentally, near the Place du Tertre, and always available if you ever need to stay there – and so, you know, being friends of *the Ed* and so forth, well, they didn't like to refuse, and then, after having kindly taken Frank back with them and performing as he demanded – exhausted though they were from a very heavy day's business – Frank, obviously still smashed and being his usual juvenile self, became a bit aggressive, not to say a bit hysterical, and started screaming that he wanted to see me.'

'Really?'

'Yes, really.'

'That still doesn't explain Torremolinos.'

'I'm coming to that, Dennis. I'm coming. This massage is just great.'

'Tell me about Torremolinos,' Dennis said.

'Thing is, Dennis, even though I was embarrassed at receiving that phone call and annoyed at Frank's lack of a sense of responsibility, well, you know me, I'm not about to knife anyone, I just felt that if I sent him back in that state you'd bounce him or something, and also, Dennis, if I may say so, knowing that Frank's trip to Paris had been a business disaster and that you would *definitely* bounce him for that, well, I didn't want that to happen and so, Dennis, it being that I had just made a very valuable connection with a certain Herr Mayer – who is, as you may recall, a formidable figure in the Scandinavian and German porno fields – and had already, with Herr Mayer, completed all the groundwork for an extremely valuable tie-up between his Company and our own, well, when I realised the fucking mess that Frank had got himself into, I decided that I didn't need recognition for my initiative, that Frank needed to save himself, and so, Dennis, you know, I gave it to him on a plate, I sent him to Torremolinos where Herr Mayer had gone to rest, and he was put up in that hotel *at Herr Mayer's expense*, and then... Well, what can I say? I mean, how much can I defend him? Frank got pissed again, had an orgy with some whores, then presented the bill to Herr Mayer, who was understandably outraged... I washed my hands of the matter.'

Dennis stared at Angelique who was still on the desk, her legs spread, her rubber breasts firm, her foam lips smiling ghoulishly. Angelique had latex skin, artificial pubic hair, a painted cunt and wig and plastic teeth, and Dennis wanted her desperately. This was clearly the end. He was down in the pits. He closed his eyes and opened them again and quietly yearned for redeeming love.

'Anyway,' the Artful Ed said. 'What's happened to the stupid bastard since then?'

'Frank Harrison?'

'Yes.'

'We've sent Rick Walker to Torremolinos to bring him back.'

'Bring him *back*?' the Artful Ed said.

'Yes,' Dennis said.

'Do you think that's wise?' the Artful Ed said. 'I mean, I know he fucked up, and that Herr Mayer is fucking angry, but Frank *might* manage to pull himself together and complete the good work that I started... God, this massage is *great*!'

'We have a crisis,' Dennis said. 'It's a very serious crisis. The printers are using "Going Down to Get It up" and your filthy illustration – *and* the fact that we haven't paid them for the past three issues – as an excuse for pulling *Suave* off their presses to make way for a new, much glossier and even filthier magazine.'

'Really?' the Artful Ed said.

'Really,' Dennis said. 'That's why we need you and the Circulation Manager back here. We need you to organise a new illustration and, more important, to find out who this new publisher is – '

'I've never heard of him, Dennis.'

' – and we need Frank to get back on the road and put the screws on our various retailers.'

'I'm coming,' the Artful Ed said.

'When?' Dennis said.

'Right now,' the Artful Ed said. 'I'm coming, I'm *coming*, Jesus Christ, oh, that's great… Christ, Dennis, that massage was really good. These New York whores are experts.'

'Are you finished?' Dennis said.

'She's wiping me dry as we speak. Thing is, Dennis, that situation sounds a mess. You'd better look for another job.'

'I *don't want* another job.'

'And what *do* you want, Dennis?'

'I want to kill myself,' Dennis said, 'but I haven't the nerve.'

'Good,' the Artful Ed said. 'I'm very pleased to hear that. I mean, the whole situation sounds tricky, so we'll need you back there.'

'We need *you*,' Dennis said.

'I can't make it just now. I mean, I've got a whole crew in Times Square and they're ready to shoot. Tell you what, Dennis: you just work out some new article to put in, and then, when you've worked it out, just call me back here and I'll dream up a suitable photograph and you can set up a shooting session right there in the building and I'll direct the whole thing over the phone.'

'And do you think I should tell the Ed you're in New York?'

'No, Dennis, I wouldn't do that if I were you. I mean, I really *respect* the Ed – a talented guy, highly imaginative, really knows what he's doing – but he *is* prone to going off his nut and you don't need that now. No, Dennis, what I suggest you do is just tell him that I'm up in the Kings Road shooting some nocturnal fashion shots with a bunch of lesbian models – he *loves* lesbian models – and that I'll ring him back at one in the morning when you've sorted things out.'

'One o'clock our time?'

'That's right.'

'So when are you coming back, Artful Ed?'

'Thing is, Dennis, that's a difficult one to answer, it being that I'm really fucking busy over here, what with this shooting session and with trying to find new models, and, of course, Dennis – and I'm going out on a limb here – I believe it would be helpful if I tried to find out, *from this end*, who that new publisher is, since, as I'm sure you know, so many of these bastards are actually Americans, or, even more insidious, American-financed, and I don't mind telling you, Dennis, that there *are* certain rumours to the effect that the Mafia or some other such organisation has been trying to move in on our lucrative and artistically excellent publishing ventures there in London, and so, you know, it could be a bit tricky, not to mention pretty dangerous, though I don't mind that, Dennis, it's all part of the job, and so, Dennis, I'll ring you back soon. Okay, sweetheart, one more time.'

The line went dead before Dennis could get a chance to ask the Artful Ed about his connection to the imposing Mzzz Cooch, and so Dennis, dropping the telephone, feeling confused and unreal, sighed and sat back in his chair, his gaze focused on Angelique. The lovely Angelique was still stretched out on the desk, her eyes blind, her teeth bared, her legs outspread in bloodless abandon, and Dennis, gazing at her, his erection steadily growing, understood that he was now in the pits and needed sweet love's redemption. Then, unable to face the slimy depths of his hidden self, his artistic soul outraged by his foul, diseased desires, Dennis pushed his chair back and walked away from Harvey's desk, and then headed down the stairs to the editorial conference in the Boardroom, where he met Rose Teasedale for the first time.

It was love at first sight.

6

Rosie Teasedale was wearing a tight, black, low-cut sweater and blue denims and pink socks and stiletto-heeled shoes, her breasts bulging out of the sweater, very creamy, so *soft*, her thighs firm in the denims, deliciously tight around the crotch, her face slightly plump and sensual with full lips and mischievous eyes, her waist slim and her hips nicely rounded. And while Dennis could by now view such attributes only as so many transparencies or colour proofs or stapled pages, and was therefore not in a position to actually accept them as being real, what made him fall in love, on the instant and most passionately, was the fact that the eighteen-year old Rosie had silvery-grey hair.

'How did you get it?' Dennis asked.

'I don't know,' Rosie said. 'I just woke up with my first period and my hair had turned this weird colour.'

'Does it bother you?' Dennis said.

'Why ask? Does it bother *you*?'

'No.'

'Fucking great,' Rosie said.

Dennis, sitting at the long conference table in another windowless, clock-deprived room, Rosie Teasedale on one side, Clive Grant on the other, Annie Bedward and Harvey and Les Hamilton seated opposite, the Ed at the end of the table, Mzzz Cooch by his side, a lot of brandy bottles and tumblers and ashtrays in use, the cigarette smoke already swirling around them – yes, Dennis, sitting there, feeling spaced out and wounded, his

175

tender soul lacerated by the horrors of this whole filthy business, felt the length of Rosie's thigh pressing gently against his own and knew, without doubt, with pure bliss, that redemption was nigh.

'Well, boys and girls,' the Ed said, smiling lovingly at Mzzz Cooch, who was there by his side, her folded hands as hard as mallets, her magnificent breasts thrusting imperiously from her sweater to challenge all takers, 'it seems to me that the first thing I should do at this *extraordinary* editorial meeting is – since some of us have surprisingly never met – to introduce those now here for the first time.'

'Hear, hear,' Harvey said.

'Thank you, Harvey, and I would just like to say that that vote of confidence is most heartening.'

'Hear, hear,' good old Stan said.

'So,' the Ed continued, a sublime smile on his chops, 'sitting at my right hand is Mzzz Caroline Cooch, famous writer from *The Observer* – which I *know* we all read – and here now to get an insight into the workings of our magazines and, in particular, into our attitudes toward the female sex, which attitudes I am sure will impress her in a positive manner.'

The imposing Mzzz Cooch offered the table a chilling sneer and the Ed, now in love with her contempt, visibly trembled with rapture.

'Also,' the Ed continued with a great deal of self-control, 'we have here, for the first time, two delightful and talented ladies, namely Mzzz Annie Bedward and Mzzz Rosie Teasedale.'

'*What?*' Rosie said.

'Pardon?' the Ed said.

'Mzzz? Did you say Mzzz?'

'M.s.,' the Ed explained.

'You poor oppressed creature,' Mzzz Cooch said to Rosie. 'You've been exploited for years and you don't even know it.'

Rosie sort of blinked, looking a little confused, then she

grinned and slid her hand beneath the table and squeezed Dennis' thigh. At this touch, Dennis trembled, his heart pounding, blood racing, experiencing, surprisingly, since his love was clearly spiritual, the naughty tinglings of an ambitious erection.

'Now, as we all know,' the Ed said, smiling adoringly at Mzzz Cooch, 'Mzzz Bedward is normally the Production Editor of *Gents*, but since the lovely Lavinia has kindly *volunteered* to man the telephones and intercoms in the Big P's sack's office in the absence of the very wonderful Mzzz Fright, Mzzz Bedward is standing in for Lavinia during this particular meeting.'

'Did you say *sack*?' Mzzz Cooch enquired.

'Secretary,' the Ed explained.

'And I suppose you think that's funny,' Mzzz Cooch said.

'Well...'

'You male chauvinist bastard.'

This unexpected conversational development between Mzzz Cooch and the Ed caused a few heads to be turned and more than a few brandies to be poured. Dennis, however, now hoping to find redemption, entranced with Mzzz Teasedale's silvery-grey hair and feeling her hand on his thigh, was beyond the human weakness for drink and merely yearned for a quick fuck.

'Ha, ha,' the Ed was saying, suffering the joys of humiliation, 'a little joke from Mzzz Cooch of *The Observer*, well renowned for its satirists.'

'Hear, hear,' Harvey said.

'And so,' the Ed continued, after introducing the male staff members, 'all formalities dispensed with, the ice broken, as it were, by Mzzz Cooch, let's get right down to business.'

The merry lads all started getting right down to business by slugging down their brandy and refilling their glasses, during which time Dennis, now above the need for drink, prayed fervently that his erection would subside because it wasn't quite spiritual. He was, however, brought back down to Earth by the Ed's sombre gaze.

'Dennis,' the Ed said.

'I love your silvery-grey hair,' Dennis said.

'Hey, you,' Mzzz Cooch said to Dennis. 'He's talking to you, you cunt-fixated snake.'

These were liberated days and the lady *was* from *The Observer*, but even so, a few eyes turned suspiciously in Mzzz Cooch's direction.

'Dennis,' the Ed repeated, dragging his gaze from Mzzz Cooch and trying to keep the love out of his eyes and look more like an Editor, 'I feel we should begin with an update on what's happening your end.'

'*My* end?' Dennis said.

'Not your cock,' Mzzz Cooch said.

'I mean, what's happening regarding the payments to the printers? I *do* feel we should know what's going on there.'

'Lavinia's organised it,' Dennis said.

'Oh, really?' the Ed said. 'Well, I must say that's truly efficient. When did the cheque go out?'

'About an hour ago,' Dennis said.

'Then it should be there by now.'

'Yes,' Dennis said. 'I would think so. She sent it by motorbike.'

'Efficiency,' the Ed said. 'There's no other word for it. I say it now, and I always *did* say it, the ladies are wonderful.'

'She's a whore,' Harvey said.

'I *beg* your pardon?' the Ed said.

'She's frustrated and she needs a length of cock, besides which she's a dumb cunt.'

Harvey chortled at his subtle joke, wanting to impress *The Observer*, and Annie Bedward, rarely short of a length, slapped his thigh and laughed raucously. Mzzz Cooch was not impressed, her lips tight, her breasts heaving, but she wanted to get *the whole picture*, so she kept her mouth shut. This surprised the Ed somewhat – even worse: disappointed him – and he felt her wrath slipping away and thus suffered true anguish.

178

'Harvey?' the Ed said.

'Yes, Ed,' Harvey said.

'I think you could show some respect for Lavinia's fine efforts.'

'Right,' Harvey said.

'And can I take it,' the Ed said, 'that since the printers have been given their cheque, this only leaves the replacement article and illustration?'

'Yes,' Dennis said.

'Fucking great,' good old Stan said. 'It's midnight and the whole city's sleeping and that's all we need.'

'Watch your language,' the Ed said.

'Watch my *what*?' good old Stan said.

'Your fucking filthy tongue,' Mzzz Cooch said. 'There's no need for obscenity.'

'Jesus Christ,' Mzzz Bedward said.

'That's *blasphemy*!' the Ed said.

'Shut your mouth,' Mzzz Cooch ordered. 'You're trying to suppress her natural mode of expression, you fucking chauvinist bully.'

The Ed blushed with humiliation and lowered his face and sighed, but then shivered with delight at the return of Mzzz Cooch's pure venom.

'My apologies,' he said.

'You weak drip,' Mzzz Cooch said.

'And of course you are absolutely right. My apologies, Mzzz Bedward.'

'Pardon?' Mzzz Bedward said.

'My most humble apologies.'

'What the fuck's the matter?' Mzzz Bedward said. 'Have a drink! Loosen up!'

The Ed did as he was told, rejuvenated through obedience, picking his glass up and slugging down more brandy and then wiping his lips. At the same time Dennis sighed, feeling fingers at his erection, and turned his head to stare at Mzzz Teasedale, his unstapled saviour.

'What's Rosie doing here?' good old Stan said. 'She should be at the switchboard.'

Dennis, feeling fingers at his trembling erection, looking deep into the depths of Mzzz Teasedale's wondrous soul, heard the hiss of a snake in Stan's voice and almost jumped up to slug him. He was, however, saved from this particular *faux pas* by the thoughtful intervention of his equally love-stricken Editor.

'Mzzz Teasedale is here,' the Ed said protectively 'because we need someone to record what we say. She has her pad on the table.'

'My *pad*?' Rosie said.

'Your note-pad,' the Ed said.

'She doesn't even know short-hand,' good old Stan said. 'What the fuck good is that?'

'Discrimination,' Mzzz Cooch said.

'Absolutely,' Dennis said.

'I can spell as good as anyone,' Rosie said. 'So shove *that* up your ass, Stan.'

'Hear, hear,' Mzzz Cooch said.

'What *I* want to know,' Les Hamilton said, 'is how we're going to fill that hole.'

'What hole?' the Ed said.

'He's being insulting,' Mzzz Cooch said.

'We have a big hole in the magazine,' Les said. 'So how do we fill it?'

All eyes turned towards Les, normally a blank space in their sight, the eyes filled with the belated recognition that he actually existed. This attention embarrassed Les, who was usually completely ignored, all his good work repeatedly obliterated by the Artful Ed's mad demon tactics.

'Hear, hear,' Harvey said.

'That's what we're here for,' Stan said.

'A most constructive comment,' Clive Grant said. 'I think we should drink to that.'

Normally not a blank space, even though he slept a lot, Clive now sat up straight in his chair and stroked his colourful tie. He then smiled at Mzzz Cooch, who returned the smile, *warmly*, and the Ed, sensing instant rapport there, was deliciously wounded.

'So,' the Ed said.

'Hear, hear,' Harvey said.

'What's *Les* doing here?' good old Stan said. 'I thought he worked for *Gents*.'

This remark cut Les deeply, making him shrivel up in his chair, his big blue eyes brilliant with shame, his little pot belly trembling.

'Les is here,' the Ed said, staring Stan straight in the eye, 'because the Art Director of *Suave*, namely that slippery Artful Ed, is obviously making his usual midnight creep, his long teeth dripping blood.'

'Ho, ho,' Harvey said.

'I don't think it's funny, Harvey. I mean, the Artful Ed's not here, we wouldn't find him if he was, and now Les, who has his own responsibilities, has to stay here all night. Now I don't think that's fair. Indeed, I think it's very selfish. Les is just like you and me – not married, but doubtless normal – and I'm sure he has his own life to live and certain beds he can sleep in.'

'Yes,' Stan said. 'His mother's.'

That remark got through to Dennis, making him sit up and think, his eyes, which felt like barbed-wire but were functioning nonetheless, focused brightly and with infinite love on Rosie Teasedale's silvery-grey hair.

'I'm corrupt,' he confessed to Rosie.

'Oh, great,' Rosie said.

'I've been in this business far too long. I've been spoilt. I've had everything.'

'Oh, really?' Rosie said.

'Yes, really,' Dennis said. 'I've been exposed to too much sex, I've had it anytime I wanted, and now *normal* sex is not enough and I'm becoming perverted.'

'I can't wait,' Rosie said.

Dennis saw her inviting smile, felt her fingers at his erection, and knew, with the conviction of the fallen saint, that he had found his redemption.

'Hey, you,' Mzzz Cooch said.

'Who, me?' Dennis said.

'Keep your filthy paws off that girl. She's not here for your pleasure.'

'Help yourself,' Rosie said.

'It's not sex,' Dennis explained. 'I simply want to suck at her breasts and find the comfort of infancy.'

'She's not a milk cow,' Mzzz Cooch said.

'Test that theory,' Rosie said.

'We have to fill up this hole,' Les Hamilton said. 'I mean, that's what we're here for.'

The silence was abrupt, all eyes swivelling towards Les, making him shrink back into his seat, beads of sweat on his baby face.

'Well?' the Ed said.

'A good point,' Clive Grant said. 'I mean, my clients wouldn't appreciate six blank pages, so we have to do *something*.'

'Any suggestions?' the Ed said.

'Let's go to bed,' good old Stan said. 'It's midnight and the whole city's sleeping, so we can't do a thing.'

'That's defeatist,' Mzzz Cooch said.

'Where's your pride?' the Ed said. 'Dennis, I think it's up to you. What we need are suggestions.'

'No more redheads,' Dennis said. 'No more blondes or brunettes. No more virgins or sluttish models or common types... My only thought is for a mother's silvery-grey hair.'

'A great idea,' Harvey said.

'A real shocker,' Stan said.

'I think it's disgusting,' Mzzz Cooch said, 'but I'm just here

182

to listen.'

'You mean *mother love*?' the Ed asked.

'The Oedipus complex,' Harvey explained.

'The Oedipus complex?' the Ed said. 'What does *that* mean? Is it *Greek* or some shit?'

'It's psychological,' Harvey explained.

'What does *that* mean?' the Ed said. 'I mean, we've never had that word in the mags? Is it obscene or what?'

'Pretty deep,' Harvey said.

'Then let's avoid it,' Clive Grant said.

'Right,' good old Stan said. 'And we don't want a silvery-grey-haired nude granny in the glories of Kodachrome.'

'Exactly,' the Ed said. 'A good point. So what else do we have?'

'Bestiality?' Harvey suggested.

'Jesus Christ,' Mzzz Cooch said.

'You're quite right to be disgusted,' the Ed said. 'And besides: we've just done it.'

They all shut up at that point, pouring drinks, lighting fags, letting Dennis put his hand on the hand that now clasped his erection. Dennis didn't care what they said, ignoring crass interpretations, now aware, in the depths of his being, that he loved Rosie's silvery-grey hair. Rosie obviously understood, giving his cock a motherly squeeze, encouraging him back along that winding road to original innocence. And was that not what he now needed? An undefiled, maternal touch? Dennis knew that this was so as Rosie eased his zip open and groped, with an instinctive, feminine tenderness at his most sacred parts.

'You little ba-ba,' Rosie whispered.

'*What* was that?' Harvey said.

'We won't have child abuse,' the Ed said. 'I mean, that's going too far.'

'Fucking typical,' Mzzz Cooch said.

'I *beg* your pardon?' the Ed said.

'I mean, just let a *woman* make a suggestion and she's

sneered out of court.'

'Well, I m-meant…' the Ed stuttered.

'It's not abuse,' Dennis said.

'Don't mind *me*,' Mzzz Cooch said, 'you rotten bastard. I'm just here to observe.'

The Ed flinched from her contempt, truly hurt and humiliated, then trembled, the pain filling him with love and the need to be pissed upon.

'I apologise,' he said.

'You weak drip,' Mzzz Cooch said.

'I haven't seen my wife for days,' Harvey said, 'so I'll want double pay for this.'

'Hear, hear,' good old Stan said.

'My wife will *kill* me,' Clive Grant said.

'*My* wife,' the Ed said, 'misunderstands me, but I know I'm to blame.'

'You weak drip,' Mzzz Cooch said.

'You haven't seen her for days,' Harvey said.

'We *never* see our wives,' good old Stan said. 'We should get compensation.'

'You rotten Philistines,' Mzzz Cooch said. 'You unprincipled lot of bastards. You're all using the wives you abuse just to rake in more money.'

'I really miss her,' Harvey said.

'And think of the kids,' good old Stan said.

'The feeling of loss can be crippling,' Harvey said. 'We're going to *need* compensation.'

'You filthy hypocrites,' Mzzz Cooch said.

'It's all *my* fault,' the Ed said. 'I never think of anything but my work, and I make my staff suffer.'

'Ring home,' Annie Bedward said.

'Ring *where*?' Harvey said.

'I think all you guys should ring home.'

'I must *insist*,' the Ed said.

This unexpected consideration for beloved wives and

offspring came at a most unfortunate time for Dennis, who, as his guilty comrades debated who should ring first, was feeling the tender touch of Rosie's maternal fingers on his now exposed cock, and, as good old Stan won the toss and picked up a telephone, felt the warmth of a pure, primal love that made that cock throb with joy.

'I would just like to say, Mzzz Cooch,' the Ed was saying emotionally, 'that your presence in this office, your wisdom and concern, has helped us to see the error of our ways and made us much better men. It is, of course, true that we were not so much cruel as thoughtless, that we ourselves felt misunderstood, but I'm sure, as you now can observe, we have all seen the light.'

'She's not answering,' good old Stan said.

'Who?' Harvey said. 'Your wife?'

'That's right, my fucking wife. The phone's ringing but the whore isn't answering, as I might have expected.'

'Wow!' Rosie exclaimed.

'I truly love your silvery-grey hair,' Dennis whispered.

'She's probably just asleep,' Harvey said. 'It's one o'clock in the *morning*.'

'You think so?' Stan said.

'It's a possibility,' Harvey said.

'The bitch is never at home,' good old Stan said. 'And my kids could be crying.'

That observation moved the Ed, almost making him shed tears, turning his head and staring straight at Mzzz Cooch to let her know he was suffering. His mistress and master rolled her eyes, her sneer deliciously brutalising, and the Ed quivered and then glanced across at Dennis, who, also, was quivering.

'I love to feel it,' Rosie whispered. 'I love it sliding through my fingers. I love it most when I pull the foreskin back and watch its eye popping out.'

Dennis' eyes were popping out, a most unusual occurrence, and his whole body quivered with release as his cock sang its love song. This all happened beneath the table, without fuss,

with great modesty, and his sacred fluid arched through the air
and came to rest on a pretty knee. Dennis stifled his gasp. Annie
Bedward glanced down. Her brow furrowed as she touched her
knee lightly and then looked up at Dennis.

'There's a bird under the table,' she said, 'and I think it's
just shat on me.'

Dennis lowered his eyes demurely, breathing deeply,
shivering slightly, thinking fondly of his mother, of the cradle
and the grave, the latter thought bringing back the knowledge
that he had not found redemption after all. Dennis sighed and
looked up, a great despair in his eyes, as Rosie tucked his weary
member into bed and quietly zipped up its sleeping bag.

'It's a start,' Rosie whispered.

Good old Stan slammed the phone down, cursed loudly and
drank more brandy, and Harvey, looking deeply sympathetic,
picked the phone up and dialled.

'Trust,' the Ed was saying. 'Without trust, it wouldn't work.
In this business, you have to trust your friends if you want to
survive. We all trust each other, Mzzz Cooch. That's the one
bond we have. It may not be much, but it's something, and I'm
really quite proud of it. You take Dennis, Mzzz Cooch. That's
the quiet one, over there. Now Dennis, he's not married – he's a
writer, an intellectual – but I think it's true to say that despite
that we trust him implicitly. He's the best of us all, Mzzz Cooch.
He keeps himself to himself. He treats the female staff with
respect and never exploits his companions. A rare virtue, Mzzz
Cooch.'

'Hello,' Harvey said. 'Laura?'

'He's found his wife,' good old Stan said.

'It's Harvey. It's *me*... Are you asleep? Yes, it's *me*. I'm
your *husband*.'

'A loyal wife,' good old Stan said.

'A real treasure,' Clive Grant said.

'So you're *sleeping*,' Harvey said. 'Wake up! I *know* it's
one in the morning!'

'Take note,' good old Stan said.

'They're all the same,' Clive Grant said.

'I'm in the *office*,' Harvey said. 'Swear to God… What do you *mean*, I'm a liar?'

'Here it comes,' good old Stan said.

'Might have known' Clive Grant said.

'Please, Laura,' Harvey said, 'stop that crying… I'll be *back* by tomorrow.!'

'She's operating,' good old Stan said.

'A real artiste,' Clive Grant said.

'What do you mean, you're having an affair?' Harvey said. 'Am I hearing right, Laura?'

'Oh, oh,' good old Stan said.

'You've got it right,' Clive Grant said.

'You *mean* it?' Harvey said. 'You actually *did* it? How many times…? *What*? What do you mean, you don't keep count…? You *what*? You want to leave home? *What do you mean, you're in love?*'

'Final curtain,' good old Stan said.

'The last rites,' Clive Grant said.

'I want to know the bastard's name!' Harvey bawled. '*You rotten bitch, don't hang up!*'

'Amen,' Clive and Stan sang in chorus.

Harvey stared at them, his bloodshot eyes now glazed, obviously stunned by the shocking immorality of his beloved wife's revelations. Annie Bedward began to sniff, her eyes brimming with tears, filled with grief that poor Harvey, so devoted to his wife and children, working day and night just to keep them happy, should have been so humiliated by that selfish bitch. Harvey blinked and stared at her, saw the tears in her eyes, dropped the phone as his pecker jumped up to dive into the rising tide of her sympathy.

'Harvey?' the Ed said

'Yes, Ed?' Harvey said.

'I want you to be a man about this, Harvey… And we're all

right behind you.'

'Really?' Harvey said.

'Yes, really,' the Ed said.

'You deserved it, you little shit,' Mzzz Cooch said. 'Go and cook it for breakfast.'

'Take your punishment,' the Ed said.

'Like a man,' good old Stan said.

'What about this hole?' Les Hamilton said. 'We've got to fill up this hole.'

'That bitch,' Harvey said.

'What's the problem?' Mzzz Cooch said. 'She just wanted a decent fuck now and then. I mean, it wasn't personal.'

'Mortal flesh,' the Ed said. 'Human weakness and frailty. Take your punishment and thus learn forgiveness. A fine woman there, Harvey.'

'Wonderful,' Harvey said.

'Dennis knows,' the Ed said. 'Just ask Dennis – he's a writer, an intellectual – he understands why we err.'

Dennis felt close to tears, moved by guilt and compassion, realising as he studied Harvey's face that his friend had been wounded. This made Dennis feel really bad, choked up with sympathy and pity, understanding that he had sinned: betraying Kathy, wounding Harvey, using Laura without acknowledging that this would bring him real suffering. And of course it had come to pass – Dennis was now suffering – and so, filled with sympathy and pity for himself, he realised that he would have to cast his selfish desires aside and return, via silvery-grey-haired Rosie's cunt, to his original innocence.

'I am speechless,' Dennis said.

'Words of wisdom,' the Ed said. 'I knew I could depend on you, Dennis, to offer Harvey moral support.'

'I'm grateful,' Harvey said.

'Not at all,' the Ed said. 'This is a grave moment of truth for as all and I think we should finish it. Les, ring your wife.'

'I'm not married,' Les mumbled.

'He loves his mother,' good old Stan said.

'I understand perfectly,' the Ed said. 'Clive, ring your wife.'

'No, thanks,' Clive said. 'I've had enough for one night. I trust my wife absolutely, but the less known the better.'

'Your choice,' the Ed said. 'I do not stand here in judgement. Nevertheless, this is a grave moment of truth and I think I should face it. I am going to ring my wife. I will show her what trust means. We haven't spoken a civil word for many months, but I won't let that stop me. I want you all to listen. Mzzz Cooch, please take note. I wish to confess my sins to my wife, and will then take my punishment.'

'You stupid berk,' Mzzz Cooch said.

Thereby wounded, thus encouraged, the Ed picked up the telephone and, his stiff upper lip trembling, dialled home to his missus. Dennis saw this and was touched, suddenly filled with brotherly love, but, wanting motherly love instead, slipped his hand between Rosie's thighs.

'Anna,' the Ed said crisply. 'This is your husband. Waken up... Don't be frightened... I know it's late, but it's me, it's your husband, and I just want to say a few words before you go back to sleep... Please be quiet, dear, I'm talking. I know it's late, but I want to talk. I want to confess my sins to you, Anna, so for God's sake be silent... Yes, Anna, I have sinned. I have stayed away from home. Worse: I have often arrived home too late to kiss my children goodnight. Nevertheless, I think about you. My concern is real enough. I just want you to know that if you're lonely you can seek comfort elsewhere. Not another man, of course. We have the children to consider. Rather, I recommend companionship of a civilised nature. Ring the office more often. I really don't mind if you do. Of course I may be too busy to converse myself, but my staff will assist you. I trust you completely, Anna. I know you won't abuse this privilege. Talk to anyone you like in the office, but please don't reverse charges. I would recommend Dennis. You might have met him once or twice. He's a writer, an intellectual, *understanding*, and I'd trust

him with anyone. So, Anna, don't be blue. Give the kids my
fondest love. Love means always having to say you're sorry, and
I'm doing that right now. I am truly sorry, Anna. You can sleep
well on that. I have sinned in the past but now it's over and I'm
taking my punishment.'

The Ed put the phone down, stared at everyone in turn,
finally let his misty eyes (pinwheels gone) come to rest on Mzzz
Cooch.

'I am ready to take my punishment,' he said, pushing his
chair back and standing up. 'Shall we retire to my office?'

'Get stuffed,' Mzzz Cooch said. 'You're beginning to like it
too much. I won't kick you if it gives you a kick, so sit down,
you dumb cunt.'

The Ed was crushed with disappointment and almost
swooned on the spot, but he bowed his head and sat down beside
her, his face pale and solemn.

'As you wish,' he said meekly.

Gazing at the Ed, and dwelling briefly on the Ed's
delightful wife, Dennis experienced a great wave of compassion
that threatened to sweep him away. Nevertheless, he was safe,
his right hand on Rosie's crotch, the young lady's thighs
clamped around his wrist and keeping him anchored. This made
him feel better. He would not be cast adrift. The pain he felt over
Anna, and over his best friend, her husband, would be eased
when sweet Rosie, silvery-grey-haired mistress and mother, held
him close to her bosom and rocked him and gave him a good
fuck.

'We've still got that large hole,' Les Hamilton said, 'and we
still haven't discussed it.'

'Words of wisdom,' the Ed said.

'An invaluable contribution,' Clive Grant added.

'He couldn't recognise the hole in pubic hair,' good old
Stan said, 'but we'll leave that point aside for the moment.'

'Pubic hair?' the Ed said.

'We've done that,' Harvey said. 'We've had sixteen spreads

of pubes in different colours, but they all looked the same in the end.'

'You're jaded,' good old Stan said.

'So my wife thinks,' Harvey said.

'You're both standing,' the Ed said. 'Why are you standing? The phone won't ring again.'

Harvey and Stan sat down, the former sitting beside Mzzz Bedward, sliding his left hand under her rump and then squeezing it and smiling at everyone.

'Okay,' he said, 'shoot.'

'Not again,' Mzzz Bedward said. 'I've just had someone's load on my knee and now my stockings are ruined.'

'I *beg* your pardon?' Harvey said.

'Never mind,' Mzzz Bedward said.

'You can never trust anyone,' Harvey said. 'I've finally learnt that hard lesson.'

'Adultery,' Clive Grant said.

'A touchy subject,' good old Stan said. 'I mean, I don't want to mention any names, but Harvey just might crack up.'

'My clients would like it,' Clive said. 'It would bring in good ads. After all, most of their ads encourage adultery, so they'd like that connection.'

'Really?' the Ed said.

'Yes, really,' Clive said. 'Blow-jobs on cigarettes and chocolate bars and ball pens, cunnilingus with grapefruits and hamburgers and pizzas, urolagia with soft drinks, ejaculations of beer and spirits, the masturbation of gearshifts and petrol pumps and electric razors, orgasms with deodorants and shampoos and hair sprays, and the good old sadomasochistic revels in denims and leather gear.'

'So how does that relate to adultery?'

'Would *you* do all that if you were married?'

'A very good point,' the Ed said. 'The marriage bonds are more sombre.'

'Classy ads,' Clive said.

191

'Up-market,' Harvey said.

'We don't want to lose our readers,' the Ed said. 'Intellectual ads kill them.'

'*Sexy* ads,' Harvey said.

'Can we get Benson and Hedges?'

'I can almost guarantee it,' Clive said, 'but it depends on the writer.'

'Okay, let's say adultery.'

'They'll buy it,' Clive said. 'On the other hand, it has to have class… I mean, we need a *real* writer.'

'Who writes about adultery?'

'Hardly anyone,' Harvey said. 'After all, it's pretty common these days. Just ask my missus.'

'Margaret Drabble?' Clive suggested.

'Are you kidding?' Harvey said. 'I mean, *Dennis* can write better than that illiterate, and Dennis can't even *write*.'

'She's a woman,' Mzzz Cooch said.

'She's a *what*?' Harvey said.

'Shut your mouth about Dennis,' Rosie said. 'His books are better than yours.'

'I don't *write* books,' Harvey said.

'She's a woman,' Mzzz Cooch repeated. 'One of the finest living writers in Hampstead, but her sex is a threat.'

'A *what*?' Harvey said.

'A threat,' Mzzz Cooch repeated. 'You feel threatened because that woman is a genius and you're all hopeless hacks.'

'What's a hack?' the Ed enquired.

'Some sort of hansom cab,' Harvey said.

'I want no photos of hansom cabs,' the Ed said. 'They're down-market these days.'

'Kingsley Amis,' Clive suggested.

'He's too filthy,' Mzzz Cooch said.

'What about Melvyn Bragg?' the Ed said.

'He's an actor,' Clive said.

'I really like him,' Dennis said.

'He's good on the telly,' the Ed said. 'I really like him when he plays the interrogator. I only wish he could write.'

'We can't illustrate it,' good old Stan said.

'Why not?' Harvey said. 'You just need a dozen nudes in a heap on a pile of spaghetti. That's real visual. Symbolic.'

'We haven't time,' good old Stan said. 'We have to shoot it by dawn. We've only got one model upstairs – and she's flat on her back.'

'Adultery's boring,' Harvey said.

'That poor woman,' Mzzz Cooch said. 'She's lying up there, the victim of rape, and she thinks she enjoyed it.'

'Rape's good,' Harvey said.

'A bit demanding,' the Ed said. 'I mean, we've all had a go at that before, but we've never been satisfied.'

'You vicious brutes,' Mzzz Cooch said.

'I don't like it,' Clive Grant said. 'The advertisers have been trying it for years, but it puts women off.'

'*And* men,' Harvey said.

'I beg your pardon?' Clive said.

'Think of COCK,' Harvey said. 'Those bitches have ensured that decent men can't walk the streets anymore. You're right, Clive: forget rape.'

'COCK?' Les Hamilton said.

'It's what you lack,' good old Stan said.

'A worthy organisation,' Mzzz Cooch said. 'Two branches, one head.'

'So?' the Ed said.

'Give Les COCK,' good old Stan said.

'A good subject for our readers,' Harvey said, 'because they all want a bigger one.'

'*That's* true,' the Ed said.

'Look at Les,' good old Stan said.

'We once ran a readership survey,' the Ed said with some excitement, 'and our readers loved our tips for enlarging them.'

'The magazines?' Mzzz Cooch said.

'No, their cocks,' the Ed said. 'That's exactly why Harvey does such good business with his classified ads.'

'What business?' Mzzz Cooch said.

'Vibrators,' Harvey said, 'and Invaders and Intruders, and Penisators and Penetrators and Pulsators and Squirmers, and Super Dongs and Double Dongs and Big Squirts and Stretchits, and any other anatomical aid that the normal guy needs.'

'Male aggression,' Mzzz Cooch said.

'Better believe it,' good old Stan said.

'I am catering to a genuine public need,' Harvey said with some dignity.

'You can get them on National Health.'

'Who said that?' the Ed enquired.

'It could only be Les Hamilton,' good old Stan said. 'He's a bit short down there.'

'A good angle there, Les.'

'Thank you, Ed,' Les Hamilton said. 'I mean, I don't actually use one myself. A friend told me that story.'

'Ho, ho,' good old Stan said.

'That's our angle,' the Ed said. 'I mean, we have all those fascists forever going on strike and then living off the fat of the land and getting Super Dongs on National Health.'

'It's a national disgrace,' Clive Grant said. 'That's why we need the Conservatives. No decent Conservative would give Super Dongs free to the uneducated, working-class masses.'

'Their poor wives,' Mzzz Cooch said. 'Now it's rape with offensive weapons. It's enough to put a woman off sex with all but her own sex.'

'We can't run it,' Clive said. 'I mean, my clients just won't buy it. The advertisers of this country won't lie down while you publicise National Health. After all, a subscription to BUPA doesn't bring you a Super Dong.'

'Double Dongs are better,' Les said.

'No politics,' the Ed said. 'It's a matter of principle. You never know which way the wind will blow, and survival is everything. I agree with you, Clive.'

'Something innocuous,' Les Hamilton said.

'Shut your mouth, Les,' the Ed said. 'You've got nothing above or below and you make my teeth grind.'

'I was just going to suggest something innocuous,' Les said quietly, 'to save us from further problems with the printers. Also, for this particular idea, you'd only need one female.'

'Les has an idea,' Harvey said.

'It dropped out of his arse,' good old Stan said.

'An article on the History of the Kiss,' Les said, whispering. 'With perhaps a single, full-page photo of Lydia's luscious lips facing the title page.'

'That's brilliant,' Dennis said.

'Dennis, you're brilliant,' the Ed said. 'You're the only bastard in this organisation who knows his job – and you've just proved it again.'

'Thank you, Ed,' Dennis said.

'Not at all, Dennis, you deserve it. One model, one photo, an easy article to knock off... What can I say, Dennis? It's pure brilliance.'

'Thank you, Ed,' Dennis repeated.

'You're so *smart*,' Rosie said.

'It's all due to my mother's influence,' Dennis said. 'And the touch of you down there.'

'My little clit's doing a dance.'

'I love your silvery-grey hair,' Dennis said. 'I also loved my mother a lot, but that can't last forever.'

'That's philosophical,' Rosie said.

'It's fucking brilliant,' the Ed said. 'Now all we have to do is knock off that article and get us a suitable photograph.'

'*The Reader's Digest*,' Harvey said.

'I beg your pardon?' the Ed said.

'I have an article on the kiss in an old *Reader's Digest*, but unfortunately it was written by an anthropologist.'

'A pervert?' the Ed asked hopefully.

'Not quite,' Harvey said. 'I mean, I doubt that he'd ever been kissed, but, you know, there's some history there.'

'How many words?' Dennis said.

'About two thousand,' Harvey said.

'Pad it out with some filth,' Dennis said, 'until it comes to four thousand.'

'Dennis, that's brilliant.'

'Thanks, Ed,' Dennis said.

'It's a thousand words per page,' the Ed said, 'so that gives us four pages.'

'Plus the photo,' Les Hamilton said.

'Shut your mouth, Les,' the Ed said. 'You haven't said a valuable word all night and I'm getting fed up with it.'

'Four pages plus the photo makes five pages,' Dennis said. 'That leaves only one page to be filled.'

'Shit,' the Ed said.

'Now we're fucked,' Harvey said.

'There's no way out of this one,' good old Stan said. 'We might as well piss off home.'

'A free ad,' Les Hamilton said.

'Shut your mouth, Les, I'm warning you.'

'I just thought, Ed, that a free full-page ad would solve all of our problems.'

'How come, you dumb shit?'

'Five plus one – '

'Makes six,' Dennis said.

'Dennis, that's fucking brilliant,' the Ed said. 'You've just done it again.'

'Thank you, Ed,' Dennis said.

'You're so *creative*,' Rosie said. 'I mean, the things you can do with that finger... Gee, whiz, I'm all *wet*.'

Bald, red and wrinkled, hungrily sucking his thumb, Dennis sheltered in the warmth of his mother's womb and knew the comfort of innocence. In a head-down position, his acrobatics now ceased, Dennis waited to be sprung forth into the light of life's numerous horrors. He didn't like that at all. In fact, he wanted to never leave. He wanted to stay inside his mother all his life and thus avoid life's teeming dangers. So, he resisted, tried to stay inside the womb, a crafty little devil, just a finger in the darkness, exploring up and down the vaginal walls, trying to find a nice hiding place. Then everything changed. In the beginning was the light. Dennis blinked his eyes and gave a muffled yelp to affirm his existence. Then the telephone rang.

'Get it out,' Rosie said.

'I beg your pardon?' Dennis said.

'Get your little bird out of my nest. The telephone's ringing.'

'Right,' Dennis said.

'Wipe it dry,' Rosie said.

'I don't feel very well,' Dennis said. 'What's happening? Where am I?'

'Is it dry?' Rosie said.

'Yes, it is. Indisputably.'

'You're really pretty cute,' Rosie said. 'We must do this more often.'

Dennis saw the bottles glinting, the ashtrays stacked with butts, the suspicious characters swimming in smoky haze around the long table. That was Harvey over there, leaning close to Annie Bedward, one of his shoulders lower than the other, his expression intense. Annie Bedward had closed her eyes and was pretending to be drinking brandy. She seemed to be squirming about in her chair, but Dennis couldn't be sure of that. Then she shivered and put her glass down. Harvey straightened up and grinned. Annie's left hand disappeared beneath the table and Harvey stopped grinning.

'The telephone's ringing,' Mzzz Cooch said.

'I need the whip,' the Ed said.

'If you'd open your eyes and pick your head up, you'd hear the telephone ringing.'

'What?' the Ed said. 'At *this* time?'

'Are you deaf?' Mzzz Cooch said.

'I won't touch it,' the Ed said. 'No fingerprints. It must be the Vice Squad.'

Mzzz Cooch threw him a sneer that turned his blood to pure ice, that filled him with the slave's fearful love as she picked up the telephone. She listened for a moment, didn't utter a word, then, with just the hint of a smile, she handed the phone to the Ed.

'It's the Artful Ed,' she said, clearly pleased. 'A *real* man at last.'

The Ed quivered like a reed, his delicate sensibilities flayed, then he placed his hand over the earpiece and spoke to the table.

'Silence,' he said firmly.

'Hear, hear,' good old Stan said.

'I have the Artful Ed on the line and I think you should hear him.' The Ed straightened his shoulders, swayed slightly from side to side, regained his balance and lowered one hand and touched a switch on the telephone. 'I will open the line,' he said. 'The Artful Ed will be amplified. As usual, the Artful Ed has come to the rescue just in time, and I think you should all hear what he has to say. I am switching him on now.' The Ed flicked the tiny switch, pounding rock music filled the room, and Clive Grant, fast asleep, awoke abruptly and shot out of his chair.

'*Jesus Christ!*' he screamed.

'I'm right here,' the Ed said. 'Good to hear from you at last, Artful Ed. And nice to know you don't sleep at nights.'

'I'm going to a party,' the Artful Ed said.

'At two in the morning?'

'It's nine in the evening,' the Artful Ed said. 'Christ, this massage is good!'

'Jesus Christ,' Clive Grant said. 'I thought a bomb had gone off. Where's my chair? My fucking head is still ringing. God, it's nice to sit down again.'

'I *beg* your pardon?' the Ed said.

'I'm going to a party,' the Artful Ed repeated. 'And don't

think I'm going for my pleasure. It's all work to me, Ed.'

'It's two in the morning,' the Ed said.

'It's an important party,' the Artful Ed said. 'Herr Mayer's just arrived in New York to discuss all our business.'

'Herr Mayer?' the Ed said.

'I can explain,' Dennis said.

'Never mind this Herr Mayer,' the Ed said. 'Where's *The York*? In King's Road?'

'No,' the Artful Ed said. 'I had to change my hotel. That Algonquin was filled with the living dead and they didn't like rock 'n' roll.'

'I don't understand,' the Ed said.

'The miserable bastards threw me out. They said they didn't like the smell of my piss and that I had to go elsewhere.'

'The Algonquin?' the Ed said. 'I don't think I've heard of it. I know a lot of pubs in Kings Road, but not the Algonquin.'

'I'm not there anymore. I've moved into the Chelsea. There's a lot of rock stars staying here, so they don't mind the music.'

'They're playing music?' the Ed said.

'They don't mind it,' the Artful Ed said. 'Anyway, I'm having this massage to prepare for the party.'

'It must be a long party.'

'It hasn't started yet, Ed.'

'You mean it's *starting* at two in the morning?'

'It's only nine. In the evening.'

The Ed blinked and glanced around him, focused on Dennis, hoping for help, but Dennis was staring thoughtfully at Harvey who was squirming most oddly.

'What time is it?' the Ed said.

'Nine in the evening. Local time.'

'We're right here in Soho,' the Ed said, 'and it's two in the morning.'

'Ah,' the Artful Ed said. 'The *York* pub... Not that. Obviously that prick Dennis hasn't told you. I had to come to

New York.'

'That's in *America*,' the Ed said.

'I wouldn't know,' the Artful Ed said. 'I embark and disembark at airports and then take taxis everywhere.'

The Ed wiped sweat from his brow, gripped the table, started shaking, blinked his eyes and stared wildly around the room, wishing Mzzz Cooch would whip him. It wasn't lust – certainly not – it was a *psychological* need: it was the need to be shocked back to his senses and the bliss of reality. He blinked again and shook his head, focused on Dennis, hoping for help, but Dennis was staring steadily at Harvey who was squirming dementedly.

'All right,' the Ed said. 'We won't discuss New York now. I'm sure Dennis knows all about New York and that it's all above board.'

'It certainly is,' the Artful Ed said. 'I mean, what the fuck do you think I'm *doing* here? Do you think I just came here for a fucking massage and the good of my health? I'm not appreciated, Ed. I want to tell you that right now. I mean, I came here to try to save the mags and now I'm getting abused. That's fucking unfair, Ed. I'm working my ass off over here. I mean, I heard about that *rival* mag when I was over in Paris. I knew that those fucking printers would try to pull some shitty stunt, so I asked a few questions, passed some francs here and there, and then found out that the bastard who was trying to do you in was being financed by some shithead over here – and so, Ed, I'm still searching.'

'I'm truly sorry, Artful Ed. Please accept my apologies. I didn't doubt you for second, Artful Ed, as I'm sure you appreciate.'

'You creeping turd,' Mzzz Cooch said.

'That's okay,' the Artful Ed said. 'I know we have these little misunderstandings, but that's part of the job.'

'And do you think, Artful Ed, that you stand a good chance of discovering who this other publisher is?'

'A difficult one there, Ed. Thing is, this is a very big city and I *do* have other business on my plate – all to do, of course, with the good of the mags – but I *am* banking, Ed, on the possibility that *Herr Mayer* might know who that other publisher is, or, indeed, might even *be* the son of a bitch we're looking for – and, of course, if Herr Mayer *is* our man, well, then, Ed – do I have to say more? – I mean, what with all that hair-raising stuff I picked up about Herr Mayer's orgiastic activities in that hotel in Torremolinos – which is, of course, why I sent the Circulation Manager there in the first place – well, I could put a little pressure on the bastard and thus ensure that he drops his planned magazine.'

'I don't want anything illegal!' the Ed said.

'It's only blackmail,' the Artful Ed said. 'You've nothing to worry about.'

'Well, that's great,' the Ed said.

There was a sudden rushing and roaring of amplified static, which lifted Clive Grant out of his chair and slammed him back down again, and then, as if coming from outer space, another voice interrupted.

'Hello! Hello! I seem to have a crossed line. Hello! Can you hear me?'

'Get off the line,' the Ed said.

'You fucking shithead,' the Artful Ed added.

'Hello, Ed! Is that you, Ed? It's Rick! I'm still trapped here in Malaga!'

'Rick *Walker*?' the Ed said.

'That's right!' Rick said, sounding hysterical.

'What the fuck are you doing in Malaga?' the Artful Ed said. 'You should be in Torremolinos by now.'

'I got lost,' Rick said.

'You stupid cunt,' the Ed said.

'I think it's a conspiracy,' Rick said. 'I mean, these Spaniards are bastards.'

'Please explain,' the Ed said.

'It's really awful,' Rick said. 'I mean, I walk out of the Malaga Airport terminal, it's all dark, the heat's killing me, my arse and my ulcer are hurting and no one speaks English.'

'Quite illiterate there, Rick.'

'*And* dishonest!' Rick wailed. 'I mean, I have the hotel's address, it's written clearly on a bit of paper, and this Spaniard smiles heartily, puts me into his clapped-out taxi, and drives me in circles for hours and then asks for a fortune. You know these damned *pesetas*, Ed – they all look like bum paper. This guy shoves great fistfuls into his pocket and keeps driving in circles. So, I change cabs. I get the very same thing. I keep changing cabs and I see the whole of Malaga, and all these bastards keeping muttering about the Artful Ed and insisting that they know what they're doing.'

'The *Artful Ed*?' the Ed said.

'Pure hypothesis,' the Artful Ed said. 'Rick doesn't know Spanish from shit, and now he's just trying to blame me.'

'It's all a conspiracy,' Rick insisted. 'I'm sure they're doing it deliberately. They're trying to keep me away from that hotel, to prevent me from getting to Frank Harrison.'

'He's paranoid,' the Artful Ed said. 'What the fuck's he talking about? Besides, why didn't he just ring Frank to get proper directions?'

'Is that you, Dennis?' Rick said.

'That's right,' the Artful Ed said.

'I tried that, Dennis. Honestly, I tried … but Frank's simply not answering.'

'Really?' the Artful Ed said.

'Yes, really,' Rick said. 'I mean, I know the Artful Ed, I know that filthy bastard's tricks, and so, you know, I used my intelligence and rang the receptionist. He said that Frank was in his room, but that he was drugged and unconscious, and that some whore, after delivering the little package, said that *senor* was sleeping. I don't have to say more, Dennis. We all know the Artful Ed. If it was a whore, the Artful Ed had to know her – and he set this thing up.'

'Why?' the Ed said.

'I don't know,' Rick said. 'I just know that I'm trapped here in Malaga in some filthy brothel.'

'That explains it,' good old Stan said.

'I'll second that,' Harvey said.

'The degenerate pig,' Mzzz Cooch added.

'No, Ed, it's not that!' Rick said desperately, his voice strained. 'You know I hate whores – particularly Spanish whores who don't even speak decent English – but the last taxi driver just dumped me here and left muttering something about the Artful Ed.'

'He's paranoid,' the Artful Ed said. 'That bastard's *always* hated me. Now he's trying to put his boot in my balls, the cock-sucking assassin.'

'Is that you, Stan?' Rick said.

'Yes,' the Artful Ed said.

'This is really most confusing,' the Ed said. 'I think I'm getting a headache.'

'What time is it?' the Artful Ed said.

'Two-thirty,' the Ed said.

'Four-thirty,' Rick said.

'The bastard doesn't even know the time,' the Artful Ed said. 'No wonder he's lost.'

'Two hours' difference,' Rick explained.

'*What's* that?' the Ed said.

'We're two hours ahead of you, Ed, which is why it's four-thirty.'

'And you've been driving all that time?'

'I was *driven*,' Rick said. 'And it's all the fucking Artful Ed's fault, I bet *he* set it up.'

'I'm confused,' the Ed said.

'He's paranoid,' the Artful Ed said. 'He's just a dumb cunt, a real cock-up, and now he's trying to blame me for his incompetence.'

'Prove it,' good old Stan said.

'I will,' the Artful Ed said. 'I'll make a quick call to Spain, find a *reliable* taxi service, and have that prick out at Frank's hotel within an hour from now.'

'Excellent,' the Ed said.

'It's the Artful Ed's fault,' Rick said. 'I mean, the Artful Ed – well, what can I say? – that bastard hates *everyone*.'

'Rick?' the Artful Ed said.

'Yes, Dennis?' Rick said.

'I'll send a taxi in half an hour,' the Artful Ed said, 'and believe me, the driver will know exactly where he's going. So, just sit tight. Keep your hands off the hookers. When the driver arrives, he'll know just who you are and he'll take you to Frank. No excuses then, Rick.'

'Oh, no, Dennis!' Rick said. 'I mean, that's really great. I'll have more confidence if I know *you're* in charge – and I won't *need* excuses.'

'Very good, Rick,' the Ed said.

'No sweat, Ed,' Rick said.

'We can expect you and Frank back by noon tomorrow.'

'That's it, Ed. We'll be there.'

There was another rushing and roaring of amplified static, making Clive Grant quiver up off his chair before settling down again.

'This is terrible,' the Ed said. 'I mean, we need Frank Harrison badly. If we don't get him back here by noon tomorrow, we could be up Shit Creek. He's the Circulation Manager, after all. We don't have anyone else. If we don't get Frank to contact his connections, we'll be dead by the evening.'

'Really?' the Artful Ed said.

'Yes, really,' the Ed said.

'Well, I'll bear that in mind,' the Artful Ed said.

'That's most kind of you, Artful Ed.'

The Ed rubbed his eyes and glanced wearily around the table, hoping to see his staff creatively scribbling, but seeing only the living dead. This particular description may not have been quite accurate, since, while it was true that through the smoky haze he could see that Clive Grant was again slumped in sleep, that Les and Stan were obviously smashed, and that Mzzz Teasedale was fixated on Dennis, he nevertheless *did* also note that Dennis' eyes were diamond-bright, that he was sitting up very straight, and that he was staring with a peculiar intensity at Mzzz Bedward and Harvey. Rubbing his eyes again, the Ed looked with more care and saw, through the smoky haze, that Mzzz Bedward was close to Harvey, that her left hand was beneath the table, and that her left arm was moving methodically backward and forward while Harvey squirmed in brazen delight. The Ed, not wishing to consider the possible meaning of such movements, sighed and lowered his gaze and looked directly at Mzzz Cooch who, with her radiant contempt, gave him comfort and hope.

'We need *you* as well, Artful Ed,' he said. 'We are *desperate* to see you.'

'What's the subject?' the Artful Ed said.

'The History of the Kiss,' the Ed said.

'Illustrations?'

'One photograph of Lydia's luscious lips.'

'You'll save money,' the Artful Ed said.

'*And* time,' the Ed said. 'Nevertheless, we have to make the lips exciting and we need you for that.'

'Let Les Hamilton do it.'

'I don't think he's up to it.'

'I know the cunt's frightened of cunt, but that shot should be easy.'

'One pair of lips,' the Ed said. 'It doesn't sound very exciting. What we need is a simple piece of brilliance to set it all off.'

'A difficult one,' the Artful Ed said.

'A Double Dong,' Les Hamilton said.

'Shut your mouth, Les, I'm warning you,' the Ed said. 'This

205

conversation's important.'

'A Double Dong,' the Artful Ed said.

'That sounds great,' the Ed said. 'You're getting there already, Artful Ed, so don't stop, keep it coming.'

'Just one lovely close-up,' Les Hamilton said, 'of Lydia's luscious lips sucking a Double Dong. It will cause a sensation.'

'Right,' the Artful Ed said.

'That's sensational!' the Ed said. 'Absolutely fucking brilliant! You've done it again, Artful Ed, as we all knew you would.'

'Thanks, Ed,' the Artful Ed said. 'I try to do my best. But it's not always easy with cunts like Les Hamilton interfering.'

'Can we let him shoot it?' the Ed begged.

'I hand it to him on a plate.'

'And *naturally*,' the Ed said, 'the finished pix will have to be passed by you, which you can do when you arrive back in the office.'

'I have my standards,' the Artful Ed said.

'But *of course*,' the Ed said. 'And so, Artful Ed, when can we expect you back here?'

'A difficult one, Ed. I mean, I have my work cut out. What with shooting all these sessions in Times Square and Greenwich Village, and what with Herr Mayer and all, it could be a tricky one.'

'When?' the Ed said.

'I'll leave at ten in the morning.'

'Great,' the Ed said. 'So you should be back here nine hours later.'

'*Nine* hours?' the Artful Ed said.

'That's right,' the Ed said. 'One hour to Kennedy, seven hours on the plane, then another hour from Heathrow to here.'

'*Five* hours on the plane,' the Artful Ed said.

'Really?'

'Really.'

'I thought you said it was seven hours.'

'Seven hours flying out,' the Artful Ed said. 'Five hours coming back.'

'How come?'

'Tail winds,' the Artful Ed said.

'Great,' the Ed said. 'That's fantastic. You'll be back even earlier.'

'Two hours earlier,' the Artful Ed said.

'Unbelievable,' the Ed said. 'That means you should arrive in the office about eleven this morning. Our time.'

'No,' the Artful Ed said.

'Pardon?' the Ed said.

'Not eleven this morning,' the Artful Ed said. 'I'll be arriving at five tomorrow afternoon.'

'Tomorrow's *Wednesday*!' the Ed exclaimed.

'Tomorrow's Tuesday,' the Artful Ed said. 'It's nine-thirty on Monday evening over here and this massage is heavenly.'

'It's *Monday* over there?'

'In the evening,' the Artful Ed said. 'It's Monday evening over here, it's Tuesday morning over there, and so, if I leave here about ten on Tuesday morning, I should be back there, given an hour on the tail end of the trip, by approximately five on Tuesday afternoon, this being summer time.'

'That's too late,' the Ed said. 'I mean, our *deadline's* five this afternoon. We've got to get this photograph set up. What the hell do we do?'

'Use Les Hamilton,' the Artful Ed said.

'A great idea!' the Ed said.

'I'll supervise him by telephone,' the Artful Ed said, 'so let me know if the cunt fucks it up.'

'What's your number?' the Ed said.

'A difficult one there, Ed. Thing is, I'm just off to Herr Mayer's party, and unfortunately I don't have his number.'

'Ring me back,' the Ed said.

'I'll do that,' the Artful Ed said.

'Okay, Artful Ed,' the Ed said, 'you've really been a great

help.'

'Anytime, Ed. I'll call you.'

The Artful Ed hung up, leaving the Ed with a dead line, so the Ed put the telephone down and offered Mzzz Cooch a winning smile. The imposing lady sneered at him, knowing the Artful Ed frightened him, and the Ed, equally frightened of Mzzz Cooch, felt better each minute.

'And so,' he said, 'the photographic session. I hope you find this instructive.'

'*Most* instructive,' Mzzz Cooch said.

This observation moved the Ed, almost made him faint with pride, lifting his head up and looking across at Dennis, his most trusted lieutenant. Yet Dennis hardly saw him, being otherwise engrossed, sitting up very straight, Rosie Teasedale close to him, both of them staring across the table, their eyes fixed on Annie Bedward whose left hand was jerking back and forth under the table while Harvey, close to her, his head back, his eyes wide, started shaking in the throes of a deep and clearly moving religious ecstasy.

'God, I just *love* it,' Mzzz Bedward was saying. 'It's so *stiff*, it's so *smooth*, it's so *hot* and what-have-you, and I've never had one of my own, which is why I miss it so much. Okay, here it comes, kid.'

Harvey's eyes were popping out, a most unusual occurrence, and his whole body quivered with release as his cock sang its love song. This all happened beneath the table, without fuss, with great modesty, and his sacred fluid arched through the air and came to rest on a pretty knee. Harvey didn't stifle his gasp. Rosie Teasedale glanced down. Her brow furrowed as she touched her knee lightly and then looked up at Harvey.

'There's something half alive under the table,' Rosie said, 'and I think it released its final desperate drip.'

'Where's that Lydia?' the Ed said.

7

The lovely Lydia was stretched out on a work bench in the studio, still long-limbed and dark-haired and bushy-tailed, a blanket thrown over her. At the far end of the studio the mysterious teetotal bisexual editor was still leaning over his desk, his eyes aflame with dementia or drugs, making one phone call after the other in a hushed, furtive voice. Since the mysterious teetotal bisexual editor worked ceaselessly at unspecified tasks for various unnamed magazines, and since he would offer the word 'Bitch!' to anyone who tried to question him, it was obvious that no man on the staff would now be man enough to talk to him.

'He's still at it,' Harvey said.

'Dedicated,' good old Stan said. 'He's seduced half the men in this city without leaving his desk.'

'Who is he?' Rosie said.

'We're not sure,' Dennis said. 'The Artful Ed hired him long ago, but we're not sure what for.'

'I like him,' Mzzz Cooch said.

'He hates men,' Clive Grant said.

'You either have it or you don't,' Mzzz Cooch said, 'and I knew he had something.'

The Ed choked back a sob, her deliberate insult cutting through him, then he turned away to hide his erection and stared down at Lydia.

'There's a woman on that work bench,' he said, 'and she has no clothes on.'

'That's Lydia,' Stan said.

'Have we met before?' the Ed said, his memory ravaged by years of dissipation. 'I ask because her face is familiar, though that doesn't mean much.'

Gorged on nudes, never shy, jaded almost beyond repair, good old Stan whipped the blanket off lovely Lydia to expose the rest of her nude body.

'I think I know her,' the Ed said.

'You disgusting brute,' Mzzz Cooch said. 'You've just disowned that poor girl above the neck and turned her into mere flesh.'

'I *like* flesh,' Harvey said.

'She wasn't bad,' good old Stan said. 'A little bit slow at the starting line, but moved well when the spurs were in.'

Stan now spurred her on again, poking her shoulder with one finger, and Lydia's lovely eyes fluttered open, distinctly bloodshot from brandy.

'Wha – ?' she murmured sleepily.

'Get up,' good old Stan said. 'You're going to be a model at last, so don't look for your clothes.'

Lydia shivered and blinked dazedly, gave a yawn and licked her lips, and then her body, which was all the lads could see, slowly uncoiled and straightened up.

'You poor girl,' Mzzz Cooch said.

'*What* was that?' Lydia murmured.

'You're being exploited and you don't even know it. You actually think it's artistic.'

'You mean fucking?' Lydia said.

'I mean modelling,' Mzzz Cooch said. 'You're degrading your sex and betraying your sisters, you poor innocent ba-ba.'

'I've never modelled,' Lydia said.

'Your time has come,' good old Stan said. 'Open your mouth when Harvey brings his Double Dong. We want to see if it fits.'

Mzzz Cooch shuddered and turned aside and glanced

210

around the large studio, now aware that the Artful Ed had been correct and that this place was a snake-pit. There were three our four work benches, an equal number of desks, two copy scanners, one large slide projector, various spot lights, and a mess of electric cables and empty bottles and used contraceptives. Les Hamilton switched the spot lights on, making everyone blink with shock: good old Stan, Les himself, that poor model and the ogling Ed, all bathed in a blinding incandescence that made them seem unreal.

'So,' Harvey said. 'I have my weapon in my hand. Open your delectable lips, lovely Lydia, and let me check your capacity.'

A veteran of numerous violent campaigns against the ravishing male hordes, Mzzz Cooch was, nonetheless, appalled to see Harvey advance upon poor Lydia, smirking, breathing deeply, his animal nostrils quivering, holding up in his right hand – oh, hideous sight! – the wobbling, impressively large Double Dong: a real two-headed serpent.

'It's really for lesbians,' the Ed thoughtfully explained.

'I *beg* your pardon? *What* was that?'

'They can both use it at once,' the Ed explained. 'When their two hearts are joined.'

'Really?' Mzzz Cooch said.

'Cross my heart and hope to die.'

'You mean two women can fuck with that thing and they don't need a man?'

'That's right. Don't be shocked.'

'That's wonderful Who sells them?'

'I believe the Artful Ed is the source.'

'My hero,' Mzzz Cooch said.

Mortally wounded and happy, the Ed glanced at his wristwatch and saw that it was four in the morning. Feeling even more wounded, and thus gaining an erection, he noticed that his bunch of merry lads were *all* gaining erections. This struck the Ed as odd until he glanced at lovely Lydia and saw that she had opened her luscious lips and filled them up with one end of the Double Dong. Harvey also had an erection – his quivering rump gave him away – but he bravely moved the Double Dong in and out, up and down, left and right, in a circle, and only stopped when Mzzz Cooch, glaring at each of the lads in turn, promptly poured the icy water of her scorn on their burning loins.

'You're all brutes,' she said.

'Gee, thanks,' they replied in chorus.

'Castration is the least you deserve. And that poor girl… God help us.'

Mzzz Cooch continued glaring, her look enough to crumble mountains, but only Annie and Rosie responded, both giggling hysterically.

'It's not funny,' Mzzz Cooch said.

'It sort of tickles,' Lydia said when the Double Dong was finally withdrawn. 'Of course, I've never had my tonsils taken out, so that could explain it.'

Annie and Rosie giggled again, hiding their pretty little faces, and Dennis, looking in particular at Rosie, felt a great deal of tenderness. Rosie's silvery-grey hair was beautiful, her gentle hands merciful, and Dennis knew in his heart that she was as pure as the love of his mother. Thus, he wanted her protection, to be flesh of her flesh, to share the very beating of his heart as he fucked her brains out.

'It's not right,' Dennis said.

'It fits perfectly,' Harvey said.

'That so-called Double Dong is in bad taste and should not be included.'

'Taste it,' good old Stan said.

'God bless you,' Mzzz Cooch said. 'You're the only decent man in this place and I don't mind acknowledging it.'

'Use a Big Squirt,' Dennis said. 'That Double Dong is just for lesbians. The Big Squirt is more to the point and also simulates come. We can have it dribbling from her lips, a frothing white against the red. I should think that would be strikingly visual and enhance the whole image.'

'That's fucking brilliant,' the Ed said. 'You've done it again, Dennis. I don't know who suggested that Double Dong, but they ought to be horsewhipped.'

'I'm so sorry,' Les Hamilton said.

'Stop apologising,' the Ed said. 'You're a creeping little turd with no balls and I'm pulling the chain.'

'Take your punishment,' Harvey said.

'Like a man,' good old Stan said.

'I'm so sorry, Mzzz Cooch,' the Ed said, 'for this regrettable lapse in taste.'

'Stop apologising,' Mzzz Cooch said. 'I can't stand creeping turds. One more sorry and I'll grab your shrivelled balls and crush them under my leather boots.'

The Ed's eyes shone with hope, but he tried to keep it hidden, understanding that his mistress would not punish him if she knew it would pleasure him. Instead, he looked at Harvey who was testing the Big Squirt, first filling it with false come from a plastic container, then holding it by its pink latex testicles and switching on the vibrator. The Big Squirt was impressive, actually splashing over the girls, and they squealed and jumped out of the way, both giggling hysterically.

'All right,' the Ed said. 'That's enough of that now. This is not a public performance, after all, and we *do* have our work cut out.'

'Right,' Harvey said.

'The Kiss,' Dennis said.

'I have the *Reader's Digest* article right here. Let's pad it out, Dennis.'

'Right,' Dennis said.

Moving away from Rosie with a profound feeling of loss, Dennis went to the nearest desk and sat down behind a large, battered typewriter. Harvey joined him enthusiastically (always excited by plagiarism) and together they studied the History of the Kiss in all its watered-down facts.

'Not much here,' Dennis said.

'Not a blow-job in sight.'

'It's all rather academic,' Dennis said.

'We might get the Nobel Prize.'

'There's nothing *new* in this article.'

'It's just lips to lips, Dennis.'

'More down-market, you think?'

'I believe that's our direction.'

'It mentions tactile sensations.'

'That's a start,' Harvey said. 'That gets us to cunnilingus and cock-sucking and the old double-eight.'

'Very good,' Dennis said.

Harvey picked up some scissors and started cutting up the magazine while Dennis patiently typed out some pornographic padding. Dennis typed very fast, in a trance of creative passion, using one page per paragraph and letting Harvey paste them down between the more intelligent, less stimulating prose of the revered *Reader's Digest*.

'It's shaping up well,' Harvey said.

'The *Digest* editors are really terrible.'

'They pay their editors highly,' Harvey said, 'but expect you to spell.'

'To *know* spelling,' Dennis corrected him.

'I'm trying to modernise the language. What we need now are a few throbbing cocks and tender clits, which, if I slip them in here, will pep up the boring *Digest* prose.'

'A nice touch,' Dennis said.

'It's a change to do some real work. I'll just add a pair of pink, quivering lips to this Eskimo nose-rubbing.'

'That should melt the ice a bit.'

'I hope so,' Harvey said. 'And I must say you're pretty damned sharp with the hot breath and labia. You're perking up this anthropological treatise beyond recognition.'

'I think you mean physiological.'

'That's the word,' Harvey conceded. 'Though how

psychiatry got into all this kissing I really would like to know.'

'You're very good with those scissors, Harvey.'

'They read better with Sellotape. I mean, putting an article together is so creative, it's no wonder we're editors.'

Dennis and Harvey kept working, scarcely looking up at all, now obsessed with the labours of *real* men while the girls poured them brandies. The brandy was beneficial, washing down the coloured tablets, and before very long the busy studio was resembling Dream Land. Dennis and Harvey kept working, true artistes at last, while the Ed gazed upon them with love and heart-warming pride. He wanted to kiss their foreheads, to bow down and lick their feet, but he sensed that if he fell on his hands and knees he would never get up again.

Stan and Les were also working, photographing the lovely Lydia, from the side, from the front, from a few seductive angles, trying to find the very best, the most *artistic* concept, bearing in mind the need for dignity and the tenets of good taste, wanting to bring out the exquisite perfection of Lydia's mouth as it formed a large O around the vibrating Big Squirter, its latex testicles now hanging down her chin, its false come on her ruby lips.

'A David Hamilton,' good old Stan said. 'I mean, we don't want Harrison Marks. What we want is something really original: a perfect copy of Hamilton.'

'All his models are so young.'

'The filthy bastard,' Stan said. 'And his books are on the best coffee tables. I don't know who he knows, Les.'

'Lydia's breasts are really nice.'

'Her damned nipples aren't stiff. Go and fetch some ice cubes from the fridge.'

'Let me suck them,' Mzzz Cooch said.

'I beg your pardon?' Les said.

'I won't have you bastards humiliate her. This is woman to woman.'

Hurt, humiliated, cast aside for another woman, the Ed turned away and walked up to Dennis for a comforting chat.

'How's the article coming, Dennis?'

'Shaping up rather well, Ed.'

'Harvey?'

'I'm giving it everything I've got, Ed… And these scissors are excellent.'

'Time's running out, guys.'

'We're doing the best we can, Ed.'

'That's not what I'm talking about, Dennis. Where the fuck's that Rick Walker?'

'He's in Spain,' Harvey said.

'He's not *supposed* to be, Harvey. He's *supposed* to be flying back right now on the five o'clock plane.'

'They're two hours ahead of us, Ed.'

'Stop confusing me, Harvey.'

'They were catching the plane at seven *our* time,' Dennis said, 'which means they should arrive here by ten.'

'Exactly,' the Ed said. 'They should be arriving here by ten. And if Frank Harrison isn't here by lunchtime we can call it a day.'

'Wiped out?' Harvey said.

'Armageddon,' the Ed said. 'If we don't get Frank Harrison back by noon, we'll never stop that new mag.'

'The telephone's ringing, Ed.'

'What was that, Dennis?'

'The telephone. Right here beside me. It could be important.'

The Ed twitched when he heard it, glanced wildly along the room, and saw the mysterious teetotal bisexual editor hissing into the other phone. The Ed shuddered at the sight of him, dropped his eyes, picked them up again, then, having picked up his eyes, he also picked up the telephone.

'Yes?'

'It's me, Ed!'

'Good. Who might that be?'

'It's me, Ed! Rick Walker. Honest to God, it wasn't my

216

fault! I mean, I did what Dennis told me to do and actually found the hotel. Then everything went wrong. Honest to God, it wasn't my fault! I found Frank Harrison in his room and woke him up and then this fat whore stormed in. Swear on the Bible, Ed! I mean, this whore had five friends. They stripped me naked and threw me down on Frank's bed, and then... God... *I can't say it!*'

The Ed stared across the room, saw the spot lights, sweet Lydia, the Big Squirt now between Lydia's breasts and being given a hug. There wasn't room for it in her mouth. Someone's tongue was in her mouth. Mzzz Cooch, a real journalist, a true *Observer* reporter, was sinking herself into her subject with commendable zeal.

'Control yourself, Rick.'

'God, I'm sorry, Ed, I'm sorry... But I'm so ashamed of what that bunch did to me, I think I'll just *die*.'

'You mentioned six whores, Rick.'

'That's right, Ed, six whores. Frank was getting ready to leave – a bit dizzy, but standing – when they burst into the room and knocked him unconscious and then threw me on his bed and had their filthy way with me. And then, when they had finished, having *degraded* me so terribly, they raised their hands above their heads and chanted, "The wrath of COCK is merciful" and then forced some coloured tablets down my throat and made my head go all funny.'

'*Coloured* tablets?' the Ed enquired.

'Some sort of filthy drug, Ed. Those tablets made my head go all funny and then put me to sleep... I remember the whores talking. I'm convinced they mentioned the Artful Ed... Then I woke up with Frank in this bed, both of us naked.'

The Ed stared across the room, saw the spot lights, Les Hamilton, the latter taking some photos of lovely Lydia and Mzzz Cooch as their lips clamped together in a frenzy of creative endeavour. This punishment was too much – the sheer anguish, the pure ecstasy – but the Ed stiffened his wilting lower member and got on with his work.

'Where are you now, Rick?'

'I'm not sure about that, Ed. I think it's called Carihuela. It's packed with seafront restaurants and Spanish fishermen and tourists, and the Mediterranean, though disgustingly filthy, is crowded with swimmers. This is where we woke up, Ed. It's a little house between two restaurants. We don't have any clothes and Frank seems to be in a catatonic trance. It's all the Artful Ed's fault, Ed.'

'That cunt,' the Ed said.

'We see eye to eye there, Ed. I've called an ambulance and I'm taking Frank to the airport, but God knows when we'll make it.'

'What time is it there now?'

'About ten in the morning, Ed. I should get to the airport about twelve and be back there by one.'

'It's a two-and-a-half-hour flight, Rick.'

'We're two hours ahead, Ed.'

'Stop confusing me, Rick.'

'We'll get to Heathrow by twelve-thirty or one – then an hour into town.'

'That's excellent, Rick.'

'I'm not saying I'll make it, Ed. I mean, we don't know what the Artful Ed's up to, but I'll try to get through.'

'You think it's the Artful Ed?'

'It's all a conspiracy, Ed. I've been waylaid and robbed and finally raped, and the Artful Ed planned it. That's the shocking truth, Ed. And now how do I tell my wife? You *know* how wives react when you've been raped: they just want to disown you. On the other hand, I don't care. I've been traumatised for life. If my wife tries to touch me up in bed, I swear to God I'll just *scream*. That's an awful thing, Ed. I'm going to need compensation. Clearly there's lots of nightmares ahead, and psychiatrists cost money. It's all the Artful Ed's fault.'

'Okay, Rick, that's enough. I can't take much more of this. I appreciate all you're trying to do, but our time is now limited. Get to Malaga airport. Keep your eyes peeled for terrorists. Don't speak to anyone suspicious, and call me from Heathrow. Okay, Rick, that's all.'

The Ed dropped the telephone and stared across the room, his heart pounding with grief and delight when he saw dear Mzzz Cooch. Her back was turned to him. She was embracing lovely Lydia. Indeed, she appeared to be sucking Lydia's pert nipples with enthusiasm. Les Hamilton was taking pictures. His little pot belly trembled. Good old Stan was looking on, drinking brandy, smoking a cigarette, and Mzzzes Bedward and Teasedale were wandering over to have a closer look. The Ed choked back his tears, let the pain wash him clean, and then, his member stiffening with pride, he stared at Dennis and Harvey.

'We're up Shit Creek,' he said.

'Really?' Dennis said.

'Frank's in a catatonic trance.'

'He always is,' Harvey said.

'I don't think that's funny, Harvey.'

'A slip of the tongue there, Ed.'

'Anyway, Ed, I'm sure Frank will recover soon and be fit enough to work when eventually Rick gets him back here.'

'You think so, Dennis?'

'I'm *sure* of it, Ed.'

'Rick swears it's the Artful Ed's fault.'

'I'm sure *that's* not true, Ed.'

'That Rick's *always* paranoid,' Harvey said. 'And the Artful Ed frightens him.'

'He frightens *everyone*,' the Ed said.

'*That's* true,' Dennis said.

'He doesn't frighten *me*,' the Ed said, 'but, of course, I'm his boss.'

'A good point there, Ed.'

'I appreciate that, Harvey.'

'This article's really shaping up, Ed, so we'll want some

more money.'

'You stole half from the *Reader's Digest*.'

'We'll want *half* of some more money.'

'Rick was raped and now he wants compensation.'

'A real Philistine,' Harvey said.

'*Bitches*!' someone screamed.

'Who was *that*?' the Ed said.

'I think it was the mysterious teetotal bisexual editor,' Dennis said, 'because he's looking rather agitated at the moment.'

'*Bitches*!' the mysterious teetotal bisexual editor screamed again. 'I'm trying to do some urgent work for the gorgeous Artful Ed and you bitches are deliberately tormenting me by letting that telephone ring and ring.'

'Ah,' Dennis said.

'The telephone's ringing,' Harvey said. 'It's there on the desk by your hand, Ed, and it could be important.'

Being punished by Mzzz Cooch, seeking comfort in obedience, the Ed picked the telephone up and continued with business.

'Yes?' he said sternly.

'Hi. I'm having breakfast.'

'Pardon?'

'I'm just having breakfast, darling… and I wanted to talk.'

'Who is this, please?'

'It's Anna.'

'*Who*?'

'Your wife. It's eight-thirty in the morning and I'm lonesome and I wanted to talk.'

'I'm busy right now.'

'You said I could ring the office.'

'I have certain responsibilities,' the Ed said, 'which by now you should understand.'

'I'm feeling blue,' Anna said.

'Take a sleeping pill,' the Ed said.

220

'You said I could ring up if I felt blue, and possibly speak to that Dennis.'

'An excellent editor,' the Ed said.

'Could I speak to him?' Anna said.

'This really *is* a nuisance,' the Ed said, 'but if you must, then you must.'

The Ed covered the mouthpiece, shrugged his shoulders, rolled his eyes, then gazed forlornly at Dennis, his voice sounding shaky.

'I must impose upon you, Dennis. I love my wife, but she's neurotic. You're a man of some culture and understanding, and I know I can trust you. Just listen to her, Dennis. I'm sure your silence will be eloquent. She just needs the reassurance of a stranger, and I'm sure you can help there. Will you do it for *me*, Dennis?'

Dennis replied with eloquent silence. The Ed handed him the phone. Dennis gazed across the room, saw Mzzz Cooch and lovely Lydia, both bathed in the blinding glare of the spot lights, their tongues making sweet slurping sounds. Les Hamilton was taking pictures. His little pot belly trembled. Stan was squeezing Annie Bedward's ripe rump and obviously telling a filthy joke. Then Dennis saw Rosie Teasedale. The light beautifully illuminated her silvery-grey hair, seeming to form a halo above her. Dennis sighed and felt a purifying love that swept his past life aside.

'Mrs Prince?' Dennis said.

'God, I miss you,' Anna said. 'I've just packed the kids off to school and now I'm feeling all horny. I've just had a banana sandwich. I almost used the damned banana. I'm sure it would be better than that bastard, my so-called husband, but it wouldn't make up for your rich fruit. God, I miss you. I *need* you!'

'I understand,' Dennis said.

'I *know* you do,' Anna said. 'It's just that you're there and I'm here and the poor bed is empty. Just leave that bastard, Dennis. He just *invents* those damned deadlines. He just wants an excuse to stay away from home and use you all as his slaves. Try to sneak away, Dennis.'

'I understand,' Dennis said.

'I really miss you, Dennis.'

'I understand,' Dennis said.

'I keep thinking it's still Saturday night. I still feel you inside me.'

'I understand,' Dennis said.

'I want you inside me. I want you all around me. I want you over me and under me and beside me. I want you to eat me.'

'I understand,' Dennis said.

'And you'll try to sneak away?'

'I understand,' Dennis said.

'I know you have to be careful about what you say – but *do* try to get here.'

'I understand, Mrs Prince.'

Anna blew Dennis a noisy kiss and then reluctantly hung up. Dennis put the phone back in its cradle and then looked at the Ed. The Ed nodded, near to tears, moved by Dennis' understanding, then he sniffed and shook his head in a judicious manner, too proud to utter clichés.

'You're a *man*,' he said to Dennis.

'It was nothing,' Dennis said.

'No, Dennis, it was much more than that... Only a *real* man could have dealt with it that way.'

'Really, Ed, it was nothing.'

'The way you talked to her, Dennis... such *eloquence*, such... *understanding*... only a *real* man could display such understanding... God, I feel so *ashamed*!'

Choking up, he turned away, deeply moved by his own clichés, and saw the mysterious teetotal bisexual editor hissing into the other phone. The Ed wondered what he was doing, shuddered with dread at the possibilities, then turned, in a desperate search for comfort, to look for Mzzz Cooch. Mzzz Cooch was a real *man*. She made the Ed feel like a *whore*. And right now she was affirming her manhood by assaulting sweet Lydia. Lydia was pressed against the work bench. Her eyes reflected the spot lights. She was bent back beneath the imposing presence of Mzzz Cooch, and Mzzz Cooch was sucking her nipples and tongue as Les clicked off the camera. The Ed knew that this was punishment. He took his punishment like a whore. Then Rosie Teasedale cracked the whip for Mzzz Cooch when she walked up and giggled.

'Where's the Double Dong?' she said.

'I *beg* your pardon?' the Ed said.

'Mzzz Cooch wants to experiment with the Double Dong because she thinks it might help.'

'*Help*?' the Ed said.

'Women's freedom,' Rosie said. 'For myself, I prefer the real thing, but Mzzz Cooch is progressive.'

Rosie giggled and turned away, stumbling into Annie Bedward, who, with tears running down her cheeks, was also giggling hysterically. This naturally appalled the Ed, filled his soul with grief and shame, but he bowed down like a whore, his satisfaction in submission, then found the Double Dong on a desk and picked it up and walked to Mzzz Cooch.

'There he goes,' Harvey said

'It's all in a day's work,' Dennis said.

'A simple kiss can lead to wondrous things,' Harvey said, 'as this excellent revamped article demonstrates.'

'Do you think it scans well?'

'A few lessons there, Dennis. We can anticipate a deluge of letters from our hard-wanking readers.'

'No need for crudeness, Harvey.'

'A slip of the tongue there, Dennis. A pity about the Ed's marriage, Dennis. He has real problems there.'

'Heartbreaking,' Dennis said.

'And yet he trusts you greatly, Dennis. That's something I think I understand. I mean, you don't fuck around.'

'Too traumatising,' Dennis said.

'That's an intelligent observation. That bitch Laura has obviously fucked around and now I feel traumatised.'

'A fine woman there, Harvey.'

'You're understanding. I'm not. That bitch is going to drive me to other women if she isn't too careful.'

'That *would* be sad, Harvey.'

'I was a good husband, Dennis. I worked so hard I rarely got home – and that's how the bitch thanked me.'

'She's just confused,' Dennis said.

'Someone fucked her brains out.'

'That's a really good woman there, Harvey, and I think you should fight for her.'

'Where's Annie?' said Harvey.

They both stared across the desk and saw Les Hamilton hard at work, his little pot belly trembling, his arse bobbing back and forth, as he weaved left and right around the two subjects now stretched across the work bench. Annie Bedward was over there, giggling hysterically with Rosie Teasedale, each clinging to the other while staring down at the pair on the work bench. Lovely Lydia was highly active, obviously working under pressure, now flat on her back, her arms and legs around Mzzz Cooch, the latter creature trying to work her denims off with one hand, the other holding up the Double Dong, which was wobbling excitedly.

'*You bitches*!' someone screamed.

'Who was *that*?' Harvey said.

'I think it was the mysterious teetotal bisexual editor,' Dennis said, 'because he's looking rather agitated again.'

'Ah,' Harvey said.

'The telephone's ringing,' Dennis said. 'It's there on the desk by your hand, and it could be important.'

Harvey picked up the phone, held it closely to his ear, listened and then rolled his eyes and passed it to Dennis.

'Who is it?' Dennis said.

'I don't know,' Harvey said. 'The voice is unfamiliar and

the stupid bitch wouldn't give her name.'

'Hello?' Dennis said.

'I'm having breakfast,' Laura said. 'That bastard Harvey didn't come home all night – and you didn't come either.'

'I know, dear. I'm sorry.'

'Are you?'

'I am. But we really have a serious deadline and we've worked through the night.'

'You don't have to defend that bastard.'

'Wouldn't dream of it,' Dennis said.

'That bastard's spent the night with some whore and now, of course, you're trying to protect him.'

'Untrue,' Dennis said.

'That's why I love you,' Laura said. 'You're so much better than him. No matter what he does, you defend him because you don't want me hurt. I mean, I think that's really sweet. You don't want me to know the truth. Just because you love *me*, you defend *him*, and I think it's just wonderful.'

'It's nothing,' Dennis said.

'So? Was he with some whore?'

'I haven't really seen him all that much, but he could have been sleeping.'

'With *whom*?' Laura said.

'Ha, ha,' Dennis said.

'God, he's such a *whore*,' Laura said. 'And now I'm all on my own.'

'I'm sorry,' Dennis said.

'Can't you sneak away, darling? Leave that bastard and all those other degenerates and then come around here.'

'I'll try,' Dennis said.

'When?' Laura said.

'I can't really say at the moment, but I'll work something out.'

'Bring some Vaseline,' Laura said.

Dennis heard the line go dead and so he passed the phone to

225

Harvey who dropped it carelessly onto to its cradle, a wicked grin on his chops.

'Another whore?' Harvey said.

'Just a friend,' Dennis said.

'And *who* could have been sleeping?' Harvey said.

'The Artful Ed,' Dennis said.

'Ah! One of *his* whores!'

'She just wanted to leave a message.'

'The Artful Ed sure gets around... and he leaves them all panting.'

'She sounded nice,' Dennis said.

'All whores do,' Harvey said.

'That's really rather cynical of you, Harvey. I think you're upset.'

'About Laura?'

'I think so.'

'I'd certainly like to get the bastard who fucked her.'

'Vengeance is mine, saith the Lord... *Do* forgive and forget.'

'She's going to drive me to other women.'

'That *would* be sad, Harvey. A fine woman there – a bit confused, but basically loving – so I think you should put up a fight and bring her back to the fold.'

'Where's Annie?' said Harvey.

They both looked across the room to see Annie Bedward visibly shaking with the giggles, holding on to Rosie Teasedale who was also giggling, the pair of them staring down at the work bench, which was now rocking dangerously. Good old Stan was aware of this, steadying the bench with one hand, his other hand holding the Double Dong between Mzzz Cooch and Lydia. Both ladies were sitting upright, embracing each other, legs entwined, and Stan was trying to place the Double Dong between them, where it rightfully belonged. The Ed was looking on, trembling, clearly in pain but strangely happy, while Les Hamilton danced frantically around them, his camera clicking methodically.

'They're hard at it,' Harvey said.

'A productive session,' Dennis said.

'That Double Dong's a bit difficult to handle. I mean, it wobbles too much.'

'You think Stan's hand is shaking?'

'Not good old Stan, Dennis. A man of great fortitude and skill, nerves of steel, which is why he's our esteemed Picture Editor.'

'How's the article coming along?'

'It makes a good read, Dennis. We've stuck this thing together pretty well, which is why we're the editors.'

'It's a drain to be creative.'

'Really hard work with the Sellotape.'

'Creativity is a gift from the gods and drives our wives up the walls.'

'A good point there, Dennis.'

'I ask myself: Is it worth it?'

'We're just victims of our talent,' Harvey said, 'and so our wives fuck around.'

'They don't understand, Harvey.'

'A worthy observation, Dennis.'

'I believe my mother understood me, Harvey, but that's now in the past.'

'God bless our mothers, Dennis.'

'She had silvery-grey hair, my mother.'

'They lose all their lustre in the end, but we have to respect them.'

'Mzzz Teasedale has silvery-grey hair.'

'I think I noticed it, Dennis.'

'The spot lights illuminate her silvery-grey hair in a most magical manner.'

'A possibility there, Dennis.'

'I think my mother would have liked her.'

'Annie Bedward reminds me of my sister, but I try to forget that.'

'She's really sweet,' Dennis said.

'A real angel,' Harvey said.

'She always looks so innocent,' Dennis said. 'And I find that appealing.'

'We all like them young, Dennis.'

'I really think that's rather crude.'

'What I want is to put my throbbing meat into Annie's hot sandwich.'

'Here comes Clive,' Dennis said.

Clive Grant was looking spruce, his hair combed, his suit immaculate, his tie knotted on his shirt, his eyes bloodshot and his chin dark with stubble, his face haggard and pale.

'Where have *you* been?' Harvey said.

'In the bog,' Clive Grant said.

'You've got blisters on your fingers,' Harvey said, 'and that can't be a bad thing.'

'Diarrhoea,' Clive said.

'Say no more,' Dennis said.

'It's a perfectly normal condition,' Clive said, 'when you're falling to pieces.'

'Ask the Ed for compensation.'

'A good suggestion there, Harvey. I'll ask him and I'm sure he'll reply by farting straight in my face.'

'He always *was* expressive.'

'We've all smelt his artist's soul.'

'You're both being rather crass,' Dennis said. 'And we *do* have our work cut out.'

'Our work's finished,' Harvey said. 'This article's a masterpiece. Les Hamilton is just finishing off his pix, and that just leaves old Clive here.'

'*Me*?' Clive said.

'Yes, you,' Harvey said. 'Les and Stan will fill a page, Dennis and I will fill *four* pages, and that only leaves one page for a fucking ad. So let's see some action, Clive.'

'I dunno,' Clive said vaguely.

'*What* don't you know, Clive?'

'Well, we charge a thousand quid per page, Dennis... I don't like to give *that* away.'

'We *have* to give it away, Clive. We can't leave a blank space. We have to fill it up with something classy, so don't piss around.'

'Nobody classy would want it, Harvey.'

'Benson and Hedges?'

'No way.'

'We could advertise some of my products,' Harvey said.

'That's too sordid,' said Dennis.

They all looked across the room, trying to think through their dilemma, and instead became engrossed with the activities of Mzzz Cooch and Lydia. They had worked through their dilemma, were now closely embraced, joined together in a frenzy of creativity by the wonderful Double Dong. The Ed was bowing his head in sorrow, Les was still taking photographs, and Mzzzes Bedward and Teasedale were giggling together while Stan steadied the work bench. Mzzz Cooch and Lydia were still upright, breast to breast, mouth to mouth, their arms and legs wonderfully intertwined, their bums rocking and rolling.

'Some kiss,' Harvey said.

'A *subscription* ad,' Clive said. 'We'll have to make up a new subscription ad and slap it down on that page.'

'A *full page* subscription ad?'

'It's better than giving it away, Dennis... And we can do it pretty simply with a photo of those two harlots humping.'

'You mean Mzzz Cooch and Lydia?'

'You've got eyes in your head, Dennis.'

'Mzzz Cooch may not approve of that, Clive. She may, indeed, be quite angry.'

'We won't tell her,' Clive said.

'She *reads* the magazines,' Dennis said.

'We'll slice off their heads and just focus on those Double-Donged torsos.'

'Rather crude,' Dennis said.

'That's what we want,' Harvey said. 'A colourful close-up of two crotches, just a hint of the Double Dong joining them together, and printed on the length of Double Dong still in sight, "It's S*uave* to be a regular subscriber; please see attached coupon".'

'That's actually quite good, Harvey.'

'I thought you'd like it, Dennis.'

'And no typing; we just need Letraset.'

'You've got the drift, Dennis.'

'Agreed, Clive?'

'Agreed.'

'I do all your work, Clive.'

'I appreciate your contribution, Harvey, but may live to regret it.'

There was, at that moment, a godalmighty crash that made the lads turn their weary, bloodshot eyes and stare across the bright studio. The work bench had collapsed, giving in under pressure, and now Mzzz Cooch and Lydia were on the floor, but still rocking and rolling. Good old Stan was unperturbed, casually lighting up a ciggie, turning away as Mzzz Cooch and Lydia bounced their bellies together, then taking little Les by the shoulder and pointing down at his camera. Les nodded his head, obviously satisfied with what he had, and then, as Mzzz Cooch groaned and Lydia yelped and Mzzz Cooch shrieked, he and Stan approached the motionless Ed to discuss some more business. The Ed simply nodded, looking down at Mzzz Cooch and Lydia, twitching slightly each time he heard another loud yelp or scream, taking his punishment as Annie Bedward and Rosie Teasedale giggled hysterically, both fixated by the sight of their two sisters on the floor, lovely Lydia still naked, Mzzz Cooch naked from the waist down, both bouncing on their bums, legs and arms intertwined, their groins thrusting in and out and meeting along the Double Dong which was, at least according to Mzzz Cooch, the Female Revolution's new weapon.

'Dennis!' the Ed shouted.

'Yes, Ed?' Dennis said.

'What was that, Dennis? I can't hear you. You're too far away, Dennis.'

'I thought you wanted me, Ed.'

'I want to speak to you, Dennis. There's far too much noise over here, so I'm coming to see you.'

The Ed crossed the studio, followed closely by Stan and Les, the latter holding his camera in one hand, the former drinking more brandy. They all stopped at the desk, good old Stan grinning lewdly, the Ed and Les Hamilton both solemn, despite the shrieking and giggling behind them.

'What's the situation, Dennis?'

'We've just finished the article, Ed.'

'And the ad?'

'No problem,' Clive Grant said. 'My department is organised.'

'And what's the time, Dennis?'

'Just going on ten.'

'You *do* mean in the morning?'

'Yes, Ed, the morning.'

'I've been a bit confused about that, Dennis, what with all of these phone calls.'

'It's morning. Local time.'

'He means London,' Harvey clarified.

'That means the other staff should have arrived.'

'With a bit of luck,' Harvey said.

'I think we've licked it, Dennis.'

'Something definitely emerging, Ed.'

'We have the film and the feature and the ad, so that's a fairly good start.'

'We have to get the copy typeset.'

'The printers can do that, Dennis.'

'What about the photos?' good old Stan said. 'They're still not developed.'

231

'A good question, Stan.'

'Thanks, Ed,' good old Stan said.

'We can send the film around to that laboratory in Holborn and have the transparencies back by this afternoon.'

'What said that?' the Ed said.

'Les Hamilton,' good old Stan said.

'One more word, Les, and I'll tear out your tongue. I'm warning you. Don't tempt me.'

'Then, of course,' Dennis said, 'while we're waiting for the transparencies, Les can get on with the layout design and the simple subscription ad.'

'Dennis, that's *brilliant*.'

'Not at all, Ed. As for the film, we can send it to a laboratory in Holborn and they'll have the trannies back by this afternoon.'

'You've done it again, Dennis. You've done the *Art Department's job*. Small wonder, every time Les opens his mouth, I feel like pulling his tongue out.'

'Sorry,' Les mumbled.

'Shut your mouth, Les, I'm warning you. Okay, Stan, ring down for the messenger and get that film to Holborn.'

'The messenger's disappeared, Ed.'

'I *beg* your pardon? *What* was that?'

'He disappeared Thursday,' Stan said, 'and has not called in since.'

'Jesus Christ!' the Ed said.

'That's it,' good old Stan said. 'We're really fucked now, I can tell you. There's no way out of *this* one.'

'I'll call a courier service,' Les said.

'*What* was that, you stupid cunt?'

'I'll call a courier service, Ed,' Dennis said, 'and get a motorbike messenger around here.'

'How can I thank you, Dennis?'

'Don't mention it, Ed. It's nothing.'

'So that only leaves the layout to be done.'

'I'm sure Les can do that, Ed.'

'Les, can you do it?'

'Yes, Ed, I think so.'

'Shut your fucking mouth, Les, I'm warning you. Now just listen to Dennis.'

'Yes, Dennis?' Les said.

'Well, I was just thinking, Les. Perhaps, while we're waiting for the trannies to come back, you could be getting on with the layout.'

'Right, Dennis,' Les said.

'Trust Dennis,' the Ed said. 'You all stand there shitless with panic while Dennis does *all* the work.'

'I'm seated,' Harvey said.

'So am I,' Clive said.

'Okay, Les,' the Ed said, 'get going. Stop pulling your cock.'

'He doesn't have one,' good old Stan said.

'*What* was that?' the Ed said.

'*You bitches*!' the mysterious teetotal bisexual editor screamed dementedly. 'I'm trying to concentrate and the phone's ringing and you bitches won't answer it!'

'Jesus Christ,' the Ed said.

'He meant *us*,' good old Stan said.

'I don't want that maniac going wild,' the Ed said, 'so for God's sake, someone pick up that telephone.'

Les Hamilton disappeared, eager to design his new layout, while Dennis, picking up the ringing phone, heard pounding rock music.

'Artful Ed?' Dennis said.

'I'm calling in like I promised, Dennis.'

'Where *is* he?' the Ed said.

'Where *are* you?' Dennis said.

'I'm in Elaine's,' the Artful Ed said. 'It's a real groovy place, pretty dark, fairly exclusive, and I'm interviewing Norman Mailer and Andy Warhol and Britt Ekland and some humourless little drip who says he can't stand his fame and keeps clutching his psychiatrist's hand and says he's called Moody Allen. You ever heard of him, Dennis?'

'I don't think so,' Dennis said.

'He's in the movies,' the Artful Ed said. 'By the looks of him I'd say he's a prop, but then he *could* be a phoney.'

'Where *is* he?' the Ed repeated.

'In Elaine's in New York,' Dennis said.

'Jesus Christ,' the Ed said. 'He's *supposed* to be at the fucking airport... And *Elaine's*... that's a real bed of snakes. All those bastards have *money*.'

'What are you doing there?' Dennis said.

'I just told you,' the Artful Ed said. 'And don't think I'm enjoying myself, Dennis. This is *your* job I'm doing.'

'You mean the interviews?'

'Correct.'

'We didn't *ask* you to do interviews. We asked you to talk to Herr Mayer about this new, rival magazine.'

'A difficult one there, Dennis. I mean, that party was really something. There were homos and lesbians and bisexuals and paederasts and Alsatian dogs and drug addicts and assorted models and really sexy whores and a few scattered perverts. It wasn't an orgy, Dennis – I wouldn't say it was *that* – but it certainly was a *noisy* affair and that penthouse was packed. Herr Mayer was there, of course. He was attending to his guests. He had jackboots and a great fucking whip, and they really enjoyed it. You understand, Dennis? It was not the right *ambiance*. What I mean is, there are times to speak out, but there are times to be silent. So I called the cops, Dennis. I think you would have done the same. Then, when I heard the sirens wailing, I got Herr Mayer out of there. I brought him straight here to Elaine's. It's a place conducive to business. We had a couple of brandies, popped a few coloured pills, and I'm sure, Dennis, that before very long he'll be sitting up straight again.'

'I'm not sure I understand.'

234

'The interviews were incidental. I mean, I have integrity, Dennis. I don't like to waste time, and so, while I was waiting for Herr Mayer to recover, I thought I'd take advantage of Elaine's by getting some hot interviews. I don't want any thanks, Dennis.'

'Thanks,' Dennis said.

'Not at all,' the Artful Ed said.

'And do you think Herr Mayer knows about our rival?'

'I'm convinced of it, Dennis.'

'When will he be able to talk?'

'His eyes are glazed, but definitely open. I should say, Dennis, that right this very minute I could get a few answers.'

'Go ask him,' Dennis said.

'A difficult one there, Dennis. Thing is, I've only an hour to catch my plane and that isn't much time. So I'm going to take him with me, Dennis. I'm going to grill him in the cab. Then, when the bastard gives me what I want, I'll throw him out on the freeway. That way I can catch my plane. I'll ring you direct from Heathrow. And I'm sure, Dennis, that I'll then have the information that will solve all our problems.'

'*It's already ten in the morning*!' the Ed screamed.

'Don't worry, Dennis, I heard that. Tell the Ed it's only four in the morning in swinging New York.'

'It's only four in the morning,' Dennis said.

'I'm going crazy,' the Ed said.

'I'll hit Heathrow at four,' the Artful Ed said, 'and be back there by five.'

'I won't confuse him with that,' Dennis said.

'With *what*?' the Ed said.

'He'll land at Heathrow at four,' Dennis said, 'and be back here by five.'

'This afternoon,' the Ed said.

'Yes,' Dennis said.

'Great,' the Ed said, 'that's fantastic. We'll have our layout by then.'

'The *layout*?' the Artful Ed said.

'That's right,' Dennis said. 'We'll have everything fixed up by the time you get here, and then you can check it.'

'Problem solved?' the Artful Ed said.

'That's right. Problem solved.'

'Fuck,' the Artful Ed said. 'I mean, Jesus, I didn't expect that.'

'We worked really hard, Artful Ed.'

'No argument there, Dennis.'

'Now we only need you, all the dirt on Herr Mayer, the name of that rival publisher and Frank Harrison and everything's solved.'

'Great,' the Artful Ed said.

'We're still praying,' Dennis said.

'Don't worry about it, Dennis. The race isn't lost yet. I'll catch that plane at five, I'll ring you direct from Heathrow, and meanwhile, keep your fucking head down and avoid all the flak.'

'I'll do that,' Dennis said.

The Artful Ed hung up and Dennis put the phone down and then stared with admirable calm at his comrades.

'Well?' the Ed said.

'He's coming back,' Dennis said.

'And...?'

'I believe he'll have the information we so desperately need.'

Great sighs of relief, the Ed choking back a sob, Clive standing up and patting the Ed's right shoulder and nodding most solemnly. An emotional moment, certainly, the mood grave with quiet pride, only broken by the giggling of the girls looking down at the floor. All the lads were thus distracted, raising eyes or turning heads, gazing across the brightly-lit studio at Mzzz Cooch and Lydia. A lot of noise over there. The naked Lydia was on her belly. She was trying to crawl away from Mzzz Cooch, who was waving the Double Dong. Mzzz Cooch was half undressed, still imposing from the waist down, her clothes strewn all around her, that impressive arse bobbing in the air as she waved her new weapon.

'I'm exhausted!' Lydia sobbed.

'God bless COCK!' Mzzz Cooch bawled.

'Where are my clothes?' Lydia sobbed.

'We're all sisters!' Mzzz Cooch bawled.

Dennis demurely dropped his gaze, his innermost thoughts hidden, and, in that moment of crystal clarity, knew that madness made sense. The white telephone was ringing, a shrill, insistent sound, and the mysterious teetotal bisexual editor screamed '*Bitch*!' at everyone. Dennis smiled with understanding, feeling compassion for his brothers, not forgetting his sisters and all mothers as he picked up the telephone. He heard the voice of his wife, steady Kathy, now hysterical, accusing him of negligence and cruelty and other, alas imagined, crimes. Dennis murmured understandingly, saying nothing too coherent, feeling stoned and spaced out and exhausted and in need of a good fuck. His wife sobbed that she was leaving, that no clever talk would stop her, and, since Dennis offered no clever talk, she slammed the phone down for good. Dennis felt tears in his eyes. He wiped them dry and surveyed the room. He saw Rosie Teasedale, her hair silvery-grey and sexy, and then, as her knockers bounced towards him, he knew that his time had come.

'All our problems are over,' Dennis said.

'No, they're not,' Lavinia said.

8

'Pardon?' Dennis said.

'It was Lavinia,' Harvey said. 'I think we left the intercom open and she heard all we said.'

'I did,' Lavinia said.

'Jesus Christ,' the Ed said.

'I don't think your problems are over. Mr Pearson just called me.'

'*Who*?' the Ed said.

'Mr Pearson… at the printers. He just called and said he wanted to speak to Dennis – and that it really was urgent.'

'Me?' Dennis said.

'He didn't want the Ed, Dennis. He said that yesterday the Ed had been abusive and that he thought the Ed was probably mad.'

'That cunt,' the Ed said.

'This sounds bad,' good old Stan said.

'Did he say what he wanted?' Dennis said. 'Did he give you a clue?'

'No,' Lavinia said. 'I mean, I asked him, but he wouldn't tell me. I *told* him I represented the Big P, but he still wanted you.'

'And how *is* the Big P, dear?'

'I don't know,' Lavinia said. 'He's been in there with that masked man all night and won't take any messages. A lot of noise there, Dennis. Groans and shrieks. I think it's disgusting.'

'So he still doesn't know about our crisis?'

'I'm still trying to make contact.'

'Well, if you *do*, dear, please use your discretion – at least until five this evening.'

'That's your deadline,' Lavinia said.

'*You filthy blackmailing whore*!' the Ed shrieked.

'Please forgive the Ed, Lavinia,' Dennis said. 'I believe he's under some pressure.'

'You'll keep your job, Dennis.'

'That's most kind of you, Lavinia. But I'm hoping, if we fix this up by five, you can temper your justice.'

'It's for the good of the mags, Dennis.'

'*You filthy blackmailing whore*!' the Ed shrieked again.

'No matter what,' Lavinia said primly, 'that bastard is going.'

'*I'm your boss*!' the Ed shrieked.

'Times are changing,' Lavinia said. 'The Big P and I won't tolerate incompetent shitheads – as you'll find out when eventually I talk to him.'

'I really think – ' Dennis began.

'*I want the Big P*!' the Ed shrieked. 'I'll get him on the phone or intercom – and failing that, I'll go down there.'

'I really think – ' Dennis began again.

'You're wasting your time,' Lavinia said. 'The Big P is not answering his phone or intercom – and his office door is definitely locked.'

'*You filthy back-stabbing bitch*!' the Ed shrieked.

'You'll be the first against the wall.'

'Please forgive the Ed's excitement,' Dennis said to Lavinia, 'and let me call you back later.'

'Okay,' Lavinia said.

Dennis switched off the intercom, clasped his hands beneath his chin, pursed his lips and studied the guys and gals gathered around him. They were all staring at him, eyes bloodshot, faces pale, the Ed quivering like a reed in a storm, perplexed and outraged. Dennis noticed this with grief, saw Mzzz Teasedale and forgot his grief, drinking deeply of her silvery-grey hair and big boobs and maternal hips, realising, on the instant, that his whole world was changing, that his wife, who had failed him, was now definitely leaving him, and that true happiness could only be found by returning to innocence. Yes, he looked at Rosie's silvery-grey hair, at her wide, child-bearing hips, and he knew, with the conviction of the saint, that a good fuck would heal him.

'That filthy whore!' the Ed bellowed.

'Come, come,' Dennis said.

'You sided with her, Dennis. You betrayed me. You told the whore to *forgive* me.'

'That's right,' Harvey said.

'We all heard you,' good old Stan said.

'I am wounded,' the Ed said. '*Deeply* wounded. I will never forget this.'

'Please forget it,' Dennis said. 'I really had no choice, Ed. It's quite clear that Lavinia is hysterical and could prove to be dangerous. That's why I did it, Ed. I simply fed her some sugar. I don't want her doing anything drastic before five this evening.'

'Some excuse,' Harvey said.

'Ho, ho,' good old Stan said.

'And, of course, Ed, if Lavinia blew her top she could really cause havoc.'

'That's true enough,' the Ed said. 'That bitch is clearly out to get me. Give her half a chance and she'd pin my balls up on a dart board. Good thinking there, Dennis. I never doubted you for a second. I always knew you had something up your sleeve and would soon pull it out.'

'Pull it out,' Harvey said.

'Let's all see it,' good old Stan said.

'You don't have to be sarcastic,' Rosie said. 'You pair of shits are just jealous.'

Glancing briefly at Rosie, the Ed then looked beyond her and saw that Mzzz Cooch was back to normal and dressing herself. A real Amazon over there, a female rapist on the loose, and the Ed, having thus defined her virtues, felt his heart fill with longing. Then he saw lovely Lydia. That shameless whore was still naked. The Ed, cast aside for another woman, was stricken with jealousy.

'I want her out of here,' he said.

'*What* was that?' good old Stan said.

'I want that naked woman out of here... There's a time and a place for that.'

'A sweet girl,' Dennis said.

'A disgusting *whore*,' the Ed said. 'She seduced Mzzz Cooch before our very eyes, and I think that's disgraceful.'

'It seemed mutual,' Dennis said.

'She *incited* Mzzz Cooch, Dennis. She's no better than a heartless gigolo taking advantage of innocence.'

'*Whose* innocence?' Harvey said.

'I don't think that's funny, Harvey. I want that shameless hussy out of here and I'll brook no more arguments.'

Lovely Lydia approached the desk, still naked from tip to toe, dark-haired and long-legged and bushy-tailed, her face revealing exhaustion.

'God,' she said, 'that Double Dong!'

'Don't be crude,' the Ed said primly.

'I don't think I really want to be a model. Where on earth are my clothes?'

'A good question,' the Ed said primly.

'They're in my office,' good old Stan said. 'I'm going in there to wait for those trannies. You might as well come in with me.'

'No nonsense!' the Ed said primly.

'It's all work to me, Ed.'

'I'm very glad to hear you say that, Stanley, but please try to *remember* it.'

Good old Stan slapped his hand down on Lydia's bare backside, gave it a friendly squeeze and then led her away.

Meanwhile, Mzzz Cooch arrived, back in her leather boots, zipping up her dishevelled denims, looking *down* on the tall Ed with contempt, her lips curved with disdain.

'Who needs *men*?' she sneered.

'Not me,' Harvey said.

'Those Double Dongs are great,' Mzzz Cooch said, 'if you don't feel like talking.'

'That whore Lydia,' the Ed said.

'*What* was that?' Mzzz Cooch said.

'Please let me apologise, Mzzz Cooch, for her appalling behaviour.'

'You dried-out turd,' Mzzz Cooch sneered.

'Absolutely,' the Ed said.

'Once the Double Dog finds acceptance,' Mzzz Cooch said, 'pricks like you will be obsolete.'

'I deserve it,' the Ed said.

'Stop crawling,' Mzzz Cooch said. 'One more word and I'll have you on the floor with my boot on your balls.'

'Really?' the Ed said.

'You look hopeful, you slug.'

'You have seen what a shameless whore I am. I *deserve* to be punished.'

'I'm really tired,' Mzzz Cooch confessed.

'Aren't we all?' Harvey said.

'Let me give you another glad-hand,' Annie Bedward said. 'That should waken you up.'

That got a laugh out of Rosie, made her grab hold of Annie, then the pair of them giggled together, their joint gaze fixed on Harvey. A pretty pair they made, angelic waifs, rather *cute*, their eyes smouldering with sin and invitation and sly, wicked challenge. Dennis chose to ignore them, now in love, not quite himself, understanding that his marriage had ended and that a new day was dawning. This was all to the good, of course. Soon his fears would be laid to rest. He looked at Rosie's silvery-grey hair, at her *motherly* hips and breasts, found relief in the knowledge that his wife had been too complex, and then, with his tingling cock stiffening, he glimpsed redemption's holy light.

'What time is it?' the Ed said.

'Just going on eleven.'

'You mean eleven London time, Harvey?'

'That's right. In the morning.'

'What's happening?' Mzzz Cooch said.

'About what?' Harvey said.

'This crisis that has you all shitting bricks. I mean, I'm here to *observe*.'

'Well, you've certainly done that.'

'Is that an inference, you little shit?'

'I merely point out that your next colour supplement should contain a great article.'

'*What* colour supplement?'

'*The Observer*,' Dennis said.

'Ah,' Mzzz Cooch said, getting her head back. 'Of course… *The Observer*.'

'A fine newspaper,' the Ed said.

'Shut your mouth,' Mzzz Cooch said.

'Love is always having to say you're sorry. I apologise, Mzzz Cooch.'

'I could kill him, the prick.'

'Please do,' the Ed begged.

'What's happening?' Mzzz Cooch repeated. 'I want to know. I mean, I'm here to observe.'

'We're on top of it,' Dennis said. 'We're pulling all the strands together. We've managed to pay the printers, we have a new feature and photos, Les Hamilton is now designing the new layout for those pages, and then, when the transparencies are delivered, we'll send it all to the printers.'

'That sounds pretty efficient –'

'You're too kind,' the Ed said.

' – but it doesn't mean your printers will actually *run* it. I mean, you still have to ring them.'

'How true,' Dennis said.

While Dennis was picking up the telephone to make this very important call, Harvey was sidling out of his chair and up to Annie Bedward's side and Rosie Teasedale, who, like Annie, had been turned on by the recent events, was slipping quietly into Harvey's chair, which was, of course, beside Dennis.

'I'm hungry,' Mzzz Cooch said.

'Here,' the Ed said, 'have a bite.'

'I'll rather bite that guy who's sleeping there, but a sandwich will do.'

'That's Clive Grant,' the Ed explained.

'He sleeps a lot,' Mzzz Cooch said. 'On the other hand, even in that condition, he's more lively than you.'

'You're so *honest*,' the Ed said.

'I'm fucking starving,' Mzzz Cooch said.

'Please come to my office,' the Ed said, 'and I'll ring for some food.'

'I should think so, you prick.'

'I'm so thoughtless, Mzzz Cooch.'

'You don't have a thought in your brain-dead head, and your dick's even deader.'

'You're *too* kind,' the Ed said.

Mzzz Cooch kneed his nuts, without malice, automatically, and the Ed let out a strange yodelling sound and then jack-knifed athletically. Dennis covered one ear, Harvey merely displayed vague interest. Mzzzes Bedward and Teasedale started giggling, heartless creatures, as the Ed hopped from one foot to the other while clutching his bruised balls.

'Mr Pearson?' Dennis said.

'*What?* Yes, yes, that's me... Pearson.'

'Ah, Mr Pearson. This is Dennis Elliot, the Chief Associate Editor of Saturnalia Publications.'

'Really?'

'Really?'

'Ah, yes, well I...'

'Mr Pearson, I'm calling because I believe you were trying to get in touch with me earlier and told our Production Editor to get me to ring you back.'

'I never spoke to any Production Editor, Mr... ah...'

'Elliot... You *didn't*?'

'No.'

'*No?*'

'No. I am not in the habit of speaking to minions. I believe I conversed with your extremely cordial and efficient Managing Director, Lavinia – '

'Ah, yes, Mr Pearson, of course.'

'A quick promotion, I believe, and well deserved.'

'Quite, Mr Pearson.'

Not wishing the Ed to learn of this recent and well deserved promotion, Dennis carefully raised his gaze and was relieved to note that Mzzz Cooch was, at that very moment, twisting the Ed's left ear and encouraging him to speak into another phone, apparently – at least according to the Ed's tortured words – to a delightful young lady who sounded American but actually came from Putney and who was, but natch, the Artful Ed's assistant and who would, she supposed, be able to rake up some sandwiches and coffee for the hard-working staff in the goddamned studio. Further, as the Ed was thus engaged in his important catering tasks, Harvey was glancing all around him in a manner most furtive and, with the gentle pressure of his creatively folded hands, easing Annie Bedward's head down towards his crotch.

''It was the Double Dong,' Rosie said.

'Pardon?' Dennis said.

'The sight of Lydia's luscious lips around that Double Dong sort of turned Annie on... I mean, she'd never *sucked* cock before.'

'What?' Mr Pearson said, sounding confused.

'Quite,' Dennis said. 'Anyway, Mr Pearson, I would just like to begin this beneficial intercourse by enquiring if you received the cheque we sent to you.'

'Yes, indeed, Mr... ah...'

'Elliot.'

' – we *did* receive the cheque, and I would just like to take this opportunity to thank both you and your new Managing Director for the extremely prompt and efficient attention you gave to this matter and to add, insofar as the cheque was actually three months late, that it is an efficiency that was never displayed by your *former* Managing Director, who was, if I may say so, rather odd and well deserving of dismissal.'

'Thank you, Mr Pearson, for those extremely kind words, and just let me add to them that while I, myself, harbour no animosity towards our former Managing Director, and that while I, during his tenure, gave him my undivided loyalty, I am delighted to note that you have already developed a certain *rapport*, as it were, with our *new* Managing Director and I shall certainly display the same loyalty towards her.'

'That's really rather decent of you, Mr... ah...'

'Elliot.'

'Elliot, and I'm sure both sides will appreciate it. However...'

'Yes, Mr Pearson?'

'... the thing is, that while we have, of course, now received the long-overdue cheque and are therefore not only morally obliged but, indeed, *willing* to go ahead with the printing of the latest issue of *Suave*, we *do*, as I have already discussed with Lavinia – '

'First names *already*, Mr Pearson?'

'First names...? Ha, ha, a good one... Well, thing is, Mr... ah... *Elliot*, that although, as I have just stated, we are not only willing but *delighted* to print the latest issue of *Suave*, there is still, as I have already discussed with Lavinia, ha, ha, the problem of that missing six pages, it being that we *do* have other contractual obligations and cannot hold the presses beyond five o'clock this afternoon, as I am sure you appreciate.'

'Indeed, I do, Mr Pearson, and may I, at this point, simply assure you that the replacement pages are being processed right now and will, beyond any shadow of doubt, be on their way to you by five.'

'They *will*?'

'Most assuredly.'

This news appeared to throw Mr Pearson somewhat off balance, and, as he paused to ponder on some equally new, diabolical strategy, Dennis took the opportunity to rest his eyes on Annie Bedward and Harvey, his attention drawn by the revelation that Harvey was, contrary to popular opinion, replete with adequate foreskin, and that Annie Bedward, helpful girl, was easing it back with her teeth in preparation for the forthcoming oral activities. Harvey was, shamefully, making free with some embarrassing gasps and groans, now bereft of all pride (if indeed he had ever possessed it) and, stretched out on his back, was now rolling his groin in a lewd manner. Taking note of this, then demurely lowering his gaze, Dennis realised that this long dark night of the soul had drained them all of the last of their sanity.

'Christ,' Rosie said.

'I beg your pardon?' Dennis said.

'Harvey's dick looks even bigger than the Double Dong,' Rosie said. 'I mean, Annie's having a real wholesome breakfast while we all sit here starving.'

'*What*?' Mr Pearson said.

'I beg your pardon, Mr Pearson.'

'Well, thing is, Mr… ah… *Elliot*, Lavinia *has* expressed certain doubts regarding your ability to get the replacement layouts together in time, and, of course, should such a possibility still exist, we *would* feel perfectly justified, albeit with regret, in putting *Suave* aside and continuing with our other contractual obligations, it being, as I'm sure you appreciate, that we cannot have our presses at a standstill.'

'A good point there, Mr Pearson, and certainly taken in

good spirit, but please, at this juncture, let me once more assure you that the new photographs have been taken, the transparencies are being developed right now, and the new article is as modest as the *Reader's Digest*.'

'Really?'

'Yes, really.'

Mr Pearson expressed no great deal of delight at this wonderful turn of events, and indeed, to the contrary, seemed a little disturbed by it, so Dennis, giving the sly gentleman time to regroup his scattered forces, lowered his gaze to Harvey and Annie Bedward. Harvey's trousers had been unzipped and pulled down in a careless fashion around his hips, thus revealing to all interested that he had a slight middle-aged spread, premature certainly, but that his lower member was still a healthy adolescent, brimming with energy. Of course it would be true to say that Harvey was not, at that precise moment, either looking or sounding too sophisticated, but Dennis blamed this understandable lapse on Mzzz Bedward's lips, which, usually grinning with disarming, juvenile charm, were now sliding up and down Harvey's member and making gurgling sounds.

'Jesus!' Harvey groaned.

'Gurgle, gurgle,' went Mzzz Bedward.

'Bite it off and spit it out,' Rosie said. 'He'll be better off without it.'

'Don't be crude,' Dennis said.

'*What?*' Mr Pearson said.

'Just a wee joke,' Rosie said, 'about Harvey's wee cock.'

'Cock?' Mr Pearson said.

'Did you say *cock*?' Dennis said. 'Are you suggesting that I'm *lying*, Mr Pearson?'

'Oh, no! Certainly not! Indeed, Mr... ah...'

'Elliot.'

' – having now spoken to you and ascertained the full facts, it *does* seem to me, certainly, that you have done everything humanly possible to get the layouts to us by five. So given this new and, if I may say so, very *heartening* information, I am sure that I can now press upon my board of directors the need for some reciprocal gesture, such as keeping our presses free until the deadline agreed between myself and Lavinia, your new Managing Director.'

'Most kind,' Dennis said.

'We would, of course, expect you to repay our good faith by keeping us informed of the progress of the new layouts and, in the event of any likely delay, pass on the news immediately to let us get on with our other work, which I feel is only fair and which *would* be of great benefit to this Company.'

'I'm sure,' Dennis said.

'And so, Mr... ah... Elliot, I feel that we can leave the matter at that, though *do* let me add, by way of congratulations, as it were, that I *am* delighted to discover that things are shaping up so well and that your problem will soon be resolved.'

'It's extremely decent of you to say that, Mr Pearson, and please let me thank you for your kind comment and, of course, for being so understanding throughout this lamentable crisis, particularly since you must have some more financially rewarding jobs to hand, perhaps even a new magazine or two which may, even as we speak, be waiting for printing space.'

'A *new* magazine?' Mr Pearson said nervously.

'Don't be modest, Mr Pearson, ha, ha. It's certainly no news to us that your printing company is one of the most respected in the industry and, as such, is doubtless fighting off a veritable queue of other hopeful customers.'

'Oh, I see... Well, yes, most kind of you to say so, Mr Elliot, but we are certainly planning no *new* magazine projects at the moment and, of course, even if we *were*, this would in no way affect our attitude towards *your own* magazines, since, apart from our policy of basic human decency in our relationships with our clients, we would, were we to weaken in our resolve and try anything untoward, find ourselves in trouble with your excellent union, NATSOPA, which would, of course, also give *you* some trouble were you to renege on our agreement.'

'Very good, Mr Pearson.'

'Very good, Mr Elliot.'

'We will keep you informed of our progress, Mr Pearson.'

'Excellent, Mr Elliot.'

Dennis dropped the telephone and saw the Ed and Mzzz Cooch, both of whom, having organised the food, were now coming towards him. The Ed was clearly in a certain amount of discomfort, his left hand over his swollen left ear and his right hand at his tender nuts, but he did, nonetheless, look at Mzzz Cooch as if wanting to worship her. Both the Ed and Mzzz Cooch, in advancing upon Dennis' desk, were forced to make a flanking movement around the embattled couple on the floor and did so, apparently, by instinct, without actually noticing them.

'Okay, Dennis,' the Ed said, swollen balls in hand, expression dignified, 'I can assume you were talking to that bastard, Pearson. What did he say?'

'He's agreeable,' Dennis said.

'What?'

'He's agreeable. We still have until five this afternoon to get the layouts to him.'

'You think he's sincere, Dennis?'

'I don't think he has a choice. On the other hand, I get the feeling that he's upset that we're actually managing it.'

'A new magazine, Dennis?'

'I think that's the picture, Ed.'

'Those cunts,' the Ed said. 'The dishonest bastards. They think of nothing but money.'

'And you don't?' Mzzz Cooch said.

'There *are* other things, Mzzz Cooch. Not all of us are motivated by filthy lucre. We have a certain integrity.'

'Shit,' Mzzz Cooch said.

'I deserved that,' the Ed said.

'You're selling out the women of this country just to line your vile pockets.'

'I am guilty,' the Ed confessed.

'I won't whip you,' Mzzz Cooch sneered.

'To deny me is to teach me humility and unburden my soul.'

'Soul?' Mzzz Cooch sneered.

'We all have one, Mzzz Cooch.'

'The only soul you have is in your dick – and it's dragging its chains.'

'Chains?' the Ed said hopefully.

'He's still asleep,' Mzzz Cooch said. 'That handsome prick slumped in the chair… He certainly does like his sleep.'

'That's Clive Grant,' the Ed said.

'I like the look of him,' Mzzz Cooch said.

'He's just another male,' the Ed said.

'A big healthy dumb fuck.'

'Did you tramp on my toes, Mzzz Cooch?'

'I don't think so,' Mzzz Cooch said.

'Harvey's head is on your foot, Ed,' Dennis said, 'but I don't think he knows that.'

This helpful comment caused all eyes to drop to the floor where, no doubt inspired by the revelations of the Double Dong, Annie Bedward was applying mouth-to-cock resuscitation in a brave attempt at keeping Harvey alive. It did appear, however, to the goggle-eyed onlookers, that this hard labour was not to be in vain, since, as they all noted, the poor victim of circumstances was making strangled sounds and rolling his bloodshot eyes in agitation.

'What a mouth!' the Ed said.

'That poor girl,' Mzzz Cooch said. 'She's being exploited by that bastard on the floor and she thinks she's enjoying it.'

The telephone rang and Dennis, picking it up, his head still in the clouds, thought that Annie Bedward looked rather cute with her cheeks bulging out that way.

'Yes?' Dennis said.

'So you're actually at work. She said you were at work, but I didn't believe her, so I just thought I'd check.'

'Who is this, please?'

'This is Kathy's mother, Dennis. And I just want you to know that while I love you like my own, I also think you're a filthy, degenerate animal who needs to be horsewhipped.'

'You're angry,' Dennis said.

'I have two daughters in hysterics. You ruined Kathy years ago and now you've tried to ruin her sister, and both of them are here right this minute, bawling their eyes out.'

'It wasn't my fault,' Dennis said.

'I wouldn't dream of suggesting it.'

'After all, I didn't know she was Kathy's sister. I'd never *met* her before.'

'And whose fault is that?'

'Are you suggesting it was mine?'

'You were married *in secret*, Dennis.'

'So?'

'And you refused to let Kathy even *tell us* she was married.'

'So?'

'You've never even met *me*, Dennis.'

'So?'

'Nor Kathy's *father*, Dennis.'

'So?'

'And that's why you never met her *sister*, Dennis, until the night of that party.'

'So?'

'And you think that's normal, do you?'

'Well, I don't think it's *ab*normal.'

'Really?'

'Really.'

'And why did you do all that, Dennis?'

'I didn't *do* anything… You're complaining about what I *didn't* do.'

'So, why *didn't* you do that, Dennis?'

'What?'

'Let Kathy tell us she was married and then introduce

253

yourself to us.'

'I didn't do that,' Dennis said politely, always respectful of his elders, 'because I felt that our marriage would stand a better chance if it was not subjected to the otherwise unavoidable interference of in-laws, because I did not want her running home to her mother every time we had a minor quibble over nothing of real importance, and, finally, because I did not want her to be exposed to the majority of my working associates, who are, if I may say so, university graduates and intellectuals who would, if unwittingly, likely traumatise Kathy by making her feel intellectually and socially inferior, which of course would be terrible.'

'University graduates, my foot.'

'I beg your pardon? What was that?'

'They're a lot of filthy-minded degenerates, those friends of yours.'

'I don't know what Kathy's been telling you, Mrs Phillips, but I really must repudiate that disgraceful accusation by reiterating that my working associates are, for the most part, gentlemen and scholars, and that the magazines for which I work, contrary to what you might have heard, are published for an upper-class, academic and *very* serious readership.'

'Tits,' someone said.

'Get off the line,' Dennis said.

'Bit tits and a hot, juicy fanny and a cunt like a coal mine.'

'*What* was that, Dennis?'

'I'm not Dennis, you filthy whore. I've got twenty inches, hard and throbbing, and you tried to castrate me.'

'Get off the line,' Dennis said.

'You don't have to be insulting, Dennis.'

'I'll give you my twenty-five throbbing inches and you'll *still* beg for more, you slut.'

'You're a foul-mouthed bugger, Dennis.'

'Please get out of that phone booth.'

'God, you slimy bitch, you're so butch, I'm almost coming

just listening.'

'*Well*, Dennis, I *never* – !'

'And don't think I don't know you, bitch. You were obviously the centre-fold of last month: that fat cow with huge knockers.'

'Get off the line,' Dennis repeated.

'Don't you *dare* mention my breasts!'

'Fat and juicy, you pagan harlot.'

'It's my *daughter* we're supposed to be discussing. I don't see why – '

'*Another* whore, you slut. Out of your syphilitic cunt. Polluting the earth with your foul, diseased twat and dragging down decent, Christian souls.'

'You're mad!'

'Get off the line.'

'You're *insane*, Dennis! And *perverted*!'

'Don't call *me* perverted, you trollop. I've got thirty good inches.'

'Thank God Kathy found out in time.'

'*Another* whore, you insatiable slut. You've been dropping one every nine months. Why not have one by me?'

'Well, I never! I don't believe it!'

'Get off the line,' Dennis said.

'I will... And if you ever ring Kathy again, I'll put the police onto you.'

'Mrs Phillips!'

'Forty inches!'

'Mrs Phillips!'

'Hot and throbbing!'

'Mrs Phillips!'

'In your cunt and up your ass and down your juicy, butch throat, you can't-get-enough-of-it harlot... Hold on, I'm putting in some more money... Fucking vandals! It's jamming again!'

'Vandals?' Dennis said.

'That's right! The little bastards! You'd think the police

255

would do something about it… Get *in* there, you prick!'

'It's not going in?' Dennis said.

'The little bastards! No, it isn't!'

'Well, since it's obvious that you *never* get it in, you shouldn't be disappointed.'

'You filthy whore! You *castrator*!'

The line mercifully went dead and Dennis put the phone down and noticed that the Ed's battered balls had miraculously given birth to a fresh erection. This was, Dennis thought, possibly due to the fact that Annie Bedward was still at work, now kneeling over Harvey, her knees and one hand on the floor for support, her other hand grasping the base of Harvey's cock with the rest of his cock in her mouth, her head rising and falling. The Ed, observing this, was clearly rather excited by it, as was the imposing Mzzz Cooch who, licking her lips and stroking her crotch with one hand, kept flicking her eyes from Harvey and Annie Bedward to the still sleeping Clive. Dennis, observing this, also gained a fresh erection, and Rosie Teasedale, observing it, gave a drawn-out, motherly sigh and started inching the low-cut sweater off her keen breasts… Then the telephone rang.

'Yes?' Dennis said.

'Dennis, this is Kathy. My mother's just told me what you said, and I must say, I'm shocked.'

'I said nothing,' Dennis said.

'She said you used abusive language.'

'I've *never* used abusive language, Kathy. That's just not my style.'

'My mother didn't invent it, Dennis.'

'Nor did I,' Dennis said. 'Unfortunately, we had a crossed line and she heard someone else.'

'One of those filthy friends of yours.'

'A deep breather,' Dennis said.

'That's what I mean,' Kathy said. 'All your friends are the same.'

'It was an outside call, Kathy.'

'Are you sure?'

'Yes, I'm sure.'

'I'll try to explain that to my mother, but right now she's in shock.'

'I'm sorry to hear that, Kathy.'

'My sister's in shock as well.'

'I'm sorry, but I met her at a party, both of us drunk.'

'That hardly excuses it, Dennis.'

'I didn't know what I was doing.'

'You always know what you're doing, Dennis... And you do it a lot.'

'I can't help myself, Kathy.'

'You're just selfish, Dennis.'

'I simply have a very strong sex drive. It doesn't mean anything.'

'I'm supposed to accept that?'

'I don't want to hurt you, Kathy.'

'Just change. At least say you'll try to change... That's all I ask, Dennis.'

'Here,' Rosie said. 'Suck this.'

'*What*? What was that?'

'I really would *like* to change, Kathy, but it's not all that easy.'

'You poor ba-ba,' Rosie said.

'Dennis?'

'Yes, Kathy.'

'Is there someone else there?'

'Mmmm. Nice. *What*?'

'I asked if there was someone else there.'

'Now suck the other one,' Rosie said. 'Make them go really stiff.'

'Dennis?'

'Mmmm... It's really difficult, Kathy. I'm trying, but it isn't all that easy and... Mmmm... I feel guilty.'

257

'I know you do, Dennis – '

'Mmmm.'

' – but it doesn't help. You've got to take control of yourself or our marriage is finished.'

'I thought you'd left me, Kathy.'

'I'm still open to suggestions, Dennis.'

'Suck them really hard,' Rosie said. 'Take them down to your tonsils.'

'Dennis?'

'Mmmm... I really appreciate that, Kathy. Mmmm... I must confess that I've been feeling really bad, but now I feel better.'

'You can always collect me, Dennis.'

'Give me tongue,' Rosie said.

'Dennis?'

'Lick down there between them, ah God, and then bite my tits.'

'Dennis?'

'Mmmm... Kathy?'

'I said you can always collect me. What I mean is, you know where I am, so it's now up to you.'

'Mmmm... Yes, that's good.'

'You mean you will?'

'Mmmm... that's nice.'

'God, Dennis, I'm so relieved to hear you say that. When are you coming?'

'Mmmm... A bit difficult.'

'Let me help you,' Rosie said.

'You're trying to put it off again,' Kathy said. 'Don't tell me it's difficult.'

'There, that's better,' Rosie said.

'Are you coming or not?' Kathy said. 'I won't beg any more.'

'Mmmm... Kathy, Kathy... Mmmm.'

'I'm coming already,' Rosie said.

'You're coming, Dennis? *When* are you coming? *Please*,

Dennis, don't *play* with me!'

'Mmmm, Kathy, mmmm…'

'You're fading in and out, Dennis.'

'I'm coming,' Rosie said. 'Swear to God! I think I'm actually coming!'

'You're *coming*?'

'Mmmm.'

'Oh, God, Dennis, that's wonderful. Don't tell me when. Just surprise me. And bring me some flowers.'

'Mmmm…So sweet… Mmmm.'

'Drop the phone,' Rosie said.

'Mmmm?'

'I want *both* your hands on my tits. Drop the phone… There, that's better.'

'Mmmm, yummy, mmmm.'

'I don't believe it! Oh, I'm coming!'

'Mmmm, mmmm.'

'Suck them, baby, keep sucking, use your tongue, lick and bite, gee whiz, oh my God, suck them, baby, I'm coming, *I'm coming*!'

'Mmmm, mutter.'

'Wow! Christ!'

'Mmmm, mommy.'

'Fuck! Piss!'

'Mmmm.'

'WOW!'

'Mmmm.'

'*Pow*!'

'Mmmm, mommy, mommy mine.'

'*No more, Jesus*, I'M DYING!'

Rosie shrieked and arched back and grabbed Dennis and shook madly, thus distracting Mzzz Cooch and the Ed from the show on the floor. Dennis opened his eyes, shook his head, blinked repeatedly, and was stunned to find Rosie on his lap, her legs embracing his hips. Dennis hardly knew what was happening, prayed to God that he was dreaming, but Rosie's shriek, tailing off to a quavering sigh, brought him back to his senses. He licked his lips and glanced around him, saw the bright lights of the studio, Clive Grant surfacing from deep sleep and muttering something about Jesus, while the Ed and Mzzz Cooch stared at him, amazed, and the mysterious teetotal bisexual editor rose from his chair, raising a clenched fist and his shrill, cutting voice:

'*You bitches!*' the mysterious teetotal bisexual editor screamed. 'I'm trying to work in this place and you're having an orgy! You bitches! You *whores!*'

Rosie gave a final shudder, shook her head and breathed deeply, then, with a beautiful, languorous smile, she dropped her head back on Dennis.

'Dennis!'

'Yes, Ed?'

'I'm shocked. I really am. You were the one person in this building that I could trust, and now look at the state of you.'

'State?' Dennis responded.

'You filthy bastard,' Mzzz Cooch said. 'You've just corrupted that poor innocent virgin, and now she thinks she enjoyed it.'

'I'm so sorry,' Dennis said.

'I should think so,' the Ed said. 'We are here to get a magazine out and you behave like a slut.'

'Oh!' Harvey groaned. 'Ah!'

'I feel hot,' Mzzz Cooch said.

'A momentary lapse,' Dennis said. 'The long night... the... *excitement.*'

'You're a whore,' the Ed said.

'What happened?' Clive Grant said.

'I feel horny,' Mzzz Cooch said. 'But, of course... the long night... the... *excitement.* I suppose that explains it.'

'I'm ashamed of you,' the Ed said.

'I'm so sorry,' Dennis said.

'Oh!' Harvey said. 'Jesus Christ! Hey, watch it... Oh, *Christ*!'

'I feel shattered,' Clive Grant said.

'The long night,' Mzzz Cooch said. 'You poor ba-ba, you've got an erection and you don't even know it.'

'The telephone's ringing, Dennis.'

'I'm sorry, Ed. What was that?'

'We can't let it go to waste,' Mzzz Cooch said. 'You poor ba-ba, let's see it.'

'I said the telephone, Dennis.'

'Sorry, Ed,' Dennis said.

'I'm absolutely shattered,' Clive Grant said. 'Hey! What are you doing?'

'Shit!' Harvey groaned. 'Christ!'

'Please pass the phone, Rosie.'

'Jesus, lover, I hardly have the strength, but okay, here it is.'

'Yes?' Dennis said.

'It's me, Dennis! It's Rick! I'm out here at Heathrow with Frank Harrison, but the Customs have grabbed us!'

'Christ, I'm coming!' Harvey cried.

'What are you *doing*?' Clive Grant said.

'Mzzz Cooch,' the Ed said, 'this is shameful. Please remember your *sex*!'

'What?' Dennis said.

'The Customs have grabbed us!' Rick repeated. 'They've hauled us in for drug smuggling, Dennis, and we could get ten years!'

'I'm coming, Annie!' Harvey cried.

'You've got a good one there, Clive.'

'Mzzz Cooch,' the Ed said, 'this is shameful. That cock is a *man's*!'

'Drug smuggling?' Dennis said.

'That's right, Dennis!' Rick said. 'They hauled us in for drug smuggling, the rotten bastards, and our cases were filled with them!'

'The long night...' Clive Grant said.

'The excitement...' Mzzz Cooch said.

'Shit, Annie, Jesus Christ, oh that mouth, oh my God, *there she blows*!'

'Did you say drug smuggling?'

'That's right, Dennis! You've got it! They opened our cases and they were filled with those coloured tablets, and I swear to you, Dennis, they weren't there when we left Torremolinos.'

'*Coloured* tablets?' Dennis said.

'That's right, Dennis, coloured tablets! And you and I know who put them there. The Artful Ed, Dennis!'

'Mzzz Cooch?' the Ed said.

'I'm waking up,' Clive Grant said.

'It's as nice as the Double Dong,' Mzzz Cooch said, 'and an awful lot *warmer.*'

'Take it, Annie! Take it all!'

'Gurgle, gurgle,' went Annie.

'Stand me up for another woman, Mzzz Cooch, but Clive Grant is *a man*!'

'The Artful Ed, Rick?'

'That's right, Dennis, the Artful Ed! That bastard put those tablets in our suitcases in Malaga Airport and then he rang the Customs in Heathrow!'

'I'm fully awake,' Clive Grant said.

'Don't lick it!' the Ed said.

'Jesus Christ,' Harvey said, 'that was great. I thought my dick was exploding.'

'Slurp, slurp,' went Mzzz Cooch.

'Watch your tongue!' the Ed said.

'Gee,' Rosie said, 'this visual stimulus really gets a girl going.'

'It tastes funny,' Annie Bedward said.

'This is disgraceful,' the Ed said.

'Whoops!' Clive Grant said. 'There it goes... Ah, Christ, wow, that tongue!'

'The Artful Ed?' Dennis said.

'That's right, Dennis,' Rick said. 'That bastard rang British Customs from New York and now they've got us hands down!'

'Do you like it?' Annie Bedward said.

'Not bad,' Harvey said. 'Hey, what the hell's going on here? Wow! Look at this!'

'Take it easy there, Mzzz Cooch.'

'Take it *out*, Clive,' the Ed said. 'I'm a whore, but I have my self-respect and I won't take much more of this.'

'Really?' Clive said.

'Slurp, slurp,' Mzzz Cooch responded.

'Jesus, Dennis,' Rosie said, 'this is far-out. I'm getting real *squirmy*.'

'The Customs?' Dennis said.

'Right, Dennis,' Rick said. 'The Artful Ed fixed it all up to keep us from reaching the office.'

'Why?' Dennis said.

'Because I *want* it,' Rosie said. 'It's poking me right where it matters and I'm feeling all funny.'

'Stop squirming,' Dennis said.

'I just told you,' Rick said. 'That bastard didn't want us to reach the office, and so he set it all up.'

'Take it *out*, Clive!' the Ed said.

'It's *already* out,' Clive said.

'What are you unbuckling your belt for, Mzzz Cooch? Leave your denims alone.'

'Wow!' Annie Bedward said. 'This is really something, Harvey.'

'I'm feeling hot again,' Harvey said. 'Take your knickers off, Annie.'

'Careful, Rosie,' Dennis said.

'I think I've got it,' Rosie said. 'I'll just adjust my clothing a little, and then, you know, we can…'

'Keep your boots on, Mzzz Cooch!'

'Pretty knickers,' Harvey said.

'I'm warning you, Mzzz Cooch… a woman scorned… Don't push your luck too far!'

'The long night…' Clive Grant said.

'The excitement…' Mzzz Cooch said.

'I'm warning you, Clive, don't lie down on the floor! I won't tolerate that!'

'Can you hear me, Dennis?'

'Yes, Rick.'

'We could get ten years, Dennis! And Frank Harrison, who's clearly still catatonic, has been buckled into a strait-jacket.'

'I'll just rub it a bit, Dennis.'

'Thank you, Rosie. Most kind.'

'Don't lie down on Mzzz Cooch, Clive. I'm warning you… You'll never get up again!'

'The long night…' Clive Grant said.

'The *excitement*!' Mzzz Cooch said.

'The telephone's ringing,' the Ed said. 'Someone answer the telephone.'

'Are you still there, Dennis?'

'Yes.'

'He's trying to kill the mags, Dennis! The Artful Ed is trying to kill our mags, and that's why I'm in handcuffs!'

'Come *on*, Harvey! I'm panting!'

'Coming, Annie! Here I come!'

'Put it in me, you brute, put it *in* me, oh Christ, you big bastard!'

'You shameless hussy,' the Ed said.

'You soft pussy,' Clive Grant said.

'It's coming up nicely,' Rosie said. 'I feel really creative.'

'Ah!' Dennis said.

'Oh!' Annie Bedward said.

'Nice and easy does it,' Harvey said. 'That's it: we're in port.'

'Put your legs down, Mzzz Cooch!'

'Put your legs up,' Clive Grant said.

'Handcuffs and strait-jackets!' Rick said. 'And a ten-year jail sentence!'

'That's terrible,' Dennis said.

'Don't you like it?' Rosie said.

'You've got to get us out of here, Dennis! You have to do something!'

'No, Harvey. Not *already*!'

'I can't stop it! Oh, Christ, Annie!'

'The telephone's ringing!' the Ed said. 'Someone answer the telephone!'

'I'm sitting down now,' Rosie said.

'Please be gentle,' Dennis said.

'You have to ring the Customs for me, Dennis, and tell them I'm innocent!'

'Oh, Harvey, you *bastard*!'

'Jesus Christ, God, I'm dying!'

'You *bastard*!'

'Your fault, little Annie... That blow-job... I was right on the edge there.'

'Keep it coming, you brute!'

'Watch your language, Mzzz Cooch!'

'Close your legs, open your legs, close your legs, give it to me, now *shake it*!'

'This is not a burlesque, Clive!'

'Every inch, Dennis! Wow!'

'They're taking the phone away from me, Dennis! Are you there, Dennis? *Answer me!*'

'Have a ciggie, Annie.'

'Thanks, Harvey. I need it.'

'Shake it to me, baby! That's it! Shake it to me, we're getting there.'

'You fucking man! You fucking *man*!'

'Watch your language, Mzzz Cooch... The telephone's ringing. I can *hear* the telephone ringing. *Someone answer the telephone!'*

'Ah!' Mzzz Cooch cried.

'Here it comes!' Clive Grant cried.

'Don't come in Mzzz Cooch, Clive, I'm warning you! *Someone answer the telephone!'*

'AAAAHHH!' Mzzz Cooch cried.

'AAARRRGGGHHH!' Clive Grant cried.

'They're taking the telephone away from me now, Dennis. *You have to come out here!'*

'Put the telephone down, Dennis.'

'As you wish,' Dennis said.

'Ah, God,' Mzzz Cooch said. 'Jesus Christ. I don't think I can breathe.'

'Oh, boy, Mzzz Cooch. Wow.'

'I always thought you were a *real* man,' the Ed said, 'but you're just a cheap *whore*.'

'That's it,' Rosie said.

'My hands are free,' Dennis said.

'Okay,' Rosie said. 'Use your hands. Pick me up and let's go.'

And so Dennis gave in, lost his image, destroyed his myth, let the members of the staff see him in action for the very first time. He hardly knew he was doing it, swept away on wings of love, swimming back to the far distant shore of his original innocence. He stood up, holding Rosie, drawn by wisps of silvery-grey hair, staggered gamely towards a whole new experience and pushed her down on the desk. Already joined, they remained as one, his probing cock in her cunt, Rosie looking up and Dennis looking down and thinking fondly of Mother. He felt her hands on his spine, at his buttocks, between his legs, then her thighs opened wide and closed again to form a shelter around him. Dennis kissed her luscious lips, slid his tongue deep in her mouth, closed his eyes and spiralled down through himself to emerge through his third eye. Here the glistening vaginal walls, the murmuring comforts of the womb, the darkness and the fear that he had left and could never escape. What truth was thus revealed? What illusions were thus destroyed? Dennis floated out of himself and glanced down and saw the bare arse of Rosie. Heave ho, in and out, groin to groin, their bodies rocking. His white bum bobbed up and down under bright lights and was watched with grave interest. Get it over and done with. Fuck her quickly and face the truth. The sacred fluid that was Dennis spurted forth and was nothing unusual. Ah, God, what sweet relief! Christ, what a disappointment! Dennis quivered and heaved, sucked a tongue, licked a nipple, poured his hot breath on belly and navel and neck, quivered again, groaned aloud, heard her cry 'Gee!' and 'Wow!', shuddered with her and then swore (*distinctly* swore) and then looked up, mortified.

'You're *all* fucked,' said Lavinia.

9

The Ed it was who finally picked up the ringing telephone and, intent on shocking his merry lads back to their senses, but lacking a loaded pistol to fire, pressed the button on the cradle and thus amplified Lavinia's voice, which, booming out loud and clear, almost blew their heads off.

'You're *all* fucked,' Lavinia said.

'*What* was that?' the Ed said.

'You're all *fucked*,' Lavinia repeated with some relish. 'I've had a call from the printers.'

The Ed, looking dazed, not himself, still in shock, glared at each of his merry lads in turn as they adjusted their clothing. All the lads seemed pretty smashed, their eyes bloodshot, hair unkempt, flies unzipped and shirt-tails hanging loose, disgusting stains everywhere. Of course, it wasn't their fault. The Ed realised this at once. It was the fault of those immoral female whores who thought of nothing but sex.

'What are you trying to say, Lavinia?'

'I'm trying to say that the mags are finished. Mr Pearson has just called to say he can't possibly print *Suave* or *Gents*.'

'*What*?' the Ed said.

'Are you *deaf*?' Lavinia said.

'I don't think I understand, Lavinia. We've just *spoken* to that cunt.'

'He rang back,' Lavinia said. 'He didn't want to speak to Dennis. He said that Dennis had made suggestions about rival magazines and offended him greatly.'

'Dennis?'

'Sorry, Ed.'

'Never say you're sorry, Dennis. We mustn't let ourselves be influenced by these women and their feminine wiles.'

'Do you mean me?' Mzzz Cooch said.

'Kindly dress yourself, Mzzz Cooch.'

'I'll dress myself when I'm good and fucking ready. Now answer my question.'

'I'm a *man*,' the Ed said.

'You could have fooled me,' Mzzz Cooch said.

'I'm a man and I won't stand impertinence even from *The Observer*.'

'The *what*?' Mzzz Cooch said.

'Did you hear me?' Lavinia said.

'Yes, Lavinia,' the Ed said, 'I heard you... And you're not making sense. Those bastards *have* to print our magazines. They made a gentleman's agreement. We'll have the layouts and trannies there by five, and that's all there is to it.'

'They won't print it,' Lavinia said.

'The bastards *have* to,' the Ed said.

'They received an unsigned telegram,' Lavinia said, 'and it scared the hell out of them.'

Rosie slid off Dennis' lap to let him adjust his rumpled clothing, carefully tucking his weary member back in and zipping up its warm sleeping bag. Rosie sighed with guiltless pleasure, rolling her eyes, the little whore, but Dennis, now relieved of his itch, could only shiver with shame. You can't go home again (Thomas Wolfe had said that) and now Dennis, having had his mystical fuck, was feeling rather deflated. It was always that way – sex was such a disappointment – and so Dennis sat up straight, composed his face and then thought about suicide.

'A *telegram*?' the Ed said.

'From New York,' Lavinia said. 'It was unsigned. But it gave Mr Pearson the information that wiped us all out.'

'*What* information, Lavinia? Please clarify that point. I cannot think of any information that could possibly help those shits.'

'Well,' Lavinia said with some enthusiasm, 'apparently Mr Pearson was informed, via this unsigned telegram from New York, that a certain Mrs Allbright of Liverpool was about to take legal action against us over a short story, "The Cleft", that we published two months ago in *Gents*. Mrs Allbright is claiming that this fictitious story actually occurred, but not to the heroine in Guatemala, as related in the story, but to her, Mrs Allbright, in Manchester in 1943, and not with a Brazilian who used a cane but with an American GI who used a whip, and her legal case is going to be based not only on the fact that the publication of the story has humiliated her, but on the claim that the copyright of the story rightfully belongs to her and that its use in our publication was therefore unlawful.'

'Good for her,' Mzzz Cooch said.

'Furthermore,' Lavinia continued, obviously power-mad, the bitch, 'the telegram informed Mr Pearson that *our* solicitor had expressed his concern, confidentially, to us, over the photograph on page sixty-six of the *Suave* presently being processed, and wanted it either removed from the film or touched up in a manner that would render it less suggestive than it was – and, of course, as the telegram, addressed directly to Mr Pearson, pointed out, neither of these instructions had been followed through by us and the offending photograph was therefore still in the magazine.'

'Good for him,' Mzzz Cooch said.

'So,' Lavinia continued, sounding more power-mad with every word she spoke, 'Mr Pearson phoned through to me to say that, given the aforementioned information from the unknown source in New York, it was felt by his esteemed Board of Directors that they could not possibly be associated with a magazine that would soon be involved in a scandalous court case and, also, that our suppressing of our own solicitor's concern over the offensive matter was a sign that we could no longer be trusted and showed that we were willing to destroy *their* reputation by sneaking through an obviously disgusting and legally dubious photograph. Due to this, and with all due respect, they are terminating our contract.'

'Good for them,' Mzzz Cooch said.

'*The filthy shits*!' the Ed shrieked.

'*You bitches*!' the mysterious teetotal bisexual editor shrieked. 'I'm trying to do some work over here and you're driving me mad!'

At this point in the proceedings, good old Stan wandered lazily back into the studio with the lovely Lydia trailing behind him. All the lads stared at Lydia, finding her sexy even in clothes, but also aware, of course, that her hair and clothes were messy and that good old Stan had obviously been all over her. As for Stan, he was smoking a cigarette and casually drinking more brandy.

'So,' he said, 'what's happening?'

'We're all washed up,' Harvey said. 'The printers are refusing to print us, and this time they're serious.'

'Really?'

'Yes, really.'

'Right,' good old Stan said. 'That's it, then. We're all due redundancy money and a fat fucking bonus.'

'You're so loyal,' Harvey said.

'*And* unemployment,' Stan said. 'We can live off unemployment for years and make a pile on the side.'

'No tax,' Harvey said.

'You've got it there, Harvey. A little black-economy job here and there and we'll be rich in no time.'

'The Artful Ed,' Annie Bedward said.

'*What* was that?' Dennis said.

'The Artful Ed was in New York,' Annie said. 'And he sends lots of telegrams.'

'Bless that man,' Mzzz Cooch said.

The Ed, now a man, gave Mzzz Cooch a withering look which did not, of course, wither her in the least but made the Ed feel much better.

'Dennis!'

'Yes, Ed?'

'We're not finished yet, Dennis. I have a few cards up my sleeve and I'm ready to deal them.'

'Really?'

'Yes, really. Cards up the sleeve, Dennis. Always keep a few cards up your sleeve and you'll never go wrong.'

'What cards would those be, Ed?'

'Frank Harrison, Dennis. That bastard should be walking through that door any minute now, and when he does, we'll make him swallow the phone and talk to all his connections. A bit of pressure, Dennis. Not *blackmail*, just *pressure*... He knows about the rake-offs that those fucking printers get, and he can drop a few names, mention an item here and there, and, without a shadow of doubt, he'll get those presses in action.'

'Charming!' Mzzz Cooch said.

'I don't think so,' Dennis said.

'What do you mean, you don't think so?' the Ed said, sounding affronted. 'Where's your confidence, Dennis?'

'Thing is, Ed – '

'Yes, Dennis?'

' – there's been a bit of a delay... Rick and Frank are being held by Customs out at Heathrow, charged with drug smuggling.'

'*What?*' the Ed said.

'The evil swine,' Mzzz Cooch said.

'They were caught with hundreds of coloured tablets in their suitcases,' Dennis said, 'after someone rang Customs and tipped them off.'

'*Coloured* tablets, Dennis?'

'Yes, Ed, I'm afraid so.'

'And who rang the Customs officers, Dennis?'

'The Artful Ed,' Dennis said.

The Ed turned a strange colour, not green but pretty close, then raised his bloodshot eyes and stared around him in a vain search for help. His merry lads were subdued, Clive silent, Harvey whistling, good old Stan staring up at the ceiling, Dennis engrossed in the opposite wall.

'Gee,' Rosie Teasedale said.

'Wow,' Annie Bedward said.

'What's going on?' Lydia said. 'You all seem a bit *tired*.'

'The telegram came from New York,' the Ed said.

'That's right, Ed,' Dennis said.

'And the Artful Ed was in New York at the time.'

'I'm afraid that's true, Ed.'

At that precise moment, as the Ed was stroking his trimmed beard and blinking his disbelieving, bloodshot eyes, Les Hamilton, who had been working at the copy scanner, emerged and advanced upon them, holding up the large layout sheets.

'I've finished the layouts, Ed.'

'Shut your mouth, Les, I'm warning you. What the fuck are you doing wasting your time when we've got a real crisis here?'

'Dennis?'

'Yes, Lavinia?'

'I had a call from that hotel. They said the Artful Ed had sent them money to cover the weekend's bill and that the Norwegian paper manufacturers, now recovering from their shock, were on their way back here to see the Ed.'

'So?' the Ed said.

'I refuse to speak to that bastard, Dennis.'

'Well – ' Dennis began.

'*You treacherous bitch*!' the Ed shrieked.

' – I understand your chagrin, Lavinia, but please tell me the rest of this.'

'The paper manufacturers are now downstairs.'

'Yes, Lavinia?' Dennis encouraged her.

'I've just talked to them,' Lavinia said. 'They're neither

paper manufacturers nor Norwegian… They're cops from the Vice Squad.'

'*What?*' the Ed hissed fearfully.

'I beg your pardon, Lavinia?'

'You heard me the first time, Dennis,' Lavinia said. 'The Norwegian thing was a front.'

'What's a *front?*' the Ed whispered.

'It was all a set-up,' Lavinia said. 'They wanted to check this place out. Apparently the Artful Ed told them that the mags were obscene, that you all took illegal drugs, and that the drugs and the sex led to orgies of the most debased kind.'

'*That cunt!*' the Ed shrieked.

'Does he mean *me?*' Mzzz Cooch said.

'He means the Artful Ed, Mzzz Cooch,' Dennis said. 'Please continue, Lavinia.'

'The cops were grateful,' Lavinia said. 'They really appreciated the information. They promised the Artful Ed protection for his personal interests on condition that he got them into our office during one of our orgies.'

'*Parties!*' the Ed shrieked.

'I'm not talking to you,' Lavinia said.

'*They were only innocent parties!*' the Ed shrieked. '*I've never* been *to an orgy!*'

'So?' Dennis said.

'You know the rest,' Lavinia said. 'The Artful Ed said the cops were only Norwegian paper manufacturers, he made the orgy worse by dropping tablets into your drinks, and then he got his whore to rip off the cops and make them even madder.'

'Jesus Christ,' the Ed muttered.

'They want to speak to the Ed, Dennis.'

'What do they *want*, Dennis?' the Ed said. 'I mean, what are they *doing* down there?'

'They want to prosecute,' Lavinia said.

'Good for them,' Mzzz Cooch said.

'They haven't a fucking chance,' the Ed said. 'They've got

nothing on *me*, boys!'

'Yes, they have,' Lavinia said.

'Jesus Christ,' the Ed muttered.

'They're going to hit you with the Customs Consolidation Act of 1876, with the Indecent Advertisements Act of 1889, with the Town Police Clauses Act of 1847, and with the Unsolicited Goods and Services Act of 1971.'

'*What?*' the Ed shrieked.

'About time,' Mzzz Cooch said.

'We're all in this together,' the Ed said. 'I just want you to know that, boys.'

'I've no contract,' Harvey said.

'Nor have I,' good old Stan said.

'In a legal sense, we've never really worked here,' Clive Grant said, 'and I'm sure my wife will back me up on that.'

'*What?*' the Ed shrieked.

'How's the attic?' Dennis said.

'I meant to tell you about that,' Lavinia said. 'I made my boyfriend go up there.'

'The doors are still opening and closing?'

'Yes.'

'And you still get the noises?'

'Yes.'

'And you'd never been up there before?'

'Yes, once. I remembered.'

'Ah!' Dennis said.

'Right,' Lavinia said. 'It was six months ago, at that party, when the Artful Ed got me high.'

'He got *you* high, Lavinia?'

'I'd practically forgotten. I mean, you know the Artful Ed, his coloured tablets... I didn't know where the hell he was taking me or what I was doing.'

'He took you up to the attic, Lavinia?'

'Yes, Dennis, he did.'

'And then?'

'The Artful Ed fucked me and then sent me downstairs again.'

'Ah!' Dennis said.

'Quite,' Lavinia said. 'Then, when he came down, he said the attic was really big and that it could come in handy in the future.'

'Why did he *do* it?' the Ed said. 'That's what *I* want to know, Dennis. The Artful Ed's drowning us in shit and you're yapping with *that* bitch.'

'He's the first to go, Dennis.'

'I understand, Lavinia.'

'I'm just waiting to have my talk with the Big P, and then that bastard walks.'

'*You filthy traitor!*' the Ed shrieked.

'Shut your mouth,' Mzzz Cooch said. 'It's because of the likes of you that COCK was formed, you rotten male chauvinist rapist pig.'

'COCK?' Harvey said.

'With *The Observer*,' good old Stan said.

'So,' Dennis said. 'You sent your boyfriend upstairs...'

'Yes,' Lavinia said. 'He surprised me. He's so brave... I sent him up and he kicked the attic door open and charged in swinging an axe.'

'And?' Dennis said.

'An instant print shop,' Lavinia said. 'They were churning out brochures and various advertising pamphlets for a new and much filthier men's magazine to be published by a company called Artful-Mayer.'

'*What?*' the Ed shrieked.

'Artful stroke Mayer,' Lavinia clarified.

'*That cunt!*' the Ed shrieked. '*The rotten bastard! The ungrateful assassin!*'

'Say no more,' good old Stan said.

'Got to hand it to him,' Harvey said.

'My hero,' Mzzz Cooch said. 'What a *man*... And he

distributes the Double Dong.'

'*The filthy bastard*!' the Ed shrieked.

'Shut your mouth,' Mzzz Cooch said.

'Get out of here, you whore!' the Ed bawled. 'I'd rather fuck a dead rat!'

'*What?*'

'Yes, you heard me!'

'I think, Ed – ' Dennis began.

'Don't worry about this mindless whore, Dennis. Who needs *The Observer?*'

'The *what?*' Mzzz Cooch said.

'*The Observer*,' Dennis said.

'Oh, *that*,' Mzzz Cooch said. 'Another capitalist, male chauvinist, regressive rag. I wouldn't wipe my arse on it.'

'Who *needs* it?' the Ed bawled.

'Not me,' Mzzz Cooch said. 'The one head and two branches of COCK never read trash like that.'

'Cock?' good old Stan said.

'She means COCK,' Dennis said.

'You *work* for that worthless rag!' the Ed bawled. 'What the hell are you talking about?'

'COCK,' Mzzz Cooch confessed.

'Cock?' the Ed said.

'The Cooch Organisation for Cunt Karma... *Praise be to COCK!*'

Mzzz Cooch threw her arms out melodramatically, and the Ed, suddenly realising what she meant, took a nervous step backward, his face drained of colour.

'You don't mean...?'

'*Praise be to COCK!*'

'Mzzz Cooch, *please* understand...'

'*The wrath of COCK is merciful and liberating and will crush all before it!*'

'If I'd only known, Mzzz Cooch...'

'*Down with men! Up their asses!*'

'And of course I always *respected* you, Mzzz Cooch, as I respected my mother.'

'Your mother?' Mzzz Cooch said.

'A fine woman,' the Ed said.

'She was enslaved from the moment you were conceived... *Nine months in hard labour!*'

'I swear to God, I didn't know...'

'You rapist pig! You stole her *life!*'

'Please believe me, Mzzz Cooch...'

'You crawling turd... *The wrath of COCK be upon you!*'

'No, Mzzz Cooch!' the Ed cried.

'Too late!' Mzzz Cooch responded.

'That's it,' Harvey said, 'I'm out of here.'

'Too right,' good old Stan said.

The merry lads started scattering as Mzzz Cooch reached for the phone and the mysterious teetotal bisexual editor screamed '*Bitches!*' at all of them. Dennis sat back, appalled, seeing the Ed's palsied limbs, hearing Mzzz Cooch hissing into the phone, 'This is it, girls! Get over here!' Her instructions made the Ed feel worse, his throat offering a strangled whimper, his eyes clouded over with the shock of betrayal as his merry band disappeared. Then Mzzz Cooch slammed the phone down, turned around, sneered triumphantly, then placed her clenched fists against her hips and looked *down* on the tall Ed.

'We're taking over,' she said.

The Ed crumbled where he stood, growing old in two seconds, seeing his whole life disappearing down the tubes, the good old days gone forever. Dennis observed this scene, entranced, being a novelist and so forth, philosophically detached (and so forth) and writing it up in his head. He did not ignore Rosie Teasedale, now being stared at by Mzzz Cooch, nor Annie Bedward, also being devoured by the ravishing eyes of Mzzz Cooch. This was life in the raw, *real* life, the truth revealed, and as the Ed started whimpering with fear, Dennis came back to sanity.

'You two turds,' Mzzz Cooch sneered.

'I beg your pardon?' Dennis responded.

'Don't give me that baby-blue-eyed innocent look: you'll get yours when my girls arrive.'

'Oh, no!' the Ed wailed.

'Stop snivelling,' Mzzz Cooch said. 'Just bend over and take it like a man and you'll feel better afterwards.'

'Not me!' the Ed begged.

'The wrath of COCK is liberating. Be a man and you will soon be a woman and never have to look back.'

'I don't *want* to!' the Ed cried.

'You disgusting coward,' Mzzz Cooch said. 'You've been raping innocent girls like these for years and soon you'll know what it feels like.'

'I *like* it,' Rosie said.

'So do *I*,' Annie said.

'You see?' Mzzz Cooch said. 'They *both* like it. So why shouldn't you?'

'I always respected you, Mzzz Cooch.'

'You grovelling, ass-licking jelly.'

'Don't hit me!' the Ed cried. 'Please, don't kick me! I never *really* liked punishment!'

'You came good,' Mzzz Cooch said.

'A momentary aberration!'

'You snivelling lump of shit, you crawling slime, I ought to do it *right now!*'

The Ed gasped and staggered backward, kicked a chair and then fell into it, covered his bearded face with his hands and bravely stifled his sobbing. Dennis observed and remained silent, taking in the *whole picture*, as Mzzz Cooch threw a sneer at the quivering Ed and then smiled invitingly at the girls. She stroked Rosie's silvery-grey hair, put a hand on Annie's hip, moved closer and looked them straight in the eye, her voice soft and seductive.

'You poor ba-bas,' she murmured.

'Wha – ?' Rosie began.

'You've both been exploited for years, and you don't even know it.'

'Exploited?' Annie said.

'Yes, dear, exploited... Like this, pet... And here... And like this... That's how they all start it.'

'I *like* it,' Rosie said.

'So do *I*,' Annie said.

'Then the swine cup your titties in their hands... That's right, dears... Like this.'

'It tingles,' Rosie said.

'They're stiff already,' Annie said.

'And you're weaker, dears... infinitely weaker... when they slip your clothes off.'

'Like this?' Rosie said.

'Like this?' Annie said.

'Then your skin starts to tingle all over and you've just got to have it...'

'Oh, dear,' Rosie said.

'I'm feeling hot,' Annie said.

'Then the evil bastards ease you down like this and stretch you out on the floor.'

'Like this?' Rosie said.

'I'm feeling hotter,' Annie said.

'Then they ease themselves between you like this... and slyly start doing this...'

'Mmmm,' Rosie murmured.

'Mmmm, mmmm,' Annie murmured.

'Then their lips – '

'Mmmm.'

' – and tongues – '

'Mmmm.'

' – and fingers – '

'Mmmm.'

'Mmmm.'

' – and before you know it you can't even think straight and – '

'Mmmmmmmm,' Rosie and Anna hummed in chorus.

The noise started far below, a sporadic shrieking and banging, doors slamming and feet pounding up various stairwells as window-glass shattered. The Ed abruptly jerked upright, his eyes again like pinwheels, his ears cocked to the sounds from downstairs, his lean body shivering.

'Jesus Christ,' he said. '*That's them*! Those rapist bitches are on the loose! I saw them on the news on the telly and they made me shit bricks! They wear boots and carry clubs, use studded gloves and thick belts, and they smash down any males who try to stop them, and then rape the poor bastards. We have to get out of here, Dennis. Rape's a terrible thing! And what's worse: they have great fucking gang-bangs, and I couldn't stand that!'

The Ed looked down at the floor, saw Mzzz Cooch and her poor victims, the latter completely naked and Mzzz Cooch half undressed, her muscular arms and legs thrown across them as their bodies collided. Dennis looked down as well, his heart pounding, his cock erect, then realised, as he observed the writhing ladies, that he wanted to join them.

'Let's go!' the Ed hissed.

'Pardon?' Dennis said.

'*Let's go*!' the Ed hissed, a wild gleam in his eyes. 'We can't sit here and let ourselves get ravaged. This is war, Dennis! *War*!'

'What about *them*?' Dennis said.

'They're perfectly happy, the whores. As for that cunt, *Miss* Cooch, she's too engrossed in her lesbian filth and won't notice for at least half an hour that we've actually left... Come on, Dennis! *Let's go*!'

The Ed grabbed Dennis by the arm and pulled him out of the chair and then pushed him, rather roughly, on ahead. Dennis didn't look back (you can't go home again, he thought) and he hurried with the Ed close behind him towards the door of the studio. The noise continued down below, yells and bangs, shrieks and thuds, and then, as they passed the last desk, they were stopped by a loud voice.

'*You bitches*!' the mysterious teetotal bisexual editor screamed. 'I'm doing work for the Artful Ed, you bitches, and that noise is distracting me!'

They opened the door and bolted, letting the door slam behind them, stopping again in the shadows of the hallway and wondering where they should go. To their right was the small room that contained the back issues and that also had contained the bald homosexual literary agent and the mysterious teetotal bisexual editor when they were going at it like two pigs in a trough during the previous Friday's party. Glancing at this room, the Ed shuddered with revulsion, then he stared fearfully down the stairs and heard the noise of battle.

'There's only one way down,' Dennis said.

'Hold my hand, Dennis... *Please*.'

They held hands rather primly and went nervously down the stairs, their souls lacerated by the distant sounds of battle, their feeling of panic increasing.

'Dennis?'

'Yes, Ed?'

'I trust you, Dennis.'

'Thanks, Ed.'

'You're the only bastard in this place I ever trusted, and I want you to know that.'

'Appreciate it,' Dennis said.

'Not at all,' the Ed said. 'I say it now, and I always *did* say it, you're one in a million.'

'I don't deserve this,' Dennis said.

'You deserve it, Dennis. *Really*. You have strength and integrity and courage, and I truly admire that.'

'It's too much,' Dennis said.

'Basic decency,' the Ed said. 'Basic decency and honesty

and *courage* are the only true virtues… *Jesus Christ, what was that?'*

The Ed jumped and grabbed Dennis, held him tight, his eyes popping, shaking and staring down the dusty stairwell at a deep-shadowed hallway. A lot of noise down there, from the administration offices: a male cry, female cheering, the drumming of clubs and collapsing equipment, the ravaging hordes of COCK on the loose and clearly victorious.

'We have to go down there,' Dennis said.

'Must we *really?'* the Ed said.

'They're in the administration area, Ed, and we have to go through it.'

'Really?' the Ed said.

'That's the way out,' Dennis said. 'We have to sneak past those offices and down the stairs before they start coming up here.'

'I'm not frightened,' the Ed said.

'Good,' Dennis said.

'Hold my hand, Dennis. Hold it tight. Please ignore the disgusting sweat.'

'Okay, Ed, let's go.'

Hand in hand, they moved forward, the sounds of cheering in their ears, passing the open-plan offices where Harvey and Dennis had worked, and then, with their hearts in their mouths, sneaking down the dark stairwell. They had to stop on the next floor, one flight above the previous exit, hearing more women down there, all shrieking and jeering, the sounds of clubs smashing glass, frantic scuffling, protestations, a man wailing, 'God preserve me! I'm just the new messenger! I was just told to deliver these photos! *Leave my trousers alone!'* His piteous plea died away, was drowned out by the shrieking women, the Ed and Dennis both shuddering at the latter sound, realising that the exit was blocked. Thus they stared at one another, true brothers, hand in hand, and then sneaked up to the glass doors of the offices and carefully peered in.

W.A. Harbinson

'*Three cheers for COCK!*'
'*Rah! Rah! Rah!*'
'*Watch that bastard! He's running!*'

Clive Grant came into view, bursting out of a crowd of women, his hair dishevelled, his shirt and trousers torn as he rushed towards the kitchen. The fierce women all pursued him, swinging clubs, their hands outstretched, but the unfortunate wretch managed to reach the kitchen before they could grab him. The kitchen door slammed shut, the clubs drumming brutally upon it, and while those holding clubs began to smash the door down, Lavinia emerged from the Big P's sack's office and was roundly applauded. Lavinia moved through the hordes of COCK, smiling victoriously, shaking hands like a politician, and then the door of the Big P's office shot open and all eyes turned towards it.

'*The Big Pee!*' all the women roared.

The Big P was extremely sexy, his/her long blonde hair in a mess, enormous breasts bulging out of a black-leather nipple-bra, his/her long legs in black suspenders and stockings, leather boots freshly polished and shining. Either a woman or a transvestite, he/she was truly voluptuous, and the sisters of COCK embraced him/her gladly, while he or she, black and blue, whip marks red on tanned skin, raised his/her hands to the heavens and let out a joyous cry:

'*It's all over! We're bankrupt!*'

The hordes of COCK roared their approval, but this roar changed in tone when the man in the executioner's mask suddenly lurched from the office. This man was carrying a golf ball, a bull whip and leather thongs, and as he reached out in a creative frenzy to drag the Big P back inside, the hordes of COCK let out a savage, blood curdling roar and fell mightily upon him.

'*Down with men! Up their asses!*'

The Ed and Dennis retreated, heading back up the stairs, only stopping when they reached the next landing, where they

285

trembled with fear.

'Basic decency,' the Ed babbled. 'Basic decency and integrity and *courage* are the only real virtues... *Jesus Christ, what was that*?'

The Ed jumped and grabbed Dennis, held him tight, his eyes popping, shaking and staring back down the stairs as glass rained on the hallway. A lot of noise down there, the bitches obviously attacking the kitchen, and the Ed, thinking of Clive, his heart going out to him, clung to Dennis and started whimpering in the most piteous manner.

'In here!' Dennis said.

'In *where*?' the Ed said.

'What do you mean, where? In here! In the open-plan office!'

'Watch it, Dennis... Booby traps!'

'They haven't reached here yet, Ed.'

'I want it out here in the open,' the Ed said. 'Face to face... like a *man*.'

'*Come on*!' Dennis said.

'I'm having a piss,' the Ed said. 'It's dribbling down my pants as we speak and I can't move my legs.'

Dennis grabbed the Ed's arm, opened the door, pulled him through, and they found themselves in the open-plan office where Harvey had once worked. Dedicated, Harvey had stayed here, had refused to leave his desk, and they soon saw him crouched low behind it, an empty bottle in one hand.

'Harvey!' Dennis said.

'Dennis!' Harvey said.

'Where's Stan?'

'Here I am,' good old Stan said, stepping out of a cupboard.

'And Les?'

'I think they got him.'

'Poor bastard.'

'Amen.'

'And Clive?'

'I think they got him as well, though I can't be too sure of that.'

'I'm here, Dennis! *I'm here*!'

'On the intercom,' good old Stan said.

'I'm down here in the kitchen!' Clive cried. 'And they're breaking the door down!'

'Poor bastard,' Harvey said.

'God!' the poor bastard cried. 'They're smashing the fucking door down with clubs and... Get off! *Don't you touch me*!'

The Ed choked back a sob, letting bygones be bygones, forgetting Clive's shitty betrayals and his quick, cowardly flight.

'A good man,' the Ed said.

'He'll soon be a good woman.'

'That remark's in particularly bad taste, Harvey.'

'A mere slip of the tongue, Ed.'

The sudden pounding of feet, a vicious drumming on the door, female shrieks as they tried to break the door down and get at the merry lads.

'Here they come!' Harvey shouted.

'*I'm not guilty*!' the Ed shrieked.

'Adios,' good old Stan said with a wave, and vanished into the cupboard.

Dennis turned around quickly, glanced across the spacious office, and then, without thinking, or thinking only of his arse, he made his way between the scattered desks, going as far away as possible. The Ed didn't see him go, being too paralysed to move, and as the door started shrieking and spitting wood splinters, Dennis dropped out of sight.

'*The wrath of COCK is merciful*!'

'*Down with men! Up their asses*!'

'What we have here is a lack of communication,' Harvey said, 'but this bottle on someone's head might make amends.'

The door shuddered and screeched, its hinges tearing from the wall, the wood panelling splitting under the blows of the heavy clubs.

'*Down with men! Up their asses!*'

'*The wrath of COCK is liberating!*'

'I refuse to be intimidated,' the Ed said with surprising courage. '*Oh, my God, Jesus Christ, they're coming in, help me Jesus they're coming!*'

The door shot off its hinges and plunged to the floor and then – oh, terrible sight! – there they were: the ravaging women of COCK. Dressed in black leather and boots, average height six-foot-one, they roared into the room swinging clubs and reaching out with rapacious hands. Dennis saw them from a distance, his philosophical detachment gone, thinking fondly of his wife, of how he loved her and cherished her, and silently vowing to love the sweet girl even more if he got out alive.

'*Down with men! Up their asses!*'

'*Not my ass!*' the Ed shrieked.

'Watch that little shit! He's swinging a bottle!'

'Take that, bitch! Ouch! *Jesus!*'

The Ed and Harvey went down, the former shrieking, the latter kicking, and were buried under a deluge of womanly flesh and thrashed soundly with hefty fists. Dennis saw it and was shocked, thinking the women quite common, outraged that they stomped on his brothers while still smoking fags. Worse: marijuana... the smoke drifted above the desks, filling the air with a sweet feminine aroma that added insult to injury. Then they dragged Clive Grant in, a pathetic figure, his clothes in shreds, his shoes missing, something that looked suspiciously like a dildo thrusting out of his backside. Clive was wriggling and kicking, a brave man, still defiant, but a quick kick to the balls made him yelp and sent his pride to the dung heap.

'*The wrath of COCK is merciful!*'

'*Not the Dong!*' the Ed shrieked.

'*All hail the Artful Ed's Double Dong!*'

'*That treacherous bastard!*' the Ed shrieked.

Dennis hid behind the desk and stared across the spacious

room and saw life in the raw in the office. All the merry lads were struggling, no longer merry but fairly lively, and the Ed, in particular, being *the boss*, let them know he was there.

'*All hail the Vaseline!*'

'*Not the Vaseline!*' the Ed shrieked.

'Keep your cool, Ed!' Harvey shouted. 'Be disdainful! Let them know who's in charge here!'

'*Oh, my god, not the Vaseline!*'

Dennis remained behind the desk and forced himself to observe the nightmare, horrified and repulsed, but still a writer nonetheless, knowing that something creative had to come out of it, lest it all be in vain. Yet how difficult it was! He had to face his own cowardice. His brothers, the poor wretches, were being abused in the most callous manner. Dennis' heart went out to them. He wanted to rise up and protect them. Instead, in his thoughts, he wrote a book around the event and then tried to dream up a title. It was the only thing to do. He knew his brothers would appreciate it. He would expose their humiliation to the world and make a packet on movie rights.

'Line up, girls! That's it!'

'Mzzz Cooch!' the Ed cried.

'Make sure they're strapped properly around your hips, and hold them steady when pushing in.'

'Please God, Mzzz Cooch, save me!'

'Five minutes each, girls.'

'Mzzz Teasedale! Mzzz Bedward! It's me!'

'Okay, Ed, bend over.'

Dennis could hardly bear to look, but bit his lower lip and forced himself, staring through the smoky haze, the sweet marijuana fumes, studying the nightmare *in depth*, thinking of the terrible human tragedy, wondering how the victims would face their wives and children when they read his forthcoming book. Yes, it was horrifying, and he accepted this as time passed, as the hands on his wristwatch crept toward five and the orgy raged noisily on. Oh, most terrible sight! Oh, the haunting, piteous cries! Dennis choked back his tears as the telephone rang and he picked it up automatically, a man in a trance.

'Yes?' Dennis said.

'It's the Artful Ed, Dennis. I'm out here at Heathrow and I've just come through Customs and I'm about to get into this helicopter, so I'll be there in no time.'

'Pardon?' Dennis said.

'You heard me the first time, Dennis. It's possible that you're in a state of shock, but some tablets should cure that.'

'I don't believe this,' Dennis said.

'These things happen,' the Artful Ed said. 'And believe me, it was for your own good: you were falling to pieces there.'

'The mags are finished,' Dennis said.

'You'll really like my new mag, Dennis. That shit of the Ed's was going downhill, but this new mag is filthy beyond belief.'

'Are you hiring me?' Dennis said.

'I need an Editor,' the Ed said.

'Do you know what you've *done* here, Artful Ed? Those whores are having a *gang bang*!'

'We're all sisters and brothers, Dennis.'

'You set it up with Miss Cooch.'

'Not *Miss*, Dennis. *Mzzz...* A truly fine woman there, Dennis, if a bit too excitable.'

'They're being *raped*, Artful Ed.'

'It will make them lesser men. They will thus be able to face their unemployment with the strength of humility.'

'I don't believe this,' Dennis said.

'You're in shock,' the Artful Ed said. 'I'll bring along a few coloured tablets and make you feel well again.'

'That orgy's getting out of hand.'

'They're just excited,' the Artful Ed said. 'They'll calm down in a couple of hours and let the lads crawl on home.'

'That's indecent,' Dennis said.

'The wrath of COCK is merciful, Dennis. Crawling home,

they will contemplate their wives with increased understanding.'

'The *Editor's* job?' Dennis said.

'I know you can do it, Dennis... And time off to write the book of the movie about this whole great event. I surrender all rights.'

'That's really most decent, Artful Ed.'

'Not at all, Dennis. You've earned it... And, if I may say so, and I always *did* say so, you're the only bastard there I can trust.'

'I miss my wife,' Dennis said.

'A fine woman there, Dennis. And a civilised man can't fuck around without a good, solid marriage behind him.'

'She's at her mother's,' Dennis said.

'I'll pick her up,' the Artful Ed said. 'I'll come down on the roof in this helicopter and I'll make sure she's with me.'

'The roof?' Dennis said.

'You'll have to get up there, Dennis. We'll throw a rope-ladder down to pick you up, but you won't have much time.'

'I'll never make it,' Dennis said.

'Don't be frightened of COCK, Dennis. I've taken care of that situation and you'll know when your time has come.'

'When?' Dennis said.

'Any minute now,' the Artful Ed said. 'Just remember to keep your fucking head down and avoid all the flak.'

The world exploded at that moment, a blinding light, a sudden roar, and Dennis shot forward and slammed into the desk and rolled across the floor. He blinked his eyes and looked up, saw it all in slow-mo, the shards of the shattered window raining down through boiling smoke as the roaring in his head became a ringing that dissolved into loud shrieks. Then a masked man appeared, swinging through the shattered window, bawling something incoherent at Dennis as he let go of the abseiling rope. He landed neatly on his feet, a masked frogman in black, a sub-machine gun cradled under one arm, throwing a smoke bomb with his free hand.

'*Keep your head down*!' he bawled.

Dennis kept his head down, but his eyes remained open as another frogman swung through the window and crashed over the desk. This man cursed and rolled off, his weapons rattling, his legs kicking, and he fell over Dennis to reach the floor and jumped up with his gun raised. Dennis tried to say something, tried to stand up, waved his hands, and the new man, every instinct finely honed, prepared to kill or be killed.

'*Don't shoot him*!' the other man bawled, his own weapon roaring fiercely, stitching a line of bullets across the ceiling while the hordes of COCK shrieked. '*I think he's one of the hostages!*'

'I am!' Dennis said.

'Shut your mouth,' the second man snarled. 'One more word and you'll be spitting broken teeth for the rest of the year.'

He swung his arm and threw a smoke bomb, then swung his weapon up and fired, the noise catastrophic, drowning out the shrieking women, as more plaster rained down from the ceiling and everyone scattered.

'*Where are the terrorists*?' the man bawled.

'What terrorists?' Dennis shouted.

'Shut your fucking mouth!' the man snarled. 'You dumb cunt, you're not worth it.'

He then raced across the office, firing wildly as he ran, and Dennis rolled onto his belly and looked through the dense, swirling smoke. The hordes of COCK were scattering, backing desperately through the doorway, swinging clubs and glittering steel-studded belts and lashing anything moving. Then the Ed came into view, a spectral vision in the murk, his hands raised and his trousers around his ankles, his bony knees knocking.

'The SAS!' Harvey cried.

'*We are saved*!' the Ed wailed.

'Shut your trap!' a charging masked trooper snarled, kicking the Ed in the nuts.

The Ed yodelled and jack-knifed, collapsed and was trampled underfoot as the daring SAS trooper raced on and swung his rifle at Harvey. The latter was rising none too gracefully, likewise ensnared in his fallen trousers, and his shaking legs gave way and he fell back to let Clive swallow the swinging rifle butt. Dennis didn't see Clive again. He sympathised but couldn't stop. He crawled away on hands and knees, sticking close to the wall, skirting around the battle area, swallowing lungfuls of smoke, and realising, if belatedly, but with patriotic pride, that those daring buccaneers in frog suits were what made Britain great.

'Slaughter the terrorist bitches!'

'Watch those perverts on the floor!'

'*I'm innocent*!' the Ed shrieked. '*I've been raped*! *I'm a victim of circumstance*!'

The Ed rose and fell again, disappearing into the smoke, and Dennis turned left at the end of the office and kept hugging the wall. The guns continued roaring, efficiently butchering the ceiling, more plaster and dust raining down as the battle raged on. Dennis smelt smoke and cordite and the fumes of marijuana, ignored the groaning and pathetic whimpering of his brothers who had suffered most grievously. Then he saw the office door, the last of the women backing out, the masked soldiers, unaware that those creatures were the gentler sex, beating them over the heads and shoulders with their rifles and forcing them back down the stairs.

'I've lost my teeth,' Clive Grant groaned.

'I've lost my balls,' the Ed whimpered.

'A close one there, lads,' good old Stan said, stepping out of the cupboard.

'Those COCK bitches,' the Ed whimpered.

'Those SAS cunts,' Harvey groaned.

'And where's the lovely Dennis?' good old Stan said, leisurely lighting a fag.

'That poor bastard,' the Ed said.

That poor bastard, Dennis, was crawling quietly out the doorway, glancing back briefly in fond recognition and then moving on. Once outside, he was careful, first looking down the stairs, then, satisfied that they were gone, he clambered back to his feet.

'Well, lads,' he heard the Ed say, 'I think we've learned our lesson. All the women, we should put them in cages and feed them some bird seed.'

Smoke was drifting down the stairs and Dennis turned around to face it, and then, feeling battered and bruised, he walked up towards the roof. The smoke swirled all around him, filling his lungs, making him blind, and he heard the sound of coughing up above and felt his blood turning cold. He stopped when he saw the lift and the corridor outside the Art Department. Blinking, he looked nervously around him and saw nothing but more smoke.

'I've really got one,' someone said.

'I don't believe it,' someone else said.

'They all say I haven't got one, but they're wrong. I mean, I'm really quite normal.'

'Come on, Les, let me see it.'

'I don't want to,' Les said.

'Yes, you do. It's poking out, Les. I think it *wants* to be seen.'

'All right, but don't touch it.'

'Cross my heart and hope to die.'

'I will if you will,' Les said. 'I mean, that's only fair.'

'Okay, it's a deal.'

'Okay, then. Don't laugh now.'

'Here, Les, I'll show you mine first. That should make you feel better.'

'Wow! Is that it?'

'Yes, Les, that's it.'

'Wow! I mean, that's really pretty. Okay, look at mine.'

'Gee, Les, that's perfect.'

'Honest?'

'Oh, yes!'

'I don't know what to do with it sometimes… I just can't control it.'

'Here, Les, let me show you.'

'That desk must be hard.'

'It's good for my back, Les, believe me. Now just lie on top of me.'

'You're not hard like the desk.'

'That's an encouraging thing to say, Les.'

'It feels really nice in your fingers, but what happens now?'

'I just slip it in here, Les.'

'Wow! Boy oh boy!'

'Very slowly up and down, Les… Yes, that's it… I think you're getting the drift of it.'

'Can this go on forever?'

'It might, Les. Let's hope so.'

'I *want* it to go on forever… Oh, my God! *Jesus Christ!*'

Dennis left Les and Lydia, demurely lowering his gaze, leaving them there in the dark room that contained the back issues and that also had contained the bald homosexual literary agent and the mysterious teetotal bisexual editor while they were going at it like two pigs in a trough. Dennis didn't like the metaphor – though accurate, it was crude – and now in love with his wife again, seeing the error of his ways, realising that he, too, in his weakness had failed, he climbed some more stairs, through the still-swirling smoke, and knew that his marriage would last and that his wife's love would shelter him.

The stairs were shaking here and Dennis heard muffled noises, his heart sinking when he eventually understood that they came from the roof. They were the noises of embattled hordes, shrieking women, bawling men, and Dennis shuddered at the thought of what was happening up there under the clear sky. Then he saw a shadowy figure, obviously creeping down furtively, obscured by the smoke and the shadows, something in its right hand. Dennis stopped, his heart pounding, his blood turning cold, then he saw frizzed black hair, a suntanned cheeky face, blue denims and an oversized grey sweater over two full, bouncing breasts.

'COCK?' Dennis said nervously.

'If you've got one, I can use it.'

'You don't belong to those other women?' Dennis said.

'Not really,' she said.

'You sound American,' Dennis said.

'I'm from Putney,' the girl said. 'But I spent a bit of time over there. A few weeks in Los Angeles.'

'You're the Artful Ed's assistant.'

'That's right,' the girl said.

'I'm Dennis.'

'I guessed that,' she said. 'Your voice is so sexy.'

It was love at first sight. Dennis simply couldn't control it. He stared at her big boobs, at her dark, frizzed hair, at her wide, audacious grin and her crotch, and knew he could not resist her.

'You've got a hard-on,' she said.

'I'm truly sorry,' Dennis said.

'Don't apologise,' she said, 'for what you've got. When you lose it, you'll weep.'

'I might lose it up there.'

'The helicopter will soon be landing.'

'He won't be able to land on that roof with all those people up there.'

'Well, he's not actually landing.'

'I'm not used to rope-ladders.'

'Just pretend it's an extension of your dick and you'll be up it in no time.'

'And you?'

'I'm here to help you. The Artful Ed wants me to help you. That's why I've got this walkie-talkie: to keep in touch with the Artful Ed.'

'You're not going with us?'

'Not today. Maybe tomorrow. The Artful Ed's going to let me be a model when he really gets organised.'

'That's what *the Ed* always says.'

'You can *trust* the Artful Ed.'

'Have you met him yet?'

'No.'

'So what makes you think you can trust him?'

'I dunno… He sounds *cute*.'

Dennis loved her trusting nature and wanted to entrust his cock to her, but the urgency of the situation – and the Artful Ed's voice – thwarted that plan.

'Mzzz Vickerage?'

'Artful Ed?'

'Has that cunt arrived yet?'

'Yes, Artful Ed. The cunt has arrived and is standing in front of me as we speak.'

'Dennis? Can you hear me?'

'Yes,' Dennis said, 'I can hear you.'

'A lot of static on these walkie-talkies, Dennis, but they'll have to suffice.'

'That's okay, Artful Ed.'

'I'm glad to hear you say that, Dennis. It's a pretty heavy number going down, but we'll pull you right out of there.'

'Great,' Dennis said.

'Don't be nervous,' the Artful Ed said. 'Your lovely wife is here beside me. She weeps tears of relief at the sound of your voice and is breathless to see you again.'

'Great,' Dennis said.

'I'm glad to hear you say that, Dennis. You will now have the courage to climb those stairs and face the massed ranks of COCK.'

'Right,' Dennis said.

'You've just said the right thing, Dennis. Now just follow Mzzz Vickerage up the stairs and walk forth to your future.'

'Right,' Dennis said.

The conversation was terminated, static rushing to fill the silence, and Mzzz Vickerage lowered the walkie-talkie and gave

Dennis a teasing smile. Thus teased, he responded, standing upright and horizontal, the bulge in his trousers utterly shameless in its need to be free. Dennis stared at Mzzz Vickerage, thought of church spires and steeples, but Mzzz Vickerage, knowing what she had to do, led him up the stairs.

They emerged to the roof, to the sounds of locked forces, the sun beaming down, flashing off the helicopter, streaming through the warm summer air to tan the hides of the warriors. The ranks of COCK were well diminished, a mere scattering of depleted forces, now venting their hatred of men by fucking every last trooper. The masked troopers were not resisting, obviously knowing when they were beaten, most starkers from their necks to their boots, displaying finely honed instincts. Dennis observed and was relieved. He now knew that he was safe. He saw the mysterious teetotal bisexual editor making merry with two agitated troopers and he felt even more relieved. Then he turned to Mzzz Vickerage. He gazed deep into her eyes. In those eyes he saw trust and true love and the light of redemption, which, of course, had eluded him.

'You've still got a hard-on,' Mzzz Vickerage said.

'How terribly inconvenient,' Dennis said.

'All this violence and excitement,' Mzzz Vickerage said, 'sort of turns a girl on.'

'Really?'

'Yes, really.'

'How frustrating that must be.'

'You'll never get up the rope-ladder with that hard-on. I can promise you that.'

The helicopter dropped lower, whipping the dust up, roaring fiercely, the rope-ladder unfurling and falling down and blowing out on the wind. Mzzz Vickerage ran across and grabbed it, her frizzed hair dancing darkly, then she turned around and brought it back to Dennis, still smiling invitingly. Dennis accepted the rope-ladder, feeling lost and forlorn, the helicopter's fierce roar and the wind blotting out his senses. Mzzz Vickerage smiled and glanced down, lightly stroked his erection, and Dennis, grabbing the rope-ladder with one hand, knew that love sprang eternal. He looked up and saw two eyes, looked again and saw four: two faces staring down upon him from a very great height.

Dennis didn't know what to do. He *never* knew what to do. He grabbed the hand of Mzzz Vickerage and stared at her as his feet left the ground. The helicopter was ascending. Dennis hung on with one hand. He clung to Mzzz Vickerage with the other and felt deeply confused. Then the helicopter climbed higher. Mzzz Vickerage was on tiptoe. Dennis thought of his wife, of the Artful Ed's mad genius, of his past and his future and his hope for redemption, and, in thinking this, caught between two fair options, his cock throbbing, his arms coming out of their sockets, he remained undecided.

'Fucked again,' Dennis said.

Revelation

W.A.Harbinson

Without warning, after a night of terrifying disturbance, an event
of unparalleled significance occurred to shake the foundations of
civilisation.
It was an event so magnificent, so extraordinary, that it would
alter forever the political structure and the spiritual beliefs of
Western society.
Bringing, ultimately,
the peace that passes all understanding…

'An extraordinary combination of love story, occult, horror and
science fiction… an electrifying read.'
  -*Bookbuyer*

'It's a great idea and Harbinson makes it work wonderfully. A
book with a difference that teases the imagination with its
ingenuity.'
  -*Sunday Tribune*

'It has the lot – love, horror, science fiction, political and
religious intrigue involving the major religions and world
powers, and an extraordinary story of the resurrection of a man
hailed by those religions as the saviour of the world.'
  -*Bookseller*

Available from
www.booksurge.com or www.amazon.com

All at Sea
on the Ghost Ship

W.A.Harbinson

In the year 2001 the son of bestselling novelist and biographer W.A.Harbinson offered his father a free trip as the sole passenger on a container ship that would sail from Shanghai to Haifa, with many other ports in between. Once on board the ship, Harbinson found that he was the only white face in a crew composed solely of Indian officers and Chinese seamen. He also realised that while he had previously sailed on passenger liners, he was 'all at sea' when it came to a working ship.

All at Sea on the Ghost Ship is Harbinson's account of his unpredictable, always fascinating voyage. Rich in feeling, acute in observation, and often very funny, *All at Sea on the Ghost Ship* is a book to give us hope and make us smile. It is also an intriguing, rare glimpse into the mind of a writer.

"Highly literate, stunningly evocative, often hilarious memoir of a lengthy voyage on a container ship made by an ageing former bestselling author in search of a personal new horizon."
    -*Freighter Cruises*

Available from
www.booksurge.com or www.amazon.com

The Writing Game
Recollections of an Occasional
Bestselling Author

W.A.Harbinson

The Writing Game is an autobiographical account of the life and times of a professional writer who has managed to survive the minefield of publishing for over thirty years.

Unlike most books on the subject, *The Writing Game* does not try to tell you how to write, or even how to get published. Instead, it focuses with gimlet-eyed clarity on the ups and downs of a unique, always unpredictable business.

On the one hand, a compelling look at a life lived on the edge, under the constant threat of failure, both artistic and financial, on the other, an unusually frank self-portrait enlivened with colourful snapshots of editors, fellow authors and show business celebrities, *The Writing Game* succeeds, as few other books have done, in showing how one professional, uncelebrated writer has managed to stay afloat in the stormy waters of conglomerate publishing.

Here, for the first time, a working author tells it like it really is.

Projekt UFO
The Case For Man-Made Flying Saucers

W.A.Harbinson

W.A.Harbinson's groundbreaking non-fiction work, *Projekt UFO: The Case for Man-Made Flying Saucers*, was widely regarded as one of the most detailed and level-headed books ever published on this controversial subject. It was also considered by many to offer the definitive explanation for a mystery that had haunted the western world for the past sixty years. Now, at last, this revelatory book about 'the world's most fearsome secret' is available to a worldwide readership. *This new edition contains updated material written especially for it by the author.*

"*Projekt UFO* does a good job in describing the history and development of the UFO phenomenon and of the known record of military attempts to build a flying saucer… fascinating."
    -*The Irish Times*

"A fascinating account of the history of UFOs, but from the perspective of their being man-made, not extraterrestrial craft… Forget ETs and invasions from space; the terrestrial scenarios Harbinson speculates are already frightening enough!"
    -*Nexus*

Available from
www.booksurge.com or www.amazon.com

Into the world of Might Be

W.A.Harbinson

Two astronauts, a man and a woman, are taking part in a scientific experiment designed to gauge the effects of prolonged isolation and weightlessness on the human body. At first everything runs smoothly, but then things start going wrong. First, the Skylab inexplicably malfunctions, then the astronauts have magical, fearful experiences. But are their experiences real or imagined? Is the Skylab haunted or not? Or are both of them simply going mad?

Into the World of Might Be is a tour de force of prose writing, an astonishingly vivid evocation of the bewildering 'new reality' of quantum physics, alternate or parallel universes, black holes and the mysteries of Time. Uniquely combining hard scientific facts with a philosophical, metaphysical and, at times, deeply religious work of fiction, this could well be the ultimate short text for the New Age... for a new generation. Read it and take wing.

"Haunting, often ethereal, always cerebral and challenging... Harbinson's most outstanding work of fiction yet... Harbinson's use of the language and fine prose alone make *Into the World of Might Be* compulsive reading."
  -*Rainlore's World of Music*

Available from
www.booksurge.com or www.amazon.com

Knock

A Novel

W.A.Harbinson

"KNOCK belongs to an Irish tradition that runs from Charles Lever and Samuel Lover, down through Joyce, Beckett and Donleavy... It is a remarkable tour de force and, like all good novels, leaves the feeling that it could have been written in no other way."
    -*Colin Wilson, Afterword*

"HARBINSON handles it like a virtuoso... A very Irish figure, this literary postman. He belongs really to the streets of Dublin - or perhaps Mr Harbinson's Belfast - not London. So do most of the other figures in this sad, moving, often beautifully funny and engagingly stately progress through a man's mind and past.
    -*The Daily Telegraph*

Available from
www.booksurge.com or www.amazon.com

More information on books by W.A.Harbinson can be found at:

www.waharbinson.eu.com

4005939

Made in the USA